DEAD TIME

BOOK ONE
AZGIEL'S RETURN

A Novel
by

JASON WILCOX

iUniverse, Inc.
New York   Bloomington

Dead Time: Book One
Azgiel's Return

Copyright © 2010 Jason Wilcox

This is a work of fiction. All of the characters, names, incidents, organizations, and dialogue in this novel are either the products of the author's imagination or are used fictitiously.

iUniverse books may be ordered through booksellers or by contacting:

iUniverse
1663 Liberty Drive
Bloomington, IN 47403
www.iuniverse.com
1-800-Authors (1-800-288-4677)

Because of the dynamic nature of the Internet, any Web addresses or links contained in this book may have changed since publication and may no longer be valid. The views expressed in this work are solely those of the author and do not necessarily reflect the views of the publisher, and the publisher hereby disclaims any responsibility for them.

ISBN: 978-1-4502-4357-5 (pbk)
ISBN: 978-1-4502-4358-2 (cloth)
ISBN: 978-1-4502-4359-9 (ebk)

Printed in the United States of America

iUniverse rev. date: 8/4/10

For

My Love
Katie

&

In Honor of
My brother Danny
Who serves his country with honor, and valor.
And to all others that are serving to protect our freedoms.

CHAPTER 1

A low-toned snort woke Tagen. He jumped to his feet, wide-eyed, nostrils flaring, all senses alert and focused on the edge of the clearing he stood in. His black oily skin twitched up and down rapidly on his chest, but years of experience took over subtly and automatically, as he quickly slowed his breathing, focusing on what could be in the darkness. Peering in the direction of the snort, Tagen could only see the thick interweaving screen of enormous trees in the ancient forest.

A loud silence filled the woods, as the snort was not repeated, and all of the normal sounds associated with the woods at night, ceased. He continued to look over each of the shadows that formed around him, seeking to identify which might mean danger, or even his life. He narrowed his dark red eyes to mere slits, in order to see farther into this forest that he had been charged to patrol, but nothing. Realizing that he could be silhouetted from the setting moon's light in the clearing, he ever so carefully began a stealthy movement to a boulder at hand. Swallowing down his fear, Tagen clutched onto the large boulder with his black-clawed hands, and hid in its shadow.

He stood only ten feet away from the border of the forest, which he became very aware of. The snort had come so quickly he hadn't been able to tell what caused it, and he didn't know what to expect. Hundreds of years had passed by since the last time something had come out, but sightings of creatures at the borders of the land were

1

starting to become more common, and everyone was on edge. The creatures within were unpredictable. Tagen alone had seen demons at the edges of their land twice in the last week. They had stood in the shadows just staring at him, but both times they moved back into the deep forest and out of sight. Both of the sightings had made him uncomfortable and feel on edge.

The eerie silence, that surrounded him, only made his fears worse. He could feel his right eye twitch slightly. A twig snapped in the woods, after a couple of long drawn out minutes had passed, followed by a couple of heavy footsteps. Pushing his back against the cold, rough surface of the boulder, he anxiously watched, waiting.

A dark figure emerged, but stayed in the shadows. Long horns silhouetted in the setting moon's light. Feeling a lump in his throat, Tagen tried to swallow. He hated demons. Nasty creatures. More then likely it would just stand at the border for a moment and then move back into the shadows like the others in the past. They knew not to come out of their land, it would only cause a war, but that's why Tagen was there. To watch.

Steam rose from the darkened figure as it breathed. Tagen's eyes widened and he went into shadow form as he noticed two more demons, all of them in close proximity. His shadow form made him invisible to most demons but not all.

Moving cautiously, all three stepped out of the thick forest. Horns pierced out from their heads. Black eyes scouted the area as they stayed at the edge of their land. Since nothing had come out of the ancient woods over the last couple hundred years, the patrols had been reduced to almost nothing and Tagen was in no position to take on three demons, especially with no backup. The dim morning light illuminated their different pigmented skin. One red, one brown, and the last black. More steam wafted into the air as the large red one snorted again.

Kaz.

Tagen could feel his muscles tighten and his breathing grow heavier. Tagen hadn't seen Kaz in over a thousand years. He pushed himself harder against the rough surface of the moss-covered boulder. *What would bring Kaz out of hiding?* He was the last demon Tagen wanted to mess with. Making maters worse, Kaz glanced in Tagen's direction tilting his head and squinting his cold, black eyes. Black tattoos in ancient writing lined the side of his face.

Instincts took over and Tagen, being in shadow form, melded into the rock face. Only his face was left, partially sticking out. Kaz looked away and the three demons marched forward, passing by. Closing his eyes for a second and taking in a deep breath, Tagen relaxed his body. *They didn't notice me.* He took one last deep breath. Now he had to quickly get back and report that demons had come out of their land. Snyp wasn't going to like this news.

Moving slowly, Tagen exited the cold stone. The rock let out a grinding noise and he froze. Holding his breath, Tagen looked in the direction the demons had gone. Nothing. He slowly let out a breath. *They're gone.*

Something moved from behind Tagen, he quickly turned, but it was too late. Green sparks and chips of rock flew in Tagen's face as a double bladed axe slammed into the boulder almost hitting Tagen in the head. The black demon had returned. White tattoos of ancient writing lined his face and right arm.

Wasting no time, Tagen tore off through the boulder. Another near miss from the axe struck next to him as he exited the opposite side of the rock, nicking his shoulder. The large axe blades had a strange, small vein of something green across them in a web-like pattern. With ease, the black demon came in for another blow. Tagen dodged and twisted, he moved with supernatural speed to the backside of the demon. He slashed him across the back with his venomous claws. Black smoke wafted from the wounds. The demon growled and fell forward against a tree.

The large wounds grew in size as the thin, black oily venom moved across the surface of the flesh. Screaming out in pain, the demon dropped his axe and reached his arms in the air. "Degnar mekna," the demon screamed in an ancient language. A healing chant.

Turning his head slightly, the demon looked at Tagen. Red flames shot from his eyes as well as the wounds. Tagen wasted no time. He bolted towards the ancient forest.

The wounds would slow the demon, but he would be healed soon. If Tagen could enter the thick woods without any of the demons seeing, he might be able to make an escape. They would never expect him to enter their domain. It was a death wish for a dark soul to go there.

Discreetly, Tagen rushed through the shadows of the demon's woods. Spots of light from the quickly rising morning sun stabbed through the canopy of leaves, which Tagen dodged. He glided with inhuman speed through the cold mist that still clung to the ground, leaving it twisting and swirling. He knew that the old powers in the woods would not hesitate to take his life if they caught him there, but he had to take the risk, there were few other options.

Something flickered by a thicket of trees in front of Tagen. He jerked to a halt and hid behind some bushes. Wild eyed, he turned around, scanning the woods. *Did I lose the demons?* The woods were empty, no demons in sight. He turned back around and rubbed a hand over his face. As long as he hadn't been seen by whatever had flickered, he might be okay.

Tagen peeked over the bushes and saw a flash of silver. He strained his dark red eyes, peering toward the area of movement.

A preel!

The demons used the silvery, beetle-like creature as scouts, to warn them of intruders, and they had the ability to see dark souls while in shadow form. The woods were filled with preels, demons, and all sorts of other creatures, all under the command of the Witch. They kept everything off their land, after they were imprisoned there from losing the wars, which also lost them their lord and leader, Azgiel.

Scanning the area, he searched looking at every shadow and object. Tagen rubbed his claws together. He looked to see if there were more preels or worse—if the demons or Witch had already been notified. Not seeing any other movement, he wondered if the small preel had seen him. Action had to be taken, and quickly. If he ran for it, the preel might see him. He had to kill it. Without another thought, Tagen dashed in the direction of the beetle-like creature, his mouth dry with fear.

The preel let out a high-pitched squeal, and turned to a dark orange. Tagen threw the beetle like creature into his mouth and tore it to shreds with his sharp, black teeth and swallowed it. As the lump of shell and legs made its way down Tagen's throat, a large shape emerged from some bushes about ten yards away. Leaves and twigs hung to the brownish skin. *The preel must've been traveling with a demon.* The large demon stood tall and broad, but slow in response to the scream of the preel.

Tagen dove through a large bush and bolted. He heard a horn sound from behind him as he darted through the trees. It echoed through the forest, signaling that the demon and other creatures were now in the chase. His life was on the line and he had to get out of the woods. *I should've never come in here.* He ran as fast as he could, making the trees look like blurs as he past them, trying to get out of their territory.

Suddenly, a being with a head of a jackal jumped out and slashed at him with large claws, splitting his right bicep. Black oily blood spattered across the undergrowth and poured down his arm. A rank, pungent odor wafted from the blood, until the wound quickly healed. Tagen didn't miss a beat—he sprinted with as much speed as he could muster. The edge of the forest could be seen where the trees were less dense and the sun shone stronger. *Faster Tagen, you're almost there.*

The jackal-headed beast breathed heavily. His paws pounding across the ground grew quieter as Tagen out ran him.

Tagen wanted to turn and destroy his pursuer, it would be so easy since it wasn't a demon, but he couldn't pause for a moment or there would be too many for him to fight.

The rising sun shone stronger, and the thick, dank air had thinned out as he exited the old growth. Tagen slowed to look back, his eyes searching the thick unwelcoming woods that he had just left behind. Nothing followed him out. A white, glowing figure lit the edge of the dark forest causing Tagen to stumble.

The Witch.

He caught his balance and ran faster. *She never shows herself, and I don't want to find out why she has.* He knew for sure there were multiple creatures and demons hiding in the shadows all around her and they would've snuffed him out like a small flame if he had been even seconds slower from leaving her imprisoned lands.

Furthering his distance from the Witch's territory, Tagen ran at a fast pace passing around trees and through breaks in the woods. He tightened his fists and let out a growl. His hasty foolish decision almost cost him his life. *No more stupid mistakes. Just get back to Snyp and report.*

A whiff of something familiar wafted up Tagen's skeleton-like nostrils and he immediately stopped. He stood in a black shadow of a large tree, sniffing the air. He dug his claws into the bark with worry. Slowly he peered around the tree, his nostrils inhaling the scents. The tree let out a loud moan from his venomous claws as he stepped forward—the lush greenness of the leaves instantly transformed to brown and fell.

The smell emanated from a small cabin that could barely be seen through the thickness of the forest. Tagen had run further then he thought. Humans didn't live close to the ancient forest, or at least he didn't think they did.

As a gust of wind ripped through the trees, Tagen jerked into the shadows and hissed, waiting to see what would happen.

After a minute passed and nothing transpired, he cautiously crept toward the small cabin, soundless as his clawed feet stepped over leaves and twigs. He glanced around, hesitated, then snuck up to the log exterior, and walked through it as if it weren't there.

Inside, a man lay asleep. His body was sprawled on top of the sheets. Next to the bed, a large yellow dog grunted in her sleep. The light coming through the windows grew dim as Tagen used his power to darken the room. A few creaks and moans rolled through the cabin, making it sound as if the foundation had shifted. Tagen stepped to the bed with his claws out. The man rustled in his sleep and moved his arm, causing Tagen to pause, holding as still as possible. After several seconds, Tagen sniffed the air and bent down, his black skeleton like face inches from the man. He jumped back.

"Mauldrin," he whispered in a scratchy voice. *How could it be? You disappeared ages ago and yet here you are, or so it appears.* Tagen leaned forward noticing something strange about him. *You're mortal and feeble.*

Tagen still remembered the day he saw Mauldrin wipe out an army with just a swish of his hand. He shook himself, to keep focused, not wanting to be distracted with Mauldrin lying in front of him. *How can it be you? It has to be some kind of trick.*

Nervously, he looked around the small barren room. Tagen twitched his fingers nervously. *Not only do you appear mortal, but you also don't have anyone with you. Not even for protection.*

He narrowed his eyes. *If you truly are Mauldrin, you're too much of a threat. I better just kill you now.*

Focusing his power, a thick darkness began to build in the room starting from the ceiling. Tagen's red eyes began to blaze. A nervous gurgle ran through his stomach. There was no telling what was going to happen if it was truly Mauldrin.

A growl from the floor broke Tagen's concentration and the blackness in the room disappeared. With amazing speed and agility, Tagen moved into a corner and became a shadow, ready to abandon the situation if it got ugly. Mauldrin sat up, pointing a pathetic handgun at him. Tagen tilted his head slightly in confusion.

Can he see me? Why is he pulling a gun? Why isn't he just attacking me?

Mauldrin had more power in one finger than Tagen had in his whole body, five times over.

Squinting his eyes, Mauldrin examined the corner where Tagen stood.

Tagen's muscles relaxed and he lowered his claws. *Mauldrin can't see me, or he would've done more then just pull a handgun.*

Still, even having Mauldrin there and awake, frightened Tagen. Moving ever so cautiously, he slipped out through the wall. *Stick with the game plan, retreat and report.* Tagen exited the cabin, anxious to get back to Snyp. *Demons coming out of the forest, and now Mauldrin? Snyp was going to be surprised.*

CHAPTER 2

In one swift movement, Caden shot up from his sleep, gun pointed in the direction of Mags' growling. His blue eyes scanned the corner of the cabin, searching. He felt a presence, but couldn't tell if it was real or a dream. He slowed his breath and patted Mags' soft, golden fur. At his touch, she immediately stopped growling.

Caden holstered the gun back on his worn, wooden bedpost. He stretched his arms up to the ceiling and arched his back. Bumps arouse on his arms, making his hairs stand on end. The cabin remained silent except for the echoes of Mags' panting off the log walls.

"What happened, Girl?" Caden asked, rubbing Mags' back. "Did you have a bad dream?" Pulling his hands away, he ran his fingers through his light brown hair and let out a big yawn, causing Mags to sit up with a tilt of her head. She lifted her butt in the air and wagged her tail right before she pounced, landing on Caden and knocking the air out of him.

"Oh, is that how it's going to be?" Caden grabbed her by the neck and flopped on top of her. Her secret weapon went to work, licking him all over the face. Letting out a laugh, he ruffled her hair and pushed her off the bed. She quickly jumped back on, diving under the ruffled cream-colored covers putting her cold nose on Caden's side. "Ahh! Hey, no fair."

His cell phone blared on his nightstand breaking the fun of the morning. Mags snuggled in as Caden stared at the phone. *Can't they leave me alone?*

After the fourth ring, Caden let out a deep sigh and answered. "What do you need Sally?" He lay back on the bed.

"Now," his secretary said in a sarcastic tone, "is that any way to answer the phone?"

"Tell me you're not calling about work and I'll answer differently," Caden responded with a chuckle.

Sally let out a laugh. "You know I'd never call you while you're on vacation unless the company tells me to. I'm afraid you'd fire me if I bothered you for any other reason."

"I wouldn't fire you. Now, what's so urgent?" Caden sat up and rubbed his forehead, knowing his vacation was over.

"Like normal, I can't say anything over the phone. You just need to get to the office A.S.A.P. I can, however, tell you that it's about your last project."

"Well, it's going to take me a good couple of hours to get into the office, and I definitely won't have my professional attire on."

"You're the boss. Talk to you soon." She hung up before Caden could respond. His cheeks flared in the back as he tightened his jaw muscles not wanting to end his vacation.

Caden loved getting away to his cabin in the mountains. He usually brought his girlfriend, Bridget, once every summer. Unfortunately, Bridget had to work this time and wasn't able to get off because Caden had been given such short notice.

Robert, his boss, had been so excited about the completion of his last experiment, he ordered Caden to take a small vacation. He had appreciated the gesture and took it willingly, since they were few and far between. He often worked long hours, either developing new equipment for SDS or going on missions.

SDS stood for Samuel D. Saints, founder of the company. To the government, the company was known as Top Hand Laboratories, a cutting-edge espionage development and sales company. This equipment, normally outdated within five years, was not the main source of SDS' jobs. SDS kept secret the actual equipment it was using or testing, as well as their secret espionage operations and agents.

The organization started almost two centuries ago. At the time, Samuel D. Saints helped develop an intelligence organization for the government, but he didn't like the governmental control. So he quit and formed SDS. The company remained independent and took out any evils that needed to be annihilated around the world, without having to sort through policies and getting permission.

A code was developed to make sure the organization always stood for freedom and human rights. If it was broken, which it never had been, the individual would be immediately executed. Caden made sure that his team followed the code with the utmost strictness.

***

The afternoon had arrived by the time Caden got to his office. He pulled into his normal parking spot and looked up at the two story, medium-sized building. A heat wave could be seen coming off the tan brick that encased the offices.

After turning the car off, he stretched in his seat while closing his eyes for a moment to release his frustration. He caught a whiff of cigarette smoke as he stepped out of the car and opened the back door to let Mags out.

"Hey Matt," Caden said without looking around. "How's it going?"

"I'm mad," Matt said with a furrowed brow. He stood a few inches taller than Caden, both in good shape. A cigarette hung from his fingers. "If they're calling you in, then we're probably heading back to the main office and I thought we were going to get some time off after the last project, especially when James and I just had to sit around all the time while you worked on the experiment." Mags jumped out of the car and ran to Matt, tail wagging. Matt placed his cigarette in his mouth, inhaled and blew smoke out of his nose while patting Mags on the head.

"Don't snap at me. Now put the cigarette out, get James and meet me in my office."

Matt took one last puff to show his defiance before disposing of the cigarette and followed Caden into the building.

After a quick elevator ride, Caden strode down a short well-lit hallway that ended at Sally's desk. She waved with a cordial smile on her face.

"Hi Sally," Caden answered her wave. Her green silk shirt swayed with her movement.

"You're looking good this morning." Caden gave her a courteous smile. "The briefing Robert sent is in your inbox. He told me to have you call him after you look things over." Caden nodded and proceeded to his room.

The fresh smell of leather lightly scented the air in Caden's office as he entered. His hiking boots squeaked on the freshly waxed black tile, echoing through the large room. Mags' nails clicked on the floor as she ran over to her doggy bed that sat on a tan rug by Caden's desk. She circled five times and then flopped down with a grunt.

Without so much as a knock, Matt and James sauntered into the office just as Caden sat down at his desk. James took off a camo helmet that matched his suit, which was chameleon-like body armor that changed colors and patterns with his surroundings.

"Have you heard any further updates about your project, Dead Time?" James asked in his usual calm voice. His suit turned black to match the leather chair.

"Actually, I haven't. My computer isn't even on yet to see what's going on." Caden hit the power button and sat back. He could tell his team members were going to speak their mind about something. Caden, unlike most team captains, allowed it to an extent as long as they weren't insubordinate, but his team was different then the others.

Matt sat on the ledge of a large window to the right of Caden's desk. "Well," he said, his brow furrowed as if deciding on the precise words. "Robert used your Dead Time equipment without you knowing about it. He furthered your work and even sent some people in. One came back dead and the other lost his mind."

"One dead and one crazy?" He noticed his computer booted with a message blinking at the bottom left corner. Caden turned from his computer and noticed Matt had an irritated look on his face.

"We leave in two days for the main office," Matt grumbled. "Robert's going to send more people in, but this time he's not doing it behind your back, he wants you a part of it. On top of that, the lovely report you'll be reading will inform you they don't think we'll be done with the next steps to this experiment for another six months or so."

"If we come back," remarked James.

"Yes, if we make it back." Matt turned and looked at him.

"Matt, there's a reason why I picked you for intelligence, but there's a line to be drawn on where you get your intel from. This is the second time you've crossed that line. I'm not sure where or how you get this information, but enough is enough. You do this again and I'm going to report you to Robert. I can't keep being lenient when you disobey rules." Caden shifted his weight, his chair squeaking underneath him. Matt turned his gaze to the floor and didn't say another word.

"Now," Caden began after taking a breath. Sometimes he wondered if he had been too friendly and nice to his men through the years, an issue Robert had gotten on him about many times in the past. "This issue is not about us not coming back. Of course we'll be coming back. We always do."

"Maybe you," James's calm voice filled the room, "but Matt found out that he and I are on the list to try out Dead Time equipment."

"They want you to go into stopped time? Well, if that's true, I'm sure it'll be fine."

"You might change your mind if you watch a video that was sent to me by another agent." Matt's eyes were stern, but cautious. Caden didn't fully understand their worry. They normally seemed gung-ho about exciting missions.

"Let me see it then," Caden responded, gesturing for Matt to get on the computer. Matt paused for a moment looking at Caden. He rubbed his hands together a couple of times.

"Do you have the video still?" Caden asked, raising his eyebrows.

"Yes." Matt swallowed as he walked over to the computer. "It's in my email." The tapping of the keyboard and clicking of the mouse only lasted a moment before Matt had his email up.

"Wait," Caden said grabbing Matt's arm. "Is that email a video of what I think it is?" He pointed to an email titled 'Orange Experiment 1'.

"It's a video of the first test of your Dead Time equipment." Matt sounded deflated, his tone flat.

Matt's shoes squeaked as Caden pushed him out of the way and clicked open the email. He opened a video clip link that was imbedded in it.

There were a couple of people in white coats, one of them being the head scientist, Allen. The director of the agency, Robert, stood along one of the plain, white walls. The room was barren of anything outside of some lab equipment and SDS personnel. Caden couldn't believe video footage of the trial existed. No one had told him it was going to be recorded.

Caden saw himself walk into the center of the room where an orange sat on a small stool. The orange was wrapped in gold fabric with little green circuits poking out of the top and bottom. Caden stood by a small machine the size of a water fountain. Three small switches were on the top. He clicked one of them and another machine in the corner, that had two rods sticking out of the top of it, made a quiet humming sound.

The small audience shifted in their chairs; one pointed to the erect hairs on his arm. Caden could remember how thick the air had felt.

"Go ahead Robert." Caden called out in the video.

Robert picked up the orange, turned to the watching audience and camera, and tossed it in the air. He quickly moved his hand away as Caden hit the middle switch. A nanosecond later, a purplish electric bolt snapped between the two rods on the machine in the corner, producing a loud crack. The orange disappeared from the air and suddenly appeared on the ground, still encased in the gold fabric. Steam wafted off it.

No one but Caden moved a muscle. The room was dead silent. Caden had felt proud of his experiment. He had demonstrated his ability to send something into stopped time and have it reappear. It had been a project that often been on his mind when he worked on experiments and at that moment he had done it.

Finally Robert broke the silence with a chuckle. A huge smile grew across his face while he stared at the orange. He walked over and shook Caden's hand. As their hands, met the video stopped.

Watching the video brought back the same excitement Caden had felt that day. His men hadn't been in the room and even though he wanted to be upset with Matt for having the video, he felt somewhat proud that they'd the opportunity to see it.

"This video shouldn't even exist," Caden began while Matt quickly clicked on the computer. Matt brought up the video that Caden had wanted to see in the first place. "Where in the world did you get-" He was cut off as the other video started.

Steven, Robert's top advisor, lay on a metal exam table, his arms strapped down. It was a peculiar sight to see. The skin on his face looked abnormally pale, but Caden thought it might be due to the video being in black and white. The graininess of the video didn't help either.

"Where did you get this?" Caden looked at Matt who was standing next to him.

"An agent who got it from a scientist."

"We shouldn't be watching this then-" A scream rang out from the video, which caught Caden's attention. Steven thrashed on the table. The leathery straps on his wrists broke and he sat up. He glanced around the small room with his gray colored eyes, peering at the seven people standing around him. Caden noticed the same fabric he had developed to send the orange into stopped time was wrapped around Steven.

"Who brought me back?" Steven shouted, his voice horse. No one moved at first, they just stood there looking at him with blank expressions. He slammed his hands down and the table seemed to disintegrate as if some type of strong acid had been dumped on it. Steven stood while the table melted away.

"Answer me!" Steven clenched his fists.

"Sedate him." Robert's voice could be heard, but he was nowhere in site. One of the medical team standing by the equipment that had been monitoring Steven's vitals moved forward, needle in hand. Steven's bare feet slapped the tiled floor as he turned and pushed his right hand out. Equipment and the man flew, slamming against the solid concrete wall.

"Steven!" Robert shouted, coming into the video. Steven's countenance changed, he stood up tall and turned to face Robert.

"Who are you?" Steven muttered. "Are you the one that brought me back?" His fists still clenched.

"Steven, we're here to help you. I need you to calm down." Robert held out his strong muscular arm, his hand opened as if trying to present one of the medical team to him.

"Steven?" Steven raised an eyebrow and shifted his head while looking at Robert. He lifted his broad hands and looked at them and then touched his face. A smile stretched from cheek to cheek. "My name is Azgiel." He narrowed his eyes for a moment and analyzed Robert. "You don't know who I am, do you?"

Caden almost missed it, but he noticed Robert move a finger and a medic that stood a couple of feet behind Steven jumped and injected a fluid into him. The drug immediately took effect. Steven fell to the ground, sedated.

"Wow," Caden said as he clicked stop on the video.

"Now you see why we have concerns?" Matt asked while moving towards the computer. "He's the one that came back crazy."

Caden didn't understand. *Why would Robert send anyone into stopped time without me there? Why was there a secret experiment done after Robert had ordered me to take a vacation right after the equipment had been shown to be successful? And why in the world would Steven be used as one of the test subjects?* He needed to collect himself. These were questions to discuss with Robert not his men.

Caden looked up at Matt. "I think you need to write me a report on who sent you these clips and how in the world they got them."

Matt quickly clicked out of everything. "Since I'm already in trouble, you might be interested in who they're calling in to test the equipment." Matt said backing away from the computer.

"Who?" Caden asked, noticing Matt had one eyebrow raised. Letting out a sigh, Caden brought his hands down on the armrests of his chair.

"Yeah, you guessed it," Matt huffed.

"Burton's team. Man! Okay, orders are orders. Forget the past. Understand?" Caden waited until they both reluctantly nodded. He turned his gaze out the window. His men had a difficult time getting along with the Burton team.

Matt and James left the room. A ding rang out from Caden's computer signaling he received a new email. At first he figured he would ignore it, he had a lot to get done and emails weren't on his priority list. Bridget needed to be informed that he had to head out of town. With the thought of telling her, he turned back to his computer, willing to procrastinate a little.

There were a number of new emails, but the latest one came from an email he didn't recognize. Normally he would delete them, but this one's title had SDS on it. Caden clicked on it. The email had one sentence.

SDS has become corrupt.

Caden hit reply and wrote one question back, wanting to know who sent it. After his finger clicked the mouse button to send, a ding rang out again. The mailbox was invalid. Grabbing a pen and paper out of his top drawer, he wrote down the email address. Matt was going to have his work cut out for him. Caden needed him to find out who had created the email address.

CHAPTER 3

Tagen dashed down the pitch-black cave, feeling the comfort of being home. The thick darkness appeared to be alive, crawling across his skin. He moved through the murky air with ease, stepping past moaning sounds that echoed through the hallway. As he rounded a corner of the cavern, a loud scream rang out, but the sound didn't faze him. He was used to the sounds, the sounds of his home.

He came to a stop at a large door. Without an invitation, Tagen creaked open the door and inched his way into the room. Snyp appeared as a black silhouette standing in front of a large gate that produced a dim light. The portal allowed instant travel to Triaad's kingdom. It was the only thing illuminating the room.

A massive beast, called a Messenger, loomed over Snyp, sent by Triaad. It was a giant rat-like creature covered in brown scales. The Messenger looked over at Tagen while Snyp kept his focus on the massive beast saying something too quiet to hear. Tagen quickly stepped forward. He ignored the fact Snyp didn't invite him.

"Can't you see I'm busy," Snyp spoke up without turning around. His black claws were stretched out ready to punish the intruder. He turned to face Tagen, his deep red eyes glaring. "Oh, Tagen, it's you. What brings your pathetic carcass back so soon?" Snyp asked. He lowered his arms to his human-like, shadowy black body.

"I have urgent news for you," Tagen said as he crouched before Snyp. He hoped his information would finally build some trust in Snyp and that he might start getting chances to eat a soul or two.

With the thought, he became even more aware of his weakened state. A state that Snyp controlled.

"I'm in the middle of listening to a message from Lord Triaad, so this better be more important for you to come barging in here and interrupt," Snyp growled.

Tagen clacked his claws. "It's about the woods. Three demons have escaped," Tagen said with a little hesitance, not knowing if Snyp would deem it worthy-enough news.

"Demon's, huh? How interesting. I wonder what would motivate them to dare and leave the protection of their woods." Snyp said as he paced around his dark shadowy servant. "Did you kill them?"

Swallowing his anger, Tagen tried to speak calmly. If Snyp didn't keep him so weak, he might have killed at least the weaker two demons. "Kaz was one of them."

"Even more interesting." Snyp stared at Tagen for a moment. "I take it you didn't do anything about it."

"I cut one of them up pretty bad." Tagen nervously rubbed his oily arm. "But no, they're still alive."

Snyp's dark red eyes shifted back towards the Messenger. "Go and report this information to Triaad and hurry back to tell me what he wants done."

Tagen tried to speak to let Snyp know he had more information, but Snyp was too caught up in trying to get the Messenger on his way. Besides, Tagen wondered if he really should tell Snyp about his findings at the cabin. He still didn't fully know if it had been Mauldrin or not. Seeing him there made no sense and if he gave a wrong report, Snyp might punish him for the misinformation.

The Messenger tilted his large rat like head, his ears flopping to one side. "You don't want to hear the last part of the monthly report? I hadn't finished it." His booming voice filled the room.

"Your report isn't as important as informing Triaad about the demons that are loose, since Tagen didn't kill them. Finish telling me when you come back to let me know what Lord Triaad wants us to do about the demons and possibly others leaving the woods," Snyp ordered, his oily body moved towards the Messenger to usher him out.

"As you wish." The beast stood on all four legs and ran out of the room, shaking the ground as he left.

Snyp looked back to Tagen. "I'm displeased you didn't do better in taking care of the matter." His claws flickered and Tagen worried he was going to be attacked for his lack of action.

"There's more news though, even more important." Tagen spoke up, hoping Snyp might let the demon matter go if his findings were correct about Mauldrin. "I found Mauldrin in the woods on my way here."

The room grew quiet as Snyp snarled at Tagen. "How? Are you sure it was Mauldrin?" He asked, moving very close to Tagen.

"Yes, I'm positive. His face is not something I'll forget any time soon." Tagen remarked feeling a little unsure of him self. Even though he had only seen Mauldrin once, it was an experience he wasn't about to forget.

"We definitely need to tell Lord Triaad. He's often speculated and wondered if he or the others would ever reappear." Snyp paused for a second, his red eyes searching around the dark room. "Did he see you?"

Tagen hesitated before answering, knowing that Mauldrin had looked right at him, but he believed he hadn't seen him. "No, he was asleep in a cabin in the woods not too far from where the witch lives," Tagen explained. Snyp flinched upon hearing information about the witch. "And as peculiar as it may sound, by how he acted I don't think he has any knowledge of who he is."

Snyp lowered his head, his brow furled in deep thought, his skin looking almost a dark gray. "What made you come to that conclusion?"

"He acted like the rest of the stupid humans we deal with, ignorant and unknowing about what goes on around him." Tagen thought back to the way Mauldrin had pulled a gun and just stared, unable to see him.

Snyp chuckled to himself. "If he doesn't know what he is, then he could be very powerful in the right hands." He paused in thought. "Very powerful indeed. Very powerful for us. Others would bow before us," he said as a crooked smile plastered across his oily black face.

Tagen cringed. "I don't like that idea, sir. If Lord Triaad found-" Before he could finish, Snyp pounced on him, plunging his claws into his chest and threw him to the ground. He stood over Tagen hissing through his sharp black teeth.

"Lord Triaad will not find out about this, and you better not tell him," Snyp snarled. "I want you to find Mauldrin and make sure he knows nothing. Test him to make sure. Once you know for a fact, come back and report. We're going to capture him." Snyp stopped talking for a moment and looked at Tagen with one eye slightly squinted. "Don't let anyone know about this," Snyp spoke sharply, standing over Tagen, ready to kill him if he refused the order.

Tagen knew Snyp could easily over power him, especially in his underfed and weakened state. Even though he didn't like the idea of following the orders, fighting back would only get him killed. "I'll check the cabin first and see if he's still there. If he's not, it might take me awhile to find him, but when I do, I'll do as you ask," Tagen said, struggling to get to his feet. The dark, sandy soil squished around his fingers as he pushed up.

A satanic smile crept over Snyp's face as he slowly removed the claws from Tagen's chest. "I expect you will keep me updated on your findings."

Tagen nodded. Pain shot through his chest. Snyp continued to smile as Tagen headed toward the exit. Before he could leave, Snyp spoke again, "If you ever let a demon get past you again, I'll be the first tearing you apart and eating you."

Tagen nodded obediently and exited the cave, not wanting to cause any further arguments. The moist air of the tunnels blew on his oily skin as he exited the cavernous room. His muscles tightened in his belly and his teeth let out an audible grind as he bit down. He hated serving Snyp, there had to be a way to get back on Triaad's good side. Snyp always kept him in a state where he could never prove himself. Possibly, if he was cautious in what he did with Mauldrin, he might do something significant for once.

Slimy skin smashed into Tagen from behind knocking him into a large rock that protruded from the cave's wall. With fast reflexes and amazing agility, Tagen spun around. The oily ground made a slurping noise under his feet. A young dark soul, a youngling, stood in front of him. A deep-throated growl vibrated in Tagen's chest as he clenched his fists. The air became hard to breath and the blackness in the cave became alive, thick on the skin.

The smaller dark soul never had a chance to say a word. His eyes darted all over looking for help as the youngling gripped his throat with clawed hands, unable to breath. Tagen's red eyes blazed in the darkness. The only audible noise was the youngling's breathing. Rage from Snyp's encounter fueled Tagen, pushing him to the limit. As the youngling dropped to his knees on the ground, Tagen let up. The air cleared. The thick blackness dissolved. Without saying a word, he walked off feeling slightly better. He felt tough for almost killing the youngling.

Tagen's red eyes widened and he stopped in his tracks. *That's it. I'll kill him. I'll kill Mauldrin and drag his body back to Triaad. Then Triaad will trust me once again.* Sharp black teeth shown through Tagen's eerie smile as he picked up his pace.

CHAPTER 4

"So you're really leaving in two days," Bridget asked, "and you think you might be back in six months?" She placed her hands on her thin waist and walked in front of the TV to get Caden's attention.

Caden leaned his head back on the sofa. He loved how she looked when she got upset, the way her nose and eyebrows crinkled. "Yeah, that's what we've been told," Caden responded calmly. He laid the remote down on the couch cushion, the soft fabric brushing on the rough skin of his fingers.

When Bridget sat down he caught a whiff of her flowery perfume. She stared at him with pleading eyes. "You just got back, and now they're taking you away for six months? Why can't the company let you try out the equipment here? You're not supposed to leave on these trips for another two to three months." Bridget waved her hands around in frustration.

Caden anticipated her response, and knew part of her frustration was the fact she didn't fully know who he worked for or the details of what he did. Even though he wanted to tell her, it could potentially cost them both their lives, so he kept his pledge to secrecy.

Bridget came close to finding out about the organization a couple of times, which always made Caden nervous. He hated the constant lies to keep his job secret, but he knew there was no other option. Besides, he loved his job.

"The project's bigger then the others and I have to go in," Caden said, hoping that Bridget might understand. "You'll have Mags. She'll take care of you."

Bridget's mouth tightened. "Very funny. I want you here. I don't want your dog to be the one taking your place. In fact, why don't you find a new job that doesn't make you travel all the time, and leave me worrying about your safety?"

Caden looked at her for a moment; he knew she was digging a little. She had already made it clear a few years' back that she knew he was in some type of military or espionage work, which he had acknowledged at that time, but he didn't tell her anything else. "I'm not going to do that. This is a really good job that doesn't come around every day. Why don't you invite some friends over and have some parties?" Caden spoke with a smile trying to get her off topic. He hated when she started pressing him for answers. "You could party until your heart's content."

Bridget's nose flared. "How old do you think I am? I'm not a teenager. I'm not going to throw parties because you're gone," she snapped.

Caden's smile increased ever so slightly. The tactic worked again. "It was just a thought. I figured you could have some fun, throw some parties, have all of your girlfriends over and do whatever girls do."

"Caden, all of my friends are married. They like doing couples things. They aren't going to come and hang out with me because my boyfriend is gone and I'm missing him."

"I'm sorry," he said as he grabbed her hand. "Look, I'll call you every night." He gave her his lost puppy dog look when he knew he pushed the topic too far. "Will that help at all?"

Bridget stood and walked away. Caden quickly jumped up and followed her as she headed for her room. Before she entered, she turned to face him. "How about you marry me as soon as you get back? That would make me feel better." Bridget's dark brown eyes stared stern and strong, almost looking right into Caden's soul. She leaned on the doorframe waiting for his response.

Marriage. The thought scared him more than anything else in the entire world. He loved Bridget and had come close to asking her to marry him numerous times, but he always chickened out. His adoptive parents fought all the time; nights of screaming, bottles smashing against walls, and him crouching under the bed. He pushed the thought away to keep it from interfering with his relationship.

"Well, how does this sound. I'll think about marriage while I'm away, and then we'll talk about it when I get back. But I promise I'll-"

"You'll think about it!" Bridget screeched. "Holy crap, are you serious? I mean, what is that even suppose to mean?" She took a breath and calmed herself down. "Caden, all of my friends met their husbands and within a year they were married to the men they loved. You and I, on the other hand, have been together for years and we still aren't married!"

"Bridget, we've talked about this…" he let his voice trail off. *What is wrong with me, why can't I commit?* He saw his father's face, the smell of alcohol on his breath, his mother crying at the kitchen table. "I just need time. I'm not ready yet," Caden said humbly.

"Well, your time has run out. Figure it out. Either marry me, or we're through. I've waited for eight years and I'm done waiting," Bridget slammed her bedroom door.

Caden placed his hand on the doorknob. He thought about asking her to go with him to his condo. He would brush off the dust on the chest in his closet and pull out a beautifully crafted diamond ring. Then he would turn to her, with one knee on the floor, and ask her to marry him.

Sweat poured down his face as he gripped the handle a little harder getting ready to push the door open. Memories flooded through his mind of times his father would smash down doors to get to his mother. Whenever his mother shut a door, it guaranteed the fight was going to get even uglier. He remembered times of his father beating on his mother for slamming the door, leaving her in a bloody and bruised state. He had tried to protect her, only to be tossed through a wall or knocked down. He could almost taste the blood from those horrible nights and he let go of the handle. Bridget sobbed softly on the other side of the door and it tore into his heart. He hated his inability to take action.

With one snap of his fingers, Mags followed him out of the house. They got into the car and started on their way to Caden's condo. The image of the diamond ring taunted him. He pounded the steering wheel. Fear that he would turn into his father made it very hard for him to act on his desire to marry Bridget. He had bought the ring so many years ago before he began working with SDS. It was the same month his adopted mother had died from a brain tumor and the last month he ever talked to his father.

Halfway to his condo, Caden pulled off the road and stared down the dark empty street. In the rear view mirror, Caden could see Mags lounged on the back seat. The idea of going to his place felt so lonely and cold. He really wanted to just go back and be in Bridget's arms. A couple of cars passed by while he sat there stuck in indecision on where he should go. Finally, not wanting to return to his place and knowing he would only make matters worse if went to Bridget's, he abruptly turned the car around. Mags moaned from the sharp u-turn.

It only took about five minutes to get to the office. When he pulled into the parking lot he saw Matt's fancy, red car parked in front. The moon shimmered on the anally clean surface. Caden thought it was rather odd that Matt would still be at the office unless he was really that bothered by the mission. Normally Matt would be off on a date with some new girl. Neither him nor James stayed at the office if they didn't have to. *Maybe he's working over time to find out who sent me the email.*

As Caden headed through the building something didn't seem right. The hallway lights were turned off and Matt's office was locked. Caden knocked, but no one answered. *Maybe he went home with James.* Even though Matt gave James a hard time about being married, he still begged once and awhile for a nice home-cooked meal.

Caden headed to his office. The lights were on in the hallway and his office door was ajar. Muffled talking could be heard, and

Caden came to a stop. He immediately reached into his black jacket and pulled his gun out. With his back against the wall, Caden slowly approached his office. The muffled voice sounded like Matt as Caden inched closer to the door. *Why is Matt in my office?* He tightened his grip around the gun handle as a precaution.

"We'll meet in the usual spot…yeah, we don't have much time. This is pretty serious," the voice said. Caden peeked through the crack of the door and saw Matt sitting at his desk talking on his cell phone. *How in the world did he get in my office, and why is he in there?*

"Okay, I'll see you at 6 a.m. sharp," Matt said. He hung up his cell phone.

Caden pushed the door open, still holding his gun. Matt made a quick move for his own gun until he saw that it was Caden. He smiled and let out a nervous laugh. "What are you doing here?" Matt asked as he got out of Caden's chair.

"What am I doing here? I think the question should be what are you doing here?" Caden put his gun back into its holster but still felt uneasy. Something wasn't right.

Matt sat down on the windowsill with the moonlight on his back darkening his face. "Well, I was staying late to finish some things when I realized that I had forgotten some papers up here in your office. I figured you had left for the day, but in the small chance that you hadn't, I came up to see if I could get the papers." Matt nervously chuckled.

"The door was unlocked? I don't ever leave the door unlocked." Caden said as he sat in his leather chair.

"Yeah. I thought it was rather strange because I know how meticulous you are about security."

"I'll have to ask Sally about it in the morning. She double checks for me before leaving the building." Caden scratched his shoulder and then situated in his chair. "So, did you find your papers?" he asked, noticing nothing in Matt's hands.

"No, I didn't. I'm really perplexed about where I left them. I came in and started looking around, but as clean as you keep your desk, I knew it was a long shot that they were even here." Matt scratched his head and wouldn't make eye contact. "And then right after I started looking, I got distracted because my new girlfriend called and talked my ear off. So I just sat here and enjoyed your comfortable chair, and that's when you walked in."

Caden bit his lip, feeling that Matt wasn't telling him the whole truth. "Want me to take a look to see if I can find them?"

"Nah, that's okay. It would've been on the top of your desk, so don't worry about it." Matt stood and paced the room.

"Well, I'll just take a quick look," Caden said while he started to sift through his little piles of papers.

"By the way, what are you doing here at this time of night?" Matt asked while turning off his vibrating cell phone.

A picture of Bridget sat next to Caden's computer. Her smile sparkled and her silky brown hair blew in the wind. Caden sighed and turned his attention back to Matt. "Bridget and I had a fight about us leaving, which turned into an argument about marriage. Needless to say, I left and came here because my condo just didn't sound inviting." He revealed a little more information than what he normally would, but it was late and he just needed to vent a little.

"Women. I'm telling you. They're not worth keeping around for very long. They lose their purpose after about two months." Matt spoke in a matter-of-fact tone.

Caden didn't say anything. He sat in his chair staring at Bridget's picture, thinking back on his first two months with her. They had so much excitement and passion in the beginning. The relationship wasn't bogged down by so much complexity. He could still remember the first time he met her. She had been seeing to wounded soldiers in the army hospital, he was there after being shot twice on the battlefield. It had happened during the last war, back when he was in the military.

Matt cut off Caden's thoughts. "Listen, take some advice from a very old friend and just leave her alone for awhile. Let her cool down and realize what a great thing she has. She'll chill out and let the issue go. Marriage will only lead to hurt and anguish, take my word for it."

Silence filled the room for a moment. Caden didn't know what to say. He did remember Matt telling him about his marriage, years ago and how devastating it turned out to be after his wife cheated on him. Shortly after that, Matt divorced her.

Mags broke the awkward silence with a whimper and kicked her feet from a bad dream. Caden stood and rubbed his neck. "Well, I think I'm going to kick you out and get some rest." Caden started making his way over to the couch.

Matt hoped off the windowsill and made his way for the door. "Enjoy the couch."

"I will. Talk to you tomorrow." Caden's words faded as Matt left the room not worrying about finishing his statement. Matt had shut off the lights when he left. Caden laid his head into one of the couch pillows.

The next thing he knew Sally called his name and the sun shown through the large windows. He blinked a couple of times to clear his vision and sat up. She held a cup of hot chocolate in a black mug and smiled.

"Girl troubles, huh?" Sally asked as she sat down next to Caden.

Lifting his left eyebrow, Caden didn't respond. He looked down at his watch and fidgeted uncomfortably. The plan had been to wake up before Sally got there.

"Still afraid to marry her?" She stopped for a second and looked at Caden with a look that made him a little uncomfortable, as if she could read him like a book. "You know, from an outsider's perspective, the two of you already act like you're married. The only difference is you haven't gone through the ceremony."

"Now what business is it of yours to be snooping and analyzing my relationship?" He spoke sharply, but not as sharp as he had planned it to be. A part of him wanted to just let go and talk with Sally about the topic. He ran his hands through his messed-up hair and cleared his throat.

"I'm a woman, comes natural." She spoke with a strong voice, surprising Caden, since she hadn't really talked to him like that before. She tightened her lips for a second and went on. "Fire me if you need to, but if I was that girl I would've left you by now if you were dragging your feet like this." Sally glanced at her wedding ring. "I mean, there are so many people that know one another a whole lot less than you and Bridget and they get married, and they do it because they love and trust each other."

Caden drank his hot chocolate to give him a second to think. She was right, but she didn't know all that he had been through. He thought back to the many times he had one-on-one conversations with his adopted mother, pleading with her to leave his adopted father. She would always say no, that he was a good man inside. That he just had some bad spots in him that needed to be worked out. She truly loved and trusted him, because he was a 'good man'. It was almost as if she was always trying to convince herself that he was a 'good man'. And then that one line she would always add, "You'll be a 'good man' some day too."

Sally took Caden's empty cup and stood staring at him in the eyes. "Look, she's got more patience than I do, but that patience won't last forever." She went to turn away but stopped short and placed the mug on his desk. "Where is Bridget right now? If I were you, I'd go fix whatever's going on between you two before you leave."

Caden looked up with bloodshot eyes. *She's at work.* He got off the couch and snapped his fingers for Mags to follow him. *Now would be the perfect time to run Mags over to her place and leave her there.* He looked back at Sally who was folding the blanket. "Thanks for the advice." The words somewhat surprised him.

"You should just let your fears go," she said, laying the blanket on the back of the couch.

The smooth, dark oak of his door under his fingers reminded him of last night. "Sally, did you leave my door unlocked last night?"

"No, sir. I make sure it's locked every night."

CHAPTER 5 -- FIRST RECORD OF TAGEN

Dead soldiers and their horses lined the ground appearing as lumps scattered across the trampled grass under the moonlight. Their simple weapons of swords, shields and archery equipment seemed laughable at best to Tagen, especially when they were fighting against Azgiel. He wasn't entirely clear why a batch of humans would fight him in the first place. To the East he could see where they had come from, which went up a large hill. From where he stood he could see a small village. *The warriors must've been an accumulation of peasants.*

The flesh on the fallen was still warm and some of them still groaned. Azgiel and his army couldn't be far off. His master and creator, Triaad, had given him direct orders to find Azgiel, see what was left of his army, and watch it slowly be destroyed without being seen. After all his tasks were accomplished, Tagen was to report back.

Tagen had watched while Triaad had worked long and hard to get to his prestigious status. He was Azgiel's top advisor. All of his power had been given to him by Azgiel, separating him from the human race, but he had refined it without Azgiel knowing. With his power, he created what he called the Dark Souls, Tagen's race. And Tagen loved serving his master.

Triaad rewards me well when I do what he asks.

Tagen looked across the uneventful battlefield. A soldier dressed in leather armor that had different colored stitching on the fringes got to his feet. Part of the leather on his left arm was melted away along with some of his flesh. He looked in poor shape. Tagen stared at him for a minute. *Humans, such curious creatures.*

Being in shadow form, the human couldn't see him. A horse pulling a wooden cart, that had spears and swords in it, caught Tagen's attention. Not necessarily the cart, but what was beyond it. A light glow could be seen through the trees. *Azgiel's camp! Only he would be arrogant enough to camp this close to his victorious slaughter.*

A dog had come to the injured human. Its fur matted with blood. The animal looked at Tagen and began to growl.

"What is it boy?" The warrior asked still on one knee.

Tagen chuckled at the lack of technology the planet had. The whole globe still used swords and spears to protect them selves. It wasn't like his home planet, where there were much further advancements with the humans.

The dog kept barking so Tagen showed himself and hissed, scarring the man to the point he fell back and sent the dog yelping. Wasting no more time, he went back to shadow form. He moved across the field with skillful speed. His feet ran over corpses and dying soldiers with ease. Keeping at the same pace, he flew through the cart as if it weren't there, as if it were an illusion. He kept his speed up until he finally heard the gruff tones of demons. Sure enough, it was definitely Azgiel's camp. He had to be there somewhere.

Large demons that looked like mounds, some with horns sat around campfires. Azgiel always kept the big ones with him. Some had wings and some didn't. Being as quiet as possible, Tagen began to circle the camp to get an idea how many were left.

Footsteps came towards Tagen and he moved to a bush and froze. A dark blue demon with a massive sword walked past him. He hadn't been seen and as the demon disappeared into the camp, Tagen let out a breath he had been holding. Some demons had the ability to see dark souls even when they were in shadow form, and some didn't. Each demon had strengths and weaknesses. Unfortunately Tagen could never sort out which demons could spot him and which ones couldn't while he was in shadow form.

Moving rapidly, Tagen circled the camp counting demons. With each step he took precautions not to make any noise or do anything that might give his position away. A strong wind whistled through the trees blowing against his backside as he came to the end where a large tent stood with demons all around it. The tent had to be Azgiel's since it was bigger and had a lot of guards around it.

He was in shock. Triaad's calculations of possibly an army over a thousand were way off. There were only about two hundred demons and creatures combined. The time came to hide out, stay out of sight, and watch. His excitement surged in him. He couldn't wait to see a good fight.

Getting out of the wind, Tagen pranced over and crouched down in several large bushes that surrounded some trees. He snuggled down in the softened ground layered with years of fallen pine needles. *There's no telling how long I'm going to have to camp out before Azgiel's army is finally eliminated, so I'll need to stay in the shadows-* Tagen's thoughts were disrupted. Something gripped his shoulder and slammed him into the tree. Blackness followed.

Tagen's vision was fuzzy when he regained consciousness. "Azgiel." The large man stood in front of him, his face showed the signs of war since the last time Tagen had spied on him. That had been back when he still lived in the kingdom, before the war. Dark bags coated the under parts of his eyes and his unshaven face bore a grimace. A large scar split his upper forehead, which was purple in the cool night air.

"At least this one acknowledges knowing my name." Azgiel's deep voice echoed. He looked at Tagen, moving closer. "Let's see if you'll die like the others, or if you'll make the wise choice to talk before we torture you to death." A sickening smile grew across his face as he turned and walked away.

Others? What others? Triaad hadn't mentioned others. Was he bluffing? Two demons held him tight. A number of other ones stood around. A greenish hued one that stood taller then the others came forward with a wooden club with spikes on it. Tagen wasn't going to stick around any longer. *Time to leave.*

Changing quickly, he went into shadow form and slipped out of the demon's hands. One step was all he got. The greenish demon clawed into his neck and slammed him to the ground. Sticks and rocks poked into his back, he was unable to keep shadow form.

"You try that again and I'll cut your legs off like I did to the others when they tried to escape," the demon said gruffly, spitting in Tagen's face as he spoke.

After three hours Tagen couldn't take anymore. The extensive torture was too much. *It can't hurt to give up and tell them since they will be dead soon.* "I'll talk," Tagen sputtered, some black blood dripping down his chin.

Grinning, the green demon gripped his cheeks and squeezed. "What are you? Who sent you?"

Tagen shook off the demon's grip. *Azgiel still didn't know anything about them? Triaad was able to keep all of this a secret?* Tagen felt both shocked and amazed. "Triaad calls us..." Tagen swallowed the oozing blood down his throat. "...Dark souls. He sent me."

The demon got in Tagen's face and squinted at him for a moment, trying to read him. Finally he stood up and looked at the group of demons that encircled them. "Take him to Azgiel and report what he said." Two demons grabbed him on both sides and carried him towards the large tent.

The morning light was dawning, while the demons pierced a sword through his right shoulder, pinning him to a tree. His dark shadowy body tensed from the searing pain, as black oily blood ran down his chest, giving off a rancid odor.

Tagen looked around at all the different demons and creatures in the camp. The demons came in different sizes and colors. A large, dark silver demon stepped in front of him and pierced another sword through his left thigh, making a hollow thud as it hit the trunk of the tree. Both of his legs dangled from being broken in a number of places. He could feel the throbbing of his muscles and bones trying to rapidly heal themselves, but after so much damage, his normal speedy healing process would take much longer.

"Tha' should hold ya," the older demon spat with a raspy voice. Tagen wanted to prove him wrong and transform into shadow form, which would allow him to move through the metal, but he knew the second he did, they would kill him. In his state, he wouldn't be able to escape fast enough.

Four demons stood around him, all large and as broad as an old tree, waiting for anything that would warrant a reason to kill him. Only ten feet away stood the large tent with heavily armored demons that gave Tagen a shiver. The old demon that had stuck him to the tree entered the tent only to come back out followed by Azgiel. The same one his master Triaad was trying to overthrow.

"I'm told you're ready to talk. And that you're sent by Triaad." Azgiel spoke with perfect calmness.

"Yesss," Tagen sputtered.

"Get on with it. I don't have much time." Azgiel rubbed his hands up and down his arms from a cool breeze, his broad muscles tightening then relaxing.

"Triaad..." Tagen took a breath to ward off the sharp pain in his shoulder. "He sent me to...spy." Another breath. "Triaad...expects you to fall...soon. He decimated your reinforcements. They're not coming...I'm...just here...to see your fall and report back to him of when it happens...so he can...be the new ruler."

Azgiel analyzed Tagen with his cold dark eyes. "Triaad has betrayed me, has he? My most trusted advisor? And my reinforcements are dead?" A smile grew on Azgiel's face. "Triaad might've betrayed me, but there's no way he could've depleted my reinforcements. You're lying. I don't believe you or the other black creatures that serve Triaad. He's not clever enough to gather followers." Stepping closer to one of the guards, Azgiel gripped the handle of the demon's sword that was closest to Tagen and began to draw it. Tagen knew he was dead.

A large, burly creature covered in thick brown hair charged into the camp as Azgiel drew the sword. Blood dripped from his arm. "We're under attack!" the creature yelled. Azgiel gave the sword back to the demon to see what the commotion was about. Tagen exhaled.

Moving back towards his tent, Azgiel spoke to the silver demon that had stabbed Tagen with the sword, "My armor!" Azgiel then turned his attention to the new creature. "How close are they?" Azgiel demanded while strapping on his chest plate. The armor was a dark metal with three diagonal red lines on the chest piece.

"They're right behind me, only minutes away," the creature blurted. "Mauldrin's army annihilated our front lines during the night."

"Mauldrin's army?" Azgiel furled his brow with befuddlement as he peered through the forest. "His whole army?" The creature nodded. "And Mauldrin himself is leading them?"

Azgiel didn't wait to hear any more. "My sword." Azgiel ordered and then turned to his small army. "To arms. Now is the time to give everything you have, it's the moment we've been waiting for. Mauldrin is here." Azgiel peered over at Tagen with anger. "So fight hard. Your lives depend on it," he yelled out to his small army while the silvery demon got Azgiel's sword from the tent.

Trampling hoof beats could be heard in the distance as Azgiel took a hold of his sword. The ground shook, inflicting more pain in Tagen's shoulder and leg.

An army could be seen through the trees. A man large in stature with light gray armor, that appeared almost white, led the army. A light glowed from him that hurt Tagen's eyes as he approached the camp with an enormous army behind him. Tagen knew it had to be Mauldrin. He had never seen him before, only heard stories.

Demons and strange creatures came out of the woodwork, charging Mauldrin from all sides. He lifted a hand producing a bright light followed by a strange vibrating sound and then the creatures and demons were gone as a wave of light engulfed them. Tagen witnessed a power he'd never seen before as Mauldrin annihilated Azgiel's army. A wave of a hand or a pointing of a finger sent more powerful waves of light smashing through trees and engulfing demons. Nothing left alive in its path.

As Azgiel drew his sword preparing to fight, Tagen felt a wave of energy hit him from the sword. The black blade appeared to eat the light that touched it. Tagen could tell from Mauldrin's fierce stare that he was intent on reaching Azgiel. He slammed through another wave of demons that tried to stop him as he persisted towards his target, but none of them were left standing.

Mauldrin jumped off his horse as he reached Azgiel, rolled once and came to his feet kicking Azgiel back with the heel of his foot. Azgiel got his balance and swung his sword, which seemed to tear through the air with black flames, but missed. Azgiel followed up with one word, "Ptarion." Mauldrin was flung back and smashed into a large boulder.

Not wanting to be around to be dealt with by either victor, Tagen tried to shift into shadow form. *Too weak.* He couldn't change.

Azgiel ran at Mauldrin who slowly got back up. The sword flew down at Mauldrin's head but he backed up and flung his hand out with a white energy at his fingertips. Sparks flew as the sword slowed down, but didn't stop.

Mauldrin screamed as two fingers were severed. He jumped back, appearing to almost fly. While tucking his bleeding right hand against his leg, he lifted his other hand in the air. Large flat boulders sprang out of the ground and imprisoned Azgiel. Demons were in the distance, more then what had been there the night before, fighting Mauldrin's army. Tagen had no idea where they all came from. The silvery one sprang at Mauldrin from behind with a large axe.

The axe blade came down hard on Mauldrin's armor, but the demon was blown backwards by some type of unseen field. Blackness began to work its way up Mauldrin's arm starting where his fingers had been cut off. Spinning his other hand around, a blue sphere encircled the wound. Once it dissipated, the blackness could still be seen, even getting worse, having moved up to his elbow.

Tagen knew Azgiel had made his sword with untold power, but he was surprised to see its effect slowly eating away Mauldrin.

Mauldrin's eyes lit up with white flames, which moved to his body. Fingers of light appeared where the two had been cut off and spots of light started to crack through the blackness. An explosion of sorts blasted outward, Tagen could feel a breeze blow against him and sniffed an interesting smell that must've come off Mauldrin. After the dust had settled, Mauldrin's hand was back to normal.

Tagen could feel his body speeding up the rate of his healing, but it was still too slow. The pain was excruciating as bones slowly realigned and grew back together.

With an explosion, the rocks that had entrapped Azgiel blew to pieces. The silvery demon got back on his feet, running back to the fight.

Moving with astonishing speed, Mauldrin dove in the air and landed in front of Azgiel, and pounded the ground. A burst of light blew everyone back, knocking over trees.

Tagen and his tree flew ten feet, crashing to the ground. His vision fuzzy, his muscles weak, he pushed his body to move, knowing he had to get out of there. He tried transforming one last time into shadow form. Success, but he was so worn out it wasn't complete. The swords that pinned him to the tree ripped through parts of his un-transformed flesh as he scurried to a safer position.

A large bush that was close by looked like a good place to hide. Tagen crawled under the bristly leaves. He peered out to see what would happen next. Mauldrin had walked up to Azgiel, who was knocked out on the ground. Azgiel's sword floated in the air, held there by Mauldrin, but Tagen couldn't see how. Only one demon could be seen still fighting, but he wouldn't last long being surrounded by Mauldrin's troops.

Leaves ruffled a small distance away catching Tagen's attention. *A demon. If they are out here hiding then they must've retreated.* He could make out his large bulky shape in some overgrown bushes. Azgiel was left alone or so it appeared. Looking back to the action, he watched as the silver demon came out behind a tree with his axe and cut down one of Mauldrin's men.

With a second swing the silver demon tried to take Mauldrin down again, aiming for his head. Tagen was fascinated, but he knew he was pushing his luck sticking around, especially with a demon not too far away from him.

Before the silver colored demon could make contact, Mauldrin waved a hand and with a white flash, all that was left was a pile of dust floating to the ground.

Azgiel awoke, as Mauldrin and his men circled around him. Tagen could barely see through a gap of men as Azgiel laid on the ground staring at Mauldrin.

"Give up Azgiel, you've been defeated. Your evil reign will go no further." Mauldrin's powerful words carried through the woods and gave Tagen a shiver.

"My evil reign!" Azgiel shouted. "How dare you accuse me of such nonsense? You're the one-" Mauldrin lifted a finger and Azgiel's voice became muted. Standing up, Azgiel placed a hand on his throat. The men around him drew their swords as he stood. He looked up at his sword that dangled above him in the air.

"Don't do it Azgiel. I don't want to fight you any longer." Mauldrin sounded calm but stern. Tagen shifted his weight uneasily, he knew he needed to bolt, but he was ordered to see what happened before he returned to Triaad.

Not listening, Azgiel jumped forward. His sword broke from the invisible power that held it and flew into his hand. Men crowded in front of Mauldrin to protect him. Five of them blew into pieces as Azgiel sliced through their shields and swords, cutting right through them. With his other hand, he waved it and everyone flew back accept Mauldrin, who stood his ground. Azgiel lurched towards him, sword ready to strike.

Tagen shifted uncomfortably. *If Azgiel wins, I'm dead. Triaad will find out I gave up information.* Mauldrin pulled back with both of his hands as a ball of light formed in his palms. He shifted forward and the light blasted Azgiel to the ground. Bands of light wrapped around him and pinned him down. Men came running up to help. One of them lifted his sword and readied to stab it into Azgiel's heart. Azgiel closed his eyes showing he was ready for his death.

Tagen smiled. His news would make Triaad happy, and rewards would be abundant. Above all, he wouldn't be in trouble for revealing the information about Triaad.

"Stop!" Mauldrin shouted and the man froze. "He's not to be killed." Mauldrin lifted a hand and Azgiel's sword floated back into the air. "Metted boenden entexted." His words were strange. Tagen had never heard them before. A deep hole in the ground opened and the sword fell into it, closing after it entered.

"None of your followers will ever be able to touch that sword. I've cursed it. Any evil touches it, they will be destroyed," Mauldrin spoke to Azgiel. Tagen knew he was also speaking to any demons or creatures that were watching. "As for you Azgiel, trapped in a cell of time for an eternity should fit you just fine." Azgiel shifted and squirmed but was unable to loosen the bands.

Brightness glowed around Azgiel and then he was gone. Something moved to the right of Tagen and he could hear heavy breathing. He turned his head, keeping his body very still. A new demon, orange in color, towered over him, but was oblivious to him lying in the bushes. His attention was focused on Mauldrin.

The demon was too close for Tagen's liking, so he turned into shadow form. His body had healed many of the wounds, but he was still in a lot of pain, making it hard to move or flee. Using extreme caution, he slipped out of the area unnoticed.

Time to report to Triaad that Azgiel is gone.

CHAPTER 6

Caden was walking through Bridget's house to put Mags out back when his pocket started buzzing. He pulled out his cell phone and flipped the lid. "Hey, Robert. We secure?"

"Yes. What'd you need Caden?" Robert's voice was cordial, but he spoke quickly.

"I wanted to make sure I understood everything correctly-"

"Wasn't the email clear enough?"

Caden's eyebrow rose, unconcerned with Robert's impatience. "You want us there in two days so my men, excluding me, plus Burton's team can go into Dead Time, right?"

"Do you want to go in?" Robert asked.

"You better believe it. I didn't create the project to sit idly by while others use it." Caden smoothed back his hair to calm down. He was letting his emotions get the better of him.

"That's fine. I just thought you wouldn't want to go in until all the bugs are worked out." Robert expressed no emotion.

Bugs worked out? Ha. You already tested the thing on humans without me there and behind my back! Once again Caden let out a breath to calm down. He wasn't fully sure why the whole thing was getting him so frustrated. "Well, that's another thing. I'm not sure if the equipment is safe to send anyone in yet. We need to do further testing. As it stands right now, I'd be worried the material wouldn't hold out and could actually hurt or kill someone." He actually had no idea that it could've, but why not add the statement to make Robert spill his guts.

"It'll be fine. Allen's already looked over the material and feels he's found all the bugs."

"Without me? You told me you weren't going to work on it until you called me back in." Caden swallowed. "Did Allen send someone in to test it? Is that how he examined it, to figure out if there were any bugs?" Caden wanted to see if Robert would lie to him or if he would do what he taught them, to be honest with one another.

"We did test it on some humans. In fact, it was Steven and Jason. And yes, you're right. The material didn't hold up as it should've and killed Jason. Steven is in poor condition." Robert coughed on the other end, but it didn't sound like a sick cough, more like a nervous cough. "Allen figured out how to try the material on humans, and my advisors were overly-excited to give it a try. So, needless to say, we gave it a try. We figured we were going to call you up for the success party, but I wanted you to get a good vacation."

"You should've told me." Caden knew he was pushing the limits on how he was talking to Robert, but he was mad.

"You've been told now. If you want to be here when the Burton team goes in for their first one, I would advise that you get in today because they've just arrived nice and early as always." Caden was surprised; it was rare that Robert spoke to him like that. He had to be under a lot of stress, that was the only times he ever spoke to Caden in harsh tones.

"I'll let my team know. We'll be in before the night is out."

"Good. We'll try to wait for you. You'll be impressed with what we've done with this thing. I think you'll like it." He began sounding like the normal Robert.

"Great. I'll see you tonight then." Caden was still frustrated and he knew he shouldn't do any chitchatting right now.

Caden closed his cell phone then flipped it back open and called Sally.

"Hey Caden?"

"Well, I have some bad news for the guys," Caden said. "The main office called and wants us to get there tonight because the

Burton team got there early and Robert wants to get going on the project."

Sally chuckled. "The Burton team got there early, huh?"

Caden slammed a cupboard door. "His team seems to constantly be a thorn in my side. Could you call Matt and James for me?"

"I'll give them a call as soon as I get off the phone with you."

"Great, just let them know they can go whenever it works best for them. We won't worry about traveling together," Caden said as he walked out of the kitchen.

"I'll let them know. Oh, and Caden, please think about what I said earlier."

"Not now, Sally." Caden said, as he plopped on the couch. Mags sat on the floor by his feet. He flipped the phone shut and let out a deep sigh, while letting his phone drop on the arm of the couch. His phone slipped off the edge and headed for the hardwood floors. Caden quickly moved to catch it, but missed, and in the process, hit the end table knocking a picture off. The glass shattered as the frame landed.

When he noticed what picture it was, Caden sat there frozen in place with his teeth clenched. Slowly he stood to survey the mess. The picture was face down, and broken glass was scattered around the frame. He carefully picked up the broken glass pieces and threw them away.

With the picture in hand, Caden sat back down. It was a picture of Bridget and him sitting on a log with the ocean crashing behind them. She was beautiful with her long dark brown hair and dark eyes. The picture was taken years ago, back at Bridget's mother's house. They went there often because it was their favorite place to walk and be together. He could almost smell the peaceful scent of the ocean and hear the rhythmic sound of the waves lapping on the beach. If only they could take some time and go there now, that might cool things down between them—it always seemed to in the past.

Caden focused on the jagged pieces of glass that encircled the picture. He picked at a piece; the glass made a horrible grinding noise from pushing up against the other broken shards. Mags let out a whine that broke his concentration.

"I don't know what to think, Girl," Caden said as he patted her head. She stared at him with a quizzical look, her head tilted sideways. "Maybe this picture says it all. Maybe Bridget and I are just broken."

Mags walked over to the back door and let out another whine. Caden let out a sigh, not wanting to get up, but he did as she wanted and let her out. Turning around, he noticed a picture of Bridget and him on the fridge. She had put it up last year and drew a heart around his face. She told Caden he was the love of her life and planned on being with him forever. *I'm amazed that Bridget has stuck by me these last eight years. She deserves better then this.*

There were so many times that he had caused problems or fights, but Bridget never gave up on him, and she stuck with him even during the hard times. A sickness ran through his stomach as he realized how much he took her for granted—keeping secrets from her about his work, leaving for long stretches of time and not communicating much during the duration. The only thing she asked of him was for an agreement to marry her.

"I want to marry you. I just can't..." Caden spoke to the picture and put his hand on it. Even mentioning the word marriage made his hands cold and clammy. Fear was preventing him from getting married. He thought about all the people he had killed or captured during his military years and his years of working at the SDS. None of them had even slightly scared him, yet he was afraid to commit to the person he loved the most and trusted with his life.

Caden balled his hand into a fist and through a punch as hard as he could into the fridge. *What's wrong with me? It's my stupid father's fault. I can't allow myself to become like him. I couldn't live with myself if I ever raised a hand to Bridget.*

Flashes of his quivering mom in corners waiting for her husband to pound on her, made Caden physically ill. His mom never seemed to see the destruction. "He's a good man" was all she ever said.

Caden touched the picture with his finger and followed the heart design. He had shared his past with Bridget about his abusive father.

She held him close and told him that he would never be that man. He had gone cold and distant when she said that because she didn't really know him. But remembering her words now sent a sense of peace and calmness through his body.

He closed his eyes and took a deep breath, pushing the fear aside for a moment and let the idea of marrying her sink into his heart. For once, he could finally see clearly what he had to do and more importantly what he had always wanted to do.

It's time to ask you to marry me. Screw my father. Sweat dripped down his forehead. If he didn't act now, it was only a matter of time before his fear would stop him. He looked at his watch. *Three more hours before Bridget gets off work.* Caden quickly made his way out of the house feeling his heart racing a mile a minute.

The fresh air rushed passed his ears as he slid across the hood of his car and got in. With his foot on the floor, he sped off down the road. Caden couldn't get to his place fast enough. He needed to stay focused on the task at hand.

The details on how Caden got into his condo were a little blurry. He grabbed the silvery knobs of his closet doors and slid them open. The closet was filled with camping gear and boxes. He moved everything off the chest. Dust outlined where a box had sat, but Caden didn't care, he grabbed the lid and tried to open the chest. *No luck.* He scratched his head.

He never locked the chest and he didn't even know where he kept the key. He bit his lip hard thinking about all the different possibilities of where the key could be.

The key was probably in his box of trinkets and junk. Moving to the small wooden box on his dresser, he quickly searched through it. *No luck.* It had to be in the room somewhere. He searched around frantically, dumping things onto the floor and bed. *Nothing.* Using his strong muscles he slammed a drawer shut. *Okay, breathe buddy. It has to be here.* A small clock on the wall ticked away as he glanced up at it. *I still have time. I'll just utilize this time to pack and brainstorm on where it might be while I get ready.*

Letting go of the drawer handle, Caden went and got his bags while exhaling a deep breath. He made short work of packing what he needed for the trip to the office. Tightness grew in his chest, as he still couldn't figure out where the key could be, and before he knew it he was done packing and everything was loaded in the car.

Caden walked to the chest and looked at it for a moment. *Screw it, you're going down.* Walking calmly, Caden entered the garage and got the crowbar. After going back in the room, he looked at the chest for a moment. *Key or no key, you're going to open.*

Metal slammed into the crack underneath the lid of the chest. With a hard push, the lock broke and the wooden lid flew open. The ring was just under a couple of books. As he picked up the black box his anxiety mounted; his breathing increased and sweat began to build on his forehead. Being so focused on trying to get the ring, Caden had been distracted from the anxiety. *Am I making a mistake?*

Taking in a deep breath and releasing it Caden gripped the small box in his hand and stood up. *No, I have to do this. At least this way we'll be engaged, we can figure out the marriage part later.*

Seeing the time on his watch, Caden realized he had to hurry if he was going to get back and be ready for Bridget. He jumped in the car and sped off. A million ideas raced through his head on how he wanted to ask Bridget to marry him. Somehow he thought it would be fun to involve Mags, maybe tying the ring to her collar. Even the old fashioned 'getting on one knee' seemed like it could be heartfelt enough since he didn't have a tremendous amount of time to be more creative. Each idea helped him push back his fear that kept trying to push its way to the forefront of his mind. He had to get this over with, and then maybe he would feel better.

In his rush, Caden hit the curb pulling into Bridget's driveway, rocking him back and forth in his seat. He grabbed the ring and darted up the front lawn only to find the front door locked. *I swear I didn't lock this.*

Confusion set in, but he needed to keep going so he shrugged it off and pulled his keys out. After entering he set the ring on the counter and headed for the kitchen.

"Mags! Come here, Girl," Caden yelled into the backyard feeling the cool breeze on his face. "Mags. Come on." He let out a loud whistle, but the only response was the neighbor's dog barking at him. *Where the blazes is she? She better not've gotten out.* He ruffled his eyebrows in confusion. Slowly, he stepped back into the house. Something strange was going on. He reached for his gun, but stopped halfway. *You're just overacting. There's gotta be an explanation for this.*

"Mags, did I leave you in the house?" He slowly walked into the front room and looked at the time. Bridget wasn't supposed to be home for another hour and Mags would never run off. His stomach dropped.

He reached into his pocket for his cell phone but it wasn't there. He rubbed his finger and thumb across his chin thinking. This was not like him. Leaving without his cell phone wasn't an option. He had to have it for work. Suddenly, something vibrated from underneath the couch. Diving down, he found his phone and picked it up. He'd forgotten to pick it up after the picture broke.

"Hey Caden, how's it going?" James asked.

"Doing well enough for the moment, what can I do for you?" Caden paced as he spoke, analyzing his surroundings, trying to make sense of everything.

"I just wanted to let you know I wouldn't be in until late tonight. I have some plans that I'm not about to cancel."

"Not a problem. I understand. Robert just wants us there some time tonight. It's not a big deal what time you get there. Anyhow, I need to let you go, so I'll talk to you later." He hung up the phone and was just about to dial Bridget's work number when he noticed a message on his voicemail.

Caden listened intently as Bridget's voice came on. Once the message was over, he lowered the phone and hung it up. The muscles in his face tightened as he closed his eyes.

I'm too late.

CHAPTER 7

Bridget slumped in her hard chair. She sat in the back corner of the doctor's office where she worked. The plain white walls around her didn't help with her depressed mood. It was difficult to even focus on her patients today.

"You're next patient is checked in," the receptionist's cold voice spoke over Bridget's shoulder. Sighing deeply, Bridget started to stand but a strong hand took hold of her shoulder, calming her body.

"Sit back down," Doctor Frasier spoke.

She could feel the heat in her face and hear her breathing shortened. *Oh crap, he must've seen me lounging.* "Yes?" Bridget asked in a meek tone.

"What's going on? You aren't focused." The doctor's calm voice eased her tight muscles.

"I'm having some problems with Caden," Bridget said while moving closer to the doctor so no one else would hear.

"Go home," Frasier said with a smile then turned and walked off. "Don't argue. Take the time you need."

She blinked a couple of times. *Should I argue with him?*

Glancing from the doctor to the room where her patient waited, she saw another nurse, her co-worker, waving good-bye to her as she stepped into the room.

I'm going. Bridget didn't allow any further debate, the doctor was right she needed to go.

Moving quickly through the office, she made short work of getting to her car. The keys jingled as she stuck them in the ignition. *Now what?*

She had been eager to leave, but there was nowhere to go. Caden was at work, so she couldn't go and deal with that situation, and home didn't sound inviting.

Finally the stale warm air in her car began to make her feel uneasy so she pulled out of the parking lot and just drove. She rolled down her windows; the fresh air blew through her hair. Something clanked together next to her. A normal sound, a common sound, but it caught her attention this time.

Caden's metals. There were two of them hanging from her mirror.

She always kept them in her car to help remind her of him. One of the amazing acts he did to get his last metal happened the same day she had met him. She had been working at the military hospital. A large number of men had just arrived from a gruesome battle. Hundreds of soldiers had died that day.

There was a long corridor lined with beds and soldiers. A soldier standing at the end caught her eye. He was on crutches with a bandaged leg and a shoulder, staring out a small window.

As she made her way towards him, believing it was the soldier she had heard some rumors about, she could see blood seeping through his shoulder bandage. "Excuse me," Bridget said softly trying to get the soldiers attention. He looked at her with pain filled eyes and then gazed back out the window. His heart seemed so heavy laden.

"Are you the one that saved these soldiers?" Her voice stumbled at the end from a strange gaze he gave her while she asked. She looked down at the blood that was seeping through the shoulder wound. There was a silence for a moment as he analyzed her, almost appearing to be staring into her soul. When he finished, he still kept his silence and looked back out the window.

"Well," she mustered up the courage to speak again. His mysterious ways only captivated her more. "If it's you, I just wanted to thank you for your bravery. You're a hero and I don't think you soldiers get enough gratitude for what you do for our country." She waited for a moment

for a response, but nothing came and she turned to walk away. She took one step and then felt his strong grip pull her back. His hand shook as he turned her around.

"I'm not a hero," Caden responded. "Men died out there today. They are the true heroes, the ones to give your thanks to." He let her go and looked back out the window. She could only imagine all that was going through his mind and the pain he was going through.

"You're right, they are heroes, and so are you." After her stern words, she left to see to other patients, but their conversations continued and grew over the next couple of days. By the end of it, she had fallen in love.

A red light brought her out of her reminiscent memory. *I don't really want to lose him. I love him. If he feels uncomfortable to marry me at this time, then I can be patient and wait.* Something choked at her throat with the thought, but she swallowed it down because the time to take some initiative was now, and she wasn't going to lose Caden. There had to be a way to sit down and talk things out without the fighting.

A meal would be nice, especially a romantic one where she could tell him how amazing he was and how much she loved him. There was one more night before he left, so there was still time to put something together. She headed directly to the store and picked up a fancy meal with lobster tails and all.

Before Bridget knew it, she was home. Once inside, she threw her purse down on the floor and kicked off her shoes. She heard scratching at the back door and jumped, startled by the noise. Slowly, she set her keys down on the little table by the door and made her way to the kitchen. Mags stood at the back door wagging her tail, her tongue flopping out of her mouth. Bridget exhaled. She opened the door and Mags rushed in, dancing around her in circles.

"Caden, are you home?" Her stomach filled with butterflies at the thought that maybe he was there to surprise her. She walked from room to room calling out his name.

"Caden, are you in here?" she asked as she entered the spare room where Caden kept his traveling gear. Clothes and some hangers were strewn on the floor and the closet doors were wide open. All of his gear was gone. She ran her fingers through her silky hair and wrapped her arms around her stomach as a sick feeling ran through her. *Did he just come by to leave his dog here so he wouldn't have to face me to say goodbye?*

"Okay, I'm not going to over react, there has to be a logical explanation for this. He doesn't leave until tomorrow," she said under her breath. She hurried outside to her car and retrieved the cell phone from her purse. After a couple of tries with no success, outside of his voice mail, she hung up and dialed Matt's number, while pacing on the sidewalk.

"Hey Matt, it's Bridget. I was wondering if you know where Caden is?"

"Nope. I actually don't for once," Matt responded with a chuckle.

"Huh, I came home early and found Mags here and no Caden." She pushed some dirt off the cement curb with her foot.

"Well," Matt started saying, "he might have left already."

"Why would he leave a day early?" Bridget asked. Her heart raced, pounding under her ribs.

"Did he not tell you? The company changed their minds. We have to report in tonight."

"So I was right."

"What was that, I couldn't hear you?" Matt asked.

Bridget heard another voice on the phone in the background. "Matt, if you're going to run this thing then run it. If not I'm going to take over. We need to go since their pushing things up." The voice was gruff and unfamiliar. She headed back in the house as she listened.

Bridget was just about to ask who that was but before she could get a word out he cut her off. "Sorry, Bridget. I got to go." A click followed Matt's abrupt and sharp goodbye.

Bridget hung her cell phone up. The room seemed to be spinning so she sat down on the couch. Feeling overwhelmed she slammed her phone down on the end table without looking and felt a sharp prick. Pain shot through her finger as she pulled her hand back and saw blood building on the tip of it. Looking over, she saw the broken picture.

Tears built at the corners of her eyes as a drip of blood fell to the floor. "Why Caden? What have I done? I love you so much," she said to herself reaching for the broken picture. "Not only do you ditch your dog, but now you leave me a message like this? That's it. It's over." She pulled the picture from the frame, tightened her eyes, and clenched her teeth. After a few deep breaths, she grabbed the bag of food and took it to the garbage can.

Whistling for Mags, Bridget picked her cell phone up and the photo. As she got into the front seat of her car, she dialed Caden's cell again and pulled out of the driveway.

Caden's voicemail blared in her ear. Hearing his voice was hard. She felt like all of her dreams had been torn away. Warm tears rolled down her cheek. The pain had become too much, she couldn't control her emotions. *You weren't even man enough to tell met to my face.* His cowardly and aggressive ways hurt and it was too much. Her dreams were crushed.

"Caden…" She sniffled. "It's over. I really don't want anything to do with you any longer. I'm over you. I'm going to go live with my mom for a while and I don't want to see you ever again. I went ahead and grabbed Mags because I know you need someone to watch her while you're away, but I'm not going to be here when you come to get her. Just so you know, I'm turning my phone off after this message and I'm not turning it back on." She paused for a moment. "Goodbye Caden, please don't contact me ever again. We're through."

CHAPTER 8

The night was dark and the only noise that could be heard was an owl in the distance singing a sad one-note song. Tagen walked up to the cabin where he had first found Mauldrin. He stood in the meadow in front of the retreat looking at the log building and the darkened windows. Putting his nose in the air, he sniffed. *Nothing.*

If he's in there, I'm going to kill him. Tagen reached to the ground and drew a squiggly line in the dirt below the meadow grass. He crouched down and looked at the cabin for a moment taking in a deep breath. *I hope I don't screw this up.* Letting out a scream, a black-like root flew through the top of the dirt and slammed into the cabin. A small ditch was left in the dirt.

The structure moaned and creaked as the entire building lost its color turning to a gray shade. After a couple of moments it began getting its brown hue back followed by a loud crack. Tagen jumped up with a smug smile on his face and put his hands to his waist. *If he's in there, he has to be dead.*

Moving cautiously he walked into the cabin, going through one of the walls in shadow form. He could sense a couple of dead mice in the walls as well as a number of different bugs. The cabin was barren of life, all of it slaughtered by his power. There was a sense of relief that Mauldrin wasn't there, but it was shortly lived as frustration quickly took over.

Everything was tidy and clean, even the bed where Mauldrin had slept. He sniffed at the blankets. The scent was old, but still useful. It led into the bathroom and then around the room. Tagen followed the trail that led out of the building. Six feet from the cabin was as far as he got before the scent completely cut off, like it was erased. *No wonder why I didn't get a strong scent out here, but who's guarding him and hiding the trail?* Something wasn't right.

His eyes studied the direction that the scent had been leading. *The Witch! If the demons had come out earlier that morning, what was to stop them from following my trail to Mauldrin?*

He had to know for sure if the ancient evil had Mauldrin; he couldn't take that kind of news back to Snyp without facts.

He followed the path that he had taken the last time, heading towards the ancient forest. Once he arrived at the wood's edge, he hid in some bushes and peered into the blackness. The demons never came this far out, but Tagen still knew he needed to be cautious. He looked behind him. *Maybe I should just leave now. I have enough evidence; I could even make some up. Who knows, maybe I saw them drag Mauldrin away. Snyp would have to believe that.* Shifting his weight, he turned his gaze back towards the woods, the prickly branches stabbed at his face.

On the other hand, if they already did the dirty work for me of killing Mauldrin, all I would have to do is get a piece of his body and take it to Triaad. I would be a hero and take the credit for the kill. A smile stretched across his face. He licked his black lips with his equally black tongue.

Tagen leaned down, getting closer to the ground and sniffed to see if he could pick up any kind of a trail that might've been left behind if they had caught Mauldrin and dragged him away. His eyes turned dark red as he sniffed and he bolted out of the bush, but it was too late.

A young beautiful woman stood in front of him casting a white glow. She took a step closer, her bare feet quietly ruffling the leaves on the ground. Her beauty captivated Tagen. Her long, flowing white hair, skin that looked as soft and smooth as silk, and her dark blue eyes that could calm the most restless ocean, left Tagen in awe. He had heard about her captivating looks, but to see her face-to-face and this close, made him forget who she was for a moment.

Once Tagen came back to his senses he quickly looked around to see if there was a way to escape. *Stupid, I should've run when I had the chance.* He couldn't see anyone else, but he could sense that her followers were all around. She moved toward him with a grin on her face. Obviously there was something she wanted from him or he would already be dead.

"What have you been doing in my woods?" the ancient, but young-looking witch asked.

Tagen just stood there listening for any noises.

The witch kept talking. "It must be pretty important for you to risk your life." There was silence as Tagen stared at her.

"You have two options," she said as she slowly circled behind him, her soft silk dress brushed against his leg. "You can tell us and we'll let you go peacefully." Her small white hand clasped his shoulder. "Or you can make it fun and we'll drag the information out of you." Her nails dug into his shoulder releasing a dribble of his black blood. He tried to break from her grasp, but he felt sluggish and weak.

Something crawled through Tagen's body as it made its way down his abdomen and into his legs. The feeling stopped just above his ankles. When the witch loosened her grip, Tagen immediately tried to run for it, but the second he lifted his leg something ripped through the skin of his calves and feet. Large brown roots shot out of his limbs, and pulled his feet to the ground. He screamed out in pain and struggled to move.

Black blood oozed out from Tagen's torn flesh. With all his might, he tried to release himself, but with every move, more roots ripped through him shooting into the ground from his stomach and hands. His face slammed into the dirt as more came through his cheeks. A few patches of grass quickly turned brown from the touch of his skin.

A thud landed behind Tagen. He could feel the vibrations, which caused more pain. *Stupid demons. I'm not ganna be able to sweet talk my way out of this situation.* He clenched his teeth, grinding them together as another root shot out from his gums. The demon behind him let out a low-pitched growl.

The witch called out to the beast in a calm voice. "Apparently he's not going to talk or he would've by now." Tagen caught a whiff of the witch's sweet intoxicating smell of wild flowers making the pain more bearable. "Do what it takes to get the information out of him. If he doesn't talk soon then just destroy the sinful little creature like the others."

The others? Had they been slowly killing off the other dark souls that had been patrolling the edges of their woods? It wouldn't be hard since Snyp had turned the patrols into skeleton crews. His anger raged with Snyp's incompetent decisions. He had to be taken out.

"It'll be taken care of." The unseen demon grunted.

A strong pain shot through Tagen's head and then everything went black. He wasn't sure how long he had been out when he came back around. His body ached and his vision blurred. Voices could be heard but his head was spinning so much that he could barely make out what they were saying. Pain swam through him and he closed his eyes. The voices said something about Domblin, and Tagen tried to focus on the conversation.

"I have this creature telling me Mauldrin's back and now you're telling me Domblin's back as well. Where's Kaz? Why isn't he with you?" the witch said in the distance. Tagen gasped. He had given up information on Mauldrin, but at least they didn't have him. Domblin. If he got out of this alive, Triaad would need to know that Domblin's here.

"He stayed behind to keep looking for-" The demon's voice stopped. Tagen heard the ground crunch as a demon walked over to him. *Crap.* He tried to breathe normal keeping his eyes closed trying to look like he was still unconscious.

"He's awake. Wait, he's the one I ran into when we left the woods. The one that gave me these pretty scars." The demon chuckled with a rumble. "Shall I kill this pathetic creature before I go back to Kaz?"

The witch took a moment to respond. "No, I have a better idea. Let his own kind deal with him. It will send Triaad a message."

She's up to something. A hard blow to his head cut off Tagen's thoughts.

When Tagen woke the second time, he could feel claws digging into his back. The ground was a couple of feet below him and he realized that he was being carried. Struggling, he turned his head and looked up. It was the same demon that had chased him into the ancient forest, his pitch-black skin and white tattoos shimmered in the sunlight.

Each large step the demon took sent pain throughout Tagen's battered body. He let his body go limp. A large leg with three white tattoos on it came up into his face as the demon stepped up a small hill. Tagen made his move and bit down into the strong flesh.

Feeling the intense strength of the demon, Tagen couldn't hold his bite. The demon slammed him into a nearby tree. Tagen's strength was spent.

"If I wasn't ordered to hand you back over, I would kill you right now."

Tagen could barely move his limbs as he was hurled into the cave that he knew all too well—home and soon to be his death. Brush crunched as the demon walked back into the woods chuckling. Tagen tried to move his arms and legs but was unable to move any part of his body. He lay there, bleeding, waiting for the inevitable. If Snyp was there or one of the older dark souls Tagen would be okay, but the younglings that sat at the opening of the cave were ruthless.

The first noise Tagen heard was some sniffing. He blacked out for a moment, but was brought back to his senses when he heard his name being called. Only one of his eyes opened. He saw three dark shadowy figures standing in front of him. They were younglings, all eager to have Tagen to themselves. With all the energy he had left, Tagen tried to move and call out, but it was useless. His body was noncompliant and most of his head and face were smashed in.

The creatures quickly made their way to Tagen, but suddenly a fight broke out. Their food was always given to them in the past and they never had to fight for it before. One of them escaped from the brawl and started crawling toward Tagen. The shadowy creature slipped over a boulder that Tagen's body was hewn against. His claws clicked across the hard surface.

Tagen understood that it was just in their nature. It was an eat or be eaten world, and if they had the opportunity to gobble a dark soul up before they died, even better for them. Being no stranger to that life—he had done the same a couple times himself—Tagen prepared to die.

The creature bit into Tagen's foot sending pain through his body as he felt teeth slowly rip into his flesh. Not wanting to feel all the pain, Tagen tried to relax and just let go.

There was no use in fighting. His life had been something great. One of Triaad's top servants until he messed up, and now he was going to die as a low grade servant for Snyp, a conniving traitor, out to overthrow Triaad.

As the dark soul took its second bite, something pulled the youngling off and the creature was thrown against a wall.

A voice boomed. "You greedy wretched things. Do I not feed you enough?" Snyp stood on top of the boulder that Tagen's body was against. His voice was heavenly, even if Tagen was mad at him.

"I need him alive. You don't eat just any dark soul without my permission." Snyp jumped off the rock and hovered over the creature that he had thrown against the wall. Through the small slits of his barely open eyes, Tagen watched the whole scene. *Get 'em Snyp, kill 'em.*

"No. Please, no. Snyp, no." The creature groveled on the floor. Snyp grabbed the creature and within seconds had killed him, biting into his neck with his deadly black teeth. The other two younglings quickly tried to make their escape but were stopped by five other dark souls, only to Tagen's glee.

"As for you two," Snyp said to the creatures, "you shall be Tagen's dinner tonight." They screamed down the cave as they were taken away. *Scream boys, it only makes me more excited to eat you.* It had been years since Tagen had been able to rejuvenate with a tasty youngling.

Snyp bent down beside Tagen. "You had me worried when you left here. I wasn't sure if I could trust you, but I'll never question your loyalty again. You've definitely proven it. Now, brother, let's get you fixed up." With a rare gentleness, Snyp slowly picked up

Tagen's broken body. Not fully buying Snyp's positive attention, Tagen tensed. The cave was beautifully dark as Snyp carried him into their home. He whispered into Tagen's bleeding ear, "Did you find him?"

With a lot of effort, Tagen shook his head, no. Snyp narrowed his eyes and tightened his jaw, but continued walking without looking at Tagen.

"For now we're going to have to let that go. With this demon situation getting worse, Lord Triaad is coming, and I want to make sure Triaad isn't here long so he doesn't find out about Mauldrin."

The news was music to Tagen's ears. *It will be so much easier to bring Mauldrin to Triaad if he's here. I won't have to try and bypass Snyp to get to him. Now all I have to do is find him and kill him.* Tagen's eyes widened. *If he's coming here, he needs to know about Domblin.*

"Domblin's here...Witch said so..." Tagen gasped in between his words, he hoped Snyp would report it to Triaad.

"I'll have to tell Triaad. There are some..."

Tagen didn't have the energy to listen any longer.

CHAPTER 9

The taxi pulled up to a large plain looking building with no windows. It often looked like a factory to Caden or more like a prison. It was intended that way to discourage people from investigating.

To get to the building there was a large metal gate with sharp posts sticking out of the top of it. Wanting to get to bed, Caden started heading towards the gate in the cool, dark air of the night. The slightly overcast moon made it harder to see.

His shoes tapped on the sidewalk. *What's that?* There was more then just his shoes tapping. He stopped, and sure enough someone was walking towards him from behind.

Acting normal, Caden kept walking but turned slightly to see who was there. The person was an older man with a beard and gray hair.

Caden had seen him before, but never this clearly and not in many years. The first time he saw him, years ago, Caden thought it had to be an agent from another country. The sightings were normally quick glimpses and were always strange. He reported the man to Robert and after an intensive investigation of looking Robert theorized it was hallucinations from stress.

After that conversation, Caden made sure he just ignored the 'hallucinations'. The man never did anything accept show up in obscure places once in a great while. So Caden figured if anything bad ever did happen he would take action then. But this was different.

The man was actually walking up to him. It was time to find out if the man really existed or not.

Caden turned abruptly. "Stop. Close enough." Without any acknowledgment, the man kept walking. Moving with moderate speed, Caden gripped the cold handle of his gun. *This is going to look bad if this guy's some crazy hallucination and someone sees this.*

"Stop." Caden pulled his gun. The stranger was only six feet away.

"You're going to shoot me?" the unknown man responded, but only slowed down. Caden prepared to fire.

"Stop toying boy, we only have a moment before they notice us."

Without another thought, Caden pulled the trigger, aiming at the man's right arm. Nothing. The gun wouldn't shoot, even as he pulled the trigger again.

"Put the thing down. I'm not here to harm you." The man stopped only a foot away. His eyes were soft blue and familiar somehow, like Caden knew him from somewhere.

"Who are you and what do you want?" Caden's muscles tensed, ready to strike. He positioned his right foot back just a smidge, in a ready stance.

"Up tight aren't we?" the man spoke with a smile. "My name is Domblin. I'm the one that brought you back into this world."

"Are you trying to say you're my dad?" Caden asked. The orphanage had never been able to locate his mother or father, and in all the years he grew up he was never able to find anything out about them.

Domblin just smiled. "Not necessarily your dad." He looked over at the gate and back to Caden with his eyes narrowed. "I don't have time to talk right now, someone's coming. Don't go any further with your Dead Time project. It's already caused detrimental issues, and it will only cause more."

"How do you-" A flashlight lit the area in their direction and Caden looked over at a security guard behind the gate.

"What are you doing out there?" the guard asked. His eyes focused on Caden's gun. The guard's free hand was on the hilt of his own.

"Just talking," Caden said in a calm tone while putting his gun away. *Even though this Domblin guy is odd, I now know he's real. I'm not crazy.*

"To whom?" The guard unsnapped his gun holster and pulled his gun out slightly.

"To-" Caden turned as he spoke, but found no one there. He blinked a number of times and even rubbed his tired eyes, but still, no one was there. Closing his eyes tight he took in and let out a deep breath. *Stressed induced hallucination. They're going to throw me in the mental unit soon. I hope this doesn't mean they are going to start up again.*

The peace he had felt a moment ago was gone; in its place was fear. If this supposed Domblin wasn't real, the hallucinations not only were coming back, but they were getting worse. The man had never communicated with him in the past before.

Domblin said he was possibly Caden's father. *Is my brain making this guy up to fill a void that I've always felt not knowing my real father?* He looked over at the security guard. *There just has to be another explanation, I can't be seeing things.*

"I have identification." Caden changed the topic as he headed towards the gate. The guard cautiously drew his gun and pointed it at Caden, just a warning that there won't be any funny business. "There you go." Handing the small black card over, Caden stepped back to give the guard some room.

After glancing at the card, he looked back up at Caden. "Sorry about that. I guess I just didn't recognize you in this darkness. And I'll admit you were acting rather strange with your gun drawn and talking to yourself." The guard held the card out to Caden. With only a forced smile, Caden took the card back and the gates opened.

"Just to let you know, Robert's ordered you and your men to head to the medical unit as soon as you get here." He put his gun away as he spoke to Caden.

Medical unit? I just want to go to bed. Don't they realize what time it is? Being polite, Caden smiled and headed into the building.

Caden dragged his feet across the plain white tile floor. He had very little energy left. There was going to be little chance for much of a nap if they wanted him in the medical unit, since they were going into Dead Time within the next four hours. Letting out a sigh, Caden plugged on, heading to get tests done, which is what he figured they wanted.

Everything became fuzzy for sometime, until a slap landed on Caden's bare back. Caden's reflexes took over and he grabbed the intruder. He looked around. He was in the medical unit. *How did I get here?*

"You can let go now," a pinched voice spoke in pain. "Didn't mean to scare-"

Caden realized he had Allen, the head scientist, by the throat. "Oh, sorry about that," Caden said with a yawn and let go. "Are we starting the tests?"

"No, we just finished." Allen said, rubbing his neck. A red mark was beginning to show from Caden's grip. "You fell asleep on me there at the end so I gave you a good slap on the back to wake you up. That was a mistake." He chuckled as he spoke. His white lab coat tightened as he put his hands in his pockets. "I honestly wondered how long it would be before you did pass out. When you came in you could barely walk."

"So, we're done then?" Caden asked ready for the softness of a bed.

"Done as we'll ever be. I'm not fully sure why we even do these tests. It's not like they show us much." Allen leaned his tall body against the white walls. "It didn't help anything when the Burton team went in."

"The Burton team already went in?" Caden snapped his head in the direction of Allen.

"Didn't you know?" Allen asked, but Caden just stared at him. "I guess not. They went in just a little while before you got here. It was a complete success unlike the other attempt, which put Steven into the mental unit. I was told you heard about that one. Good.

Either way, I made a couple of modifications, that I think you'll be impressed with when I show you, which worked." The conversation was waking Caden up. Between the frustration that the Burton team already gone in and the reminder of Steven, he was feeling more energy as anger set in. The mere mention of Steven's name prodded Caden to go pay him a visit.

"Thanks, Allen." Caden said, changing topics. "I'm going to head to bed now."

"You need it." Allen patted Caden on the back and walking away.

The Burton team! Always a thorn in my side. They're always about themselves and being in the spot light. In fact, that was partly why both teams were at such odds with each other. They were on a mission together that had started out rather rocky and it had almost gotten James killed. Toward the end of the mission, a huge glitch had come up. Caden could feel his chest tighten as he thought back to the experience.

Bain, the head of the Burton team, stared down a dark hallway his tall body a shadow on the wall. Palmer, one of his men, had already cut the power to the building and everything was pitch black with an overcastted night. All the guards that had been in the hallway had been killed. Flashlights could be seen moving around in the room they were going to, and footsteps could be heard behind the door. Bain made a sign for Caden's team to move through the doors.

With a nod, Caden led the way. He adjusted his night vision lenses and pulled out a small instrument to look through the wall to see what they were facing. Three men stood on the other side with semiautomatic guns. Caden held up three fingers, his hand and body were covered in the black bulletproof armor. He used his hand to mark the general direction where the men were located. James moved fast and kicked down the door and dove to the ground. Three quick shots ended the problem.

"You could let others help you once and awhile," Matt said into his mic while walking into the room behind James. As he finished speaking an explosion went off behind them knocking everyone over that was still in the hallway. Caden grabbed Palmer, and pushed him through

the doorway where Bain and Mike had already run into. Bullets were flying all around them.

Palmer let out a yelp as one of the bullets pierced through his armor. "They aren't using regular bullets."

"James, take lead," Bain ordered. James didn't budge, watching Caden who was using the instrument to look through a wall.

"Not ours," Caden said. "Too many. We need to find an exit and get out of here. They're setting up something big and it doesn't look pretty. This is a trap."

"Nonsense," Bain said, holding guns in both hands. "James, take lead. Let's take these guys out."

"We're not entering that fight," Caden demanded, "It's time to find a way out of here before they finish setting that weapon up or we're toast."

"I'm in charge here and I'm sending James out in front," Bain ordered. "We'll take them out before they can set up this weapon. Now move James." Bain pushed James in the back. With a quick movement James turned and landed his fist in Bain's face knocking him to the ground. A fight broke out, but it was short lived as an explosion broke it up from Caden blowing a hole in one of the exterior walls. Caden's team made their escape, with the Burton team not far behind. Before they could get across the front lot, the room they were standing in disintegrated. The escape wasn't the prettiest with a verbal fight carrying on all the way back to the office, but they at least lived.

Caden stopped, quickly coming out of his thoughts after almost running into a garbage can. From a doorway behind him he heard a deep voice call out his name. He turned and saw Bain sitting in the game room with a newspaper opened on his lap. "It's been a long time," Caden said while entering the room and sitting down next to him. *There was the man himself. I need to talk to him anyway before seeing Steven.*

Bain smiled. "It has been." He closed his paper. "How have things been going for you?"

"I'm doing okay, a little tired. How about you?"

"I can't complain," Bain said as he leaned back in his brown-leathered chair. "I heard through the grapevine that you arrived. Was it an okay trip?"

There was a level of smugness to his words and Caden knew why, but he wasn't going to get sucked into the drama. "I heard your team went into Dead Time. How was it?"

"Yeah, we did, but we were only there for a minute. Robert wanted our visit to be quick." Bain shifted in his seat. "Robert ordered us to go in. He wanted us to go first, to make sure it was safe for your team. He was worried that if you went in and something bad happened then he wouldn't have you to fix it."

"Good to know." Caden responded feeling a little better about the situation, but still frustrated that Bain's team went before him.

"I'll tell you what Caden, Dead Time is something else." Bain spoke more natural, as if he wasn't guarded any longer. "It's the most surreal experience you'll ever have."

"What made it so surreal?"

When he was a child he used to think about how amazing it would be to stop time. He used to make believe he could stop time in his bedroom. He also imagined being able to communicate with things like trees, but then he grew up and realized he just had a wild imagination. Even though it was make-believe, the whole idea about stopping time thrilled Caden and he had strange ideas flow into his mind on how to do it. In fact some of his friends growing up used to tell him he was fixated on the topic. Now, it was a reality.

With a smile Bain replied, "You'll just have to wait until you go in because I can't describe it." Bain suddenly changed the topic. "By the way, did you ever end up marrying that girl you were always talking about?"

Silence seemed to fill the room; Caden was surprised by the question, it had come out of nowhere. He thought about shrugging off the question as he stared at the doorway.

His lack of a response must've made things obvious. "Ah, girl problems. Never good."

"She left me." Caden wasn't sure where his response came from, possibly his lack of sleep. It was time to go, he was getting tired and he wanted to talk to Steven about his experience in Dead Time before he crashed.

"That's tough," Bain said as he toyed with the pages of his newspaper. "I-"

Caden cut him off. "I'm having a real difficult time keeping my eyes open." As Caden finished his sentence he stood up and stretched.

Bain smiled. "I hear ya. I think I might do the same as soon as I finish going through the paper." He sounded relieved that Caden stopped the conversation. By his response, Caden figured he probably didn't expect the answer Caden gave.

"I'll see you later," Caden said as he left the room.

It didn't take long for Caden to get down to the holding cells. There was only one guard at the front desk.

As Caden approached, the large gentleman raised his gun and said, "That's far enough." Caden stopped, and raised his eyebrows in surprise. The guard kept talking, "No one is allowed down here so you might want to turn around and go back."

Caden thought he knew all the guards, but he didn't recognize this one. Robert must have just hired him.

"Do you know who I am?" Caden said with a smile.

"I could care less. My orders are to let no one down here." Caden looked him up and down. He had to be new. Everything he wore was pristine. The black glistening boots had zero wrinkles in them and looked like they had only been worn once or twice.

"I'm here to examine Steven. If you don't let me through I'll have your job."

"Do you have some identification?" the guard asked.

Caden nodded his head and pulled his identification card out, which the guard examined closely. He pulled his radio close to his mouth. "Can someone verify a Caden Agent 3-Z for me." None of the cards ever held a lot of information and never their last names. A quiet voice could be heard from the earpiece in the guard's ear. With a wave the guard ushered him past.

"I'm glad I'm not in your shoes. I wouldn't want to deal with the freak," the guard mumbled as Caden walked passed his large desk.

"Thanks," Caden responded with a half smile. "Which cell is he in?"

"He's down at the end. We actually moved him from his normal cell and put him in the isolation cell because Robert ordered it."

"Well, I didn't know where his normal cell was," Caden started, "but I do know where the isolation unit is."

"Oh, I almost forgot," the guard said as he unclipped a flashlight from his belt. "The power is out down there and we're not sure why, so you'll need this once."

Caden flicked on the flashlight and headed towards the isolation unit. An uneasy silence filled the hallway and gave Caden a chill. The darkness seemed to increase with every passing step. Even the light from the flashlight didn't seem to brighten the area. Fear began to seep into his body. Caden stopped in his tracks. His lack of sleep was messing with him. He shook his head and began at a normal pace toward the isolation room.

A small square window in the heavy steel door was the only way to see into Steven's room. Light entered under the door from Caden's dim flashlight, which only gave shape to a few of the larger objects in the room. Caden peered in but was unable to see Steven. He leaned up against the door and saw something dark move in the back corner. It just stood there as if it were looking at Caden. *Steven?*

Slowly, Caden tilted the flashlight up to the window. The door shook as if someone pushed up against it. He leaned even closer, his eyes almost pressed to the window.

Steven popped up on the other side of the glass breathing heavily and fogging up the glass. Caden, a little startled, jumped back and kicked the door out of reflex. Fading back into the darkness, Steven moved away and disappeared. *If that was him in the back, how in the world did he get from the corner to the door so quick?* Caden could tell that this wasn't the normal calculated and professional Steven he had known before.

After a deep breath Caden walked over to the keypad to unlock the door. Before he pushed the last button, he placed his hand on his gun ready for anything. The door creaked open, and strangely the lights came back on, flickering at first. Caden turned the flashlight off, the click echoed through the hallway and cell.

Steven was crouched on the floor in the center of the room tapping on a small metal drain covering. He didn't look up or acknowledge Caden at first. Caden peered into the corner looking for the dark figure that had stood there before. Unsurprised, Caden found nothing there accept some carved initials that had been there for years. Besides the mat on the floor and a bed along the wall, the room was barren.

Caden felt like he was losing his mind because he just didn't understand how the dark figure could've been Steven. Two possible hallucinations in one night, he was beginning to get concerned. Shaking it off, Caden drew his attention to Steven.

"Are you the one that brought me out?" Steven asked as Caden moved closer. "Have you come to finish what you started so long ago? Is that why you've brought me here?" Steven looked up, still hunched down, but appeared ready to attack. His skin was pale and his eyes looked void of any irises—just black pupils.

Caden could feel himself breathing rather heavily. Whatever went wrong in Dead Time really messed Steven up and not only mentally but physically. The man looked creepy. *No wonder the guard didn't want anything to do with him.*

"I think," Caden started, "you may have me confused with someone else."

Steven grimaced and relaxed his muscles. "Do you know my name?" Steven asked while standing up. Color began to enter into his eyes and his skin began to look normal.

"Steven," Caden responded, "Right?" His breathing was still heavy even with his effort to calm himself down. Ready for action, Caden still kept his hand on his gun, just in case Steven went into a psychotic rage.

With a big smile and a chuckle Steven moved over to his pad on the floor and lay down. "Yes, it's Steven." He paused. "You just keep thinking that."

"So, who did you think I was?" Caden asked while he moved over to the wall and leaned against it. He finally felt his body start to relax a little, but was still ready should anything happen.

"Why did you come to visit me?" Steven asked, completely ignoring Caden's question.

Not knowing how sane Steven was, Caden decided to answer. "To find out about your trip into Dead Time, the stopped time."

Steven rolled over to his side. "You want to know what happened in there do you? You want to know what caused me to be locked up, right?" He looked up at Caden for a moment with almost a twinkle in his eye. "They think I'm crazy, but I'm not. It was that stupid Robert. He made the whole thing up and pumped me full of drugs to make me lose my mind."

"You seem to be doing okay right now," Caden said, not believing Steven's story.

"They didn't give me my meds this morning," Steven responded. "I'm not sure what's going on, but somehow they forgot."

Caden frowned. "Why would Robert even care about putting you on drugs and keeping you captive?"

Steven's jaw muscles tightened with anger. "Look, all I know is that I came out of Dead Time very dehydrated and starving. Robert and the scientists immediately injected me with something that made me lose control of my body." Steven's voice rose as he continued, "From that point on, they kept giving me drugs. If you want answers go talk to Robert because I don't have them for you."

Caden backed up to the door. He was worried that if Steven got too loud he might create attention and that was the last thing Caden wanted. "I think it's time for me to go." He was going to have to come back another time. It had been a mistake to come that night.

"Good," Steven shot back and took a step forward. "Get out of here. You weren't really looking for the truth, were you? You're a part of this whole thing, aren't you? You just came to harass me." Steven seemed frantic, his eyes darting like a frightened bird. "Get out of my cell! Get out! Get out!"

Caden gladly exited the cell taking care to lock the door securely behind him. As he peered in once more, he noticed a menacing smile on Steven's face.

There was more to this story and he was curious to get some answers, but now wasn't the time. Sleep was calling his name, he would find Robert later and ask him. Even the guard might have a couple of answers.

The flashlight rolled across the guard's desk as Caden pushed it over to him as he walked passed, forgetting that he was going to ask him some questions. The guard, who was reading a book under a small lamp reached a hand out and took it.

"Have fun?" the guard asked with a peculiar smile. Caden raised an eyebrow and exited through the double doors. He had reached the next floor on the stairwell before he realized he was going to ask the guard some questions. *Crap.* He looked at the stairs he had just climbed. *Sleep can wait Caden, it'll only take a couple of minutes to get back there and ask him my questions about the medications.*

Caden quickly made his way back to where he had come from. He pushed down on the handle of he double doors to the cellblock and it seemed to explode out at him. The blast slammed him backwards against the concrete wall.

"Can you hear me?" a voice asked. Caden blinked a couple of times, his vision blurred as he became coherent, realizing he had been knocked out. One of the guards was sitting in front of him and had Caden leaned against a wall. Having a hard time producing words, Caden nodded. "Good, stay here for a minute and let your body recuperate.

"Get explosives down here, now." Robert's voice was loud to Caden's pounding head. His director had just come out of the doors from the stairs.

Shifting his position slightly, he saw five men gathered around the large set of double doors that led to the holding cells, prying with a crowbar. The metal doors blocked their view to anything going on behind them. *How long had I been out? What in the world is going on?*

"Move." Robert demanded as he approached the situation, his voice stern and harsh. The crowbar dropped and the men moved to the side as Robert pulled his gun. Bullets flew and seven shells fell to the white tiled floor. Holes circled the door handle. A strange bright light could be seen through them. Caden's head throbbed.

"What is that?" one of the men standing by the door asked, leaning down to peer through the holes. Caden tried to move, but he was still struggling to get up. *Stupid legs work.*

"Knock it down." Robert's long shadow stretched down the hallway from the light as he backed up. He signaled with a wave. A loud bang rang out as one of the guards kicked near the spot Robert had shot up. Before the others had a chance to join in, a loud, low toned thunder reverberated through the hallway. All the men covered their ears as it rang out. One of them lurched forward and fell to his knees. Caden's vision went blurry.

The doors appeared to be bulging inward. A current of wind sucked through the bullet holes, whistling as it went through. The bright light dimmed.

Silence.

The noise stopped. Light glowed through the holes once again. Moving cautiously, the guards took their hands away from their ears. Each one looking back and forth at one another, unsure what had just happened. Caden blinked a couple of times. His eyes strained to refocus. He needed get up and help. Muscles in his legs were beginning to respond better, but they still shook.

"Knock the doors…" An explosion from within the room cut Robert off. The doors blasted open, throwing everyone backwards and Caden into a pole that lined the wall. His vision blurred and he passed out.

CHAPTER 10

The darkness was comforting to Azgiel in his quiet cell. An old, worn bed creaked underneath him as he rolled on his right side, trying to relax after Mauldrin's visit to him. Being held as a prisoner was getting old, but his curiosity kept him there. If he truly wanted he could just leave, it wouldn't be hard. Leaving would mean he wouldn't get answers to his questions, so he patiently waited. *Time is on my side.*

There wasn't much to complain about, the cell was far better then where he had been. Sooner or later someone would have to explain who brought him back and why, as well as why Mauldrin seemed dumb.

Turning again, the bed let out another creak. It seemed louder this time as if his cell door opened. At first Azgiel shook it off, but then he heard a snort from behind him. Not knowing who was there, he twisted in his bed and sat up. An enormous beast stood in the doorway. Horns stretched out from the creature's head.

"Azgiel?" A deep scratchy voice rumbled off the concrete walls.

"Kaz," Azgiel said as he stood up, "Is it really you?"

"Sir," Kaz said with a respectful tone while lowering his large body to one knee. "I've been waiting for this day for too long."

"It's nice to see you, too."

"Thank you sir," he growled. "The Witch has sent me to get you. She is eager to have you back."

"I'll be anxious to see her as well." Azgiel smiled and raised an eyebrow. "Is she the one that brought me back?"

"No. We couldn't figure out how to bring you back." Kaz stood. His dark red body engulfed the entrance to the cell, his long horns almost touching the ceiling. Eyes shifted up and down, analyzing Azgiel's new body.

"How did you know I would be here?" Azgiel didn't understand how or why Kaz would be there, if he wasn't part of bringing him back.

"The Witch. She felt your return and sent us in the direction she felt you were in. As we drew nearer, we picked up your scent. It led me here to find you in some strange, wimpy human body." After he finished he snorted to show his disgust with the body.

"We? Where are the others?" Azgiel asked looking past Kaz.

"I sent them back. We aren't alone here. Domblin is on the grounds. He didn't see us, but we saw him and as such, I sent the other two back to inform the Witch." Kaz took two nervous steps as he eyeballed Azgiel.

"Strange that Domblin's here." Azgiel put his hand up to his chin while he paced for a moment. "Mauldrin's here as well, in fact you just missed him. He's gone stupid. He had no idea who I was. Did you see him on your way in here?" When Azgiel first saw Mauldrin he had been worried not knowing what he was going to do to him. The situation grew stranger when he found that Mauldrin didn't have any recollection about who he was. His mind was gone. Questions rolled through Azgiel, and he wanted answers.

"No, but I didn't use the conventional way to get in here," Kaz remarked as he looked behind him and then back to Azgiel. "Sir, we should probably get going." He backed up and gestured for Azgiel to go first.

"No, before I go I want to find out who brought me back and why, as well as finding out what is going on with Mauldrin." Azgiel explained.

After being imprisoned in a cell of time for centuries upon centuries, Azgiel wasn't too worried for his safety. He wanted to understand why he was brought back; it fascinated him to no end.

There would be plenty of time to get back to his followers, but if he left now he would never find out what was going on.

"Do you want-" A shot rang out, cutting Kaz off, followed by a thud. Kaz roared, baring his sharp teeth and long fangs. He turned around quickly his wings being held close to his body.

A man's scream rang out and Azgiel could see the snidely, rather plump guard standing outside the entrance holding a gun, shaking in place from the sight of Kaz. The man was a fool for bringing a gun to fight a demon.

"Intelligent," Azgiel remarked sarcastically, but his words fell short as no one was listening to him.

With intense speed, Kaz dove at the guard as he fired another shot. Kaz didn't slow up, he only grew more aggressive. Azgiel couldn't help but let out a chuckle. Claws tore into the man's chest penetrating through the skin. Screams and yelps filled the empty cellblocks as Kaz picked the guard up and carried him towards the security desk.

"Some...monster has me...I need back up," the guard called out into a radio attached to his shoulder. Azgiel followed behind Kaz, fascinated to see what his old friend would do. He had no idea how much time had gone by, but it had been numerous lifetimes since he had seen a good fight.

With a loud thud, the man stopped his screaming and slid to the floor after Kaz threw him against the wall with incredible force.

"Are you okay?" Azgiel asked, not fully knowing what the guns could do to Kaz since he had never really seen them in action.

"I'll be fine." Kaz shook his brooding muscles and clenched his fists as he let out a snort towards the dead guard.

"What is that?" Azgiel asked, feeling a strangely familiar presence near him. He couldn't quite identify the source or the direction it was coming from, but something was near. Something from long ago.

"Domblin." Kaz growled and turned only to be blasted into the wall. His large feet smashed the desk as he went over it. He collapsed to the floor, knocked out.

Azgiel turned as well, moving at a relaxed pace, only to find Domblin standing there, holding some type of bright staff. *So, Domblin had been the source of the familiar feeling.*

Loud laughter started echoing down the corridor. Azgiel couldn't help himself; it was a laugh of joy that it was Domblin who let him out. "So, you're the one behind all of this. The one that got me out?" The large doors to Azgiel's left creaked slightly distracting both of their attentions. He noticed Mauldrin only for a splint second before Domblin jerked forward causing the doors to blast shut. A barrier of light remained on the doors after the explosion.

Azgiel smiled as he turned his focus back to Domblin. It was rather nice to see Domblin put Mauldrin in his place, and very impressive that he had become so powerful.

"So, you're the one that brought me back then, right?" Azgiel questioned.

"Not a chance." Domblin barked holding his staff a little higher. "But I am the one that's going to put you back in your prison, where you belong."

A knot developed in Azgiel's throat and a pain seemed to pinch at his heart. Out of all those who had ever betrayed him in his life, he hadn't foreseen Domblin being one of them. He swallowed once. "Tell me little brother, when did you become one of them?"

"You still don't understand do you? You lied to me and betrayed what we stood for. I'm not going to stand by while you deal out more death and destruction," Domblin snapped.

Even though he was hurt, Azgiel was thoroughly impressed. At least his little brother finally found a backbone.

A blast of white light shot out from Domblin's free hand. Chuckling out loud, Azgiel held a hand up and the energy was absolved into his palm. "Tickles." He took a step forward. "Now was that really necessary?" Azgiel knew the blast was only a test; Domblin was sizing him up. *If you were anyone else I would've killed you for that.*

Still smiling, Azgiel lifted a hand. "Do you know how nice it is to have a body again? I mean really. You begin to take it for granted until it's been taken away for years upon years." He wanted to get him talking.

"Enjoy it while it lasts." Domblin snapped.

Azgiel stared at Domblin for a second. His staff was growing increasingly brighter. A stronger attack was on its way, which disheartened Azgiel. "Are you sure you want to go down this road?" The smile drooped slightly; he could feel the foreign muscles of the new body loosen in his face.

"Time to go back," Domblin spoke with a subdued tone. His eyes watched Azgiel like a hawk.

Gunshots rang out distracting both of them. Bullets smashed through the door and the white barrier, which instantly mended itself after each bullet. The interruption sent Domblin into action. He jumped forward ready to slam the staff to the ground.

Knowing the attack was coming, Azgiel held his hand in the air and Domblin slowed, but didn't fully stop as Azgiel had intended. He was in shock. Domblin had never been that powerful. The staff flew out of Domblin's hands and smashed into the ground. A thunders clap vibrated the floor and kept roaring through the room causing Azgiel to put his hands to his ears.

A strange black line went up from the floor after the staff fell to the ground. The noise stopped but the line turned into something strange. It appeared to look like a tear like in a picture. *Domblin's really going to put me back in.*

"Enough!" Azgiel shouted. The tear kept growing. It was the size of a human now. "It's time for you to see what true power is."

Azgiel raised his hands and he floated off the ground. Black lines began to circle around him forming a ball with him in the center. Domblin ran at him, picking his staff up in the process. The concrete floor under Azgiel cracked and bent in from the sphere that was building around him. "Goodbye, Domblin." He spoke loudly through the darkness that was accumulating.

"No!" Domblin threw his staff into the sphere. Only an inch of it penetrated the field, but it was enough, and Azgiel knew it. Grimacing, he pulled his hands in as quickly as he could to cover his face. The ball exploded, launching Domblin across the room into a wall. Everything close was blown backwards. Walls and doors were taken out. Azgiel was smashed to the floor, his right leg and side taking the major blows. Pain shot through him. He knew he had a couple of bones broken.

Something with incredible strength grabbed his shirt and lifted him up. "It's time to go, sir." Kaz spoke as he turned Azgiel around. His thick arm flexed as he held him up. Azgiel could see that the desk had somehow covered Kaz from the blast.

"Get us out of here, my power is too weak." Azgiel stammered, feeling almost ashamed. Kaz lowered him to the ground. His right leg throbbed even with him keeping it in the air. The Witch would fix him up, as soon as they got back. He was too exhausted to do it himself; his power had grown weak during his time locked away.

Peering through the settling dust and rubble, Azgiel looked for Domblin. Searching to see if he was still alive. Nothing. Kaz took a hold of his shoulder and a ball of blue light encircled them. Concrete bubbled up over the electric shield as it zapped and twisted. With a loud snap they were gone leaving the bulging pile of concrete behind.

CHAPTER 11

With a jerky movement, Caden threw himself forward into a sitting position. He breathed fast and heavy, feeling very disoriented and sore in a number of places. *How did I get from the hallway to a regular dorm room? My room?* The lights were on, the door was cracked, and before he could get his bearings, a voice from the corner of the room called out his name.

"It's about time you woke up," Domblin whispered from the back corner of the room. "I was beginning to think I would have to jump on you."

Caden blinked a couple of times to clear the fuzziness from his vision. A strong pounding in his head made it hard to open his eyes with the lights on. His muscles ached as he turned to look at Domblin, who was covered in dust and spattered with cuts.

"You again." It wasn't the smartest remark to make, but it was the first thing that popped out, as Caden stared at what he thought was a hallucination. He lowered his head from a pain drilling through his brain. *If I don't acknowledge him maybe he'll disappear, besides I have to figure out what's going on. How in the world did I even get in my room?* Caden looked up at the door that was still cracked open.

With a smile Domblin pulled Caden's attention back to him. "Listen to me. Right now I don't have much time. I understand that you still plan on using your Dead Time equipment even after our last talk. It's not safe for you, stay out of it." A noise came from the hallway. "I'm not going to be able to explain things to you now.

It will have to be another time." Domblin stopped talking after he heard footsteps coming down the hallway.

Caden looked to the door, a sore spot on his ribs gripped at his chest and he placed his large hands on his dusty shirt. The soot was grimy under his fingers. Closing his eyes and letting out a deep breath, Caden decided to engage in conversation. "What do you mean it's not safe for me?"

No response came. He opened his eyes and turned. Domblin was gone. He shakily stood, looked under the bed, but there was nothing. The closet door was open but no one was there. His concentration was interrupted as Robert and Bain barged into the room.

Robert was speaking the second he walked through the door. "Good you're awake. Now tell me what happened down there?" Outside of a large cut on Robert's arm that was stitched up, he appeared to have walked away from the blast with little damage. Obviously he had already been cleaned up and taken care of, unlike Caden.

"I'm not too sure, sir." A throbbing pain pounded in Caden's head as he spoke. He lifted his hand to rub his right temple. "I visited Steven. Left, and forgot to tell the guard something so I headed back. When I got to the doors, some explosion knocked me out. The rest of it you were there for." Under his nose itched so he rubbed it with his finger only to feel crispy, dried blood stuck to his skin. Caden tried to wipe it off.

Narrowing his eyes, Robert studied Caden for a moment without saying anything. Bain still stood behind him at a respectful distance. "Why did you go see Steven in the first place?" Robert's voice was gruff. Caden stopped rubbing his lip. *He's questioning me?*

"I wanted to get my own assessment of what Dead Time did to Steven since it is my project." The headache seemed to disappear with the adrenaline pumping through his veins, fueled by the anger. *How dare he question me!* "I'm not behind this." Caden's words were cold.

Robert chewed on the inside of his lip for a moment. His eyes still narrowed, analyzing Caden's every move, and Caden knew it. "The Dead Time project has been compromised. We were attacked in three different places last night. I have reason to believe Steven's behind it all, but I don't fully know who's with him. The facility is in lockdown right now and I want both of you and your teams ready to go in Dead Time by oh nine hundred." Robert reached into his pocket as he finished.

"You're being rather vague. Can you fill me in on what's going on?" Caden asked as he watched Robert pull out a small injection gun.

"I'll tell you the details as long as you agree to let me inject you with a T-13."

Pursing his lips, Caden stared at the injection gun. The chip would allow Robert to listen to his conversations anywhere he went, and would track his every move, giving Robert knowledge of where he was at all times. "What are you trying to pull? You're not supposed to inject any of the agents with those, that's SDS policy."

"Make your choice." Robert's tone was cold. His right hand moved in a better position to draw his gun. Caden looked down at his trigger finger twitching. Scars were scattered across his fingers from all the years of being in the field before he became Director of SDS. He looked back up at his dark eyes that analyzed Caden.

"We can't trust each other anymore? Is that what it's come to?" Caden could feel the heat in his face as he spoke. He looked past Robert. "And you Bain? You agreed to this too?" Neither of them said a word. "Fine, if that's the only way you feel you can trust me, then do-" Before he could finish Robert popped the injection into him, right behind the left ear.

"Wow, that thing packs a punch," Caden said as he rubbed just behind his ear. "Now I know why my prisoners in the past always whined about it."

"Sorry Caden, it's a crude way for me to know if I can trust you. When this is all said and done, I promise we'll deactivate it. But right now we have to weed out those that are double agents. Both of you are to take these injection guns with the T-13 chips in them and put them in your men. If they refuse then they need to be locked up, and that's an order."

Both of them were handed small injection guns. Caden shifted his weight holding the gun in his hands and looking at it. He clenched his teeth together, angry about the request. "Fine. I'll do as you order. But you told me you'd fill me in on what's going on. So?" The gun fit nicely in his pocket. He could feel a bruise on his leg as he put it in his pants. There were probably many sore places yet to find.

"Fair enough. You know about what happened in the prison. After the explosion we went in and all we found was the dead body of the security guard. Steven was gone and the place was blown to pieces, with some rather peculiar things left behind that we're still investigating. Two other attacks happened at the same time. A couple of scientists were killed along with some guards. The attackers took Dead Time suits and a computer that had information about the suits. I have reason to believe that Steven was a double agent and they were after the Dead Time equipment all along."

"What's the point of us going into Dead Time so soon after the attacks? Shouldn't we be out there tracking these suckers down?" Caden snapped.

Caden shifted his weight looking at both of them. *How in the world did Steven get a shot at being an advisor to Robert if he was a double agent? Robert must have has his reasons to hide some information from me, but things just aren't adding up.*

"No, I have a team already working with the guards to find them. I need your two teams to be ready to fight when we find them. If they're one step a head of us, you'll just be wiped out. Your equipment is just that good Caden." Robert patted Caden on the shoulder and walked out, even though Caden had more questions. Bain nodded and followed Robert. Caden squinted at him as he left. *Butt kisser.*

Moving quickly, Caden changed out of his tattered clothing and dressed some of his wounds. Surprisingly, all he came away with were a couple of scratches and a few sore bruises. *That must've been why they just left me on my bed. There were probably others in much worse condition and needed the medical beds.* He washed the last cut on his leg.

"Caden?" James voice called out from within his room. He put the washrag away and exited the bathroom. "What's going on around here?"

Walking over to his bed, Caden picked up the injection gun, where he had left it. "Robert's ordering everyone to be injected with a T-13."

"Excuse me?" James furrowed his brow and popped some of his fingers. "He can't ask that of us."

"He did and I have to take you into custody if you refuse." Caden struggled with his own words.

"That's not right Caden, and you know it."

"Right or wrong, he's just trying to find out who he can trust. We have nothing to hide so it's not going to hurt anything. Robert gave me his word that he will deactivate them as soon as he finds double agents that have broken into the facility. So, I see you've heard," Caden said noticing James nodding. He lifted the small injection gun up for James to see.

"You know just as well as I do that even if he deactivates it, he can turn it back on at any time." James responded without taking the injection gun.

"We're going to have to trust him. Besides, orders are orders."

"No, Caden. Orders aren't always orders, there is a line," James said while letting out a deep breath, eyeing Caden. After a moment, the anger in his face seemed to let up a little. "If you say it's okay, then I'll trust you. You've never led me astray." His voice was softer, but Caden could tell he was still frustrated.

The words made Caden uncomfortable and he let his hand lower, moving the injection gun away from James. *You're not making this any easier.* After a small hesitation, Caden lifted the gun up to James. Shifting his weight, James raised an eyebrow and gave Caden a stern look as he took the gun and injected the chip.

"Ooo. That hurt." James said as he flinched and handed the gun back to Caden. "Good luck on Matt being as compliant."

"True enough." Caden knew it was going to be hard to convince Matt. "Robert wants us ready to go into Dead Time by oh nine hundred. So, get what you need to do done, and head to the lab."

James left without saying another word. Caden finished getting ready and headed out as well. It was time to find Matt.

On the way to his room, Caden ran into Matt in the hallway. He was out of breath and sweat dripped down his forehead. "Caden, I'm glad I found you," Matt said to him as he approached. "Have you heard we were attacked yet?"

"Yeah, it looks like you were part of the fight like I was." Caden responded as he walked past Matt, motioning for Matt to follow him.

"What's the plan of attack? It seems like no one has a bloody idea of what is going on around here," Matt growled as they walked into his room. The room was immaculate as if he hadn't been there yet.

"Close the door," Caden spoke quietly. "Good. Now Robert-"

Matt spoke at the same time. "I have to talk to-"

Both of them stopped talking. "Let me go first." Caden stated. "Now, Robert has ordered us to be injected with a T-13. A refusal will place you in a holding cell." His tone and language was harsher then it had been with James, knowing he couldn't be as nice with Matt.

Rubbing the back of his neck, Matt shook his head. "That ain't gonna happen."

"Matt, Robert said he would deactivate them after all of this. It'll just be for a short amount of time." Caden knew this argument was inevitable. Matt always had to have things his way and Caden wasn't going to put up with another 'no' because he needed his team to stick together with all that was going on.

With a look of disgust, Matt eyeballed Caden just as James had. "You already have one in, don't you?"

"Of course I do. I wouldn't ask you to do something I'm not willing to do." A little stress left. Caden could feel his shoulders relax. *The conversation might actually go okay.*

Matt wrinkled his nose and walked over to his nightstand. The drawer squeaked as it opened. He pulled out a pad of paper and a pen, basic items in all of their rooms. Caden walked over as he heard the pen go to work on the paper. Crinkling, the paper was thrown in Caden's face.

There's a lot more going on then what you know. We have to talk, but it's not safe here. Caden read the scribbled handwriting.

"Why not?" Caden asked. Matt took the pad out of Caden's hands and began scribbling once again. "This is silly Matt, just talk to me."

Matt gave him a scowl and then finished writing. *You have a T-13 in, anything I say will be heard. I researched where the email came from that you got. Steven isn't who Robert says he is.*

"Robert's already mentioned something about that. I'm sure he'll fill me in more." There were a number of questions Caden wanted to ask, but he also knew it wasn't the right time. Matt often went through a lot of back channel ways to get information and if Robert found out, Matt would be gone. It was time to get Matt to take orders for once without the argument. There was no telling if the conversation thus far had been heard, and if it had, Matt was walking on thin ice. "Now, let's inject this stupid thing and head to the lab so we can go into Dead Time or you might end up locked up. We don't have anything to hide," Caden said as he looked back towards the door to make sure it was still shut.

"Lock me up then."

Caden looked back to him, he could feel the sweat build on his forehead and heat burn in his cheeks. "I'm ordering you to let me inject it." Caden demanded while he reached into his pocket for the gun. "I need you to be compliant."

"Not a fat ch-" Matt stopped as three men entered the room. Two of them with guns pointed at Matt. All had on black guard uniforms. With a smile Matt looked at Caden. "You should've listened to me."

Moving in front of Matt, Caden put his arms up. "He's going to take the injection. Let me handle this."

"Sorry, sir. Orders from Robert. We have to take him in." The men moved right past Caden. He didn't put up a fight, even though everything inside of him wanted to take action. Clicking from the cuffs showed they were on. Matt was going willingly. As they walked out of the room, Matt gave one last glance back to Caden.

'We'll talk later,' Matt mouthed.

Caden's gut turned over, he wasn't sure if they truly would get a chance to talk later. With the T-13 in, everything was going to change for a while. Silence dominated the room. An emptiness filled Caden's heart. *Why couldn't you just let go for once and take the stupid injection?* With a hollow thud, Caden kicked the bed. *Time to talk to Robert.*

The walk to the lab was a blur from the anger that clawed at Caden's chest with intense pressure. Huge machines of all shapes, sizes, and colors lined the walls. Most of them Caden was very familiar with. There were a couple of new items here or there, not enough to catch his interest. He was intent on looking for Robert.

A scientist was working on a large computer next to Caden as he walked in the lab. His shoes clomped on the hard concrete floor, echoing in the expansive room. "Brogan, where's Robert?"

"Huh?" Brogan quickly looked up. Huge black bags hung under his eyes. "Oh it's you. Robert? Bain, Robert, and Allen are in the first office on the left wall." He responded pointing to his left.

After a hard knock, Robert opened the door. "What!" He looked at Caden and smiled. "Oh, Caden, come on in. Just the man we needed." Bain and Allen sat at a large wooden conference table. A gun sat in front of Allen with gold Dead Time suit material wrapped around it. "Have a seat. We were just about to debrief Bain on what's going on." Robert walked back over and sat down next to Allen, Caden followed and sat next to Bain.

With a nod Robert signaled Allen to begin. Clearing his voice with a growl, Allen complied, "I'll start by explaining the gun." He lifted it up. The Dead Time material glistened. "We're trying to see if we can get you guys a working gun since we now have enemies with Dead Time technology."

Caden's eyes narrowed and his fist clenched involuntarily. Robert and Allen had taken over his whole project.

Bain leaned in to look at the gun closer. "So is that the big secret that I need to keep confidential?"

"No, there's more." Allen said. "We're going to replace the suits. We have something that we think will make you far more effective in Dead Time. We actually thought of the concept while we were working on this gun."

After looking in Robert's direction, Allen went on. "Robert had asked why the metal of the gun wouldn't work to be the conductor for it to go in, why we needed the Dead Time material. I explained that it wouldn't work because it isn't like a circuit board or human body that can carry some type of electrical signal." Bain raised in eyebrow as Allen continued. "Well, we both had an epiphany at that moment. We're going to develop the technology to run through the human body so you won't have to have a suit on."

Caden shifted in his seat and rubbed his hands together. *How could they keep working on this behind my back? This is my project.* He took a deep but silent breath.

With his deep voice, Robert added to what Allen was saying. "As you both know, we've already developed the technology to make some of the equipment that we've invented compatible with the body. So, as you can imagine, all we have to do is reprogram the actual Dead Time receiver to respond to the body."

"When do you think you'll have this ready?" Bain asked while leaning forward.

Allen sat back in his chair. "The longest? Two days. We hope we can get it done today. That is if Caden's willing to help us. Our plan is to start on the project as soon as we finish with you guys going in. Well, I mean, to start the actual process to make it work with a human body, we did do a couple of tests already, but we can show you that after the Dead Time run."

Tension eased out of Caden's shoulders. *That's more like it. It was about time they bring me into my project.*

"About going into Dead Time," Robert began taking the gun out of Allen's hands. "Part of the reason why I'm sending you in is to test the guns while you're in there. But it has to stay confidential, even from your men because we still don't know who the spies are." With a stern look, he glanced over at Caden.

At some point before we go into Dead Time I have to figure out how to pull you aside. I have some questions for you Robert. Caden eyed Robert.

"I'm liking that idea," Bain said with a smile. "It's about time we get to shoot a gun."

"We believe there are going to be some complications with the gun though," Allen explained. "I personally don't think the bullet will go very far once it penetrates the time suit. We're not even sure it's going to fly straight."

"Sounds like it'll be fun," Bain joked.

Noticing the clock, Caden spoke up. "Robert, did you notice the time?"

"Oh shoot, we need to get out there." Robert turned to Allen. "Put the guns where we already discussed earlier. Let's head out gentlemen." The chairs squeaked across the hard floor as they all stood up. Allen put the guns in his white lab coat and was the first to get out the door with Bain following behind him.

Moving quickly, Caden grabbed Robert's arm. His silk blue shirt, slid in his fingers. "Hey, really quick. About Matt."

"I wondered if you were going to bring that up or not. I'll admit I was surprised you didn't say something when you first came in here."

"You know he's just being Matt, right? He's not one of your spies."

"He wouldn't accept the injection, so I'll hold him for now. When I get around to questioning him, I'll let you be there." Robert put his hand on Caden's shoulder. "Fair enough?"

"I'm okay with that." Caden smiled in return. *That's all I needed to hear.* "Oh, and about Steven."

"Leave it alone." He pushed Caden out the door ending the conversation.

CHAPTER 12

Azgiel held his leg as he sat on the hard ground. Everything around him was black in a circular diameter of six feet, burnt from their arrival. A large tree that stood close to them crackled and popped from a small fire. With a thud Kaz snuffed it out with his large hands.

Crack! Azgiel healed his leg, realizing the witch wasn't around to do it for him. "Oh, that feels better." He chuckled as he spoke. "I forgot how painful it is to have a body." Pushing himself up with his hands, he stood. "So, where did you land us?"

"We're about a five minute walk from our forest. We have to move slowly through here. There are dark souls patrolling the borders. It's partly why we couldn't just zap back into the Witch's lands." Kaz's voice was deep, but he kept his voice at a whisper.

"Dark souls?" He tried to remember if he ever learned of such a creature, but he couldn't quite recollect.

"Do you remember the creatures we were capturing the last couple of months you were here? I was told you even had caught one the night before you were put into a cell of time. The nasty thing that told you Triaad had betrayed you?" Kaz wasn't looking at Azgiel while he spoke. He peered through the brush on high alert.

"Ah, yes. So, you heard about what happened that night?" Azgiel responded while crunching through the charcoaled grass, moving closer to Kaz.

"Yes, sir. Everyone knows what happened that night. We started a war against Triaad after we found out. Unfortunately we lost and there are only a small number of us left. We hide in these trees. His cowardly dark souls are too scared to come in after us so it stays as our refuge." The large red demon stood. His muscles rippled as he shook, looking one last time to make sure the coast was clear. "Let's go."

Moving quickly they both bolted, Kaz leading. Azgiel ran faster then a normal human, but he had to, in order to keep up with Kaz. Leaves from bushes slapped Azgiel in the legs and arms. A strange high-pitched scream rang out, catching him off guard. They both looked around. Azgiel saw him first. A dark figure with strange red eyes stood in front of a large tree. The creature let out another scream and some movement could be heard all around them.

"Keep moving!" Kaz barked, no longer whispering. They moved quickly. After passing around a large boulder, Azgiel could see an edge of a thicker forest. It was darker, and it had the Witch written all over it.

A sharp pain drove into Azgiel's back and shoulder as something jumped on him, knocking him to the ground. He reached back and grabbed oily skin, pulling off the creature that was attacking him. Its teeth tore at his flesh leaving a strange sensation that something was burning into his body like acid. Using brute force, he squeezed the creature's neck, holding the dark soul out in front of him. Claws sprung out, slashing at Azgiel's arm. Blackness filled the wounds, but instead of letting go he tightened his grip.

Screaming, the creature went from black to translucent and back to black. Dark souls stood off in the distance, watching. Azgiel knew they were surprised and waiting to see what was going to happen. He tilted his head a little and smiled. Black liquid from the wounds dripped off his arms almost tickling as it rolled across his arm hair. Energy flowed to all of his cuts from an internal surge of power and they quickly healed.

Another dark soul charged. Kaz saw him coming and quickly drew his sword, slicing the creature in half. The two torso pieces melted away into an oily puddle only leaving a black rubbery skeleton.

Going limp, the dark soul In Azgiel's hands gave up, only keeping up a low toned growl. His dark red eyes stared at Azgiel. "Who are you?" It hissed, choking as he tried to speak.

"Just a simple man." He could see the fear in the creature's eyes. It was the same fear he saw in the other dark souls that were still standing in place, watching his every move.

"A man couldn't…" The dark soul tried to swallow. "Keep me held."

"This one can." As Azgiel spoke he drew from the power within that was slowly coming back. Smoke wafted out from where his hand touched the oily skin. Another scream rang out from the creature as it began savagely clawing and biting Azgiel. Each wound healing after every attack.

"You're not so tough." Azgiel smiled. The dark soul exploded into dust and blew across the under growth. A couple of dark souls hissed as they departed, but none of them were willing to continue the attack.

A shiver that went up Azgiel's body as he looked at Kaz who towered over him. "Oh, it feels good to be back." The excitement of killing something ran through his veins. His mouth salivated and his muscles flexed. *So much power. I've missed this.*

"I'm worried they're only regrouping. We need to move," Kaz spoke while looking all around them. His heavy footsteps landed with a thud on the forest floor.

"Lead the way my faithful friend. As much as I would love another good fight, we needn't waste time when there is so much to do." Azgiel patted Kaz on his thick red arm feeling the leathery hard skin. After a quick snort they made they're way into the dark forest that stood only a short distance away.

The air grew thicker as they entered, and the sounds changed around them. There were no birds singing any longer or frogs croaking in the distance, the place was void of the sounds of life.

"From here we can move quicker." Kaz grabbed Azgiel's arm. After a quick zap, they were in a very dark part of the woods. There was no undergrowth and the trees that stood around blotted out the sun in its entirety.

A bright glow illuminated the area around them. Azgiel could feel his rough skin wrinkle as he smiled. "Maselda."

"It's been a long time since I've heard that name." The Witch responded as her bare feet stepped on the barren ground, slowly circling around Azgiel. Her dark blue eyes looked him up and down, analyzing his new body. "Is it really you, Azgiel?"

She circled to his right. Before she could get behind him, he reached out, grabbing her thin arm, the soft dress smooth under his worn fingers. He pulled her in pressing his lips against hers. Pushing her body into him, she wrapped her arms around his shoulders and kissed him back. Kaz shifted his weight and accidentally brushed against a tree. They pulled back and Azgiel looked up at his uncomfortable servant and then back to the Witch. "Tonight." He raised an eyebrow.

"It's nice to have you back, my husband." She smiled, her white skin showed no wrinkles.

"It's nice to be back." He looked around. There was nothing in the blackness that surrounded them. "Where is everyone? Why are you here in a forest, not in a kingdom? Was Mauldrin behind any of this?"

"No. It was Triaad. He betrayed us," she answered, her eyes looked away from Azgiel.

"How?"

"After you were locked up, we looked into the report about Triaad destroying your reinforcements. What we found was a fight. Triaad was ready for us and tried to kill all of us when we showed up at the castle. We fought for almost a year trying to take back your kingdom, but he had just grown too powerful with an army of dark souls that grew daily." Sorrow showed in her eyes. Azgiel assumed it was for all those that had fallen. "Needles to say, we retreated to here where we've been able to keep him and his filthy creatures out for thousands of years, using some tricks you had taught me." She winked.

"Dark souls. What are these dark souls anyway?" He shifted and looked at Kaz as well, desiring one of them to answer.

"A perversion of nature," Kaz grumbled and tightened his fists.

"Triaad stumbled onto some powerful…dark matter, I believe he calls it. The stuff alters humans into those creatures. They're fierce and powerful." The Witch's sweet intoxicating voice was magical, and filled Azgiel with a peace he hadn't felt in a long time. He had truly missed her. Her beauty captivated his mind, a true work of perfection.

"Focus Az," the Witch whispered while brushing her soft hand across his cheek. "Like I was saying, Triaad keeps an army of them here. Some of them patrol our border continuously. Others are out doing strange missions for Triaad, tempting and manipulating the stupid, blind humans. What they're doing with them, we're not sure. And lastly, there are an unknown number of them in a cave where they guard the gate to control who comes and goes."

"We'll have to hit them first, before they come into these woods." Azgiel once again looked at the dark empty woods around him. "Now tell me, are there others?"

The Witch smiled and looked up at Kaz. "Get everyone assembled. Let's give Azgiel a chance to say hello."

"As you wish." The large demon turned, and vanished. Azgiel saw the opportunity and drew close to his wife, pulling her into him. She smiled and her glow seemed to brighten the darkness around them.

An hour passed before Kaz returned. "They're ready and excited Your Highness." Kaz tilted his head as he spoke, peering down at the two of them lying on the ground holding each other. Azgiel ran his fingers up and down the Witch's soft silky dress. The fabric almost seemed alive as he touched it, flowing under his fingertips. He kissed her forehead one last time and stood. After brushing off a little dirt, he held a hand out and helped his wife off the ground.

"Let's not keep them waiting." Before Azgiel could even fully get ready to go, Kaz grabbed both of them and they were carried away to a small hill at the edge of the thick forest that led to a type of valley, which was encircled by the Witch's magic. The morning light glowed in the sky with light red hues popping over the treetops. A sight Azgiel awed at, it had been too long.

The Witch walked up the small hill first, to address those that had been following her for so many years. "Azgiel has returned." The crowed screamed with excitement. Azgiel couldn't see the masses yet because the hill blocked the view. "Once again, brothers and sisters, we will begin our path to victory. We'll no longer be captive in these woods. He'll lead us out to destroy our enemies." The crowd cheered with pleasure. War horns and different types of banging filled Azgiel's ears, he could feel the excitement.

"But enough from me, I give you Azgiel." With those words she opened her hand and a ball of light emerged. She threw it down causing a bright flash leaving behind an intricate web-like design of glowing white lines on the ground. Holding her hand out, she called for him to come up. The audience had quieted after the flash leaving the only sound Azgiel could hear was the heavy breathing Kaz made while they walked up to the Witch.

Azgiel stood on the small cliff's edge looking out over his small number of followers numbering almost a thousand. Light from the web-like veins below lit the audience and himself. As he looked out, they began talking to one another. The numerous whispering created almost a low hum as they all looked up at this man that looked nothing like Azgiel.

Steven's body was far smaller then his original one, and much less muscular. They needed to know he was still the same. It was time to show them he was back, to unify them under his direction once again. His army would then follow him to destroy Triaad, starting with the dark souls on this planet.

The crowd silenced as Azgiel raised his hands in the air. "I have returned." Azgiel's voice boomed, but there was no response. The whispering kept up and he lowered his hands. *Time for the show of my power.* A sting in his eyes made him blink. He could feel the darkness fill the eye socket as they turned to black. His soul within flexed against the outer flesh shell. White skin turned to a dark gray. Energy zapped at his fingers and the crowed stopped whispering.

"You dare doubt it is I, Azgiel?" Azgiel snapped. "I will not have this." He threw his hands forward and a blast shot out in a bubble-like shape. A combination of a thick black-like air and a small amount of electricity knocked the audience back zapping them as it went. Random screams of pain rang out as the explosion made its way through the creatures. It was only enough to get their attention, not enough to actually do harm.

A clatter went through the gathering as they threw themselves to the ground, bowing before Azgiel. He smiled as he relaxed and his body went back to normal. "Good! With all of you behind me, we will rise up and destroy the traitor and oppressor." Cheering broke out as the crowd got back on their feet.

"We'll start with the army of dark souls that plague this planet. We will no longer be captive in these woods." More cheering rang out as well as horns. "We will collect ourselves here and build an army like no other, and then we will crush all that oppose."

Raising his hands, Azgiel tried to calm the excitement. "My followers, it is good to be back, even if our reunion has to be with me in this puny human's body and not my own. Fear not, I still hold my power within and nothing will be able to stop us."

CHAPTER 13

Caden thought about Domblin. *Why is my mind hallucinating about Dead Time and warning me not to go in?* He looked around at the scientists and men getting ready to go in. *Am I subconsciously scared?*

Robert walked past him and headed over to a group of scientists to talk to them. *If I get through this project alive, maybe it's time for me to get help before I totally lose my mind, even if it is a job killer.*

He tightened his jaw and let out a deep breath, to look at what was going on around him. Everyone was there and the place was alive with excitement. All but Bain were suited up. Caden watched all the scientists run around hurriedly. Surprisingly, Allen was nowhere in sight. While Caden approached the area to suit up, a hand grabbed his shoulder.

"The guns are in the drawer next to the switch that sends you into Dead Time," Robert whispered into Caden's ear.

Without looking, Caden responded, "Have you told Bain?"

"He knows," Robert sounded distracted with his comment. He let go of Caden's shoulder and walked away quickly to get everything up and running.

"Caden," James called out from the left of him. He looked over to see him dressed in the gold suit. "Come on, your suit is right here." Caden walked over focusing in on James to bleed out all the noise around him.

James gave a dirty look to one of Bain's men, Palmer, as they walked past. Caden leaned in. "If you start a fight, I'm not going to back you up," Caden said just loud enough for James to hear. A large smile grew on James' face, which Caden hoped meant he would behave.

Caden was surprised at how odd looking the suits were. The mask was not fully see-through and had micro wires running through it. Gold chain-link armor kept everything protected along with a large oxygen tank that was underneath the suit. It made the men look like hunchbacks. Picking up the suit, he was surprised to find it was lightweight for being gold and very flexible.

James ignored Caden's last comment and kept smiling. "You need to lighten up."

He finally spoke up. "They're all hot heads, and you know it just as well as I do."

Caden shook his head in agreement, but didn't want to say anymore, it was time go. They walked over to a small platform. All the scientists stood around watching and holding their breath. Knowing their fears with the experiment, Caden could feel himself sweating and breathing a little heavy, both from worry and excitement. Robert lowered his finger to a button, and then silence. All noise stopped. Robert stood with his finger still pressed to the button, frozen in place.

Never before had Caden heard such silence, he felt deaf. The void of sound seemed to put a pressure on his eardrums. Everything in front of him stood completely motionless as if it were an enormous picture.

Palmer's voice came over the mic breaking Caden's focus. "So, what are we supposed to be doing again?"

"Just getting used to things," Bain responded as he walked to the center of the room. "We could do some practice sparring and some basic moving around just to get the feel of things."

Caden was amazed by everything he saw. Their shadows didn't follow them. They stayed in place from where they had been standing when they entered Dead Time. Ripples were being created behind

Bain as he moved—like thick heat waves that came off roads during a very hot day.

Caden moved his hand upward creating the same waves. There was a blackness that followed right behind his arm that would last for a second, just like air bubbles when moving an arm into water. Movement was a little more restricted by a small amount of resistance, but Caden wasn't too worried about it. He was more fascinated by the blackness that followed his arm.

Bain noticed him. "It's the light that does that. You're moving the light particles around. They come back together like water does when you move through it, but if you notice it stays a little foggy afterwards. That's caused by the particles not coming back together in the same position they were in, which distorts the image you see."

"I'm impressed," Caden said as he looked up at Bain.

"Don't be," Bain responded. "I only know because that's what Allen told me after we went in last time. He came up with a pretty good theory."

Mike dove at Palmer from the stand and began to spar with him. They moved in slow motion and looked like a fight scene in an action movie. Their speed was rather slow and they were able to jump higher and float through the air for longer periods of time. Palmer did a Super Man dive toward Bain, which to Caden looked like he was flying. He chuckled to himself.

The whole world seemed to have changed, which fascinated Caden. It was nothing like he had ever experienced before.

Palmer's arms were out straight as he tackled his boss to the ground. Bain pushed him off, throwing him up in the air with his legs. Palmer seemed to be as light as a feather slowly floating back to the ground. He positioned himself like a ballerina with one foot coming down on his toes and the other foot up in the air. His arms were pointed upwards with the palm of his hands pressed together. Bain started laughing and then everyone joined in. The teams were surprisingly getting along fine.

The timers were going to click off soon and make them leave Dead Time. Robert had only wanted them in for a couple of minutes.

"Now remember," Bain explained, "the exit button is under the armor on your right shoulder. All you have to do is hit that and time will start once again. So, go ahead and do that now." Other then Bain and Caden, the other three hit their shoulders and became frozen like everyone else around them.

Bain looked over at Caden. "You ready to try the guns out?"

"You bet," Caden said as they walked toward the drawer that held them.

Caden loved walking. He compared it to what it must feel like when walking on the moon. His whole body was lighter and felt amazing as he lifted his legs and would almost float a little until he pushed them back down. He felt like a child at play, exhilarated and excited.

"Since you've had time to talk to Allen, I'm wondering if you'd answer a question?" Caden asked with a smile. "Since the oxygen tanks have a limited amount of air in them, how is it that Steven was able to stay in Dead Time for so long?" He tapped on his oxygen tank making a clanking noise.

"Allen said they have no clue," Bain said, holding his gun up to the target that Robert had hung on the wall. "You ready?"

While lifting his gun and aiming it, Caden nodded. They both fired. There was no kick as the gun went off and no sound. The bullets exited the barrel about an inch before they came to a dead stop. "Wow, that's pretty ineffective." Caden said.

"Yup." Bain lowered his gun. The bullet hung in mid-air. "Well, you ready to head out?" Caden nodded and reached for his exit button. He turned to Bain as he went to leave. His hand was in motion and he wasn't able to stop himself quickly enough when he noticed a dark creature move in the corner of the room. He blinked. The shadow was gone.

A loud bang rang out and echoed through the room as time started again. Scientists dove to the ground to take cover. The sound of the gun firing seemed to be magnified once they came out of the Dead Time. James, Palmer, and Mike seemed rather confused by the noise and the fact their bosses were on the other side of the lab holding guns.

Caden looked around to see if the dark creature was still there, but it was nowhere to be seen. He blinked his eyes. *Did I see what Steven had seen or are my worries getting the best of me?* He took a deep breath and closed his eyes for a moment. *Keep it together Caden. You have to keep it together.*

"You forgot to put them back," Robert said distracting Caden from his thoughts.

Bain tossed his gun to Robert. "It doesn't matter. They're useless. The bullets don't move once they exit the suit material. We would never be able to use them in Dead Time. I think it would be best if we just stuck with knives," Bain said as he looked where his bullet should've been on the floor.

"Or swords." Caden said with a chuckle picturing himself with a sword and his gold armored suit. "Ones that match our armor maybe."

Robert was just about to respond to Caden's sarcastic remark when Bain spoke up. "Our bullets. They actually shot the target."

"They what?" Caden said with surprise. The last he had seen of the bullets, they were hanging in mid-air.

"Wow," Robert said as he put his finger into one of the holes made by the bullet. "Not only did they hit the target, they must've been going at an incredible speed to put a hole all the way through a concrete wall."

"Hopefully we didn't hit anyone or anything behind that wall," Caden said while looking through one of the holes. He would've felt horrible if he had.

"I think," Robert began to say with excitement, "we can still find a use for these guns even if they don't shoot far in Dead Time."

Caden leaned up against the wall with his head lowered. The room began spinning. His vision blurred, but after blinking a couple of times they cleared up.

"Everything okay?" Bain asked him.

"Yeah," Caden responded while trying to get his helmet off. "I just got to get this suit off." He walked over to the stand where they had gone into Dead Time to take it off. As he was finishing with his oxygen tank, Allen walked up.

"After you're done, get Robert and Bain and remind them that we need to meet downstairs in the lower lab," Allen said rather quietly and then walked off.

Caden finished taking the oxygen tank off and then took a deep breath to try to clear his spinning head. He looked over at Bain and Robert who were talking over by the target. Bain almost had his suit off while the other three still had theirs on. Caden walked over and whispered to both Bain and Robert what Allen had told him. Without looking to see if they were following, Caden made his way down to the lower lab so he could sit down. His head started throbbing half way there.

It didn't take long for Bain and Robert to get down there even though Caden felt it took them forever. Once they sat down Allen stopped tinkering on some pieces of equipment and started talking.

"Ok, so to get you up to speed, I ran a couple of tests on some rabbits last night." He looked at Caden. "Before the break-ins. Anyhow, the switch that sends you into Dead Time, converted perfectly over to the rabbit's body. It connects simply to the back part of the spinal cord. We had a one hundred percent success rate when we put every single rabbit into Dead Time."

"So how did you get the critters out?" Bain asked.

"We put a timer on the device," Allen explained. "It was fun to see where the rabbit would reappear after putting them into Dead Time." He looked over at the rabbits caged against the wall. They twitched their pink noses.

"Would the human ones be on timers as well?" Robert asked.

"No," Allen said. "They would have a controller that they wear that looks like a watch. This control can get them in or out. It can also be set so the whole team can go in together. Bain and Caden would have the master controls for the team."

Robert raised an eyebrow and smiled. "You said you could have this thing up and running within a day?" From the way he spoke, Caden could tell Robert was getting excited.

"With Caden's help. I believe so. You know how fast our engineers can produce stuff once we give them the basic idea, so I'm figuring we could have the chips installed before the nights out in both of their teams. The watches, if you don't mind me calling them that, should be able to be ready in the same time if you can get the engineers in here working with us."

"I'm not sure if I want one put in Matt at this time." Robert remarked losing his smile. He eyed Caden for a moment while biting at his inner cheek. "Second thought, go ahead and install it, but I want him kept locked up. So when you do his, do it in his cell." He looked over at Allen. "But for now, let's get the other five agents ready to go."

Caden was still sitting there quietly trying to pay attention. His vision kept getting fuzzy and his head pounded. He had wanted to say something about what Robert said with Matt, but he couldn't formulate words at the moment.

Robert looked over at him and said something, but Caden couldn't make it out. Sounds seemed to disappear and then everything went to black as he passed out, his head thudding on the table.

CHAPTER 14 -- SECOND RECORD OF TAGEN

Between the demons putting Tagen through all the torture, and being blasted by Mauldrin's powers while he had been pinned to the tree, he was in poor shape. In his weakened state, there wasn't a chance he could take on the demon that he heard next to him, nor any other demons that might've been roaming around. It was time to make a discreet escape.

He looked back one last time at Azgiel's camp where Mauldrin and his army still stood, ready for any other attacks. Some of the tents Azgiel's troops had been staying in were on fire or knocked down. A couple of horses were kicking and trying to get loose from being tied to trees near the fires. Mauldrin's men had already been gathering some of the weapons and shields from the fallen demons and were piling them up.

Wanting to stay alive, Tagen continued to retreat. Azgiel was dead and Triaad was bound to reward Tagen for his efforts. The torture slowed him down.

He only made it halfway to the gate that would allow him to travel back to Triaad before he collapsed in utter exhaustion. His side was bleeding badly and he could barely step on one of his legs, thanks to one of Azgiel's demon's crushing it. Between the damage done to his body and all the running, he wasn't healing. In fact, he was getting worse.

Knowing he should be safe so near the gate, he gave into sleep. *Hopefully when I wake, I'll be healed enough to get back.*

A noise woke him. The night had set in, but the darkness had little impact on his sight. Whatever it was, it moved quickly, so Tagen knew it wasn't a demon.

"It's Tagen," a voice called out. Two dark souls plopped down beside him.

"So it is." The other one spoke with amusement in his voice. "Let's get ya back to Triaad. He's been waiting for your report."

"Or we could just eat him," the dark soul whispered so quietly that Tagen barely heard him. He quickly gathered enough strength to get up in order to defend him self. One of them turned his head and looked at him, the closest dark soul helped him up and threw him over his shoulder.

"Let's move." Pain shot through Tagen's leg and body from the bumpy ride. His wounds were taking a long time to heal.

The trip was fast and before he knew it, the dark souls that had found him, flopped him down on Triaad's stone floor in his room high in a tower. Feeling the coldness on his back, Tagen tried to stand.

A pale white man stood in the corner of the room.

Triaad.

He walked over—his steps a slow rhythmic beat that almost put Tagen back to unconsciousness. Before he could slip back into the sweet blackness where he felt no pain, Triaad pushed Tagen over on his back using his foot.

"What happened?" Triaad asked.

Tagen didn't understand why he was being treated this way. Triaad seemed colder then he had ever been to him before.

"I...was... captured," Tagen struggled to speak taking in breaths between his words.

"And tortured by the looks of things." Triaad took a couple of steps back.

"Yes," Tagen pushed the word out with one of his exhales. Pain shot through his ribs from talking. He took a deep breath to add what he felt was good news. "But he's gone...Mauldrin won...Azgiel is...dead."

"I've already been updated on Azgiel's condition. Now what information did you tell them?" Triaad asked sounding almost angry. He also didn't understand how it mattered on what information he gave. Azgiel was gone—he was no longer a threat. He thought Triaad would've been happy.

"Everything...I knew..." Tagen gasped for air, struggling to get out the last bit of information.

"You fool." He said as he gripped Tagen's throat and lifted him in the air. Triaad's eyes became pitch black and his fingers felt as if they were starting to tear through Tagen's skin. The room began to spin, and Tagen could tell Triaad was sucking or pulling the life out of him.

"Azgiel isn't dead." Triaad barked. "They merely put him into a cell of time. Do you not realize how stupid Mauldrin is? It's only a matter of time before someone figures out how to get him out and when he gets out, he'll be coming for me. I'm going to need to watch my back at all times, never knowing when he might return. Besides that, his army will be out to get me, instead of joining us." He ground his teeth. "The trouble you've caused. You should've let them kill you, because when I'm through with you, you'll wish they had."

Triaad dropped Tagen to the floor, sparing his life. Tagen could feel small holes in his neck as his blood seeped out of them.

A lot of energy had gone into making sure no one knew of Triaad's attempts to overthrow Azgiel. Triaad only existed because of Azgiel. He had given Triaad his powers and immortality. He had been Azgiel's right hand man, top advisor, and even governed Azgiel's kingdom for him while he was at war.

Tagen had thought it wouldn't matter that he had given up all the information with Azgiel gone. He hadn't thought of Azgiel's army turning on Triaad, but he really hadn't had time to think of anything for that matter, except to stay alive.

"I didn't realize..." Before Tagen could finish his plea Triaad lifted a hand and squeezed his fingers together. Instantly Tagen's skin around his mouth joined together, pulling tight enough that it stretched his eyelids further open. He was unable to speak or close his eyes.

Frantically, Tagen reached for his mouth to tear it open with his claws. The pain ripped through his skin as he dug a claw in. Triaad pursed his lips and threw a hand up. Tagen was thrown through the air and slammed into the hard stonewall.

Something sticky grabbed a hold of him before he slid all the way to the floor and the wall began to pull him in. Liquid rock wrapped around him. With all the strength he could muster, he fought against the pulling. *No success.*

Acting quickly, he shifted to shadow form in hopes of moving through the wall and escaping. His plan failed. Molecules of the stone began intermixing with his and he could feel himself pulling apart. He tried to shift back, but it was too late, the rock solidified.

"If you're still alive when I decide to come back up here, I might let you live as a slave. By then maybe you'll think twice before giving into torture ever again. But I wouldn't count on living. I don't ever plan on coming back up here now that this kingdom is mine. Enjoy being eaten by the rats." Triaad moved out the door leaving Tagen stuck in the wall with only his head, hands and one foot hanging out. He tried to shift again, but it was no luck his body was too mangled. Despair sunk in.

What a way to go.

Months passed, and then years. The rats had only been able to figure out how to get to his one foot. They piled on the floor, a rotting flesh heap, killed from his toxic blood. Almost all of his foot had been chewed off. His body grew weaker with every passing month.

No one knew how long a dark soul could go without eating, but it looked like Tagen was going to find out.

After many years, Tagen realized he was going to die from starvation, he only wished he had the capability to kill himself.

One day, no different then any of the other horrendous days, Tagen heard a different noise other then rats. There was no strength in his body to respond. After the many years, his skin had stretched and he had been able to close his eyes. He couldn't even remember the last time he had tried to open them. Hope of someone coming through the door was gone and he didn't normally respond to noises any longer after being disappointed so many times by rats and the wind. But there was something different about the noise.

Dust that had collected around his skin flaked off as he opened his stiff eyelids. His eyes felt like sandpaper had just ripped over them. The light burned making his vision blurry and he closed his eyes once again. In the blackness he felt peace.

"Are you alive?" An unfamiliar voice hissed. Tagen reopened one eye and looked. His vision was still blurry, but he was able to make out a dark personage.

"Ahh, so you are. Good in deed."

Wanting to speak, Tagen tried to open his mouth but was unable to. His jaw was locked from being held closed for so many years after Triaad had bound his lips together. With some effort he could finally focus his vision. A younger dark soul stood in front of him, one he had never met before.

"I've been assigned a mission," the dark soul began. He scratched at the stone wall that encased Tagen. "Some would call it a suicide mission. Personally, I think it's a perfect mission to show how great I am. The problem. I need a servant." Prancing, the dark soul made his way back towards the door. "A servant that knows his way around. Unlike these mindless beasts." Clanking of a chain could be heard as the unknown dark soul reached out the door and dragged in a youngling.

From the looks of the shininess of his skin the youngling probably just got pulled from a dark matter cell.

Crawling on all fours the creature darted in the room. His eyes moved all about, taking in information. Tagen could feel his heart beat a little stronger. If he could only take a couple of bites, he would feel so much better.

"You want it, don't you?" Lifting his clawed hand, the dark soul reached out and snapped the youngling's neck. They were easy to kill when they had just come out of a cell, not being fully developed.

A small wave of dust blew towards Tagen as the tar black body fell to the ground. "If you pledge to serve me, I'll feed it to you so you can repair and get yourself off that wall. All I need is a yes."

Wanting to be let off the wall at any price, Tagen fought with all his might to open his mouth, but it wasn't budging.

"I guess it was a shame to kill this little fella after all. Triaad told me you might be willing to serve if you were still alive, but I guess he was wrong." The dark soul reached down and picked the corpse of the ground.

I'm not going to lose this chance! Tagen put the last of his strength into opening his mouth. His jaw let out a squeak while his skin that had been sealed tore open like brittle leather. "Yes." It came out raspy.

Smirking, the dark soul turned back to him. "I'm glad to hear you came around. I would've hated to leave you up here to die." As he spoke, he tore off an arm of the youngling and held it up for Tagen to take a bite.

The flesh was soft and melted in his mouth. Along with all the other bites that kept coming. After about half the corpse was eaten, Tagen found he could start talking again.

"What's the mission?" His voice was very soft and still raspy.

Letting go of the left leg that he was trying to rip off, the dark soul looked at Tagen. "To hunt down rogue demons that are in hiding. At least, one of them is outside of their territory. Oh, you probably don't know what the territory is. Well, it's where the Witch and her followers have put up a stronghold, which we can't infiltrate. Instead we keep them contained." He leaned back down and tore off a foot instead of the entire leg with a slight crunch.

Insanity, fighting demons! "What's your name, so I know who..." Tagen coughed a couple of times. "Who I'm serving and will be dieing next to."

"Quite the wit on you, isn't there?" He responded while holding the foot up for Tagen to eat. "First off, you'll serve me, but Triaad is still your master. And the name's Snyp."

"Tell me Snyp..." Tagen lost his voice. His throat burned. He cleared it with another cough. "What about Mauldrin and...his followers..." It was tough to talk so he focused on finishing eating the foot offered to him.

"'They're gone. Decided to leave after they put Azgiel away." Snyp spoke as he got the other foot, black blood oozed out where limbs had been taken off, pooling around the body.

"Leave?" A foot was shoved in his mouth after he spoke.

"Yeah. I don't actually know all the details. All I was told was Mauldrin and the other lords thought everything was going to be fine after Azgiel was taken care of and then they disappeared, reportedly never to return. They were too stupid to know about Triaad."

Even though Tagen had more questions, he was beginning to feel his blood circulate once again, and he wanted to focus on healing. There would be plenty of time to ask questions, but it was time to get off the wall. Pain throbbed in his limbs as his veins and arteries began working. He could actually feel his fingers once again and gave them a twitch. Thick dust cracked and broke off from his black skin.

A strange pain began to develop in his shoulders, chest and stomach. At first Tagen wasn't sure what he was feeling, but then he remembered, his body was interlaced with the stone.

Blood began dripping from his chewed off foot. After a few drops, the new droplets began to string outwards like veins. Flesh began to build around the veins and capillaries. Bones began to grow back, and the black fibers wove together.

"Excellent." Snyp spoke as he approached Tagen with another piece of flesh, noticing the healing foot and his black pigment growing darker. "Once you are strong enough to shadow, do so. Triaad told me it should pull you back together."

Tagen held back his anger. *That's all it would've taken! Shadow form, and I would've been free. If only my stupid body hadn't been so weak!*

Nodding his head in gratitude, Tagen bit into the next serving of meat. His foot was almost repaired. It only had the skin left to mend. Being tired of the wall and having the new knowledge, he tried to shadow. Surprisingly his left arm did as he wanted, but the rest of the body stayed the same.

The coldness of the stone moved through his arm as he stretched it forth. *A miracle.* Fingers and arm were free. He waved it about, uncaring of the overly excited smile on his face. Wanting to be completely free, he closed his eyes to focus inward.

"Keep it up and we'll be out of here and on our way to slaying demons. Demon hunters. I'm going to be famous," Snyp spoke, but his words trailed off.

Letting out a grunt, Tagen was able to get his right arm to shadow. Aching muscles limited some of his movement, but he didn't care, he twisted both arms back and forth. Snyp had stopped bringing flesh, distracted with his own conversation about how Triaad was going to someday see his true potential. Snyp's feet splattered in the oily blood on the floor as he paced.

Most of the pain was gone in Tagen's foot as he looked down to see it was fully healed. A grin ran across his face and he went completely into shadow form. His upper body felt whole as he exited the stone that had been home for many years. With a scream, Tagen turned and scratched into the wall, digging his claws deep into the rock. Blackness began to fill the cracks in the stone.

With a loud crack the wall split from the floor to the ceiling and broke apart falling outwards. Tagen watched as the pieces of large stone fell many stories to a frozen courtyard below. He hadn't even realized it was winter.

"How many years have I been here?" Tagen demanded as he spun around. Snyp was staring at him with his red eyes wide open.

Anger flowed through Tagen's veins, but he knew he needed to cool down. Especially if he was going to ever get back on Triaad's good side.

"I think Triaad said something like a little over ten years." Snyp walked over to the gaping hole in the wall. "Why did you do that?" Tagen wasn't really paying attention. His clawed feet made short progress of the gap between him and the corpse on the ground.

"STOP!" Snyp demanded as Tagen took a large bite. The juices were so enjoyable, now that he wasn't stuck in a wall. "You're not allowed to eat anymore. Triaad said you could only have enough to get out of the wall. The rest is for me."

Tagen swallowed and turned his head slightly. "I'm still weak, I need more to get my strength up to full potential."

"That's the point. I can't fully trust you, so I'm not allowed to feed you enough for you to fully restore." Snyp tried to stand taller to look intimidating. Ideas raced through Tagen's mind, trying to think about what to do, if anything. "If you don't agree to comply I'll be heading out now to inform Triaad of your choice. So, what's it going to be?"

Using his claws, Tagen ripped one more large chunk out of the body and moved back to show his partial compliance. Snyp looked at Tagen for a moment. Tagen figured he was debating if he wanted to make a fight out of the flesh in his hands or not. Finally, Snyp looked back towards the corpse and dug in. After filling his mouth he looked back towards Tagen.

"Once I'm done we're leaving. You're not to leave my side unless I order you to." Snyp showed his black sharp teeth as he spoke.

"I hear you." Tagen bit into his last bit of corpse. *You're lucky I don't kill you right now, while you're still relatively young. I'm only going to play along because if I do I might gain favor again with Triaad.* He gazed out the hole in the wall that he had made to look away from Snyp who was ravaging the last of the body. *A demon hunter, we'll see if we live through that.*

CHAPTER 15

There were a few dim lights on, in the small medical room. A quiet hum came from the machine that was hooked up to Caden, producing the only noise that could be heard. As he slowly opened his eyes, he could see the monitor displaying his vital signs. The rhythmic beating of his heart made lots of jagged mountains go up and down on the screen.

He tried to blink away the blurriness in his vision, but it wouldn't go away. Even though Caden was under some blankets he felt very cold. There was no one else in the room to ask what was going on or even what time it was, leaving Caden feeling strangely alone.

Caden kept staring at the glowing screen to his left, which was the brightest light source in the dark room. The low toned humming was getting to him and he felt like falling back to sleep, but the screen started to fizz out like a wire was coming loose, bringing him back to his senses. He went to look around but was unable to sit up. As he tried he thought he heard someone come through the door behind him.

Caden gave up his futile efforts to move so he could listen intently to see if someone had really entered his room. The door creaked open. The silence that followed alerted him that this wasn't going to be a pleasant visit. His vision seemed to be getting darker and a thick blackness settled over the room. Caden struggled to take in air but his lungs felt stiff. He wanted to call out, but it was a struggle to even think about saying something. Maybe he was going to pass out again. He started giving into the darkness until he heard something move.

With his neck muscles barely responding, Caden slowly turned his head to see who it was. His whole body fought against him, but he pushed harder. He heard heavy breathing. With one last push, he caught a glimpse of a dark shadowy creature.

"Mauldrin." The hiss sounded evil.

Caden was unable to get a good look before he felt a crushing pressure on his body. Something slowly increased the pressure as though something was sitting on him, causing him to wheeze with each breath as he fought for air. His heartbeat grew weaker. He lost feeling in his hands and feet. A deep exhale came from his lungs followed by a peacefulness that he had never felt before, which ran through his entire soul. There was no pain, as if a weight he never knew he had, lifted, and freedom took its place. His heartbeat disappeared along with the pulsing of blood through his body. He felt himself being lifted in the air, but the feeling didn't last as a scream pierced his hearing.

With a powerful rush he went back into the heaviness, making him feel disoriented, but he could tell whatever was attacking him had stopped. His heart pounded once again and he began taking breaths—gulps at first, almost choking on the incredible amounts of air he took in. He became very aware of his entire body functioning. Each muscle and organ used the resources they needed.

Caden felt so contained. A part of him wanted to go back to what he had just felt, the complete freedom and peace without the physical limitations.

He briefly saw the dark creature go through the wall as if it were a ghost. A noise drew his attention to the end of his bed where he saw Domblin standing.

More hallucinations.

A flood of energy surged through Caden's body giving him the strength to sit up. Domblin still stood at the end of the bed. "You need to watch out for those little buggers. They'll be the death of you. As well as your Dead Time project, if you don't stay out of there," Domblin said as he approached Caden.

Caden felt the room spin, at least he felt like it was spinning. He swallowed down the nausea.

"I have to leave for awhile so I won't be able to protect you. Take this. It will keep you safe while I'm gone." He held out a white chain with a dark blue gem on it.

The chain was ice cold to the touch, but the gem had a strange warmth to it that captivated Caden. Surprisingly, the metal was very light.

"Hurry up and put it on." Domblin turned and looked at the door. "Hurry, I have to go."

Not even sure if he was truly awake, he followed the directions and moved the chain towards his neck.

"Oh, and Caden, find a way to marry her, you may never get another chance," Domblin's voice was stern. Caden slowed his movements startled by Domblin's comment, but he proceeded to wrap the chain around his neck and the gem landed on his chest. A blue flame lit up and disappeared in a flash causing a warming sensation throughout his upper body. Suddenly, he felt invigorated, full of energy and strength. He looked down, reached for the necklace but it was gone. In shock he looked at Domblin wanting to ask what happened, but he was also gone.

Caden quickly ripped his IV out. He needed to know what was going on. Throwing the blankets off, he ran out the door, but Domblin was nowhere to be seen. The hallway was empty.

He rushed down the empty long hallway to the stairs. *This isn't a dream.* Caden wondered if he was loosing his mind. Needing to know the answer he pushed on, his bare feet slapped the cold tiled floor.

As he approached the door to the stairs, he heard voices coming from the other side. The talking stopped as he cracked the door open. Someone grabbed Caden by his shirt and threw him to the ground.

"Get up slowly," a voice called out.

Caden pushed himself up and saw three men standing around a laptop. A scientist lay on the floor, bruised and bleeding, while a man stood over him holding a gun to his head. All of the men wore black outfits that almost looked like thick wetsuits. Hoods hung off the back of the suits and knives were strapped to their right thighs. The man who had thrown Caden down circled around him, knife in hand.

"What's going on here?" Caden asked as he estimated the distance between him and one of the men that stood by the laptop. He was ready to pounce and grab the knife.

"That might get you killed, Caden," the man standing over the scientist said. His baldhead glistened with sweat under the florescent lights.

"Do I know you?" Caden asked.

The man smiled, his dark brown eyes were empty and cold contradicting the smile. "All professionals know their targets. Don't tell me you don't know every detail about the people you've killed." Caden understood what the man meant, he did learn every detail about his targets, and now he knew someone had a target on him. With a smooth motion the blond haired man standing next to Caden lunged at him.

Dodging the thrust with little effort, Caden grabbed the guy's fist and twisted, pulling him down, and brutally kneeing him in the head. Caden spun him around and slit his throat using the man's knife and proceeded to throw the knife at the bald man. Not fully ready for the attack, the man tried to dodge the knife, but it clipped him in the shoulder. His actions were second nature, and his heart beat at an easy pace.

A man pulled a gun and pointed it at Caden. "That was a mistake."

As he went to pull the trigger someone from behind Caden yelled, which sounded like Matt's voice. *Can't be Matt. He's locked up.*

The gun went off, but the bullet stopped and fell to the ground right before it would have struck Caden in the chest. All the men quickly pulled their hoods over their faces and vanished. Caden ran over to the scientist and rolled him over to see if he was okay. Robert and a guard came running through the door.

"What's going on here?" Robert asked rather harshly while the guard ran to help with the scientist. He scooped the man up and rushed off to the medical lab.

Caden stood and looked around, knowing the situation wasn't going to look good. The body of the man he killed was gone along with the gun that had dropped to the floor. All that was left was a puddle of blood and a bullet. He quickly informed Robert what happened.

Robert furrowed his brow as if he didn't believe him.

"I think these are the men we are looking for," Caden said knowing he needed to get to the point. "They had some modified Dead Time suit on. That's how they were able to disappear." There was an awkward silence. Robert looked at the blood on the ground and then over to where the scientist had been laying. He pushed a little button next to his small radio in his ear. "Surveillance check stairwell 5, floor 3, during the last ten to fifteen minutes."

Finally, Robert looked at Caden with no expression. "Follow me." He led him down the stairs.

"Where're we going?" Caden asked as his bare feet moved down each cold concrete step.

"To the surveillance room." Robert didn't look at Caden while he spoke. "I want you to tell me what's going on around here and why your T-13 chip stopped working for a little bit."

"I didn't think there was anything that interfered with those."

Robert nodded. "There wasn't supposed to be." They exited the stairwell and entered the security surveillance office.

"Everyone out," Robert ordered as two guards quickly got up and left the room. He sat down at one of the monitors and hit a couple of switches. A video of Caden lying in the medical unit asleep came on the screen. "Now help me understand what happened here, and if your explanation isn't believable, I'm going to be locking you in a cell, so no B.S."

The video showed Caden slowly wake up and look at his monitor. Then the screen went to static for almost half a minute until a loud scream came over the speaker. The static changed to lines while the scream rang out, and then went back to normal static once it stopped. Another moment or two went by, and then the picture slowly came back. Caden grabbed at his chest, with a panicked look scanned the room, then ripped the cords out of the medical machine and ran out of the room.

"And here's how I know your T-13 wasn't working," Robert said as he rewound the video and turned the volume up so the static noise almost hurt Caden's ears. Right before the static completely went out a voice could be heard. "...have to go."

It was hard to make out, but Caden could understand it. *Is it my voice? Am I talking to myself and hallucinating?*

"Did you see anyone enter or exit the room?" Caden asked, feeling the perspiration build under his arms and on his forehead.

Robert stopped the video and leaned back in his chair. "No." He scratched his nose and turned his chair a little more to face Caden. "When security tried to pull the tape to watch what happened in the stairwell a glitch came up, there was no tape. Someone took it out." With a deep sigh Robert went on. "I've worked with you a long time, Caden. We have a good relationship, but if you're apart of all of this I need to know, and I need to know why."

Caden tried to cut in, but Robert kept talking, "If you're with Steven on this and both of you are trying to bury me, it won't work."

"What? Sir, I don't under-" Caden tried to interject again. *What in the world was Robert talking about?*

"You're in a room where everything goes to static on our monitor. We catch you talking but it doesn't get picked up on your T-13, which I would love for you to help me know how that happened, only to find you standing over a nearly dead scientist." Robert kept going, "Telling a rather unbelievable story with the only evidence a pool of blood." Caden kept trying to interject but Robert wouldn't let him. "You go and visit with Steven without any authorization and moments later the place is in chaos with Steven gone. Plus one of my security officers tells me that you've been logging into files you have no business getting into."

"Robert," Caden said rather forcefully. "You have to listen to me. I'm not part of anything against you or this agency. Obviously, I allowed you to put in the T-13." He never thought he would need to explain himself to Robert. Normally they got along really well. "The story in the stairwell is true—the scientist will be able to verify that as soon as he wakes up, I guarantee it. And about visiting Steven, I was just trying to find out what happened to him when he was in Dead Time because this thing is my project and you went behind my back." It felt good to finally let loose his feelings.

Taking a quick breath to calm him self so he wouldn't look even more guilty, Caden continued. "This whole thing about the T-13 not working, I haven't a clue. Oh, and about getting into files, I've never gotten into anything that doesn't pertain to my team or me. The only person I can think of that might've accidentally done something along those lines is Sally, but even then I would've a hard time believing that. I will check into it though."

Silence followed Caden's comments making him feel more uncomfortable. Robert just sat there with his lips tightened. Caden could feel himself breathing a little heavier, knowing that his story didn't sound great with the evidence against him. But maybe their past eight years would weigh in his favor.

Robert finally spoke. "Your story is far fetched and, if it was anyone else, I would just throw you in a cell to be on the safe side." Robert paused for a moment as if he were debating the next part. "I'm going to trust you and get you down to the lab to have the Dead Time chip inserted into you. But," Robert said with a flat tone, "If I find out you're lying to me, I promise it'll be me that puts the bullet through your head. You won't be going to any holding cell."

"On that positive note," Caden said, "don't you mean that I get to go help develop the technology for the chip?"

"Allen finished the work up while you were out for the last twenty four hours. In fact, he's already put it in some of the men." Robert didn't look at Caden any longer, and Caden knew he wasn't trusted anymore.

There wasn't much else to say and Caden always knew when it was time to stop talking. Even though Robert threatened him, Caden knew his story was true and was confident he would prove it. Either way he was just happy that Robert was giving him a chance to provide proof. Robert was never very gracious if he suspected someone of fowl play. He would just lock them up like Matt, which worried Caden. Robert's leniency could be a trap. It was a tactic they've used before on enemies. Trap or no trap, Caden had to utilize the time to his advantage.

"I have other things to do," Robert said as he turned his attention back to the monitors.

"Thanks for trusting me," Caden said. Robert nodded his head in response. As Caden went to step out of the room, he turned knowing his next question could get him into trouble, but he had nothing to lose anymore. "What's going on with Steven that you think I'm part of that has the potential to bury you, as you put it?"

"I shouldn't have said anything. Just forget it. Look, all I can say is he isn't who you thought he was. It was just a cover so he could do the things he was doing. That's why we had such a hard time sending him into Dead Time, and now with the way he's acting..." Robert stopped and looked at the floor. "I've said too much. Just with that information, your life is now at risk along with mine. But there will come a time that I will fill you in, but not now. Don't push the topic again." His final comment almost sounded like a plea.

With a nod, Caden walked out the door leaving Robert in the darkened room with his only company being the surveillance monitors. There was a sense of loneliness about Robert. Caden wanted to push, but he knew better. Another time. He headed to the lab for the implant.

CHAPTER 16

Tagen moved through a building, following Mauldrin's scent. It had come as a surprise to find his scent in the first place, especially when his mission was to locate Domblin. Snyp ordered him to stop the search for Mauldrin since Triaad was coming to personally get Domblin.

Knowing the demons had been in contact with Domblin, Tagen started there. He had become almost an expert on hunting demons from his past with Snyp. Their trail had been easy to follow. Domblin's scent was all around. The strange part was he picked up on Mauldrin's scent once he got in the building. From there it just seemed logical to go after Mauldrin and see if there was a way to drag his dead body back to Triaad. Caution was needed as he searched the building since Domblin was close by.

He kept in shadow form and double-checked before he went around any corner. A group of men walked down the hall towards him. Four out of the five wore uniforms, which Tagen figured were guards. The man in the front was larger then the others and had more formal clothing on. Two young dark souls followed the group in shadow form, unbeknownst to the men. One of them creped along the wall, the other walked behind them.

Luckily for Tagen, they were both too young to be able to identify Mauldrin or Domblin's scent.

Snyp had dark souls all over, influencing powerful men and women for some grand scheme Triaad had planned, which Tagen wasn't privy to. Looking at the group, Tagen figured they were there for the man dressed in professional attire. Snyp would never waste time sending dark souls out for guards.

"I want more security around the lab now that the project done," the nicely dressed man demanded.

"We'll get right on that Robert." The guards headed back the other direction.

Tagen knew how it felt to be ordered around and even felt a little spite towards the man called Robert. He hated being told what to do by Snyp.

As the dark souls passed, they paused for a second to look at Tagen and then moved on. They stayed very close to Robert as they followed along.

Mauldrin's scent grew stronger in the direction they had come from. Tagen moved down the hall and went up a stairwell. There was a medical unit on that floor, Tagen figured out from the signs on the walls and doors. He quickly passed through a door with no effort.

Perfect. Tagen smiled as he looked at Mauldrin unconscious on a medical bed. The machines began to act up as Tagen approached, from the darkness he caused to flood the room to control him. He needed Mauldrin paralyzed for the attack. As he approached, he realized Mauldrin was awake and was pushing through the paralysis, turning his head slightly to look at Tagen.

"Mauldrin," Tagen hissed. There was no time to waste. He jumped on Mauldrin and dug his shadowy claws into his chest.

At first it seemed too easy. The tables quickly turned and to his surprise, he found a strong resistance. Using all of his strength, he pushed his claws deeper into him trying to overcome Mauldrin's soul. But Mauldrin was too powerful. He wasn't sure how Mauldrin was doing it, but he was overpowering him.

Mauldrin's soul had a strength that Tagen hadn't expected. He awed at the power, and began to understand why Snyp wanted him so badly.

His soul was brilliant white and glowed around his claws. The moment was short lived as something hit him from the side, knocking him over the medical equipment that was connected to Mauldrin's body. Unable to keep his shadow form, Tagen positioned himself for a fight. Surprised, Tagen saw Domblin running at him.

Knowing he couldn't defeat Domblin, Tagen changed immediately into shadow form and dove through the wall. He had no idea if Domblin followed him, but he wasn't going to take any chances. Mauldrin and Domblin teamed together would be a bad idea. Besides his orders were only to find Domblin, not capture him, which he had done.

Tagen didn't wait to see what would happen next, he did what he knew best, he ran for it. With all the energy he could muster, he sped out of the building, moving through the walls and making his way back to Snyp. Even though the demons talked about Domblin and he had picked up on his scent, it was still a surprise to see him. Triaad had locked the old man up years ago, on a different planet.

As soon as Tagen made it out of the building, he checked to see if he was being followed. To his relief there was no Domblin. But the situation had drastically changed, since Domblin was together with Mauldrin.

Moving at amazing speed, Tagen arrived back at the cave within no time. Once he entered the cavernous labyrinth, he finally slowed down. The dark tunnels were comforting. The usual screams echoed through the cave, which was music to Tagen's ears, for it meant safety. Nothing and no one dared to enter the caves, not even Domblin.

His shadow-like body was fully restored, and was even a little more powerful, after devouring the younglings. Snyp had never allowed him to eat ones that were as old as the two had been, and now he craved more. The revitalized energy was empowering for Tagen. He had been a slave for so long to Snyp that he had forgotten what it was like to feel strong. He was tired of serving Snyp. He wanted to be respected again. He wanted freedom. Those enslaved dark souls at the building were pathetic, and Tagen was done.

Using his strength, Tagen pushed the large doors open to Snyp's spacious throne room and entered. He resented the idea of reporting to Snyp, but knew there was no other option right now. Domblin had to be dealt with if he was going to kill Mauldrin and get him back to Triaad.

The large transportation gate that Triaad's messengers came through was closed, making the room very dark. "What do you have for me?" Snyp's voice called out, but Tagen was unable to see where he was.

"During my search for Domblin I not only found him, but stumbled upon Mauldrin at the same time and attacked him, figuring that's what you would want me to do." Tagen stepped further into the room to find Snyp. He hoped to get some recognition for his efforts.

"Tagen," Snyp said, still unseen, "you have become priceless in a time when few can be trusted."

"Mauldrin is still very powerful," Tagen said, knowing he needed to start building up the reason on why he didn't have him in his hands. "But I'm positive he doesn't know who he really is." He took a breath waiting to see if he would be praised for his conclusion. When no comment came he went on. "I went after him, and he was able to evade me as if it was second nature, but his moves were awkward. His actions weren't controlled."

"It might be harder to catch him than we thought," Snyp said as he suddenly appeared in front of Tagen. "We might have to get a group of younglings together to help you catch him at some point, especially if his paths are crossing with Domblin. We need to move cautiously if he's hanging around Domblin now that Triaad's coming." He peered off in the distance for a moment. "We need to separate them somehow before Triaad gets here."

"Agreed." Tagen knew that if Triaad stumbled onto Mauldrin, he wouldn't get the chance to deliver him and reconcile his past. "Domblin's the reason I don't have him in hand. He attacked me and ran me out of the building."

Snyp waved his hand and a throne of bones erected next to him. He slunk down. "Domblin is protecting him then."

"That's how it appeared to me."

The throne dissolved back into the ground as Snyp stood and paced. "We're really going to have to watch ourselves. If Lord Triaad gets a whiff of our plan, we'll be done for." Snyp's eyes blazed red as he spoke. "I want you to keep on Mauldrin. Figure out his weaknesses so you and some younglings can catch him. I'm going to send some others out to take Domblin down before Triaad gets here. So don't worry about him any longer. I'll just need a location of where to send more dark souls."

While holding a hand out, a large map flew up into Snyp's palm. The old thick paper crinkled as he opened it. Tagen was familiar with the map. It was the same one Triaad had given Snyp when he and Tagen had first come to the planet. Locations shifted ever so slightly, following the continual changes in the land and city. One of the surrounding forests next to the city was shrinking from a logging crew cutting trees down. A dirt lot was developing with concrete pouring into it.

Tagen impatiently pointed out the building. "That's where they are."

"Really?" Snyp said as he slid a claw down the map and it zoomed in a little more. "I have a number of dark souls working that area. I'm surprised none of them reported anything about Domblin."

"I couldn't tell you why either. I even saw some there while I was in the building. I'm just letting you know where he's at," Tagen responded moving a small amount backwards because he wanted to get out of there. Snyp was acting rather strange and even his tones were just a little more off then normal.

"I'll gather some dark souls and send them. When they get there, I'll have them meet up with the others that are already there to work on getting Domblin." Snyp was still analyzing the map as he spoke.

"I'll get back there immediately so we don't lose sight of Mauldrin like we did Domblin." Tagen felt pretty good about himself, and respected. Snyp rarely treated him this well, but he still wanted to get out of there.

"And Tagen, next time, take care of Domblin if he gets in the way. Don't let that lazy bum push you around. And if you do come back, either have Mauldrin in your hands or you better have a plan on how to get him. In the mean time, I'm ordered to take an army of dark souls to the ancient forest and deal with the demons." Tagen halted.

Snyp never dealt with anything anymore, he always sent his servants. The whole thing was rather strange that Triaad would specifically order Snyp to deal with the issue. Now he understood the strange behavior.

"I'll do my best." Tagen responded carefully, while stepping backwards.

He wanted to get away from him, uncomfortable with Snyp's often-erratic behavior. His commander nodded and disappeared back into the darkness. Once he was gone, Tagen turned and wasted no more time getting out the door.

If Snyp was leaving and Triaad was coming, the whole situation could fall right into Tagen's hands. He could snatch Mauldrin somehow and get him back to Triaad before Snyp got back. Excitement made him run faster. The problem was getting Mauldrin. His strength had been incredible last time, but it was uncontrolled. So, if he could just snatch him up like a regular human, it might work. A smile grew across his face and he began to plan.

Before Tagen even knew it, he was back at the building. Time had gone by fast. The night had rolled in, which made better opportunities to attack Mauldrin. He began the path down the hallways, moving through some walls to get to where he had seen Mauldrin last, but he wasn't there. He picked up on the scent and began jumping through walls. After going through a really thick wall that led to the hallway just outside of a number of rooms, he saw Mauldrin heading into one of them.

Smiling because Domblin was nowhere in sight, Tagen moved fast. His shadow form prevented anyone from seeing him. As soon as Mauldrin entered the room and closed the door, Tagen dove through it. He tore into him with his shadowy claws. Mauldrin collapsed to the floor.

"Mauldrin!" Tagen shouted.

Fighting with all of his might, Tagen picked Mauldrin up and slammed him back down, in hopes of weakening him. Something strange happened as he reached into Mauldrin and gripped his soul to end the battle, a flash of light ripped through Tagen.

He screamed and everything went white.

CHAPTER 17

Even with the painkillers, pain still crept down Caden's neck from the implant. Allen had told him everything went perfectly well and he could get up and move around right after the procedure. Caden completely disagreed; his neck was throbbing. *How in the world was Allen able to know everything would be okay? They hadn't put the equipment in humans before.* Arriving at his room, Caden pushed the door open and saw his welcoming bed. He felt the bandage that wrapped around his neck.

As soon as he closed the door, Caden saw something dark move to the right of him. Before he could act, an unseen force knocked him down. His room went pitch black. The air was thick and hard to breath. Caden felt his body stiffen and become unresponsive.

"Mauldrin," a voice hissed.

Blood pulsed stronger through Caden's veins. There was something in the name that he identified with, as if it had been his name. But that couldn't be true, unless he had been called that before he was adopted as an infant.

The name gave him a surge of power that Caden had never felt before. A rush of energy fired through his chest where the necklace had landed. Slowly he was able to move some of his fingers and his neck.

A dark shape materialized on top of him and the creature thrust itself at Caden's chest. Caden felt his heart clench and his breathing became difficult. His body lifted into the air and then plummeted

125

back down against the floor. While struggling to get air, Caden was crushed down even harder.

The same peace he had felt earlier came to him again. There was a sense of freedom from the physical heaviness of his body. This time Caden understood what was happening—he could feel his soul exiting his body as death overtook him.

The walls seemed full of life. He pulled up his hand. There was clearness to him, as if he was partially translucent. A loud scream broke him of his wonderment and the creature that had been attacking his body, clawed frantically. For the first time Caden saw his attacker clearly. The creature had multiple sharp, black teeth that gnashed wildly in the air. Large claws gripped Caden's chest.

A smoky whiteness started to rise from where the creature was clawing into him. Caden wasn't sure what was going on, but he did understand that he needed to act. Moving with a great deal of difficulty, Caden tried to move his hand towards the creature. He saw his ghost-like hand move out of his physical hand and move towards the black being.

Something calming took over once he saw what he was. With a smooth motion, Caden clasped one of the creature's claws. The second he touched the dark shadowy beast an explosion knocked the creature across the room and into a wall. Caden smashed back into his body and the heaviness returned. Breathing was difficult. The body became a heavy weight. Aches and pains that he had become accustomed to, now seemed tedious. His eyes drooped, and it was a struggle to move, but he lifted his head to see if the dark shape was still against the wall. The room was empty, and there was no sign of any type of struggle. Caden's chest hurt from where he was clawed, but there were no marks.

The room went quiet. *Was I really attacked or was it all just a bad nightmare?* He raised his hand to his brow and rubbed above his eyes. The back of his neck and head throbbed from the implant. He closed his eyes to lessen the pain.

I'm loosing my mind. What do I do? I don't want to be locked up like Steven. If I tell they'll put me away, what will happen with my Dead Time project?

Caden knew he needed to do something. He was tired of strange nightmares and hallucinations. He could only imagine what his team and Robert would think if he told them about the crazy things he was seeing. Like seeing his spirit outside of his body, boy he would be the laughing stock once he brought that up.

The doorknob clicked as someone entered the room.

"Hey, what ya doing sitting around on the floor?" James asked. "Get up. Let's get going."

Caden opened one eye and lowered his hand so he could see him. The throbbing only got worse. He looked around and then at his watch. *When did I fall asleep? I slept here all night? No wonder why I'm so stiff.*

"In case you haven't heard…" James picked a pair of pants up off the ground and threw them to Caden. "We get the day off. We don't have to be back until early tomorrow morning."

"Why? They just put the implants in." Caden pushed himself up.

The situation almost seemed contrived, like it was a setup. But his throbbing headache made it hard to think too much about his worries and paranoia.

"Does it matter?" James said while throwing Caden's suitcase on the bed to hurry him up. "We can get out of here, so let's do it before they change their mind."

Caden just stared at James. If it was a setup, it could be dangerous to leave. Not only that, he was sick and tired of them working on the Dead Time project without him. Lowering his gaze he focused on James's wedding ring.

Bridget.

Thoughts of what his hallucination or Domblin had said, ran through his mind. *'Oh, and Caden, find a way to marry her, you may never get another chance.'*

This might be his only shot for a long time to marry Bridget. If the whole thing were a setup to find dirt on Caden, Robert would be sadly disappointed if he took off to marry Bridget. Unable to contain himself, Caden let out a chuckle.

"What's funny?" James asked.

"We'll talk about it later." Caden said, trying to focus his pounding head. When he had arrived at the office, the hallucinations started so maybe getting out of there would make them go away. Besides, getting away gave him a chance to investigate some of Robert's accusations and clear his name. "Is everyone getting the day off?"

"Just the Burton Team and us," James said as he sat at the end of the bed. "Well, except Matt, he doesn't get to leave his cell."

Caden shuffled some things around and saw his picture of Bridget. It was an old picture of her, taken back when they first got together. She was standing on their favorite spot at her mother's house along the beach. Unable to fully control his flooding thoughts, his mind took him back there, to their first kiss eight years ago. At the beach house, where Bridget's mother lived.

After dinner, Caden stood and motioned for Bridget to follow him. She walked beside him, their hands intertwined, as they passed through brush and trees going up a hill that led to a small cliff. Bridget tried to ask where they were going but Caden only shushed her. He suddenly stopped in front of a large bush that rustled in the ocean breeze.

With a smile Bridget looked at Caden. "You wanted to take me somewhere to hide?"

"No, close your eyes," Caden said as he took hold of her hand. He gently pulled her towards the cliff's edge and passed the bush. The breeze blew their clothing, making it flap against their skin. An oceanic fragrance filled the air as the day cooled down. The moment was perfect. "Okay, open your eyes."

Red and orange filled the sky saturating the clouds that hovered over the ocean. The brilliant glowing sun sank into the ocean. Caden clasped Bridget's other hand, turning her towards him. The colors brightened her face and fired up her blue eyes. He peered into her, pulled her in close, and placed his arms around her.

There were no words, instead, she moved in closer to him. He gently pressed his lips against hers as she ran her fingers through the back of his hair. Nothing seemed important any longer except Bridget. Caden didn't ever want to let go. He had kissed many girls before, but there was something different about Bridget that made Caden feel alive.

The waves crashed on the sandy beach as Caden looked out over it, not wanting to take her back to the house. He held her while listening to the rhythmic beating that surrounded them. Bridget surprised him by pulling his face to hers and letting him taste her sweet honey lips again.

"Caden. Hey, Caden!"

Caden jerked. He blinked at James, not wanting to leave the memories. Remembering the moment was such a nice contrast with all the pressure and stress that he had been feeling the last couple of days with the project and hallucinations. It furthered his desire to want to be with her permanently. To marry her.

"Stop dragging your feet and let's get out of here."

The ride to the airport took forever. James was on the phone the whole time talking to his wife, leaving Caden to deal with the pain in his head and neck. They arrived a little early for their flight. James finally got off the phone after they sat down in the terminal to wait.

"So, I hear through the grapevine that things aren't going well with Bridget."

"I don't want to talk about it." Caden closed his eyes and slouched in his seat.

"Caden!" James elbowed him.

"What?"

"I'm your friend. My wife told me the basics of what happened. So, how are you going to fix this?" James said eagerly.

Feeling his jaw muscles tighten, Caden looked at James. *Your wife knows!?!* He took a deep breath and let it out. James was always a talker, a more sensitive man. It's what made him easier to talk to, but Caden was still reluctant. *But!* Caden squinted. *He might know how to get her back.*

"Well, it's a rough idea, but basically I'm going to ask her to marry me," Caden responded. The words felt funny to say. He could feel his cheeks get warm with embarrassment and his chest tighten.

"Great," James remarked with a little sarcasm in his voice. "So, you're going to propose, but when would be the wedding? I think you might just piss her off more with an engagement that doesn't have a date."

"Well, what would you suggest than?"

"Marry her."

"I thought that's what I just said."

"No," James said with a smile. "I have a friend who's a minister. He can get the legal stuff all situated. You call Bridget's mom to get Bridget out of the house and we'll get some friends to help set something up on the beach. As soon as Bridget gets back you not only propose, but if she says yes, you marry her right then and there. That will show her how serious you are. Trust me, its full proof."

Caden could feel his heart rate increase. His initial feeling was to say no way, but James was right. It's something Caden should have done a long time ago. *Yes, let's do it.* But the words weren't coming out, he struggled to vocalize them. All the fear pushed his heart to beat faster. *I'm not going to be run by fear any longer.* "Let's do it." His shoulders relaxed and he felt a peace come over him.

"Okay, you call Sally and who ever else you want to be a guest and I'll call the priest." After Sally was mentioned, Caden remembered he needed to call her anyway about who was accessing Robert's files.

"I'm going to go get a drink while I call the minister, you want anything?"

"No thanks." Caden pulled his cell phone out and called Sally.

"Hey Caden," Sally said as she answered the phone. "What can I do for you?"

"Can you hop on my computer and check out the logs to see when Robert's files were accessed last?"

"Sure thing, just give me a second." The phone went silent for a couple of minutes while Caden watched busy people hurrying past him to make their flights. "Okay, so the last time it was accessed was the night you slept here. In fact there's even a couple of other times two weeks before that, which happened in the late hours as well."

"The night I slept there?" He never accessed Robert's files that night. "Any chance you got on there that day before you left?"

"Nope. I stay clear of those files. I know that's a big no no."

Caden scratched his head in confusion until something clicked. He stopped scratching. *Matt.* "Sally, what time was it that someone logged into the files?"

"Umm, about eight that evening. In fact they were on for a couple of hours."

"Thanks Sally, I need to let you go." Caden said and was just about to hang up until he remembered the wedding. "Oh, and Sally, I'm setting up a wedding for tonight, I'll give you a call later with the details."

"Really?" Sally said with excitement in her voice. "Don't leave me hanging too long. I want to hear the details about this one."

"Okay, I'll call you as soon as we have the details." Caden needed to talk to Matt, but he was going to have to wait until he got back to the office to question him. There was a lot more that Matt knew. *I'm going to kill...* His thoughts were cut off. He had completely forgotten about the T-13. *How stupid can I be? Here I am incriminating Matt and myself by talking with Sally on the phone.* The only hope he could have is that they hadn't been listening, but he highly doubted it. *There's nothing that can be done now. I have to stick with the plan and stop making stupid mistakes!*

"What's wrong?" James sat, interrupting Caden's thoughts.

"Just a little nervous about the wedding." Caden showed a fake smile hoping James would buy it and let the topic go.

"Well, I got a hold of the minister and he's in."

CHAPTER 18

Azgiel stood at the edge of a deep pit, too deep to even see the bottom. Demons and creatures stood all around him waiting in anticipation. Ropes hung around the large eight feet diameter hole. Clanking could be heard echoing from down below along with a squeaking as one of the ropes moved upwards over a pulley system. The wind blew against Azgiel moving the ropes back and forth.

"It's down there, huh?" Azgiel asked, looking down into the darkness.

"Yes, sir. It will just take a little bit to get it out, especially with this wind." A small human-like creature stood next to him, encased in an odd assortment of armor. It was a bark gnome.

"Keep me updated on when you get it up here." Azgiel backed up as he spoke and tripped over a rock landing on a fallen tree. Pain shot through his back and chest. Creatures quickly surrounded him.

Looking down, Azgiel saw the broken limb that was stabbed through him just below his rib cage. Warm red blood flowed down his torso saturating his new gray weaved shirt that had been made for him since his old armor and clothing didn't fit his new smaller body. The feeling was strange. It had been so long since he experienced the physical pain, he almost didn't know what to do about it for a second.

Movement increased the pain. Azgiel reached down and clasped his hand on the log. With a flash, the broken branch puffed into smoke and the fallen tree launched away from him. His body slouched forward only being stopped by a demon that held a hand out and helped him stand up. Twisting his head and popping his neck, Azgiel took in a deep breath and closed his eyes.

He focused his attention on the wound. Flesh began mending and his body made short work of healing itself. After his wound was taken care of, he reopened his eyes. Creatures stood all around him, looking at him with curious eyes. Azgiel knew they were trying to understand.

Their master was showing weakness and making stupid mistakes. Ones he would've never made in the past. If they found out how weak he had become in his cell of time, they wouldn't trust him to win the war against Triaad.

Giving a smile, Azgiel turned to the fallen tree. *Let them question this.* With a raised, hand the tree melted into a pile of black sand and parts of it blew away in the wind.

"Azgiel," Kaz's voice rang out over the crowd's whispering. His broad red body pushed through the creatures. "You sent for me?"

"Yes." He looked at the dispersing crowd. "Walk with me." They headed into the woods, getting out of earshot from anything listening. Kaz was someone he knew he could fully trust.

Stopping under a large tree, Azgiel did one last check to make sure nothing was watching them. "Do you remember me telling you Mauldrin was back at that facility?"

Kaz nodded, his horns rustled a branch.

"He's the key to unlocking the curse when we get the sword out of the ground. Without full use of the sword we're in trouble." Azgiel shifted his weight, a twig snapped under his feet. "I need you to go back and get him. We have to find a way to get him to take a hold of the sword, to break the curse."

"I'll go quickly and be back before you know it." His long wings spread outwards. A couple of tears could be seen in them from the years of fighting.

"Wait," Azgiel quickly added. "There's more. He needs to take the thing willingly, or I'm afraid it won't undo his curse."

Pulling his wings back in, Kaz lowered slightly to look in Azgiel's eyes. "How will we do that?"

Azgiel could tell by the way he spoke, he didn't have confidence that it could be done. "He doesn't remember who he is, remember? What I need you to do is figure out a way to get on his good side. To make him think we're his allies. His friends." Azgiel's eyes wandered, looking around the woods that surrounded them. His mind raced with ideas. "I have it. Once you get on his good side and he trusts you, without Domblin finding out, let me know. We'll set up a situation where he will have to draw the sword to protect himself."

"Will you tell him what the sword is then?"

"We'll inform him of who he was. A king of this world, and we're his faithful followers. We'll tell him the sword was his and holds the power for him to rule once again." Chuckling, Azgiel continued, "Play your cards right Kaz, and the plan will work out."

"What situation are we going to put him in, to get him to draw the sword?"

"Leave that up to me. I'll have it figured out before long." A small jackal headed creature walked towards them. Azgiel looked at him and then back to Kaz. "For now, go. Don't waste time."

Kaz's large red wings extended, stretching his muscles. With a large step, he left the coverage of the tree and dove into the air. A gust of wind blew pine needles and twigs at Azgiel.

"Sir," the jackal-headed creature whimpered. "The item is on its way up."

"Excellent." Azgiel turned to look at the creature that only stood as tall as his chest. Blood raced through his veins, excited by the idea that they finally had his sword.

As they approached the site, the ropes turned slowly and a light shone from the pit. The pulleys squeaked loudly and could be heard even with the wind blowing hard. There was a chill in the gust that gave Azgiel goose-bumps. After a moment, he could see the Witch's head emerge and then the rest of her body. Two small troll-like creatures, both the color of dark mud accompanied her. They all stood on a wooden platform surrounding a crystal clear boulder containing the sword.

Pushing past a couple large demons, Azgiel got to the platform and held a hand out to help his wife down. "I'm impressed," he spoke as she stepped off the wood, making it creak as her weight shifted.

"It was nothing. Like I said, we've had it locked up down there for some time." She turned to watch the two troll creatures lift a cloth under the clear boulder to get it off the platform. The wind blew them back and forth as they quickly made their way to stable ground.

"Is there a specific way to get it out of the diamond shell, or can I just blast it off?" Azgiel asked while putting a hand on her shoulder.

"Leave it to me." She walked over to the diamond rock and slid a fingernail down its solid clear surface. The wind blew her white dress, which flapped in the opposite direction of her workings. A bright line appeared where she had touched it. Light poured out and the surface began to crack. Finally the shell shattered, breaking into small pieces of clear rock all over the ground. One piece hit Azgiel in the leg, which made him jump slightly.

After the explosion, the sword dropped to the ground. With a strong rumble something like a heartbeat shook the ground. The sword called to him, he could feel a pull from inside. One of the trolls that helped uncover the sword ran for it, to take it to Azgiel.

"No!" the Witch called out, but it was too late. Moving quickly, the creature tried to grab the sword by its handle. A blast that looked like a lightening bolt cracked about him and threw him backwards. His skin began to dissolve as he screamed in pain, but there was nothing that could be done. The curse from the sword made short work of him.

"Don't anyone else touch it!" the Witch yelled. Azgiel moved closer to the sword. He missed it. The power that would surge through him, if he could only have it in his hands again, was something to be desired. *Patience, I will have you in my hands soon enough.*

From a strap in her dress, the Witch pulled out a strange brown matt. It wasn't made of fabric, but it appeared to be made out of a reptile skin of some sort. She bent down and placed it over the sword, then picked it up while wrapping the sword in the scaly skin.

"Your sword, Lord Azgiel." She held the sword out with both hands while lowering her head. He looked her over. The two greatest things that he had ever had in his life stood before him.

A scream broke his concentration. He looked out in time to see one of the jackal headed creatures get knocked down by a dark soul. Three demons quickly drew swords and the closest one of the demons split the dark soul in half. More screams rang out and in the distance a thick blackness moved, covering the floor of the woods. Dark souls. Hundreds of them.

"Hide it!" Azgiel ordered. She nodded and made her exit back into their ancient forest. Grunts and yelps could be heard all around as his demons and other creatures fought. A large sword with strange green writing on it was shoved in Azgiel's face. He turned to see one of his demons, a dark orange one handing him the weapon.

Screams kept echoing across the open meadow that stood between them and the woods where the dark souls were coming from. Azgiel made his way to the front where his troops were fully prepared. Now was the time to show his power.

Stabbing the sword into the ground, Azgiel lifted both of his hands in the air. The wind blew against him. Feeling within, Azgiel tapped into his power that was slowly growing stronger by the day. A large ball of fire tore through the clouds, quickly making its way to the planet, leaving a large smoke trail behind it.

Leaving little time for the dark souls to react, the enormous ball of fire struck the ground, landing on top of their enemies. The explosion threw everyone backwards. Azgiel felt sore from all the power that had surged through him. A smile stretched across his face and he folded his arms as he looked over the destruction.

I'm back!

His troops slowly got up and looked over the destruction as well. Fires burned on many of the trees and the wind spread it. Smoke filled the air and made it hard to see anything. Walking back towards the sword he had driven into the ground, Azgiel picked up a handful of dirt. He closed his eyes and the wind began to pick up. Slowly he let the dirt sift out through his fingers blowing away in the strong gust.

The small amount of dirt grew as it approached the fires, looking like a thick sand storm. It blasted through the woods, extinguishing the fires. Most of the smoke cleared out from the meadow. A small crater was left from the ball of fire.

"No way!" Azgiel said under his breath. A dark soul sat upon a large rat-like creature in the middle of the meadow. *How could anyone live through that?* Shadows moved along the land heading towards the dark soul. At first he wasn't sure what they were, and then he realized they were all the dark souls. His attack had done nothing.

"My Lord, you need to use the sword." A gruff voice spoke from beside him. He turned to see a large black demon standing next to him. "They don't die easy, but the Witch did discover some magic that she put into our swords that kills them. The green stuff, my Lord."

Looking down at the strange sword with green lettering on it, Azgiel took it by the handle. The cool well-worn leather felt soft in his hand. *I can't look weak!* He lifted the sword high in the air and turned to the gathering creatures. "Let nothing live."

His words produced a cheer from those around him and all of them pulled their weapons. Screams began to echo towards them from the dark souls and Azgiel turned to face them. Black spots moved across the charred ground and quickly moved to the green landscape in front of them.

Gripping the sword tight, Azgiel charged his enemies. He could hear the loud running behind him of his small army. Two demons ran beside him, one black and the other a burnt red. Their massive bodies towered over Azgiel.

The dark soul on the rat creature pointed and more dark souls charged, screaming as they moved. Azgiel found his target, the commander. None of the dark souls would stop him.

A dark soul came out of nowhere and jumped in the air to attack Azgiel, a flash of green went by his face as the black demon slammed the creature into the ground with his sword. The blade sliced through the chest splitting the creature in half. Azgiel didn't take the time to see if it was dead. He had to get to the commander of the dark souls.

Something powerful hit him from the side and another from the front knocking him down. He could feel the invisible dark souls cutting into his skin. One of them bit his neck. Trying to unpin his arm to swing his sword, he realized he was getting nowhere fast. The demons that had been by his side were gone fighting their own battles. More weight bore on him as unseen dark souls kept piling on.

"Enough!" Azgiel yelled and a black explosion blasted outward from his body launching the dark souls into the air. Gapping wounds lined his body. A thick, black tar substance filled each cut. Flexing his muscles the wounds healed letting off a strange smoke from each cut, which helped Azgiel feel a little queasy.

Another dark soul ran at him, but this time he could see him. Azgiel sliced his head off and put himself into action, running for the commander. Seeing more dark souls make their way to him, Azgiel knew he needed a different plan, especially after he watched the dark souls disappear. He only had seconds before the invisible attack would happen.

Azgiel held out his left hand and a bright light shot out, engulfing the dark soul that rode on the beast, knocking him to the ground. In its path a glass like hallway was left. *See if you can get through this.* He ran into the chamber. Loud bangs hit the walls as dark souls tried to run through it, but were unable to. At the end he could see the dark soul he had trapped, clawing at the walls to get out.

Realizing the inevitability of his situation, the dark soul turned to face Azgiel. He let out a scream and then disappeared. The ground turned black and a liquid tar like substance wrapped around Azgiel's legs gluing him to the spot. Screams echoed from behind him, dark souls were making their way to him. Knowing they move extremely fast, Azgiel had to think of something and quick.

Turning at his waist, Azgiel lifted his hand and another glass-like wall broke out from the ground, closing off the backside of him. No dark souls would be able to get to him now. A pain shot into his stomach, he could feel the flesh tearing apart. Knowing it had to be the commander, he turned to see a larger dark soul. His eyes blazed red as he screamed in Azgiel's face, reverberating in the small chamber. The black teeth sharp, ready to bite into him. His claws kept tearing upward, moving towards his chest.

Azgiel smiled.

The dark soul stopped and closed his mouth, giving a look of confusion. Gray smoke wafted up between them. Azgiel could feel the itching of his stomach healing back together. Power flowed through his body followed by a blast that threw the commander backwards. Metal ground against bone as Azgiel drove his sword through the creature's chest, pinning him to the ground.

"You try to move through that and it will slice you in half." Azgiel took a moment to look around. Demons and other creatures stood all about. There were no more dark souls in sight.

Victory.

"Who are you?" the commander hissed. He held perfectly still staring at Azgiel with his red eyes.

"I'm the one that's here to protect them." He pointed towards all the creatures that stood just outside the glass barrier. "But the real question is, who are you?" The commander said nothing. A snap of the bone could be heard as Azgiel pushed the sword a couple of inches upward.

"Snyp," the dark soul squawked. "I'm the one that is in charge of this planet."

"Excellent. Then you might live." Azgiel smiled. It was time to cause some controversy with Triaad. To send some fear down his spine with a beautiful lie. "Tell Triaad, Mauldrin is back and pulling all of us together to overthrow him. It's only a matter of time before we tear his beating heart out." With a wave, the glass enclosure evaporated and Azgiel pulled the sword out of him. Weeds bent over and moved sideways as Snyp ran off in shadow form.

Cheers broke out all around Azgiel from his loyal army. Unfortunately, as he looked around, he could see that many had died. Some of the jackal-like creatures and a handful of bark gnomes were being pulled off the field, killed in the fight.

The green veins in the sword glowed strong as Azgiel lifted it in the air to show his excitement. He couldn't help but let out a chuckle, being proud of himself. *Triaad will now be off on the wrong road, looking for Mauldrin while we prepare to kill him and his dark souls. And while they're after Mauldrin, It'll give Kaz a chance to show him we are the good guys by protecting him.*

CHAPTER 19

The morning was cold and Bridget didn't want to get out of bed. She could smell breakfast and hear the sizzling of sausages. The thought of getting up went through her mind, which brought a grimace to her face and she pulled the blankets over her head. Mags was still passed out in the corner of the room on her dog bed. The phone rang and she heard her mom pick it up.

Wondering who could be calling so early, she threw the blankets off to listen. Her curiosity got the best of her and she got up. Fuzzy slippers warmed her toes and a thick robe helped fight the chill in the air. A creak came from behind her as Mags stretched and slowly followed her out of the room.

"Oh sure that would work just fine." Bridget heard her mom say as she walked down the short hallway that led to the kitchen. As she came around the corner, her mom smiled. "Morning honey," Elizabeth said while she motioned for Bridget to have a seat at the table. Elizabeth hung the phone up and set it on the dark tiled counter. She picked up a mug and walked over to Bridget.

"Who was that?" Bridget asked, accepting the mug of hot chocolate.

"Phone solicitor," Elizabeth said, and proceeded without missing a beat, "Sleep well?"

"I slept well. But it sure is cold this morning." She took a sip of hot chocolate. The warmth of the liquid warmed her insides and made her smile.

Elizabeth sat down. Her old chair creaked underneath her. "I'm going shopping this morning. I'd like you to join me."

Bridget hesitated, but she knew it would be rude to decline, so she kept her smile and responded, "Yeah, that would be fun and I probably should get out and about. Maybe it can take my mind off things for a little bit." The thought of just lying around and watching all the lame TV shows sounded better then being around people. She let out a quiet sigh not wanting her mom to catch on that she wanted to stay home.

"I think you'll feel much better," Elizabeth said with a huge smile on her face. "Let me go get you some breakfast and we'll get out of here."

Bridget felt the shopping trip took forever, but she enjoyed getting out, even though they didn't get home until a little past noon.

Before Bridget had everything unloaded, Elizabeth already had the grill going with Mags standing guard waiting for anything to fall to the ground. "How about I do the barbequing while you make a salad," Bridget asked as she came out on the back patio. She was feeling useless and the shopping trip had motivated her to start doing more around the house.

"No," Elizabeth said without looking up, "I like barbequing and the salad is already made."

"What would you like me to do then?" Bridget asked.

Since Bridget had gotten there, Elizabeth kept bugging her about getting up and doing things instead of moping around and watching TV. Now that Bridget was actually in the mood and offering to do something, Elizabeth refused. She didn't understand why her mom was acting this way.

"Why don't you go take a walk along the beach," Elizabeth said. "Go. Relax. I have everything covered."

"Are you sure?" Bridget asked.

"Yes," Elizabeth said, "I'm fine, now go take a walk. I'll call you when it's ready." The sound of the waves was inviting, and Bridget wasn't in the mood to argue.

As she walked up to the water, she picked up a smooth flat rock and threw it into the ocean. It skipped once before a wave engulfed the stone. With a sigh Bridget lay down in the warm sand.

She used to skip rocks with Caden along the beach, but that was years ago. The last time they skipped rocks was also the last time Caden brought up marriage in a positive way. He had told her he wanted to marry her some day. Hope had stayed with her ever since, until now. The hope was completely gone.

That moment had been something that never left her memory. It was the first time he'd ever talked about marriage in a positive way, and not only was it positive, but he also said he liked the idea of getting married to her. Normally when anything about married couples or marriage in general came up, he only had very negative things to say. He did make it clear that he loved her and always wanted to be with her, but she knew he had strong fears of marriage. At that time she had thought about asking for clarification on what he meant, but she was afraid that if she said anything it might make him feel pushed.

After years went by with him never bringing the topic up again, she often regretted not talking to him right then and there about it. There were multiple times she brought it up later, but he always said he didn't even remember the comment, which frustrated Bridget to no end.

A tree creaked next to Bridget, bringing her out of her thoughts and back to reality. She looked in the direction of the noise and saw the cliff where she had first kissed Caden. The breeze picked up, rustling the trees and bushes around her.

The thought of that kiss made her heart beat faster. Caden, and the dream of being together always was what she wanted, but it was gone, somehow it all unraveled.

She got up and walked toward the cliff, heading to the path. The breeze that blew through her hair was cool on her skin. She took a few steps then collapsed to the ground, her tears quickly making their way down her cheeks.

Life used to be perfect, but something happened along the way and now Bridget didn't know how to fix anything. The life she wanted had slipped through her fingers.

Bridget looked to the sky with her tear filled eyes. "Please." She let out a deep sigh and lowered her head.

"Bridget," a voice that sounded like Caden's called out her name. Wiping her tears away, she stopped crying. She was unable to tell where the voice had come from. There was nothing but a bush in front of her so she turned to look behind. The breeze blew her hair into her face, and a hand took her wrist, startling her a little bit. The skin was rougher, like a man's hand. She quickly turned around to see who it was.

Tears of joy threatened as she saw Caden kneeling in front of her holding her hand, but the joy was conflicted with the tremendous amount of anger that she felt. The warmth of his strong hand only made the internal conflict worse. There was so much comfort and peace that pushed through her body with just his single touch. She wanted him back, with all her heart, but she couldn't go through the emotional ups and downs any longer.

His eyes asked for forgiveness, telling her how truly sorry he was. She looked down and felt a small black box move across her palm. Caden opened the box to reveal a diamond ring.

Am I daydreaming?

"Will you marry me, Bridget?"

A ton of thoughts ran through Bridget's mind as she blurted, "How did you find me here? How did you know I would be in this spot by the bush?" The whole thing was too surreal. She closed her eyes and then reopened them only to find Caden still kneeling in front of her.

Caden's warm smile disappeared. "Umm, Bridget...would you answer my question?"

The sun's rays that came through the trees caused the ring to sparkle. Reality began to set in as she processed the question. "Are you serious?" she asked, not meaning to say it out loud.

Caden let go of her wrist, not knowing how to respond. "More serious than I've ever been in my life." He sat in the cool sand. "I don't want to lose you. I can't lose you. I've been an idiot and I let my fears get in the way of what I want more then anything else in this life. You."

Without another word, Bridget jumped forward into Caden, wrapping her arms around him. Caden fell backwards landing on the sandy ground. Her lips pressed against his, while her fingers ran through his hair. His strong fingers gently took a hold of her left hand and put the sparkling ring on her finger. Bridget's eyes filled with emotion.

"Will you marry me?" Caden asked again with a confident voice. Just the sound of it made Bridget's hair stand on the back of her neck. The question that she had dreamt about finally was asked.

This time she didn't hesitate. "Yes. Yes. YES!" She kissed Caden again. Suddenly, she stopped, her lips pressed against Caden's. Her eyes opened.

Caden pulled back. "What?"

"How did you know that I would be right here?" she asked with a mischievous look and a smile in her eyes.

"I just know you that well," Caden responded with a chuckle. He stood up and helped Bridget stand. Holding her hand he tried to guide her past the bush, but she didn't budge. He turned back around to face her. "What?"

"Do you really want this?" Bridget asked. "I mean, are you really wanting to get married or are you just trying to resolve everything so we can get back together?"

Taking her by both hands he stepped closer to her. "Bridget, I realized a little while back how much of a fool I've been." He stopped for a minute then continued. "Look, I'm not that great at explaining how I feel. I never have been. I want you, and I want this. I never want to lose you again." He pulled her closer.

"But how do I know? How do I know this won't be one of those never ending engagements?"

A big smile came over Caden's face as he pulled her out onto the small cliff. "I know this is all kind of cheesy, but…" He motioned to the beach below where there were a handful of people with a priest and a small setup for a wedding.

"You've waited long enough," Caden said holding Bridget in his arms. "The engagement is over. It's time to get married."

"But I don't have a ring for you."

Caden pulled out a silver ring. "We can use this for now and get a real one later." He led her down toward the group of people that were waiting for them. Elizabeth had tears in her eyes as they walked up to the group.

"Phone solicitor, huh?" Bridget said in a fun-loving, but mocking tone to her mother as they approached. She looked over at Caden and spoke to him with the same mocking tone, "and you say you just know me that well. You had this all planned out, didn't you?" Caden just smiled.

The ceremony went fast for Bridget. She was so excited that it all seemed to just fly past her, except for the part where she said 'I do'. The reception was back at Elizabeth's home. Caden and Bridget walked slower than the rest, holding each other as they made their way back.

"So, where are we going for our honeymoon?" Bridget asked. She felt as if she were walking on clouds. The whole world seemed to be lighter.

"Well," Caden hesitated, "your mother's beach house for tonight."

Bridget stopped and looked at him then laughed, he had to be joking. "Come on, where are we really going?"

"For tonight it'll be here at the beach house because I have to get back to the office early in the morning," Caden explained. "I plan on taking you somewhere amazing when I get back, but that destination is a surprise."

"You aren't done with... with whatever it is they need you for?"

"I'm sorry, but no," Caden said trying to pull her in close. "This was just an unexpected day off, and since I decided I couldn't wait any longer, we're now married."

Bridget took a deep breath to cool herself down.

Her first impulsive thought was to get mad at him, but with the breath, she ran through her mind everything that had just happened. She looked down at her amazing ring. She was married; the honeymoon could wait even if she wanted it now. If she got mad, it would only tarnish the perfect wedding.

Bridget stopped and pulled Caden in close to give him a big kiss. "Thank you. Thank you so much. You have made me the happiest woman alive."

CHAPTER 20

The next morning Caden got up extremely early to get ready to head back to the office. He bundled up in one of Bridget's bathrobes to keep warm as he packed his things in the car, his arms extended far out of the sleeves. Mags followed him out and ran off to the beach.

Caden had gotten up extra early just in case Bridget wanted to just hang out, but she didn't budge. He had a half-an-hour before he had to leave, and lying next to Bridget in a warm bed seemed like the best way to fill his time.

Quietly Caden slipped under the covers. He stretched and cracked his back and then scooted over to cuddle with Bridget. No less then a minute had gone by before he was asleep.

Something awoke him—a feeling that somebody entered the room moving along the wall past his feet. Caden tried to turn but his body wouldn't respond to any of his desires. The mattress sunk a little at Caden's legs as something put its weight on the edge.

"Bridget," a voice hissed, "very fine indeed."

A surge of energy flowed through Caden as he forced some of his muscles to respond. He turned toward the creature that was crouched by his legs. Caden saw the same creature that had attacked him before. At first he felt fear as he looked at the dark shadowy skin, the sharp black teeth, and the burning red eyes. The creature was frozen in its spot, looking like a deer caught in headlights.

They looked at each other for a moment before the dark shape smiled and crouched, ready to attack. Caden clenched his jaw and said through his teeth, "Bring it on."

Rage fueled Caden's actions. He was not going to allow anything to touch Bridget. Without a sound, the creature dove at Caden, but something hit the creature and sent it slamming against the wall. Caden tried to look at what protected him but was unable to turn far enough to see anything.

A loud snort emerged from something in the back corner of the room to the left of Caden. Without any effort, the dark creature moved up the side of the wall. Black veins grew from behind the figure as if there were roots growing along the wall and ceiling. Caden was intrigued as he watched the oily substance move swiftly towards his side of the room.

Metal rubbed against a sheath. Caden knew it was a sword being drawn. The steel blade was held out in front of Caden. Dark green writing was inscrolled, leading to a small hole at the tip of the sword. There were scratches on the well-worn blade.

A scream came from the shadowy creature on the wall. Its black teeth seething.

Caden heard a heavy footstep as the sword moved forward. He was finally able to see a part of the beast that lurked behind him. A large, red hand held the handle of the sword and dark black tattoos ran up his arm. The rest of the beast's body hid in the shadows, but he could tell that it was large and had horns on its head that had strange carvings in them. Breathing heavy, Caden felt his eyes widen in shock.

"I'm surprised you're not dead," the red beast said in a very deep, scratchy voice to the creature. "You're the one that I heard was left for your own kind to eat?"

"What are you doing here?"

"I'm here to protect Mauldrin. I won't allow you to harm him."

The dark creature said nothing in return. Instead, it dove off the wall, releasing its claws. A sheet of blackness followed the dark shadow, pushing a dresser out of the way, and knocking the bed against the wall. Caden tried to move his head but with no success. He was worried Bridget might be dead since she hadn't responded to anything. The beast's sword flew across the room stabbing into the wall. Screeching and crashing echoed in the room as the two creatures fought.

A massive red wing extended over the bed and then retracted. Parts of the wing were torn with little holes. A fiery ball smashed the dark creature into the wall causing him to disappear into a puff of smoke. Caden felt freedom from his paralyzed state, but before he could move, his body stopped responding and he passed out.

As soon as he became responsive he opened his eyes, Caden was surprised to see the room back to normal. Everything was quiet, and there were no signs of any type of fight.

Quickly, Caden got out of bed. He leaned over and checked on Bridget who was sound asleep. His heart pounded, the hallucinations weren't getting any better; they were getting worse.

After kissing Bridget on the forehead he left.

Fear ran through his veins—fear that Bridget was going to get hurt if he stuck around like Steven had done to one of the staff at SDS. He had to get back to the main office as quickly as possible and talk to Robert. His secret had to come to an end.

By the time Caden arrived at the airport, he was beginning to second-guess the idea of talking to Robert again. He didn't want to be locked up like Steven. He had some time to waste before he could board the plane. So he sat down at the gate and thought about what had happened that morning. His heart rate slowed. His eyelids felt heavy.

A kick to Caden's foot woke him up as James stood over him. "Time to get up sleepy head. They're boarding the plane."

Caden blinked a couple of times. He stood and stretched. "I must've been tired."

"I bet you're tired after last night," James said with a big smile on his face. Caden gave a halfhearted smile.

They both found their seats without saying a word, and most of the flight they kept to themselves, with James every now and again giving Caden a strange look that Caden didn't understand.

"Okay, tell me what's going on," James asked after a long time.

"What do you mean?" Caden asked as the seatbelt sign came on.

"You're acting like…" The pilot announcing that they were approaching their destination cut James off.

"You're not your usual talkative self," James said bluntly, ignoring the pilot.

"It's nothing," Caden said, "I'm just tired." He looked down at his hands. *What if I tell James instead of Robert? James has always backed me up in the past and maybe he could help me figure out what was going on.*

"I don't think so," James said while crumpling up his trash. "You're not just tired. There's something more going on. Did Bridget do something?"

Caden pulled out a pen his pocket and a magazine from the seat in front of him. He quickly wrote, "It's not Bridget," he rubbed a hand on the back of his neck while he wrote. "You can't tell anyone, not even Matt." He scribbled quickly, not wanting to speak the information because of the T-13.

"Sure thing," James said moving in a little closer to him. "You know you can trust me."

"Yes I do. Something keeps happening to me and I can't tell if I'm going crazy or if I'm having realistic nightmares or…" Caden couldn't even finish writing that he might be seeing hallucinations, it sounded too stupid.

"What's been happening?" His eyebrow lifted.

"I've been seeing creatures-" Caden stopped writing again. He felt completely crazy and James was going to see him that way.

"Creatures?" James asked. "What do you mean exactly? Like animal creatures?"

"No." Caden spoke under his breath. He felt like a fool and wished he had never started telling James. "Like, monster creatures," he whispered.

"Monsters?" He gave Caden a half smile. "Seriously? Monsters? What do they look-"

A scream cut James off. Seatbelt latches clicked as people ran from their seats. A man stood over James and Caden pointing a gun at them.

"Are you going to shoot us?" James asked nonchalantly.

"I'm only here for him," the man said, pointing at Caden. Beads of sweat rolled down the man's forehead dripping off his short brown hair. He wore a black body suit. "But if you get in the way I'll kill you as well." His hands trembled as he waved the gun back and forth between Caden and James. The man talked into a mic on his wrist. "I have him in the second cabin."

Seeing the perfect opportunity, James hit the gun causing the man to shoot at the ceiling. James snatched the gun and tossed it to Caden. The man threw a punch only to be knocked down as James grabbed his arm and slammed him to the floor. Blood gushed from his nose.

"Fool. Do you even know who you're messing with?" James rested his knee on the guy's head and twisted his arm almost dislocating it. Caden watched from his seat as James did his thing. He was impressed, and ashamed. Normally he would have been just as quick as James, but he had been so caught up in his fears of losing his mind, he couldn't pull himself into the action.

"I know who you are," a voice said from behind. Caden turned around. It was the same man he had seen in the stairwell holding the gun to the scientist. Caden started but before he could make a move, he was thrown against a seat and James was hurled down the aisle by an explosion on the plane. Both men in the suits disappeared at the same time.

Caden grimaced as James rose from the floor. "They stole the suits. They broke into the main office."

"Do they have Dead Time suits?"

But before Caden could respond, another explosion rocked the plane knocking both men back down.

Looking out the window, Caden noticed a jet flying toward the plane as a missile launched. It hit the wing, blowing the engine to bits. Pieces of metal and debris pelted the side and window.

Passengers rushed to the front of the plane panicking. James pushed his way through the aisle toward Caden.

"They're already off the plane, aren't they?"

"Yeah." Caden said as he tried to keep his balance. The plane plummeted toward the ground.

The pilot blared over the speakers, "Please, everyone stay calm and seated with your seatbelts on. Stay seated!"

James' eyes met Caden's. "What do we do?"

Caden glanced at the ground and then to his wrist. "This." He pushed the switch to stop time.

The silence was loud after all the screaming. The passengers looked like they were being thrown forward, frozen in that moment. Caden had hit the switch so quickly he hadn't even noticed the front of the plane touched the ground.

"Let's get these people out of here!"

"How?" James asked. He glanced at the frozen people.

"Not sure, any ideas?"

James looked around for a moment then walked over to the emergency exit and kicked it open. "This way."

"Good thinking." Caden grabbed a young man that was being thrown out of his seat. He dragged him to the exit. The passenger's body was frozen like a statue but was very light, like Styrofoam. With little effort, Caden pushed the guy out the door, but he just stayed in one spot, frozen in mid-air, high above the ground. Caden made a face.

With a huff, Caden jumped out of the plane, seized the floating man as he passed and pulled him slowly to the ground. Once his feet gently made contact, he walked the passenger a little ways away from the crash to make sure he would be safe when they started time again.

Caden saw the outside of the plane for the first time. The front end was crumpled. A thin trail of flames moved along the underbelly of the plane and pooled in some of the ripples from the impact. One of the windows was smashed out and glass fragments were frozen in mid air just above the roof of the plane. Caden quickly made his way to the cockpit. James, with an arm full of passengers, was just barely getting to the ground when Caden reached the front end of the jet liner.

The metal was cold to the touch as Caden began climbing up the side of the plane, using the bent and broken metal as a type of ladder. A strange sensation went through his fingers as he took a hold of a ledge. His nerves seemed to not know if they should be signaling pain or comfort. Pulling himself up, Caden noticed that his fingers were in a pocket of fire. Quickly he pulled his hand away, more out of surprise then anything. His fingers looked just fine, no burns, and he turned his focus back to the flame.

The yellow, reddish flame, which looked like a liquid in the stopped time, seemed to be alive. It seemed to almost call to him. With doubt in his mind, Caden moved his hand close to the fire, but still kept at a safe distance. He whisked some of his fingers in the air and immediately stopped; the flame had responded to his movements, changing to a darker shade and growing.

"Are you going to play all day or help me unload this thing so we can get out of here?" James asked.

"Did you see that, the flame…" Caden trailed off noticing that the flame looked the same. His hallucinations were getting the better of him and now wasn't the time to deal with them. "I…I'm just still getting used to this Dead Time stuff."

"I noticed," James said with a smile on his face. "Now, can we get back to work, or am I going to need to crawl over you so you can stare at the fire?"

Lifting himself up, Caden reached the window and climbed into the plane. Both of the pilots were pretty beat up from shards of glass hitting them and being slammed forward into the plane's instruments. Caden watched as James grabbed a piece of glass that was floating in front of him. The cockpit was littered with them, along with other objects that were loose inside the small area.

"Want to help me with these guys?" Caden asked.

James poked and toyed with the pieces of glass in the air. James looked over at Caden. "Sure thing." They quickly got the pilots out, but it took some time to get the rest of the passengers off. Fortunately since it had been such an early flight the seats were only half filled.

"Could you imagine how much harder this would have been if we weren't in Dead Time and we had to deal with actual body weight compared to their weightlessness?" James took a deep breath as he looked around. People were strewn across a parking lot near where the plan crashed.

"No. I couldn't even imagine, nor do I want to, you ready to start time ag…" He stopped short and sprinted toward the plane. "Someone at the emergency door," Caden screamed over his shoulder. If one of the men in the black body suits was still on the plane, Caden was going to get him. There wasn't going to be any slow responses this time.

He climbed through the open window of the cockpit and headed up the plane. It took him a minute to get to the seating area where he had seen the movement by the opened emergency door.

At the corner of the doorway, Caden stopped and looked around. Not seeing anything, he slowly made his way up each aisle looking down the seats and around them. He bent down to look under the seats. He could see nothing in the main section of seats, but further on he noticed someone crouched about five rows up from him.

The lights in the cabin dimmed and he could sense something was wrong. Being as quiet as he could, Caden moved backwards. He heard the soft sound of someone rubbing against the leather seats; what sounded like claws slid across the hard floor. Caden took a couple of steps backwards to the open emergency door.

"Where ya going?" a scratchy voice croaked from behind the seats. Caden took another step, realizing that it was the same dark creature that had attacked him just a few hours ago. The creature sniffed then scratched at the seats. "MAULDRIN!"

A weakness surged through Caden's entire body making him collapse to the floor. The overhead lights shut off and the light in the cabin seemed to get sucked out. A dark colored hand reached out and grasped the seat and the figure began pulling itself up.

Caden tried to move, but couldn't. A strong force pinned him to the floor.

"You're not going anywhere," the creature hissed. A cold liquid began moving across Caden's legs making its way towards his head. It tensed his muscles as if he had just stuck his legs into ice water.

"To bad your big, red friend can't save you this time. He can't follow us into a cell of time." The creature slowly moved down the isle.

With one last effort Caden focused on his muscles. He first moved his fingers, and the rest of his body quickly followed, fueled by adrenalin. Not wanting to stick around and find out what the creature was planning on doing with him, Caden jumped up and dove out the emergency exit.

Unable to look behind him to see if he was being followed, Caden yelled, "RUN!" Caden hit the button even as he flew through the air. The explosion hit Caden, launching him forward and slamming him to the ground. He curled instinctively. His back and right shoulder took the brunt of the damage from the tumble, but overall he was bruised and scraped up. He huddled until the plane stopped crashing into the ground. Screams and cries rang out as people ran around frantically not understanding how they got out of the plane.

James helped Caden up. "That was some crash landing you did."

Caden smiled.

"Why did you start the time back up so soon?" James asked while brushing off some of the dirt on Caden's back. "Why didn't you wait until you were on the ground?"

"Didn't you see it?" He thumbed back toward the plane. "The thing that was after me?"

"I only saw you but you did have me worried for a minute with that horrified look on your face."

"That's because there was something after me." Caden shot off. He felt frustrated. It had been a chance to prove the hallucinations were actually real.

"What *thing* are you talking about?" James asked, "We were the only ones in Dead Time. There wasn't anything else in there but us."

Caden looked around at all the screaming, and the chaos. "I'm not sure what it was, but it creeped me out, and it's not the first time I've seen it."

The blaring sirens grew louder as they approached the crash site.

"Well, whatever it was, I'm sure it's dead now. Especially after a crash like that," James said with a chuckle.

Caden could tell James didn't really believe him. He knew he better drop the subject or he was going to start sounding crazy. Once again, he still didn't know if he was hallucinating or if things were real.

Dust lightly clouded the air next to Caden as he padded the last little bit of dust off his clothing. "My wallet's gone. They must've taken it. It had all my key cards and access cards."

"You think they took it?" James asked. "The guys who attacked us on the plane?"

"I bet that was the reason for being on the plane and attacking us," Caden said angrily.

"If that's the truth, then we need to get to the office now. Let's find a car."

"Good idea," Caden said following James. "I'll call the office to-." Before he got a chance to dial, his cell phone showed someone was calling. He didn't recognize the number.

"Caden." Matt's voice.

"Did Robert let you out?"

"Yes, but-"

"Good. Tell security and Robert that the people who stole the Dead Time suits were on the plane with James and me. They stole my key cards and access cards. I'm figuring they're heading your way."

"I'll tell them, but I need to tell you-"

"Talk to me when I get there. Right now James and I need to figure out how to get over there. We're probably about forty-five minutes out if we can obtain a ride." He hung up the phone.

Police cars and emergency teams pulled up to the scene. James quickly made his way to a back alley with Caden right behind him. James pointed. "I see a car that we can high jack."

CHAPTER 21

Bridget sat at the bar in her mom's kitchen stirring her hot chocolate and staring off in space. A pot sitting on the stove bubbled over and her toast was getting cold. *Is there something I did to upset him?* Bridget thought. She looked down at her hot chocolate. *Why would he leave without saying goodbye?*

The hot chocolate didn't look appetizing any longer so she pushed it away accidentally spilling it. Snapping out of her thoughts, she leaned over to grab a washcloth. As she reached she noticed the water boiling over and with a growl ran over to the stove.

Not only was Caden's early departure frustrating, but a nightmare she had before she woke up was bothering her as well. She had been lost in some dark house and something dark and evil was there. The only exit was a big black door, and when she opened it, something attacked her and that was when she woke up to find Caden gone. The nightmare had left her sweaty and feeling terrified most of the morning. She wanted Caden by her side even more.

"Bridget," Elizabeth yelled from her bedroom. "Come in here for a minute."

"One sec," Bridget yelled back while shutting the stove off and moving the pot. She walked o her mother's bedroom and stopped in the doorway. "What ya need?"

"There's a plane crash on the news," Elizabeth said without looking away from the TV. She was sitting on the end of her bed. "Do you remember the flight Caden was on?"

"Flight 239," Bridget said while walking closer to see the news report, "but I don't think it would've been his because it was an earlier flight then this." Bridget sat down next to her mom. "Do they know what happened yet, or how many dead?"

"The engines had blown out at least that's what the pilots are reporting. They say that everyone was able to mysteriously get off the plane before it crashed."

"Well, that's good." Bridget said.

"Yeah, but the odd part is that they don't know how they got off. The crew and pilots are saying they were on the plane and then right before the plane crashed they were off and safe. It has the emergency teams and news media totally perplexed. Some of the passengers are giving credit to the creator, calling it a miracle. Others say it was aliens and they remember odd figures carrying them around on spaceships. I'm sure they'll come to some logical conclusion but now they're still going through the wreckage to make sure everyone got off the plane." Bridget stared at her mom, surprised with her rambling. Curious, she looked to the screen.

Bridget gasped when she read the scrolling banner on the channel. "Oh my gosh." Bridget said as she turned up the volume. "It was Caden's flight."

"All but three passengers have been identified," a newscaster announced. "The emergency teams are still looking through the wreckage to find the missing passengers." The TV screen switched to another news anchor that was out in the field. "This man who lives in the town says he saw the plane wreck and everyone get off. Can you tell everyone what you saw?"

The anchor lowered a microphone. "It was the strangest thing I ever did saw," the man explained. "The plane came crashing down. Then people were all over the place and one dude was like flying out of the plane, almost like some type of superhero saving all the passengers."

The reporter pulled the microphone back. "Thanks Tom. These other people standing next to me are passengers that saw the same thing, of some person flying out of the plane. We haven't been able to locate this man. According to some witnesses, he walked away from the scene with one other passenger."

The news cut to the wreckage showing a smaller window at the bottom of the screen. "Emergency teams have found a body on the plane, but it is too badly burned for them to identify the person, it appears they had been in the restroom. Right now we have to go to our sponsors but stay tuned. We will continue following this story throughout the day."

Bridget nervously tapped her foot on the floor. "Do you think Caden is okay?" she asked. Her mother muted the TV.

"I'm sure he's fine," Elizabeth responded putting her hand on Bridget's leg. "In fact, knowing Caden, I wouldn't be surprised if he was one of the men that walked away unfazed by the crash."

"I can't believe he would be that stupid," Bridget said. "Why would he walk away from a crash without being checked out or even stopping to help the others?"

"I don't know dear-".

"In fact, why hasn't he called me?" Bridget asked. Elizabeth wrapped her arm around Bridget and pulled her in close. Both of them sat there in silence for a minute with the TV muted. A sick feeling went through Bridget's body as she imagined Caden being the one that died in the wreck.

Only a couple of minutes had gone by before the phone rang. Elizabeth reached for it, but Bridget took it out of her hands and answered.

"Hello," Bridget said with panic in her voice. "Caden, are you okay? Are you hurt? Where are you?" She still shook in fear.

"I'm fine," Caden responded.

Bridget let out a sigh. "I'm so glad you're okay. We saw the wreck on the news. We were so worried about you."

"No need to be worried, James and I left the wreck immediately after it happened."

"It was you and James that walked away?" Bridget said, her voice rising a little louder. She couldn't believe it. Anger began taking over her emotions. "How foolish can you-"

"I just wanted to call to tell you we're okay," Caden said rather bluntly. "We're on our way to the office right now, so-"

"You just survived a wreck," Bridget began, "and now you're on your way to work. Why would you even think about going to work after you were on a plane that crashed, and how will you even get there?" She looked over at Elizabeth with wide eyes.

"I just wanted to let you know we're okay," Caden said again, "but I need to get going."

"No," Bridget yelled. Her heart rate was going crazy. "You need to come home, now! You're not thinking clearly. Obviously that crash jarred something loose in your head."

"I'm not coming home. Not right now. Bigger things are-"

"If you're not willing to come home, I want to come to you."

"No." Caden said, almost pleading with her.

"You've put work over us in the past; you're now putting it over our honeymoon." She took a breath to cool down a little, which didn't help. "You then put work over your health after going through a plane crash. You aren't going to push me out after all of this, using your work as some kind of excuse. I'm coming!" She realized at the end she was almost yelling.

"Bridget." Caden said in his tone that showed his frustration. "The answer is no. You cannot come out and meet me. I'll explain the best I can later, but right now there are lives at stake and I have to go."

"Caden-"

"I love you. I promise I'll call you later." With that, Caden hung up.

Bridget hung up the phone and looked over at her mother. Tapping on the phone with her fingernails, she looked back at the cordless black phone and back to her mom. "I need to run to the airport and get a seat on a plane. He can't stop me if I'm already there."

CHAPTER 22

Crunching could be heard as Tagen approached Snyp's large room. As he entered he saw Snyp eating a youngling that had been created for the purpose of food.

There were many cells throughout the caverns that contained people they caught. Normally the cells contained bums, drug dealers, people that wouldn't be missed when they disappeared. Once they caught a human they were thrown into the cells where their souls would be unable to leave their bodies as their bodies died. Slowly darkness seeped into their souls, and the soul—out of survival—absorbed the body. Most of the dark souls were created for food, which not only rejuvenated them, but also gave them more power depending on how old the soul was and the knowledge it had. There were also the souls that Snyp decided to keep alive, which only happened if his ranks were growing small.

As Tagen approached, Snyp looked up. A black oily substance squirted out of Snyp's mouth as he crunched down on something between his teeth. "What news do you bring?" Snyp asked after swallowing. A large wound split up the middle of his back, oozing black blood pooled on the ground.

"Are you ok?" Tagen asked quietly.

Snyp reached back and touched the wound. "It will be fine shortly. Things didn't go as well as I had hoped."

Knowing if he pushed for much more information Snyp might get irritated, Tagen decided to move on with his information. "I know a way we might be able to capture Mauldrin," Tagen responded while eyeballing the half-eaten corpse. The thought of sinking his teeth into the juicy, black flesh made him hungry.

"Well go on," Snyp said, reaching for a severed hand and biting off a finger, crunching through the softened bone that hadn't been fully absolved by the person's own spirit.

"I followed Mauldrin into stopped time."

Snyp stopped eating and lifted both eyebrows at Tagen. "Mighty brave of you to venture into a cell of time like that."

"I was nervous," Tagen said quickly, "but I made sure I was careful." Tagen looked at the hand Snyp was still holding, craving to have it. "I think the cell was empty, I never saw a thing."

"So how do we capture him?" Snyp asked. With a small toss, Snyp threw the hand to Tagen.

Tagen ripped into the hand making short work of it. He finished the last bite and wiped the black oily liquid that dripped down his chin. "He's much weaker in the stopped time. I was able to control him for a little bit with just his name. I believe if you give me a group of younglings, we can capture him the next time he goes into a cell of time."

"And what if the next time there is something in that cell?"

"I feel confident that we'd be okay," Tagen responded in a hissing voice. "Besides, if there was anything there it would go after Mauldrin to try to make its escape."

"Very true." Snyp tore a piece of shadowy flesh from the corpse and chewed. "Go and pick some younglings that you trust. Make sure they don't know who Mauldrin is and then bring him back to me."

"There's more." Tagen hesitated. The last time he had reported information about someone trying to stop him, he got in trouble. Snyp stopped chewing for a moment and looked up at Tagen. "One of the times that I attacked Mauldrin, Kaz was there, protecting him."

Snyp's black muscles glistened as he flexed them and stood. "Demons can't go into time cells."

"It was before I attacked Mauldrin in a cell of time."

Turning away from Tagen, Snyp walked further into the darkness of his cavern, mumbling to himself. All Tagen could understand was something about what the human had said was true that Mauldrin was joining the Witch.

"This is getting complicated," Snyp spoke while he paced. His mumbling increased in volume. Finally he stopped and looked up at Tagen. "What about Domblin? Where was he?"

"I'm not sure. He was nowhere to be seen, but I wasn't at the location where I had shown you previously. I attacked Mauldrin in many different places outside of that building, hoping I could get him with Domblin not around."

"No matter, I'm sure my scouts will find him and keep a trail on him." Snyp finally raised a hand and his throne of bones formed out of the ground. The bones grinded as he sat. "Let's stick with the plan. Get some younglings and catch Mauldrin as quickly as possible. I'll try to hold Triaad off as long as I can, to give you a chance to get Mauldrin out of there, so he doesn't find out. I'll also inform him that the demon thing is resolved, so I won't have to keep losing battles out there and wasting my time with them."

"Is it resolved?" Tagen asked, not meaning to ask out loud. Snyp just glared at Tagen for a moment. His red eyes blazed.

"Is the plan clear?"

"Yes," Tagen said. *I can't wait to bring you down, you backstabbing...* Stepping away from the carcass that he wanted to take, Tagen left the room.

The usual emptiness in the hallway, with the normal occasional scream, seemed hollow to Tagen. He hadn't always lived like this. There was a time when he lived with Triaad in his kingdom and was treated with respect. Everything had fallen apart almost two thousand years ago and he was going to get it back. As soon as he could prove Snyp's terrible plan, then Triaad will love him once again.

Soft dirt sifted through his toes as he slowly walked. His plan was going to have to change now that he would have younglings involved. *I'll have to catch him alive and bring him back here as Snyp requested. But then...then I'll inform Triaad before he leaves. We'll catch Snyp red handed. I'll be recognized for my heroic efforts.* Smiling, Tagen began to walk faster.

Liquid dark matter dripped over the opening where the older younglings slept. Tagen looked around at the large numbers of creatures lining the holes in the walls and the floor. He only wanted the fanatical younglings, ones that were almost too much to handle. They would be strong enough to fight Mauldrin.

"Who wants some flesh?" Tagen yelled, looking for the overly anxious ones that drooled for blood.

He knew he was flirting with disaster if one of them grew too desirous and hurt Mauldrin, but he felt strong enough to keep them in line. There was going to be a fight for Mauldrin and he needed to be ready with dark souls who would fight, even if it meant their lives.

A large crowd of growling younglings crowded around Tagen.

"You may eat anything, or anyone that stands in the way of the one person that I must capture and bring back to Snyp," Tagen said to the large group of younglings. He was pleasantly surprised, almost the entire cavern of younglings had gathered around him.

Even though Tagen wanted to take them all, he knew if he was going to keep order with the younglings he needed a smaller group. He could come back for the others if the stupid demon got in the way again. It would be hard enough to make sure the ones he took didn't attack Mauldrin even though they would be told not to.

"I can't take all of you right now," Tagen said as he looked at the seven closest younglings. "You seven. Let's go. If I need more, I'll come back for the rest of you."

"Meat," one of them hissed as they made their way out of the cavern and through the tunnels.

CHAPTER 23

The streets were empty as Caden sped down back-roads to get to the main office. James sat in the passenger's seat, and was on his cell phone talking with his wife. They had hijacked the car; it was old, but still had a kick to it. A skull on a necklace string hung from the rear view mirror and the seats were covered with black fabric.

"Okay hun, I'll talk to you later," James said as he closed his cell phone and put it back in his pocket.

"Everything good with the wife?"

"Yup," James said with a smile. "She thinks I'm nuts, but she's grown used to it and wished me well."

"That's really cool of her," Caden said, still feeling a little frustrated from Bridget's response.

"What about Bridget," James began, "how does she feel about the whole situation?"

"Oh," Caden hesitated. He really didn't want to talk about it. But he knew if he didn't, James would start bugging him, and he really didn't have the patience for that. "She's not too impressed with my decisions." He pulled down a street a couple of blocks away from the office building. They could see it at the end of the street.

Suddenly, in the distance, a huge explosion blasted the SDS office building. The explosion gave the illusion that time had slowed down. Cars were thrown around in front of them as the blast quickly approached. Caden slammed on the gas and steered for a side street, but it was too late. The enormous blast clipped the back of their car, knocking all of the glass out of the windows and slamming the car against a concrete building. Caden's ears rang and his heart pounded. Dust filled the air. Explosions from small buildings and other structures echoed down the roadways.

James had cuts on his face and a piece of glass sticking out from his left cheek. Blood trickled down his lips from his nose. "You okay," Caden asked while putting his hand on James's back.

James sat up a little and pulled the glass out, "I'll be alright, how about you?" The small glove box creaked as James found napkins to put on his face and nose.

"I'm fine," Caden said restarting the car. "But I have a bad feeling we don't have an office anymore." Anger brewed inside of him, but this is what all of his years of training were for, to keep the anger subdued. He could remember Robert teaching him techniques over and over on how to keep anger contained because it would blur thoughts and make his work sloppy.

Both rear tires were flat, which gave the feeling that the car was driving on a very bumpy road. Most of the buildings around them were destroyed as they drove to the office. The windows were blown out and some of the buildings were on fire. Only a couple of minutes passed before they got to the building, or what used to be the building. It was just a pile of rubble and some fires here and there.

James and Caden got out of the car. An explosion rang out behind them and they both quickly ducked down. In disbelief Caden examined the situation, looking across the rubble. He took deep breaths; he had to stay clear minded so he could effectively help any survivors.

Vibrations came from Caden's pocket. Reaching in, he pulled out his cell phone. He didn't recognize the number and started to put it back. There wasn't time to be wasted on a phone, but something inside prodded him to answer. "Hello?"

"Caden, it's me…"

"Matt, you're alive." Caden said louder then he expected. James quickly looked at him. "Are you buried in the rubble? We'll get down there as fast as possible."

"No, I'm not in the building." Matt sounded out of breath. "I have something important to tell you. Can you meet me?"

"Meet you? The office just blew up. Not sure if you knew. But I'm here now and I'm going to help get survivors out."

"I know the office blew up. I don't have much time. Meet me at the building on the corner of 4th and Denk Ave. Come in through the blown out wall."

"You come to me. I have to get out in the rubble to see if there are any survivors."

"There won't be, trust me." Matt sounded almost remorseful. "Caden, I need you to meet me. It's about Robert. You can't trust him. He's betrayed all of us."

"What do you mean?" Caden asked. "How did he betray us?" Something moved in the rubble just a little ways out from where Caden was standing.

"I can't tell you over the phone."

"I'll call you back in a minute. There's someone alive out there. I have to get them help."

"That's impossible-"

Before Matt could finish, Caden hung the phone up. Without a second thought, he instinctively jumped up to help whoever was there. He had to move slower then what he wanted from the small fires and spots in the rubble that looked unsafe. As he got closer, the figure moved in rather bizarre ways, arms bending in ways they shouldn't. It even appeared to Caden that the figure was growing a leg back, but he figured it must have been from the rubble falling down and heat waves from the fire that was burning rather closely to the survivor.

"Caden, stop," James called out. "You could fall into the basement areas."

Creaking noises came from under Caden's feet as he kept going forward, ignoring James. He knew that whoever was out there needed help immediately. Fire shot up out of a large hole in the ground, and Caden had to backtrack to maneuver around it. Sweat soaked through his clothing. The intense heat caused his eyes to burn. But he was getting closer and he could hear the person moving around.

"Hello!" Caden yelled, hoping to get their attention.

"Don't come any closer," a voice muttered. Caden could barely hear over the fires and things crashing to the lower levels of the building. Ignoring the warning, Caden kept moving forward.

"That's far enough." Steven said. He was huddled in between two walls that had been smashed to pieces. "You shouldn't be out here." His left hand was shredded—only his thumb was left—and large chunks of skin were torn off of his face. Caden was surprised to see him. Robert had said Steven escaped, but there he was, and somehow had survived the explosion.

"I'm here to help," Caden responded, taking another step forward. He could tell Steven needed medical attention immediately, and more than likely, he wasn't going to be in the right frame of mind to let Caden help him.

"No you might get hurt."

"Everything's going to be okay." Caden tried to sound calm and reassuring even though he wasn't fully sure Steven was going to be all right. He took another step closer.

"Fine, have it your way," Steven said in a voice that didn't sound like his. "I didn't want you to see this, but I can't stay here much longer and neither should you."

Caden stepped closer. As if by magic, the cuts on Steven's face began to heal along with the bones, muscle fibers, and skin on his left hand. Caden thought he could see particles in the air coming together to heal Steven's wounds. A crack sounded from Steven's broken leg as it mended itself. Caden took a couple of steps back feeling the rubble move under his feet. Steven slowly stood up and Caden noticed a steal bar sticking out of his side. With a quick motion, Steven pulled the bar out and tossed it to the ground. The hole filled in and healed. Caden didn't know what to think.

"It's time for you to get out of here." Steven said taking a step closer to Caden.

"How did you do that?" Caden asked. He tried to rationally break down what happened. "Did Robert and Allen do this to you?

Did they perform some other type of experiment that he didn't tell me about?"

"It's unsafe for you out here. You need to go back," Steven said again.

Caden took a step back and the flooring gave out on him, and he began to fall back into the lower levels of the building. Miraculously, Steven caught him by the shirt and pulled him out like Caden was as light as a feather.

"Leave," Steven demanded after putting Caden down. Without another word, Steven walked through a small wall of flames that parted out of his way as he went through. "I'll find you later. Right now I have to find someone."

After Steven disappeared Caden quickly turned and started back, moving rapidly across the rubble, knowing he couldn't follow Steven because it was too unsafe. To the side of him, large sections of the building collapsed, which motivated him to move even quicker. James wasn't by the car when he reached it. Caden looked back to the rubble. *What had happened to Steven?*

"James!" Caden yelled out. The air filled with sirens and fire trucks converged on the scene, so he figured James must have gone to talk to the emergency teams. "James," Caden yelled again.

With no response and not being able to see him anywhere in sight, Caden walked over to the car door. He paused to look at the damage to the vehicle. The body was bent where it had slammed into the corner of the building. He reached out for the door handle and felt a gun push up against his back.

"Why did you do it?" Robert asked.

"Why did I do what?" Caden asked, frozen.

"Don't play stupid with me," Robert snapped. "I'm giving you a matter of seconds to answer before I shoot." Robert drove the gun into Caden's back. Caden noticed one of James's feet sticking out from behind the car. Time for conversations was over. With a swift move, Caden hit the Dead Time switch. He felt something driving into his back.

Robert had fired the second Caden had moved. Reaching back, he felt the bullet that was stuck halfway into his skin. Pulling it out, he put it in his pocket. He then checked on James who was breathing and there was no sign of blood, so Caden figured Robert had only knocked him out. It was time to take care of Robert.

Blood spots hovered in the middle of the air from where he was bleeding. Noticing a shirt and some worn out tennis shoes in the back of the car, Caden took the shirt and tied it around his left shoulder to block the bleeding. If the bullet had actually run its course, it would have hit Caden's heart and killed him. Anger surged through him. He trusted Robert and now Robert tried to kill him. Caden ripped Robert's gun from his hand. *I have to tie him up.* Pulling the shoelaces from the old shoes, Caden tied Robert's hands together. Caden turned Robert and pushed him against the car, if he didn't, Robert might be in an advantageous position to run or attack. Robert wasn't a person to mess around with. He had seen more action than Caden's whole team put together. Caden could hold his own with most people, but Robert was known to take down agents within seconds.

Beginning to feel paranoid of what might be in Dead Time with him, Caden was ready to leave especially with James knocked out and no one to watch his back. He was already on edge after talking to Steven.

Taking a deep breath, he hit the button. Sirens from all around flooded back into Caden's ears as time started. Lights flashed all around the scene and fires blazed.

"Now," Caden snapped, "tell me what you're talking about." He pointed the gun at Robert's temple.

"Do you really think I'm that stupid?" Robert asked. "Matt calls me from some building and tells me you not only sprung him, but you want me to meet you at some location a couple of blocks from here. And the moment I arrive at the place this happens. When I get back James and you are still standing around. Obviously, you blew it up and you wanted to keep me alive for some odd reason. And by the look of things, you've learned how to use that Dead Time pretty well. So, I'm guessing you're team is the one that sabotaged all the equipment."

Robert relaxed against the car and then looked at Caden with his jaw tightened. "Come to think of it, you were always there when things were going bad. I trusted you and told security not to worry. Now look at you. Why did you do this?"

Caden stood speechless. He couldn't understand why Matt told Robert to leave or even the bigger question how Matt escaped. There was no way Matt could have been apart of this, or could've he? Sally had told him that Matt was the one getting into Robert's files, but he needed to keep that information to himself for now, until he got the chance to talk to Matt himself. If he admitted his own suspicions about Matt, Robert might conclude he was guilty as well.

Looking Robert up and down, Caden remembered that Matt had told him not to trust Robert. He was getting to a point where he didn't trust anyone.

"I wasn't behind this," Caden explained, lowering the gun a little. "And nor was my team. James and I arrived after getting attacked on a plane and had barely survived that."

"Then why did it show on our system that you had entered the building?"

"Like I said, we were attacked on a plane. It was the same guys that attacked the scientist in the stairwell. They took my I.D. and pass card to get into the office. And my only guess in having you alive would be to frame our team so they could get away without being hunted down."

"You expect me to believe that," Robert argued. "Someone was able to just steal your I.D. and pass card. You of all people! They just attacked you and stole it? I find that hard to believe."

"They were able to because they stopped time," Caden responded with a heightened tone. He was frustrated with the fact he had to be arguing with Robert about this, they should be working together to save those in the rubble, not fighting.

"They stopped time," Robert said mockingly. "Your story, once again, seems flawed to me."

"Robert," Caden began, "you have to believe me. I'll give you all the details later. Right now we need to help save anyone that's still trapped out there." Caden paused for a moment remembering his encounter with Steven, which reminded him how Matt had said that Robert was betraying them. "By the way, I saw Steven out there, and I want to know what other tests you guys did to him?"

Robert's face changed from angry to surprised. "You saw Steven? Where? Where was he? If you saw him, why aren't you with him, or getting him out of here since you're obviously with him?"

"With him? I might've gone out to help him, but as far as I'm concerned, he's lost his mind and I'm not going with him anywhere."

Robert sighed and looked relieved. "So, where was he?"

"He was out in the middle of the rubble," Caden said, pointing in the direction where he had seen him. "He survived the blast, but he was really beat up. The strangest part was that he grew back a hand and healed the rest of his wounds within seconds. So once again, what tests did you do on him?"

"We didn't do anything to him," Robert said, sounding very sincere, "we only sent him into Dead Time just like we did with you guys. Can you tell me what direction he went in?"

Caden bit his lip. "I'm not fully sure-"

"Caden," Robert pleaded, "I need to know where he went. I'm worried he might hurt people if I don't catch him. So, can you please untie me and let me go find him?" Robert held out his tied hands.

"How do I know I can trust you?"

"The same way I'm going to have to trust you," Robert said.

Caden knew he was right, they had to trust each other, and if Robert were willing to trust him then he would do the same. Besides, Robert had never led him astray before. Matt was the one Caden felt needed to be questioned.

Signaling for Robert to turn around with his finger, Caden scanned the area to make sure he knew all of his options in case Robert decided to attack. He pulled the string apart and dropped it to the ground.

"Thanks," Robert said as he rubbed his wrists. "Now, which way did Steven go?"

Seeing that Robert wasn't going to fight, Caden felt reassured. It appeared Robert just wanted to keep Steven from hurting others from his insanity, like he said.

"That way," Caden pointed. "To your knowledge, who was in the building when it exploded?"

"Everyone."

Caden could feel his heart drop as a pressure began to build in his chest. "What do you mean everyone?"

"I mean everyone but us three," Robert sounded depressed. "I had all the teams fly into get Dead Time chips while yours and Burton's teams were away. Burton's Team had already arrived, and I thought you were there, but obviously you weren't. Either way, because of your little incident with the plane, you and James were the only two that I know survived."

Caden didn't know what to say. He just couldn't believe that everyone was in the building when the bomb went off.

"I'm sorry Caden, but believe me, I know how hard it is."

"I'm sure you feel worse then I do," Caden said rather flatly, pushing his emotion away. "It makes sense why you were so abrasive when you found us."

The amount of guilt that Robert had to feel, and anger, loosing all of his men, his entire agency-destroyed in one blast had to be tearing him apart. Caden knew once things were cleared up, the three of them were going to go hunting for those who had done this. For now, Caden needed to make sure James was okay and get some answers from Matt.

"Tell James I'm sorry."

"Yes, sir. Don't worry Robert, we'll find who did this."

Robert gave a halfhearted smile and ran off into the debris.

Walking over to James, Caden was trying to push away the pain he felt inside. With little effort, Caden picked up James and leaned him against the car.

"Wh…what happened?" James asked.

"Robert thought we blew up the building and so he attacked you."

James rubbed his eyes. "Okay."

"He attacked me too, almost shot me in the back." Caden could feel the sticky blood pooled in the shirt he had wrapped around him.

"Ouch." James stood up.

"Listen, you can do what you want, but I have a gut feeling there are some bad things that are coming our way. If you want my advice, I suggest you get back to your wife and disappear. I have one thing to take care of, and I'll be following right behind you."

Some rubble crashed from the building and Caden stood to look at the mess. The whole situation was overwhelming. The entire agency, blown up in an explosion. Steven miraculously healed himself, and Robert attacked him. Caden took a deep breath, but found it hard to breath from a hot blast of smoke that drifted in his direction.

"Are you serious?"

"I don't know what all is going on James, but I fear our lives are going to be on the line next." Caden didn't even look up. He kept staring into the rubble.

"If you really believe so, I'll trust you on this. You've never led me a stray."

Looking up at James's trusting expression, with his eyes a little wider, Caden knew they both needed to go. "Get out of here. We'll meet up later when it is safer and we actually know what is going on."

With a nod, James acknowledged the order.

"Oh and James," Caden added. "Call Sally, tell her to disappear."

Once again James gave another affirmative shake of his head and took off down the street.

Caden figured he was trying to get far enough out where he could get a taxi and head to the airport, which he would be doing soon himself. Matt was on his priority list first.

CHAPTER 24

A light breeze blew against Azgiel as he stood on the small wooden balcony of Maselda's home. He was amazed by what they had built. An entire village made in towering trees. Hand crafted wooden bridges connected the trees. Balconies extruded at each dwelling with the same careful craftsmanship as the bridges. Ornately carved designs were in all the work, with ancient symbols that gave the dwellings power and protection.

It was nothing like his old kingdom and castle, but after all of his time being locked away, his tastes had changed. There was a peace that seemed to flow through him just being there. The world he had known before he had been sent away was full of war, pain, hate, anger, and revenge.

"Do you like what we've done?" Maselda asked from behind.

"I do." He turned to face her. She seemed to glow in the shadows of her home. "Does everyone have a place to live up here?"

"No, the Anubite's have developed an interesting tunnel system in the ground." She pointed over at one of the Jackal-headed creatures, the Anubites, who was walking down a worn path.

"The trolls live in small homes down by a lake not far from here, and the bark gnomes have developed small huts that burrow partially into the ground and snug up against the trees. You can even see one just down there." She pointed to an interesting bump that circled at the base of one the giant trees. A bark gnome was working on something just outside of it. His strange armor, that they always wore, shimmered in the sunlight.

"And the rest are up in the trees?"

"That's correct." She stepped closer to him, her bare feet moving softly along the smooth wooden floor. With a gentle touch, she placed a hand on Azgiel's shoulder, followed by her head. "A lot of things have changed while you were gone. After Triaad almost completely wiped us out, we isolated ourselves here." They both kept looking at the bark gnome. He began using a small broom to sweep the front area of his porch. It was a strange sight to Azgiel. The small human-like figure, fully covered in metal armor, sweeping a porch.

"A lot of time has gone by since the wars," she continued. "Outside of the demons and I, the rest of them don't really know what it was like. They follow the traditions of their great, great ancestors, but I'm afraid they will need work done to be ready for a war. They aren't immortal like the demons and us. They weren't there to see what happened. And you, you're only a person in a story to them. "

"Speaking of demons. Has Kaz returned or sent word?"

He was getting sucked into the calmness of the world around him and was forgetting of the war that was brewing. It was vital to stay on task. They were able to get the sword, now it was Kaz's turn to do his part, and if he needed help, Azgiel needed to get out there.

"No. No word yet, but he will, I'm sure of it." She spoke softly.

Comfort came from her words along with her soft touch. Azgiel appreciated the small things more then he had before. A simple thing as a touch from his wife was a blessing. Again he was becoming distracted.

"I'm going to go back there and help him. We can't take too long on this or we could lose our window to get Mauldrin. The sword is the answer to defeating Triaad, and only Mauldrin can break the curse on it."

"I know." She stopped resting on him. "Do you want any backup to go with you, especially since you weren't ever able to see what's all going on with Mauldrin and don't know what exactly you're getting into?" Her light eyebrows furrowed in, with a worried look.

"No, I'll be fine. It will be easier by myself." Sensing her worry, he reached down and took her soft hand.

"Do you remember how to get there?" Her dark eyes appeared to look into his soul.

"Yes."

"And-"

"I'll be fine. Most of my power has come back." A smile stretched across his face.

"I just got you back. I don't want to lose you for another two thousand years or even longer." She tightened her grip on his hand.

"No need to worry. I'll be back before you know it." Azgiel was surprised by her response. It was the first moment she had shown any strong emotion about his absence. He raised his hands to begin the process of transporting. Soft lips pressed against his as his wife quickly put something in his pocket.

"A charm for good luck." She stepped back as a ball of energy zapped around him.

Her glowing skin and dark eyes imprinted in his mind after he zapped into the same cold building he had left only a couple of days ago. Walls were still smashed in the prison area and everything seemed quiet.

"Don't move or I'll shoot," a short, pudgy security guard barked. Azgiel raised an eyebrow while he looked the man up and down. The guard pointed a small black gun at Azgiel.

"Steven?" the man mumbled and tilted his head.

There wasn't time for this. Azgiel lifted a hand and the guard was flung against the wall, and instantly died from the severe impact. Kaz needed to be found and soon. Hopefully he was with Mauldrin, but if he wasn't, Kaz was his top priority. Mauldrin second. If Domblin or the others had done something to him, they would all pay dearly.

Not wasting time, Azgiel left the area, and went into the hallway. A voice echoed down the corridor from the stairway. Azgiel could barely make it out.

"I'm not sure why he's not responding, but I'm almost there to find out." No one replied to the voice that Azgiel could make out, but the man kept talking. "Yes, sir. Even if he's not there I'll check to see if Matt's in his cell." The words grew louder and Azgiel could make out the hard-soled shoes tapping down the steps.

"If he's really out there…" The guard came around the corner and stopped as his eyes made contact with Azgiel. "Steven's here. Steven's back, sir." The man tried to draw his gun at the same time he spoke into his radio on his shoulder.

Azgiel let out a sigh. He really didn't want to spend his time fighting bloody humans. There had to be another way. The guard looked more important then the last one by the amount of metal pins on his chest. He could possibly use the man to help him. Raising his hand, Azgiel was just about to silence him but a loud explosion rang out and the building shook. Both of them braced themselves. Another explosion followed, even louder.

Azgiel raised his hands to put a field around him. Blue light encircled him, just as a third explosion, far louder then the first two, went off. The walls around him blew to pieces and a wall of fire followed, swallowing everything in its path including the guard.

The force was even too much for Azgiel in his weakened state. Between the fire and explosion, the blue sphere that protected him tore into shreds, and Azgiel was thrown backwards. Blackness followed.

When he woke, he could feel pain throughout his body. He wasn't sure if seconds or hours had gone by. Large chunks of concrete and other debris were all around him, chunks of it pinned him to the ground. Some of the concrete shifted, making a strange groaning noise as a large piece fell on his left hand ripping his fingers off.

Azgiel yelled out in pain. He pulled his hand out. All that was left was his thumb. Closing his eyes he tried to command the debris to take him up, but it didn't work, he was too weak.

"Get me out of here." He demanded. It was pathetic that he had to use words since it was a weaker form of control over everything around him.

Concrete and steal shifted around him. Grinding and a couple of loud crashes sounded through the rubble. Sunlight broke through, and he knew a hole had been made. Beneath him, concrete came together to make a table like structure and pushed him up through the hole that had been made.

Pain shot through his abdomen, something was sticking through him. Once he came to a stop, he stood and looked down. An iron rod had pierced through his body. His leg was giving out, being broken in half and he knelt back down.

"Hello!" Someone called from behind him. He slowly turned to see Mauldrin heading his way. *Stupid human! Doesn't he realize what danger he's in? I can't have him die, not now.*

"Don't come any closer." Azgiel struggled to speak or move. "That's far enough. You shouldn't be out here."

"I'm here to help," Mauldrin still walked in his direction. If he had enough power, he would just zap him out of there, but that wasn't going to happen.

"No," he demanded, "you might get hurt."

"Everything's going to be okay," Mauldrin took another step closer. Azgiel could sense the structure getting worse and more unsafe, he couldn't wait any longer, they both needed to get out of there.

"Fine, have it your way," Azgiel snapped. "I didn't want you to see this, but I can't stay here much longer and neither should you." Closing his eyes and focusing, Azgiel began the process to heal himself, using what energy he had left. An itching sensation ran up his arm and leg. Feeling came back to his fingers that grew back. A crack rang out as his leg mended and the bone reformed.

It was time to get the bar out of him. He stood and gripped the bar, still warm from the heated explosion. Moving quickly he pulled the bar out with a slush noise and tossed it to the ground with a clank. Itching began in his side as he could feel the wound heal.

"It's time for you to get out of here." Azgiel made his way to Mauldrin.

"How did you do that?" Mauldrin stumbled on his words. "Did Robert and Allen do this to you? Did they perform some other type of experiment that he didn't tell me about?"

He ignored him. "It's unsafe for you out here. You need to go back." Azgiel watched as Mauldrin looked in shock. His eyes were huge and his mouth was slightly open as he stepped backwards, away from him. The flooring gave out from under Caden, and he began to fall back into the lower levels of the building. Using as much energy as possible, Azgiel moved at a superhuman speed, and caught him.

It was rather strange for Azgiel to be saving such a pathetic, backstabbing being such as him, but he had to. The man contained the power to get his sword back, even if he didn't remember anything of the past.

"Leave." Azgiel pointed. Not wanting there to be any further discussion, he turned and walked away. A large wall of flames was in the direction he wanted to go. "Part." He spoke under his breath, and it split as he walked through. Not wanting him to follow he needed to add something. "I'll find you later. Right now I have to find someone." He yelled just as he passed through the flames.

I need a place to mend and strengthen myself, if I don't Domblin or any of the others will be able to kill me with ease. After that, it's back to the hunt for Kaz.

A building stood in front of him with a large part of it blown away. He could make out the first couple of levels being a parking garage. *That will do for a little while. But you can't lay low too long Az. I didn't see Kaz around Mauldrin so that must mean something has happened. I also can't go up against any of those guys until I get my strength up.*

Small chunks of concrete grinded under his feet as he came to an immediate stop. *Azgiel you're arguing with yourself, get a grip. Let's just get to one of those cars and get a nap.*

Making short work of the distance, he climbed into the back of a large van and closed his eyes. Exhausted, he was out in seconds.

A loud voice, yelling, woke him up. Once again, he wasn't sure how much time had past while he was out. The sun had moved much further a long in the sky, so it had been at least a couple of hours.

"Are you guys, okay?" A familiar voice called out from down below. It was the same voice that woke him, but he wasn't too sure where he recognized it. Stepping out the open door to the van causing it to squeak, he looked down below. *Ah yes, Robert.*

Robert had yelled down through a crack in the debris. Other stragglers were around him, obviously people he had saved. *What a hero.* Azgiel grimaced.

"I'm going to get you guys some help," Robert said as he stood up and looked around. He stopped and headed down a street. Azgiel looked to where he was going and saw some fire trucks.

Robert ran up to two firemen and pointed back to where he found the trapped people. The smaller of the two nodded and Robert started to return but stopped in his tracks. His eyes glared at Steven.

Now I've been spotted, time to go. Azgiel stood there for a moment watching Robert run to the building he was in.

There was something about the man that intrigued him, something that he had noticed the couple of times he had talked to him, but had shrugged off. Even the first time when he had just come out of his cell of time, Robert had caught his attention. Knowing it might be the last time he saw him, he decided to wait for him. *Maybe he has some answers for me, and now that he isn't surrounded by others maybe he'll talk.*

Once he heard the tapping of footsteps coming up the stairs, he moved into the shadows behind a pillar. Running too fast, Robert got to the floor and tried to stop only to slide on soot and slam against a car. He pushed himself up. Azgiel could see a dent left in the small white vehicle.

Moving slower and more methodical, Robert began looking around. He walked over to the ledge and looked over it. "Where did you go, Steven?" Robert called out.

"I'm not going to make it easy for you," Azgiel said. "I don't believe I'll be showing myself to you at this moment." Robert searched, even looking in his direction, but Azgiel had made the shadows darker to conceal himself.

"Steven," Robert spoke loudly, "I'm not going to hurt you. I just want to help you." Loose debris fell on a car and Robert headed in that direction. "Listen Steven, how about you just come out and we can talk?"

"Your lies are very obvious," Azgiel said calmly. His voice reverberated all about the parking area. "It's just like a child covered in mud pleading that he never stepped in the mud puddle."

"Steven," Robert began, "you've known me forever. You were one of my top advisors. I just want to help you."

"Stop your begging." He could feel a sense of power coming from Robert, and it was sad to see him so pathetic. "You have no idea who I am. You don't even know my real name."

"What are you talking about?" Robert asked turning in place. "We've known each other for a long time."

"Shush you fool. You have no clue who I am, which was an odd surprise when you brought me out of my cell."

"Steven, what have you done? If you're trying to reveal everything that's been going on with this stupid mission of Jason's and your's, I'll take you down with me. Besides, it was your deal in the first place. I had no idea what you guys were really doing."

"Now it makes sense. You're blinded by your corrupt ways and lies. You don't even know who I am. Did you develop the equipment to let me out of stopped time?"

"If you're referring to the Dead Time equipment then no. It was Caden, don't you remember?" Robert responded. "And I'm not blinded by anything. I'm just here to make sure you're going to keep your mouth shut."

"Is Caden by chance the one that came and saw me in my holding chamber before I so brilliantly escaped?"

"That would be the one."

"So he has a new name," Azgiel spoke to himself. "It will make it much easier to talk to him now, knowing his name."

"Come out and let's talk like men," Robert shouted. "I need to know that you're sane enough to keep your mouth shut. Tell me I'm blind-"

"Yes, you are blind," Azgiel added, beginning to enjoy the stupidity. "I can sense the greatness that you once held. But your corrupt ways and lies have diminished it, that's why you have become blind. Blind to what you could've been. The power you could've held." The power reminded him of Mauldrin and who Mauldrin used to be. All humans were born with a certain amount of power, some used it and some didn't.

"What are you talking about?"

"Obviously things that are over your head. Just like who I really am, or who Mauldrin is."

"Ok, then tell me, who are you really?" Robert's voice was sarcastic.

Azgiel jumped on the roof of the car that Robert was leaning on. Robert moved back and positioned himself ready to fight. "Now that is the question."

"I would like to know who it is you think you are."

"Since it will be fun to tell you, my actual name is Azgiel," he smiled as he answered. "I was imprisoned in a cell of time."

Robert let out a chuckle. "A cell of time, huh? And how in the world do you get imprisoned in a cell of time?"

"For doing lots of things that people like Caden, and others felt were wrong and evil."

"This is getting better by the moment," Robert said having a hard time choking back the laughs. "So, now you're blaming it on Caden for putting you in a cell of time. Are you sure you aren't referring to the holding cell you were in at the headquarters before it blew up?"

"It was actually Caden that put me there." Azgiel debated how far he wanted to take the conversation. He needed to get back to searching for Kaz, but something intrigued him about Robert, possibly the fact he reminded him of Mauldrin, so he continued. "Caden took a very powerful sword of mine and put a curse on it that if any evil thing touches it, they die instantly. He holds the only power to release the curse. After he took the weapon, I was powerless to fight against him. It was shortly after that he imprisoned me, but not before I killed a couple of the five that were left. And no, I'm not as foolish as you. I know the difference between a concrete cell and a cell in time where I have the entire planet to roam."

"Why would someone use stopped time for a prison cell?" Robert began circling Azgiel.

With a smile, Azgiel let him, looking forward to the fight. "Those who get locked away can only get out through stealing a body because it's their souls that are imprisoned, so you're pretty much stuck there," Azgiel started. "And, if your soul is locked away in a cell of time, you have no power over anything. Trust me; it's bad being locked away."

"So," Robert began, "you're telling me that you're some evil soul that was locked away in a cell of time by Caden when he was in his previous life, and we just happened chance to release you by sending Steven into your specific cell?"

"I think you're catching on." Azgiel slid one foot back getting ready for the fight. "Maybe you're not as stupid and clueless as I thought you were. I can reverse whatever Domblin has done to you and Mauldrin and bring your memory back. You might actually serve a use. Would you like to join me on my mission?" He still wasn't sure what was going on with Mauldrin and could only assume Domblin had done it.

Robert smiled. "And what mission would that be?"

"To kill the man that gives you directions. A man by the name of Triaad." Azgiel exclaimed, "My mission stretches over galaxies."

"That's enough Steven," Robert said, his smile fading. "You've clearly lost your mind, and I can't trust you to keep information secret. The Dead Time just messed up information in your head and I think it's time for you to come with me."

"You don't understand," Azgiel said tilting his head a little. "I'm not going with you, but I'll give you the option of coming with me and joining my ranks. It would be nice to have other humans by my side once again...I miss those times." Without another word Robert dove toward Azgiel, reaching for his arm to pin him against a car.

Azgiel moved at inhuman speed and grabbed Robert by the hair and slammed his face into the windshield. Glass shattered inward.

"I'll give you another chance," Azgiel said, backing up from Robert, "because I think you would be a very powerful addition to our ranks, in the right hands. Will you join us?"

Robert was getting in a better stance to strike. Blood trickled down his face in a couple places from the glass. "I'm not going to join in your crazy delusions." The rubber on Robert's shoes squeaked as he attacked Azgiel more forcefully.

Azgiel, with little effort, gripped Robert's oncoming fist and pulled him forward, slamming Robert's face into his knee. Blood dripped from Robert's mouth and nose as he broke the hold and threw an elbow at Azgiel's jaw. Backing up, Azgiel dodged the blow and Robert lost his balance and missed. Quickly moving Azgiel kicked him, knocking him to the ground.

"I can offer you more power than you could ever imagine." Azgiel said while taking a couple steps back. "And wealth like you've never seen before."

"You're just delusional." Robert wiped the blood from his mouth. "You're not some creature from Dead Time. Caden didn't put you there. And if you're not going to come easily, then I'm going to have to dispose of you." He spat blood on the ground. "I can't have you telling people information during your crazy spells. You know too much."

Shifting his weight for a more powerful kick, Robert lunged forward smashing his foot into Azgiel. The kick knocked him back a couple of steps.

"That will be your one and only." Azgiel smiled, he was impressed. Robert quickly moved to attack again, throwing a fist, only to have it knocked down. With little effort, Azgiel blocked the next set of blows that came at him and finally took hold of Robert's fist, spun him, and slammed him against the floor. Knowing the cold concrete couldn't be too comfortable, Azgiel decided to help the situation and put his knee on Robert's head. Dust from the floor choked Robert's lungs as he tried to breathe, making him wheeze.

"Listen to me, Robert. I could easily kill you if I wanted, however, I'm going to make my offer again and then I'm going to give you some time to think about it. But first let me show you an image."

Azgiel lifted a hand and black claws grew on his fingers. He reached down and clawed into Robert's muscular neck. Energy rushed through him into Robert.

Wanting him to get a taste of what he was talking about, Azgiel shared memories. The images flowed through his mind and into Robert. He showed him the wars between him, Mauldrin and the others. Even more importantly, he graphically showed what happened at the end, when his sword was taken and he was put in a cell of time.

Finally, pulling his claws out and retracting them, he got off Robert.

"I hope that helps you with a decision." Azgiel chuckled.

"I'm not sure what I just saw. Everything seems so confusing," Robert replied. He tried to move, but fell back to the ground. Azgiel knew it was foolish for him to try to get up after his brain had just gone through so much.

"As I said before, my offer still stands if you ever want to join me. I would honor your power and give you the glory you deserve, unlike the society that you live in, which will punish you for your crimes."

Caught off guard, Robert kicked Azgiel's legs knocking him to the ground. An elbow slammed down on his nose and blood splattered across his lower face.

That's it. It was time for Robert to share the same fate Mauldrin is going to face after he rids the sword of the curse.

Azgiel hopped to his feet. Robert's large fist flew at him, which he barely dodged. Moving quicker then Robert was able to, Azgiel grabbed the arm and pulled him in. Another elbow hit Azgiel in the side, something snapped inside. Azgiel was shocked that Robert could get back to moving so quickly after what he had just gone through.

A powerful amount of electricity flowed out of Azgiel and into Robert, sending him convulsing for a moment and then nothing. The limp body fell to the ground as Azgiel let go.

"One less future Mauldrin to deal with." His skin was black from where the electrical current had come through. Looking up he saw the firemen getting the people out of the rubble.

Time to find you Kaz. I've wasted enough time here. Running, he took a leap off the ledge and jumped a far distance, defying gravity. He landed on a wall that had been knocked down that was close to ground zero. Looking around, he debated which direction to go. There were no visible tracks that he could sense. He frowned. *So, I guess I'll follow Mauldrin's tracks for now.*

CHAPTER 25

After James left, Caden pulled his phone out and hit redial, hoping Matt would answer.

"Caden. I'm glad you decided to call me back." Static made Matt's voice hard to hear.

"Are you still in the same location?" Caden asked looking down the street.

"No, I've moved. It's too dangerous to stay around there, for both of us." More emergency teams could be heard coming down the streets as they talked, quickly making their way to the scene.

"I already told James to get out of here for that same reason. But I'm still here. Where are you?" Police cars led the way for the fire trucks and other emergency personnel. Two police cars pulled up right next to Caden. The sirens made it hard to talk.

"If I were you, I would just get out of there for now. We can meet up later." Matt sounded urgent. The policemen got out of their cars and one of them said something while pointing at Caden.

Caden turned and ignored them for the moment. "How about you tell me what's going on. No more games Matt, we've known one another for far too long to keep any more secrets."

"Put your hands where I can see them." One of the police officers yelled. More cars were pulling up, cutting their sirens. Confused, Caden slowly turned around, putting his hands in the air, the phone still in hand. He could hear Matt trying to say something, but he couldn't make it out.

"What's your name?" Another officer asked while walking over to him with a piece of paper in his hands. Three other cops had their guns drawn, pointed at Caden.

"I think there's been a mistake here. I'm with you guys. I'm here to help." Caden responded very calmly. If they searched him they would find his gun, and that was the last thing he needed at the moment.

"It's him. Take him into custody," the officer holding the paper ordered. Caden finally saw what it was. It was a headshot of him with specific details of his name, age, weight, height, etc.

"Wait one second." Caden lowered his hands slightly, while a number of officers approached him.

"He's got a gun."

That was enough for Caden, he moved his arm to hit the Dead Time switch, but before he could an officer knocked him down from the back. The cell phone hit the ground in his fist while a handcuff slapped against his left wrist. He quickly put the phone in his pocket to get it out of the way.

Pulling inwards, Caden yanked the cop down that had cuffed him, hitting his face against the hard pavement. Another officer charged and Caden swiftly kicked him down using the ball of his foot. More officers charged, he wanted to hit the switch but the first officer hadn't let go of the handcuff.

A club swung at him. Dodging, he grabbed it and brought the cop in only to land a strong kick to his chest. From his right he heard a gun drawn. He spun, kicking a piece of rubble at him. Caden kicked the gun out of his hand. The officer holding the handcuffs pulled Caden backwards. The cop that had drawn the gun charged at him with a nightstick. Reaching out, he grabbed a road sign and using brute strength, slung the cop that was pulling him, into the one charging him. He could've killed them, but they were just trying to do their job. They weren't the bad guys.

Three more came at him with nightsticks. It was only a matter of time before there were enough to take him down. Using a tactical defense, he blocked the onslaught from the first man while hefting off to the side of him. The second was almost too easy, being uncoordinated, Caden spun him into the sign.

A clang rang out from the third officer barely missing him and hitting the sign. More officers had arrived and some of them had guns out waiting for a shot. Knowing it needed to end, Caden kicked the man's wrist after he had hit the metal sign. His wrist snapped and Caden took a hold of the cop's new weak spot. He pulled him in close and drove his fingers into his neck.

"Stay with me or I'll kill you." There wasn't a second to lose. The officer nodded his head in compliance. They scrambled to an alley, the cop being a human shield. Once he entered his rubble filled exit, Caden kicked the officer back out towards the street and ran for it. A large brick barrier stood in his way and he jumped up, snatching a metal later that hung down. From there he threw himself over to the top of the bricks, grabbing the top and pulling himself up. A slight prick hit him in the shoulder.

Not wasting time, he jumped and ran around the building. Everything began to grow foggy. He saw Matt approaching in a car and jumping out. Sounds began to get fuzzy as he reached back and pulled out a tranquilizing dart from his shoulder. He fell to the pavement, hitting his head. Everything went black.

"We're going to need to figure out which shelter the president's heading to." Caden could hear Matt's voice as he woke. Pain shot into his head where he had hit the pavement. Reaching back, he could feel the crusty dried blood in his hair.

"Good, you're alive."

Caden pushed up on the leather couch and turned to see where he was. Someone walked out of the room that Caden didn't recognize and Matt walked up to him. The room was barren outside of some furniture along the walls and a large chalkboard that had all kinds of information posted on it.

"Where am I? How did I get here?" Caden spoke softly.

"I overheard what was going on over the phone. I brought you back to a secret office that I developed." His tone gave Caden the impression that Matt was proud of his office.

Noticing some pain in his left wrist, Caden looked down and noticed the handcuffs were gone, but he had some nice bruising left in its place.

"I'm not sure if secret is a good word to use." Caden felt awkward, realizing for the first time, the man he had known for so long was a complete stranger. He wasn't sure if he could even trust him.

"Fair enough," Matt said as he sat down in a chair about four feet away. "Are you okay? You look pretty beat up."

"I'm fine." Caden lightly rubbed his head as the pain increased. He debated which would be the best way to address Matt's strange behaviors and the situation.

"I'm glad to hear," Matt said leaning back in his chair. "I was worried the explosion might've gotten you."

"How did you get out of your cell?" Caden figured it was time to stop beating around the bush. It was time for some answers. He tensed.

"Some of the men that now work for me busted me out," Matt answered reluctantly.

"Your men?" Everything was getting worse. Caden felt like he was in some kind of nightmare. Matt had been building some kind of team behind his back.

"Oh, don't seem so surprised, you were catching on by the end... weren't you?"

"I knew you had back channel methods to get information that I didn't like to know about, but no, I had no idea you were developing some type of group. And what is it that you and your team do?"

"Simple. I created this." Matt held his hands in the air as he spoke. "All of it was for the sole purpose to take down SDS and overthrow the government?"

"Why?" Shocked, Caden struggled to find the right words. His chest felt like something had taken his breath away. He had figured Matt was up to no good, but nothing like this. "Why would you do such a thing? Are you behind the bomb?"

"So many questions." Letting out a sigh, Matt shifted his weight in the chair. "Yes, I blew the building up. And why?...Well, to make a long story short, I tripped over some information one day about what Robert was involved in. He's been taking orders from the government, and their plan is an ugly one."

"How in the world could you blow up the building?" Caden knew attacking now would be a poor choice at the moment. He had to wait for a better advantage. "Are you sure you didn't just get some bad intel? I mean, this is Robert you're talking about." He stood up while he spoke, unable to keep himself on the couch.

"One of your weaknesses is having too much trust in friends," Matt said. "You never learned how to keep an eye on those close to you. And in this business, you shouldn't trust anyone."

Caden disagreed, he normally was observant. The memory of Matt being in his office passed through his mind, and the different things that Robert was doing lately entered in as well. So he had been ignoring some things, but it had a lot to do with everything on his plate like Bridget and the hallucinations. *Matt's wrong.*

Caden's heart pounded. *How could Matt be behind this? He had always stood by my side even in tough times, standing for good not evil.* Anger raged inside Caden, but he subdued it again, knowing once again he had to keep thinking rationally. His eyes searched the room, spotting a letter opener sitting next to a large lamp on the end table.

Matt pulled out his gun. "Don't get any stupid ideas. I didn't bring you here to fight. I brought you here to offer you a proposition."

Caden looked at the gun. "I can't believe you're the spy. I trusted you whole-heartedly. How can you betray everyone like this, especially me, your friend? I mean, were you the one that sent the men to kill us on the plane?"

"I'm not betraying anyone. It's Robert who's betrayed all of us. And about the whole plane thing, well Justin got a little carried away. He was only supposed to get your information and divert the plane, not crash it."

"This Justin I take it, is bald and one of your men?" Caden calculated his ability to get the gun out of Matt's hands. The odds were not good.

"That's the one."

"The same one that tried to shoot me at the office?"

"Yes, but I stopped the bullet before it got to you. So, no harm, no foul. He's just a little too gung-ho. I'm working on that, I've told him he's not to hurt you or James." Matt had a smile on his face, as if he were proud of his man.

Caden moved on to the bigger questions. "So what was this terrible thing that Robert and the government were doing, that made you willing to kill everyone in SDS?"

"That was an accident. I had no idea that Robert was going to call everyone in, but in the end it saved us some time, since ninety percent of the agents were part of the plot."

Matt's smile disappeared. "It had to be done either way." He stood up and lowered the gun to his side. "Like I said, Robert can't be trusted. That's why I ended his reign and there'll be others that are going to fall with him. I'm sure you can't even begin to comprehend all that has been going on behind the scenes. Robert sold his soul for money and power, he has become intertwined with political corruptness, and it has come time to show the world what's really going on. This goes beyond Robert. It goes to the very top, to the President." Caden shook his head in disbelief as Matt spoke. "I know it's hard to believe, but in time the truth will be revealed."

Matt scratched his arm and looked at the floor. Caden could tell that whatever information he was about to give bothered him, if it were even true. "Robert was part of a secret plan to create a perfect society, or at least that's what they called it. The plan was to slowly kill off people they deemed not good enough. You can imagine what that list looked like. Criminals, mentally ill, political opponents and the list just goes on from there. They're using all types of methods to slowly kill them, from tampering with water systems in towns where a high percentage of the population are targets, to using isolated assassinations."

"You're right," Caden said folding his hands together. "That is rather unbelievable, even if there was something like that going on, which I doubt there is, Robert would be completely against it."

"Believe who you want." Matt sounded irritated. "But as soon as the records are uncovered from the office, we plan to lead a revolt to get rid of the government and start a new one. And then Robert will pay for the terrible things he's done. That's why I kept him alive; to make sure he faces what he's done. I didn't want him to get off easily with being killed in the blast."

"You're going to build a new government? I can't believe what I'm hearing…I just don't know what to say. I mean, wow, so you're basically setting up to take over this country." Caden knew he might be having hallucinations, but at least he hadn't totally lost his mind like Matt had.

"No." Matt tightened his jaw and slightly narrowed his eyes. "I'm not doing this for power. We'll hold a vote and make sure honest people that want to take care of this country are voted in."

"So, you're going to wipe out an existing government so you can rig the election for a new one?" Caden asked. He rubbed his left temple. "Why in the world didn't you just bring this information to the proper authorities? That could've put an end to the whole thing and then allow the democratic process work without you tainting it."

"You don't get it." Matt raised his voice. "There isn't a single person in government right now who isn't in on this, at least not any longer. They just killed the last one not too long ago. Also, most of those so-called proper authorities are also involved. This thing is huge. You've just never wanted to see it. And the only way to get rid of all the corruptness is to wipe it out. And the only reason why I'm planning on helping the voting process is to make sure someone trustworthy gets into the seat."

"Even if you're telling the truth," Caden said after taking a deep breath, "your plan is idiotic. Manipulating the people to vote for someone, takes away the freedom of the people in this country. That's the beauty of democracy—people can choose who they want without someone else mandating them to pick who they feel is best for whatever reason." Caden took another deep breath and let it out. "I'm in shock right now."

"The system is already corrupt; I'm trying to help fix it. Our democracy doesn't work anymore. You're wrong and you'll find out soon how wrong you are." Matt sounded deflated and agitated. He kept using his free hand to point at Caden while talking. "I came here to offer you a position on my team. This world is going to praise us for doing all of this and I want you here with me."

"I...I must not be awake. Maybe I never woke after I passed out from going into Dead Time and I'm just dreaming all of this because nothing has made sense since I came out of that place."

"No Caden," Matt said gruffly, "this isn't a dream. I've been planning this for a very long time. For the last year I went to your office late at night to steal information. That's how I always knew about things that were coming up, and Robert made the mistake to put that much trust in everyone not to get into his files. But I hacked into them. So, when we heard about the Dead Time suits, I knew that would make our whole mission too easy and it was time to act."

Matt smiled as he continued. "I'll have to admit, I thought you finally caught me when you walked in on me at your office a couple of days ago. But once again, your trust blinded you. And all of those supposed phone calls I was having with girls... those were people on my team. However, I have to give a ton of credit to Justin. If it wasn't for him, I don't think we would exist. He's been my right hand man."

"Robert sold his soul for money and power," Matt spoke harshly as he continued, "he's become intertwined with political corruptness, and it has come time to show the world what's really going on." Caden shook his head in disbelief. "I know it's hard to believe, but in time the truth will be revealed. We planted the explosives so that when the lower part of the building is dug up, they'll find proof in the records."

Caden hit the Dead Time switch and everything went silent. He lowered his head into his hands and let out a deep breath. Confusion swarmed through his tired, drugged filled mind.

"I'm not sure what the point of that was."

"How the..." Caden started while quickly looking up.

Matt pointed to his neck. "You forget that I'm plugged in as well. If you go into Dead Time, I go with you. And I'm sure James is trying to figure out why he's in Dead Time right now, just like I was when you guys used it on the plane."

Swiftly Caden grabbed the letter opener next to him and threw it at Matt causing him to flinch. The letter opener stopped in mid air, but Caden dove at Matt knocking him to the ground while he was distracted. Caden's speed was slower in Dead Time, but he was still more skilled then Matt at combat. Within seconds he had Matt pinned to the ground in a hold that could kill him. Matt didn't move a muscle; Caden could tell he knew the position he was in.

"I take it that you won't join me," Matt said with his face smashed against the floor.

"You can take it that way. Why didn't you come to me about this when you found out about the supposed conspiracy?" Caden snapped.

If Caden was a crying man, he knew he would've let the tears start rolling down his cheeks. He felt so betrayed and hurt. Now he was standing over one of the few men he had trusted with his life, not knowing if he was going to kill him or not.

"You would've never listened, just like you're not listening now," Matt said then coughed. "Listen, I'm really not here to fight. I just wanted to offer you a spot on my team because I fear for your safety." Caden pushed his knee deeper into Matt's neck. As he eased up, Matt coughed again. "I'm worried for your safety as soon as all the information is released about what's really going on. This nation is going to revolt against everyone on those lists that are trying to develop a perfect society and our names are on the list. I can keep you safe if you join me, and I can clear your name so that people will think you're a hero."

"I don't want any part of this Matt," Caden responded loosening his grip a little more.

"Then I suggest it's time for you to disappear." His tone changed, and Caden could tell he was disappointed.

"And what if I just kill you now?" Caden asked pushing his knee harder into Matt's neck.

"That won't solve anything..." Matt coughed. "What's done is done and the truth will be out soon. Then you'll see that I'm not lying."

Caden got off Matt and stood. His muscles flexed from the adrenaline. Rubbing his neck, Matt stood as well. "If you were anyone else, I would kill you right now and not even bat an eye. But I'm going to give you a chance."

"And there's your wonderful second weakness that even Robert documented in some of his reports." Matt smiled and leaned against a table, which let out a creak.

At first Caden was going to ignore the comment, but it just rubbed him the wrong way so he decided to bite. "Which is?"

"You don't do what it takes to get the job done when you're afraid of someone close to you getting killed. I mean look at you. You think I'm wrong, and yet you won't do what it takes and kill me." Looking a little nervous on giving the information, Matt was rubbing his hand up and down his leg. "Didn't you ever wonder why Robert only sent you on very specific missions? He did send us on the one with the Burton team, but I mean look how that one ended. No offense, but you bailed on that mission. Robert even wrote it up in a report that I confiscated."

Truth or a lie, Caden knew Matt was right. He did give in too easy on that mission. It often ran through his mind that he had made a mistake, even though he kept that information to himself. After the horrible incident that happened when he was in the military where he led an army into battle and almost lost all of them, he had become gun shy of losing men ever again. From time to time he worried others noticed, but he did his best to keep it a secret.

Hearing the words Matt had to say angered him and hurt. Caden wasn't fully sure what Matt was trying to get at. *Is he trying to manipulate me into not liking Robert or is he trying to tear me down in the hope that I'll submit to him, or...*

Matt kept talking, never losing a beat. "The report I found, Robert had sent it to someone high up in the government to give a summary on why we weren't successful. The report he got back basically ordered him to get rid of you and your team. Funny part was he wrote that he was going to keep you because of your inventing capabilities, but you wouldn't be involved with anymore of their missions to push their plot. Personally I thought it was a positive thing. You were able to stay out of the corruption."

"Prove yourself. If you say you have all these reports that you've confiscated, show them to me. Surely you must still have them." Caden was tired of the games. He was getting to the point where he was ready to kill Matt, which made his stomach drop.

Swallowing, Matt shifted a little. "I don't have it here. It's all on my computer back at the office."

Caden clenched his fists. "That's what I thought."

"Caden, I give you my word. It's all there. At least give me the benefit of the doubt that it's there. My password to get into it is luckyseven, all spelled out with no spaces. Go to the search and find the folder called Over Reaching. The folder is password protected so you'll need to type in truthtolight, once again all one word." Matt stopped leaning on the table as he spoke and had a desperate look in his eyes.

"It's hard to trust you. Look around. This has all been one huge lie. A secret that you've kept from me." As Caden spoke Matt walked up closer to him and even put his hand on Caden's shoulder. Emotion ran through Caden and he let his fist fly, punching Matt squarely in the face, knocking him to the floor.

Getting back up, Matt rubbed the left side of his face where his skin was quickly turning red. "I deserved that." He twisted his head a little to pop his neck. "I'm not going to fight with you, if that's what you're looking for."

He wasn't looking for a fight either. The punch had come out of nowhere. Fueled by the tremendous amount of hurt and anger that was tying his stomach into knots. "I think it's time for me to leave before I sort through my confusion and decide to kill you," Caden said while tightening his jaw.

"Maybe this will allow you to trust me some," Matt began as he wiped the blood that ran down his lip. "I won't act until either the news has dug up the information about everything going on or until you call me that you have gotten into my computer and found everything that I was talking about."

Rolling the information over in his mind, Caden decided that it was fair enough for the time being. They were both in a stalemate and something had to give. "I'm going to leave here and get Bridget and her mother in a safe place first. After that I'll run by our office back home to look at your computer, but if you're lying, I'm coming back for you and all of your men. And my supposed second weakness won't stop me!" He tightened his fists.

"That works for me." Matt picked up his gun from the floor. Caden raised an eyebrow, but wasn't too worried since it was worthless in Dead Time. "When you find out that I'm not lying, my offer will still be on the table. You're my friend, Caden. I would never lie to you." Matt holstered his gun.

Seeing the gun put away helped relieve some of the stress. "I don't think I can ever support you," Caden took the letter opener out of the air and kept it in his hands, not knowing what he would run into while he tried to get out of the building. "Even if you're telling the truth. The way you went about this was wrong. There are a lot of innocent people that you've killed."

Matt didn't have a response, he stood next to the chair he had flipped over, dragging a finger across the back of it. Caden back stepped towards the door. The door was already cracked so Caden just had to push it open. After opening it he found a hallway with an exit sign that glowed at the end. All he would have to do is stay in Dead Time until he got out of the building to make sure know one would seize him.

Right before Caden left, Matt added, "By the way, congrats on your marriage. It's about time."

Unable to formulate any words, Caden left the room and closed the door behind him. More pain rushed into his heart as he walked away from Matt, knowing the next time he saw him he might be shooting at him.

Caden exited into the empty hallway and quickly ran to a stairway door and stopped. He was surprised to see that Matt wasn't following him or exiting the room. As he turned back, he noticed something move down an adjacent hallway. Turning to see what it was, he stopped. There were eight black creatures lining the floor, walls, and ceiling. One of them let out a scream and Caden hit the Dead Time switch. The void of sound was gone and the normal sounds returned. Nothing was there. All the creatures were gone, but his breathing was elevated.

The door handle was cold as Caden urgently grabbed it, wanting to get out of the eerie situation. Something seemed to call out to him from the hallway once again, sending shivers down his spine. At first he didn't want to look, but he needed to know.

Turning, Caden watched as the lights flickered off, but it was still empty. He was about to shake off the feeling when he saw something move out of the corner of his eye. A dark shape slithered across the ceiling slowly making its way towards Caden. At first Caden thought he was seeing things and closed his eyes for a second. *It can't be real. It's just a hallucination.*

When he reopened them, the creature began moving very rapidly. It was the same type of creature he had just seen in the hallway and in times past, but it was smaller this time-it was a different one then the one that had attacked him before. Caden threw the letter opener at it, but the creature easily dodged it, letting it fly past him and stab into the dry wall ceiling.

A guard of sorts with all black gear came out of a door just in front of the shadowy figure. "Halt," he yelled as he drew his gun. Before Caden could say a word, the creature dropped to the ground behind the man and jumped on his back. A dazed look came over the guard as his skin turned pale white. His veins protruded from his skin looking as if they were filled with black liquid. Void of any expression, the man dropped to the ground and the creature let out a scream.

Caden quickly opened the door to the stairway and slammed the door shut behind him. As he turned around Caden froze. In front of him stood the same large red creature he had seen in Bridget's room. His horns towered upward, and his black eyes were cold.

The demon pushed Caden to the side smashing him into the wall. Moving past him, the creature ripped open the door, and ran into the hallway. While the door slowly closed in front of Caden, he watched the red monster pin the shadowy personage against the wall.

Caden waited in silence, debating if he should run or see what happened. If he opened the door and the large red beast was still there, he might be able to get some answers, but death could be waiting for him as well.

Caden's hand shook as he reached for the doorknob but there was no turning back. He opened it but there was nothing there. No demon, no black creature, no guard. Now he understood why no one came running into the hall after the scream, it had to be another hallucination.

Across the hallway the door to the room Matt was in began to open. *Got to go.* Caden quickly made his way down the stairs and found an exit from the building at the bottom floor.

"Freeze." A guard all dressed in black gear called out as Caden exited the building into an alley. He was only a couple of feet away.

I don't have time for this. The man was obviously an amateur by the way he held the gun. Matt probably only put him out there to scare people away. *Another one of Matt's inept people.*

Caden dodged right while grabbing the man's wrist with his left hand. The gun shot off, barely missing Caden's stomach. Using his right fist, he smashed it into the man's elbow, dislocating the joint. Screaming in pain the man kicked him in the leg, while Caden seized the gun. With a quick spin Caden drove his elbow into his opponents face, knocking him to the ground.

"Get up and I'll kill you," Caden's voice was sharp as he pointed the gun at the man. The guard scooted on the ground backwards. His chin trembled as tears formed at his eyes.

Amateur. Caden decided to let the man live, just in case they turn out to be the good guys. "Turn over and put your face on the ground with your hands behind your head." The guard moved quickly. He let out a whimper as Caden gave him a kick to the rear.

"If I see you turn over, I'll kill you." Caden ran out of the alley and was surprised to find himself on the other side of town where the city was more run down. He needed to find a taxi and get back to the airport.

CHAPTER 26

Once Caden was a block away, he slowed down a little. If Matt wanted to follow him, there would already be men on top of him. Caden figured he had nothing to worry about, accept trying to get a taxi where taxis didn't normally go. The streets were lined with random piles of garbage and junk. Screaming and fighting could be heard down one of the streets from a domestic dispute.

An old, beat up car drove by with a couple of men dressed in black clothing. Caden didn't want trouble so he kept his eyes looking straight ahead. The last thing he needed right now were the cops called on him.

His phone vibrated in his pocket and he flipped it open. The casing was cracked. "Hello."

"Caden," Bridget answered. "Tell me where you are."

"I'm not fully sure right now, but I'm heading back to you, so don't worry about it." A large rat made a hissing noise at Caden as he walked past a pile of garbage. He walked a little faster. He had heard stories about rats, especially ones that size. "I should be in some time tonight."

"Tell me where to meet you and I'll come get you so we can both go back home together." She spoke calmly, but Caden could tell the tone could change at any moment.

"That would take too long. I'm going to get to the airport and fly back to you as soon as possible. Trust me. I'll be there as soon as

I can, because some serious things have come up." Caden could see a major street ahead while he spoke.

"I'm at the airport. I flew over here, so just tell me where you are and I'll come get you. It'll only take me a moment to get a rental." The tenseness in her voice was starting to show.

Caden stopped in his tracks. "I told you not to come."

"Did you really think I was going to sit around at my mom's house when you had gone through a plane wreck? Come on Caden, you know me better then that. When have I shied away from something?" She was right, even when Caden had first met her at the military hospital so many years ago; she wasn't a nurse that shied away from danger.

"Look, just stay there and get us a flight back. I should be there within an hour. I need to get you and Elizabeth to safety."

"What's going on Caden? Does this have anything to do with the building that blew up that's all over the news?"

"I don't have time to explain right now. I give you my word; I'll explain everything to you later. And I mean everything." Caden hoped that would get her to do what he was asking.

"About an hour?"

"Yes, about an hour." A black tattered stray cat gave a warning hiss as Caden accidentally kicked some garbage. The old wooden crate looked like it had been sitting there for years.

"I'll get the tickets." Bridget was short, and Caden couldn't blame her. He wasn't being too pleasant either.

"I love you."

"Love you too."

As soon as he hung up, he was on his way to the main street. Ironically, two taxis sat at the corner he was headed to. It was in front of a large bar. Looking for passengers.

The trip to the airport seemed long because of the strong pungent odor in the cab. Quiet and cold, the driver seemed almost awkward around Caden. He was eager and grateful to get out of the taxi and into the airport to find Bridget. But he didn't have to go far. Bridget was sitting on a concrete bench outside, waiting.

"Did you get the tickets?" Caden asked as he stepped out of the cab.

She jumped up and threw herself into his arms, holding him tightly. He snuggled into her hug feeling the comfort that she had to offer.

"I did, and you're lucky you made it in time to get on the plane. They'll be taking off here in a minute. They've already started the boarding."

"I'm glad to hear it. I was worrying I wouldn't make it. I was further then I thought."

"Now tell me what's going on." Bridget said.

"No," Caden tried to sound reasonable, but he knew he was going to come off gruff. "It won't be safe to talk about anything until we're off the plane and alone. I'm worried about standing out in the open right now." Bridget grew a little cold. They walked to the terminal in silence. Caden worried that security might stop him, if they already knew who he was.

Through the whole process, he was surprised to only run into two security guards and neither of them was paying attention. Caden realized there must not be an alert out yet. Getting on the plane was a cinch.

The plane ride was awkward as neither of them spoke to each other, which made the trip feel long. To Caden it seemed like there was even a physical void.

When they landed, Caden rented a small car and they headed toward Elizabeth's house. Tired and hungry, he let Bridget drive, which she was more then okay to do. As they drove through the tree-lined streets, Caden caved in unable to take the silence any longer. It was time to talk. He had prolonged it long enough.

"I don't quite know where to start, so I guess I should say that I'm a secret agent for a group called SDS." Caden stopped to wait for a response but nothing came. "I ran a small group that included me, Matt, and James. We ran missions once and awhile, but we would also test a lot of equipment throughout the years and you might be surprised by this but I even developed equipment."

He waited again for a response but there was nothing. Rubbing his hands together, he knew he had to keep going. "That's why I would be gone for a couple of days here and there. I was sent on missions, developing equipment, or testing it."

Bridget just sat there silent, not saying a word.

"Okay, can you give me any feedback?" Caden asked. She looked over at him but didn't say anything. "Like, how you feel about this so far?" She shrugged. Caden let out a deep breath in frustration, but figured he deserved what he was getting. He would be upset as well if Bridget had lied to him for so many years.

Struggling to look at Bridget any longer, he turned his gaze out the window and watched as the sun went down. The light flashed as each tree passed. Knowing he needed to tell her everything, he took another breath and pushed forward. "The building that was blown up on the news was ours." He paused for a moment to see if that would get a response, but still nothing. "Matt believes in some conspiracy theory that deals with my director, the agency, and almost our entire government. According to him, they're trying to kill off a large chunk of our society to create a superior population. So, Matt took it into his own hands to destroy what my director was doing and get the information out to overthrow our government, which included blowing up the building." Caden paused. His words were sounding almost sarcastic. Seeing Bridget not giving responses, made him decide to lay it out thick to see if he could get her to talk.

Caden cleared his throat before he went on. "Our latest project allows us to stop time. I actually invented that one." He raised an eyebrow as he looked at Bridget. "It's called the Dead Time Project." Scratching his chin, he moved a little forward to look at her eyes, but she stayed focused on the road. "Oh, and just to let you know, I'm a wanted man now and I'm back here to get you and Elizabeth in a safe place. I don't know what all is going on out there, but I've always known that if things went down my first responsibility would be you and your mother."

Bridget lifted one of her hands off the steering wheel and rubbed her temple. Caden stopped talking for a minute to let Bridget digest everything he had told her. Turning his focus to the glove box, Caden realized he had pushed her a little too far. He looked back up at the road and watched each line on the road speedily pass by as they glowed under the headlights. "Bridget, I know it's a lot to take in, but could you at least tell me what you're thinking?"

Lowering her hand, she took a deep breath. "I don't really know what to say. I mean, I knew you had some things to explain, but I didn't expect your explanation to have parts that seem so unbelievable." She looked at Caden. "You say you're a secret agent and your agency can stop time. Stopping time! Do you know how ridiculous that all sounds?"

"I didn't think it would sound ridiculous," Caden responded with a look of confusion on his face. "A little unbelievable, sure." He bit his lower lip. "Either way, I'm telling you the truth now, and I apologize for keeping it from you. The agency demanded secrecy. You of all people should understand that. And don't act like you didn't have some idea that I was doing secret things, you had to've seen the signs."

"I believe you to an extent, I mean you're right, we even had a couple of conversations about your work. It's just hard to fathom because it sounds like something out of a science fiction novel. I mean stopping time, being a part of a secret organization, your director possibly being caught up in evil things, and Matt blowing the office up. I had actually figured you were doing secret missions for the government, not a secret agency. And about you having to keep it a secret from me, I'm mature enough to understand that. I'm frustrated because I would've rather been kept in the loop, but I do understand keeping information like that secret."

"But it's hard to believe?"

"Well yeah," Bridget said. "What if I told you the same information? Would you believe me?"

Caden nodded. "It'd be hard to believe. If it helps at all, I'm betting every news station is airing the information right now. I can turn on the radio. It would be nice to hear if Matt was actually telling the truth or not." He leaned down to turn on the radio but stopped short.

"No," Bridget said, "we're close to mom's house. I believe you, I guess. It's just shocking. I really don't want to talk over the radio. I just want to talk with you."

Caden paused for a moment in thought. "There's something else I want to talk to you about before we get to your mom's house."

"I'm not sure if I can handle anything else." Bridget sounded a little stressed. She began rubbing her temple again.

Caden took a deep breath. Bridget was the only one he felt would understand everything, if not, she would at least have empathy. After finally expressing so much truth, he felt a pressure to keep going. "I'm scared I'm losing my mind. I keep seeing demonic creatures and they seem so real. I'm not sure if it's from some experiment they did to me or if I'm just going crazy. I see them one second and then the next, they're gone with no evidence that they were ever there." As Caden finished, they pulled down the small gravel road that led to Elizabeth's house.

"What do you mean exactly?" Bridget asked. The rocks from the gravel road could be heard underneath the tires and clanking on the undercarriage of the car.

"Well," Caden began, "it was happening whenever I would take a nap or when I came out of one. But the last couple of times have been when I'm fully coherent. I tried telling myself it was just dreams at first, but now I'm really starting to think I'm losing it. And I wouldn't be the first. They had another guy named Steven lose his mind after he had gone into stopped time."

Bridget pulled up to her mom's house and put the car in park. The headlights from the car lit the front of the house.

Bridget looked over at Caden. "Even though everything you're telling me is a lot of information and I'm feeling overwhelmed, there is one thing I know for sure. I love you, and no matter what, we'll get through all of this together. I married you because I love you, and I'm not going to let some secrets or hallucinations keep me from what I finally have." Bridget smiled and took his large, warm hand.

Emotion flooded Caden. He could see what a true relationship was, unlike what he had seen growing up. Bridget was there for him, and she wasn't going to let issues get in the way of their marriage.

"I love you too," Caden said as he leaned over to give her a kiss, wanting to be as close as possible to her. His hand touched her soft cheek, and he ran his fingers over the back of her neck. The second their noses touched, Caden heard a loud crack followed by a popping noise from the windshield. Bridget was thrown back into her seat as she struggled to let out a scream of pain. Caden's reflexes took over; he pulled Bridget down and ducked over her.

He quickly felt for his Dead Time switch, and pushed the button. Nothing happened. He hit it again and again and again, but nothing. With all of his strength he slammed it against the dash. It must've been damaged when the large demon had thrown him against the wall. There was no more time to waste he had to take care of Bridget.

Adrenaline pushed through Caden's body. The warmth of Bridget's blood covered his hands as he found where the bullet had entered her chest. With as much pressure as he could muster, Caden pushed on the wound directly over Bridget's heart. He knew she didn't have long if he didn't act quickly.

"Please don't let me die, I don't want to die," she pleaded. Her tears dripped on his arm as she gasped for air.

Caden pushed harder on her chest, but it was no use. The blood was rushing too fast, and he couldn't stop it. He knew there was nothing he could do for her. Her quiet whisperings, her pleading, her heavy breathing and crying came to a stop. Bridget's lifeless hands slid down his arm. Her eyes, those dark brown eyes, glazed over.

He couldn't move. His body was paralyzed.

Death was no stranger to Caden. He had faced it many times in his job. In the past, he had always known what to do, but this time he was useless. He held Bridget's lifeless body. Choking back his tears, he slowly began to release his grasp. He was soaked in her blood. He tried to swallow the lump in his throat but there was no saliva in his mouth. Slowly, through tears, he kissed her on the cheek. It was still warm.

Caden felt like he was going to explode. There was so much he wanted to tell her and do with her, but now it was too late. He laid his forehead against hers and quietly whispered, "I'm sorry. I'm so, so sorry. I failed you." Tears welled up in his eyes and slowly made their way down his cheeks. "Please forgive me."

He squeezed his eyes shut as tight as he could while the warm tears kept flowing.

Reality of his situation began to sink in and his anger flooded him. A pure rage. The sniper wasn't going to just stop with Bridget. Lying low, he reached between the front seats and unzipped one of the side pouches of Bridget's suitcase. He pulled out the handgun he had taken from the security guard. Another bullet shot through the glass almost clipped him in the head. Stuffing from Bridget's seat flew into the air as the bullet tore through it. The sniper had moved toward the right of the car.

Getting into a better position, Caden opened his door and dove into some bushes that surrounded a large tree. A bullet ripped into the tree trunk. The sniper was extremely close, closer then Caden had expected. He didn't move. He just sat there in silence, ready to spring into action at any moment.

A very quiet snap came from about five to six feet away in the direction of the sniper. Caden dove to his left, and then shot in the direction he heard the twig snap. Each shot rang out along the coastline getting lost in the slow rhythmic beating of the waves. Caden's shots seemed to follow the rhythm, even after he ran out of bullets. He kept pulling the trigger, clicking away as he took his last step to the bush.

Lowering his gun, Caden could make out a body limp in the foliage and a large sniper gun on the ground. He took a hold of the man's black coat and dragged him out. The sniper, who Caden didn't recognize, was a very young man, probably in his mid-twenties. Moving quickly, not knowing if there were others, Caden searched him and found another handgun, which he took. With nothing else of use, Caden dropped the body to the ground and spat on it. Black clothing covered the man, just like Matt's men. *Did Matt do this?*

He went to turn, but couldn't. Too much anger filled his mind and he kicked the man one last time as he yelled at the top of his lungs.

Slowly, Caden turned, and walked back to the car. He ran his fingers through Bridget's hair. That shot was meant for him, not her. Guilt rushed through his body. This was all his fault. Bridget dead, and it was all his fault. *Who ever did this was out to kill me. It couldn't have been Matt.* Caden froze for a moment. *But Matt was the only one that knew where I was headed. I had told him where I was going before I left.*

Caden took a deep breath. If his training taught him anything, it was to think through each situation. He needed proof it was Matt. *Don't jump to conclusions.*

Before the pain could really sink in, headlights glared in the rearview mirror. He lovingly swiped his hands across Bridget's eyes, closing them finally to the world. The dirt road crunched beneath his feet as he walked towards the car. Rage and hate flowed through his veins. There was no subduing it this time. He wanted revenge on everyone that had a part in Bridget's death and he only hoped whoever was coming down the drive was a part.

The light breeze blew through Caden's hair as he walked. Caden thought about the Dead Time switch on his arm and felt anger. If it had worked earlier, Bridget would still be alive. The car came to a stop while Caden tore the Dead Time switch off his arm and tossed it to the ground. Everything went silent. Puzzled, Caden looked over at where he had thrown the switch. It had fallen into a small puddle on the side of the road. He walked over to the puddle and picked the switch up. The shadow he had created from standing in the headlights stayed as he moved away.

A strange feeling went through Caden as if he were being watched. He looked behind him but saw nothing.

He thought he saw something move in the tall grass past the bushes, but that was impossible—time had stopped. Pressure built in his chest. *I hate this place.* The car, still sat to the side of him, eerily silent. Trying to shake off the feeling, Caden thought of Bridget and anger filled him once more. He tightened his fist around the switch. *Why couldn't it have worked before?*

A loud scream rang out from behind Caden, then another from the left, followed by something hitting him in the leg knocking him to the ground next to the car. Using the strength in his arms, Caden threw himself back to his feet but there was nothing to be seen. He crouched low and looked under the car. A dark creature screamed in his face, grabbed his arm, and tried pulling him under the car.

A blow hit him in the back as another scream was let out. Claw-like hands grabbed his arms and legs. The flesh of the creatures was uncomfortably cold. A voice called out to him through the screeching and scurrying.

"Mauldrin," the voice hissed and then something sharp tore into Caden's back. His body went limp. He tried to fight, but he couldn't command his body any longer. Sharp rocks in the gravel tore against his face.

Another voice hissed. "Why isn't he gone yet?"

Something else was said in response, but Caden couldn't understand. He began to give in to the painful feeling of the rocks digging into his face and the claws tearing at his skin. It was hard to tell if his eyes were open or closed, and breathing became too much of a burden. Darkness started moving through his veins and taking over his body, but he could feel some type of power at his chest that seemed to hold him there. As he finally began to give in and stop fighting he saw a bright flash that strained his eyes. Feeling seemed to rush back into his body, and he was quickly aware of the blast that had knocked all of the dark creatures off of him. The creatures screeched in pain.

Caden began to make an effort to stand up, getting to his hands and knees first, but stopped when he saw a man standing a few feet away. A brilliant light glowed all around the man making it hard for Caden to look at him. The man held a staff; purple electric shocks zapped around the bottom of it.

The glowing figure quickly slapped his staff down on the Dead Time switch that Caden had dropped on the ground, smashing it to pieces. He took a step closer to Caden standing over him. With one quick move he grabbed him by the neck, and lifted him in the air. Caden tried to look at him, but time started again, and he fell to the ground. Waves crashed once again, and the engine of the car idled by him. The man was gone, along with the dark creatures.

The car engine turned off and Caden reached to the back of his neck where some blood dripped out. Pain shot through his back as he touched the spot where the Dead Time chip had either been damaged or taken out.

Hearing the car door open, Caden rolled to his side. The driver stepped out, and Caden took a couple of steps back, staggering. The man emerged like a dark shadow.

"Who are you?" Caden asked while trying to control his nausea. His legs and fingers trembled from the attack in Dead Time.

"How ya doing?" the man asked as he closed the door. Caden recognized the voice but wasn't sure where he had heard it before.

"Who are you? And what are you doing here?" Caden asked. He didn't know if the man was there to kill him, but he clenched his fists ready to attack if needed.

"Boy, you sure have some spit to you, don't you," the man said. "I'm honestly surprised you're still standing after such an attack."

Confused, Caden just stood for a moment. *Was he talking about the attack in Dead Time or the sniper?* The man took a step closer. *Domblin?* It had to be another hallucination.

"Either way, we need to get you out of here," Domblin said.

"You're a hallucination. And I'm talking to you." Caden said. He felt like giving up after everything that had happened. Having another hallucination was a breaking point.

"I'm very real," Domblin said with a big smile. If he weren't a hallucination, it would've been a strangely comforting smile.

"So what are you doing here?" Caden asked still unsure if he was really just hallucinating.

"I'm actually here to get you to a safe place. I need to get you out of here and soon."

Maybe he should just shoot him, he would find out really quick if he were hallucinating. But on second thought, if he was real he probably shouldn't kill him right then and there. Caden tried to analyze the situation the best he could. Either Domblin had to be a hallucination or the person behind Bridget's death had sent him. There was no other plausible reason for the man, if he was real, to show up right after Bridget had been shot.

In the slim chance that Domblin was real and worked for whoever killed Bridget, he could be used as a tool. Revenging Bridget's death would become easier. "When I'm done with what I need to do, you can take me to your safe place. Until then, you make one wrong move, I'll kill you-"

"We don't have time for these games," Domblin cut him off. "I'm worried about your safety."

"You've had a fair warning," Caden said still pointing his gun. His head was beginning to hurt from the idea that he might actually be standing on a dirt road talking to himself with his deceased wife in the car, with who knows what bad guys headed his way to kill him.

"Caden, please. I know you don't trust me, and you shouldn't. But look at all that has happened." Domblin glanced over to his car.

Caden's jaw began to tremble. *Bridget.* He could hear her laugh in his mind, and smell her sweet perfume. And those brown eyes. So alive. He clenched his fists. "I don't have time for you…" He muttered as he walked back to the car.

He gently pulled her out. Her body was limp in his arms. Domblin stood with his forehead crinkled. If he was there to kill Caden, and not a hallucination, then he might as well do it with Bridget in Caden's arms. But Domblin made no aggressive moves, and Caden didn't care. *What was Elizabeth going to think when I have to tell her of Bridget's death?*

Elizabeth!

He walked up the dirt path to Elizabeth's house, Bridget's limp arm swung back and forth. The front door was cracked, and Caden paused for a moment, knowing it wasn't a good sign. He pushed it open with his knee. And there she was, Elizabeth, sitting in her recliner with a bullet hole in her head.

Caden carefully laid Bridget on the sofa and took a step back, leaning against the wall and sliding down to the floor. He couldn't hold back his tears. The pain was just too unbearable.

Elizabeth had been watching the news before she was shot, which was still on. The news flashed pictures of SDS members and that they were wanted dead or alive. Most of them had died in the blast, but there were still some out there. They showed pictures of James, Robert, Matt and then his face flashed on as well.

The TV screen changed to the nation's capital where there was a massive mob. The army was doing their best to protect the white building, but the uprising was huge. Before the news anchor could even say a word, they cut to the President.

The president looked ill as sweat dripped down his face.

Screaming rang out in the background and the camera fell. There was gunfire and more screaming. Someone picked up the camera and pointed it at the President. He was lying on the ground, and someone's foot dug into his neck, pinning him down. The camera zoomed out to reveal Justin, the man who tried to kill Caden on the plane, holding a gun to the President.

"Now Mr. President," Justin said, "explain to the world the truth of what you were doing."

"Caden, we need to go," Domblin said calmly. "We have to get out of here now. I'm worried for your safety, if we don't."

Closing his eyes for a second, Caden debated whether he was going to answer what he started believing was a hallucination since Domblin hadn't attacked him yet. In the end he decided to answer in the slim chance he was wrong. It was hard to care. There was so much emotion Caden was going numb inside. "Do you think I care what happens to me right now? And if you think I'm going anywhere with you before I bury my small family, you're wrong. You'd have to kill me first."

A gunshot rang out from the television. Justin had shot the president. The screen went black.

"We've wasted enough time. We have to go, now!"

Caden was just about to argue when a creaking noise came from the entryway. A dark shape crouched on the ground, the same creature that had attacked Caden. He recognized it. Not from just sight, but the feeling that came in the room was so familiar.

"Mauldrin," the creature hissed. The lights in the front room flickered.

Domblin stepped in front of Caden. "You're not going to touch him."

"One way or another he'll be mine." The creature moved closer to Domblin, showing no fear. "Triaad will be here soon."

"I'm not going to allow Triaad to get near him either," Domblin said.

Caden raised an eyebrow. *Great now my hallucinations are going to fight again.*

"You're correct," Tagen hissed, sounding amused. "He's coming for you, and I'm taking Mauldrin with me, before Triaad gets here." Black roots began to grow throughout the living room.

Domblin's hands started glowing white as he positioned himself to fight. Caden moved to stand up, curious to what was going to happen. Domblin turned to him. "Sleep now," he demanded making a motion with his hand. Caden tried to protest, but before he could get a word out, darkness took hold and he fell asleep.

CHAPTER 27

The park was empty. Azgiel was grateful for that. Running through streets for two hours had grown tiresome, but he could tell he was finally getting close to finding Kaz. His scent was getting stronger along with Mauldrin's. Through the park, he could make out a city that was more run down then where he had just come from.

"Turn around slowly or I will shoot you," a man's voice said, breaking Azgiel from his concentration of staying on Kaz's scent. At least twelve men, clad in body armor, held semi-automatic guns all pointed at him.

"It's definitely him," the closest man said into a mic on his shoulder.

Azgiel let a smile stretch across his face. *Ignorant, stupid mortals.* He eyeballed each of them individually to see if they posed any type of threat. From his assessment, the odds were easily against them. "And who do you think I am?" Azgiel asked to strike up a conversation, more to humor himself.

"Steven Torn."

"And who might you be?" Azgiel asked, chuckling.

"You don't need to know that information," the man responded.

Azgiel scanned the men and their equipment. Their body armor was black and their faces were painted black. "So what's the plan," Azgiel began, "Are you just going to stand there all night with your weapons pointed at me?"

"Until the President tells our commander what he wants done with you," the man answered snidely.

"Oh come now, you have to take orders?" Azgiel decided it was time to end his fun and get back to his search for Kaz. It was nice having actual interaction with someone once again, after many lifetimes over, being locked away.

"We're done talking," the man said. His face transformed suddenly. "What? The President has been assassinated? I can't believe… Okay…we'll take care of it." His trigger finger twitched.

"Well gentlemen, this has been fun, but I must get a move on."

"Stop or I will shoot," one of the guards, ordered. Azgiel didn't say a word he just kept walking away.

"Last warning. Stop or I will shoot you."

Azgiel kept walking, and the man shot a warning that flew past him. Stopping, Azgiel smiled menacingly and turned around, but kept walking backwards. Another shot rang out, this time meant for Azgiel.

With a quick motion, Azgiel caught the bullet in mid air. He turned his hand over and reopened it. The bullet turned into a small white flower. Letting go of it, it floated to the ground.

Without hesitation, the man motioned with a finger to let bullets fly.

Azgiel threw up his hands, and the bullets turned back on the gun holders, killing a couple and knocking the rest of them down from the impact on their body armor. One of the men pulled a knife and ran at Azgiel. The blade sliced at him, but never made contact. Azgiel moved in strange ways dodging the blade. Finally, the knife made contact, hitting Azgiel's hand. It shattered into pieces as if it were made of flimsy glass.

Three of the men ran off, fleeing the scene. They had seen that one of the men that had been hit pulled a grenade and let it roll towards Azgiel.

Azgiel felt the energy from the fire as it rapidly approached him. He quickly threw up his arms and felt a surge go through his body. The blast didn't harm him, it bypassed him. The smell of smoke wafted up his nostrils. Heat could still be felt even after the blast had gone by.

Taking a step back, Azgiel observed the destruction from the blast. Bodies were strewn on the ground. A couple of bushes and trees were on fire. Feeling something warm move down his leg, Azgiel looked down to see a wet spot began to show on his black pant leg near his knee. Touching the spot, he found the hole and tore it bigger. Digging into the wound with his fingers he pulled out a piece of sharp metal from his leg about the size of a small pencil. Once the metal was out the small wound quickly mended. A frown grew on his face. *I guess my power is still weak.*

Azgiel looked up to find that all the living soldiers were now completely out of sight. A dark shape to Azgiel's right caught his attention. *Kaz.* The demon's large human-like frame slammed to the ground with his long wings outstretched.

"Sir," Kaz growled. "I didn't expect you to be out here."

"I'm here to help with Mauldrin, but this whole time I've been trying to locate you."

"I've got good and bad news."

"Go on."

"The bad news is, the dark souls know about Mauldrin and have been going after him. The good news is, they've given me the opportunity to protect him twice now, which I think will help him believe we're the good guys." Kaz pulled his wings in as he spoke.

"Good." His plan had worked then. He looked behind Kaz. "So, where is he?"

"I've lost him right now. It's actually the second time I've lost him. Both times I fought with the dark souls, I chased them off and he's always gone by the time I get back. I was just in the process of hunting him down again when I ran upon your scent."

"Let's-" A gunshot cut Azgiel off as a bullet pierced through his shoulder, knocking him forwards. Kaz dove into the air. Before he had a chance to turn around, Azgiel heard a thud hit the ground behind him. Spinning around, Azgiel saw that one of the soldiers had come back. The man managed to hit Kaz twice, which only made him angrier.

Kaz moved with un-human speed as he ducked down while drawing his sword and swung at the gun. With ease, the sword split the gun in two and sliced off the man's left index finger and the tip of his left thumb. The soldier screamed in pain. Using the butt of the gun, he tried to hit Kaz in the face, but missed. Kaz grunted at him and picked the man up.

Baring his fanged teeth, Kaz drove his sword through the soldier and tossed him into some large, red-leafed bushes. While putting his sword away, he growled in the direction he had thrown the body.

"Let's go," Azgiel ordered as he took a couple of steps closer to him. "How long has it been since you lost Mauldrin?"

Picking at a couple of his wounds from the gun, Kaz said, "We're about an hour behind him, and as long as he doesn't get on a plane like he did last time, we should catch up quickly." He looked back down at his wounds and spoke in his ancient tongue, "Degnar mekna." The wounds slowly closed up.

"Which way do we head?" Azgiel looked towards the old rundown town in front of them and took a step in that direction, stepping over a dead soldier.

"I believe we could move faster if I flew us. It's getting dark enough with the sun going down people shouldn't see you too well and I'll just alter my state so they won't be able to see me." Kaz held out his hands, ready to pick Azgiel up if he agreed.

"Let's get going." Azgiel answered holding his arms out to be taken. The pure force that Kaz took him and bolted them into the air startled him. His head and stomach felt strange from the fast change in pressure. Not needing to pay attention, Azgiel let his mind go as his legs dangled above rooftops and city streets.

His wife's words ran through his mind that his followers had lost their edge for war. Azgiel knew the only reason they won the battle with the dark souls the other day was the intense power and strength the demons possessed. The others were somewhat awkward on the field, not used to the fighting. If it had been a long battle, they would've been destroyed. Concern ran through his heart, not fully knowing what to do. There would have to be time before they were prepared to fight Triaad, unfortunately that time may not exist with Triaad starting battles. It was just a matter of time before a large army was brought against them.

As Azgiel brainstormed and got lost in his thoughts, time seemed to slip away. They made it to an airport where Kaz grumbled about Mauldrin getting on a plane. He took a quick break and then they were off again. The trip was longer and they both were quiet as they flew.

Before Azgiel knew it, they were landing. In the distance the ocean could be seen and the waves could be heard crashing on the beach. A small house sat in the middle of some trees where Kaz brought them down.

"Is he in there?" Azgiel asked. "Wait! Is that who I think it is?"

"Domblin," Kaz answered. "I'm not sure if they're still here, the trail becomes strange."

"I sense that too." Azgiel didn't wait around to talk any further. He quickly ran towards the house. A car was out front with two bullet holes in the windshield, but he kept going. Once in the home, he saw two dead bodies, but no Mauldrin or Domblin.

"That's his wife." Kaz spoke from behind as he bent down to enter the home. The floor creaked from his weight.

"There's been a fight here. It was Domblin, with something, but I'm struggling to place it." The floor was black with streaks through it, along with the walls. One of the back walls was completely blown out and a broken TV had been thrown through a side wall.

"It's a dark soul. They must still be after Mauldrin, but I'm assuming Domblin was successful in stopping its attempt." His deep voice seemed to fill the small entryway.

Moving towards the young lady on the floor, Azgiel gently picked her head up. Blood stained her clothing, and a pool of the red liquid covered the dark wooden floor. "And you say this is his wife?" As he spoke, he lifted the eyelids and looked at her dark brown eyes.

"Yes," Kaz answered leaning over Azgiel. "I saw them together before the dark souls attacked him the first time. They were in bed together."

"If we aren't too late, we might be able to use her to get Mauldrin." Azgiel spoke as he moved his hand over her chest. Whispers came from his mouth and his hand began to have a bluish glow. Her heart became clear to the eye as if her skin had become translucent. A small and very dim white light lit, and Azgiel quickly closed his hand, ending the glow.

"We still have time, but we have to move fast. Get us back to the Witch. NOW."

CHAPTER 28

The cabin room was dark when Caden woke. In a panic he sat up quickly. *Bridget.* She died in his arms. He had tried to save her. Looking around and searching the room Caden realized he was in his cabin. *Everything must have been a terrible nightmare. It had to've been. None of it had been true— the Dead Time, Matt overthrowing the government, Robert doing evil things, the hallucinations, Bridget dying.*

Closing his eyes and taking a deep breath, he tried to let go of all the emotions that swirled through his body. The nightmare was over. As he began to calm down, he felt a sharp pain in his neck. He leaned forward, turned on his lamp, and looked at his clothing he was wearing.

"NO!" Caden screamed. The rest of the scream was primal, letting out as much pain as possible.

Finally he stopped. He collapsed back on the bed. He didn't want to believe it. "No…Bridget, what have I done," he said quietly through tears.

Caden punched his headboard, snapping it in half. He just wanted to wake up. Nothing seemed to make sense. Evil dark creatures chasing him, demons protecting him, Bridget and Elizabeth being dead, Mags missing. He couldn't understand how he woke up in his cabin. *How in the world did I get here?*

As Caden tried to pull himself together and think straight, he noticed a strange light coming from outside the cabin window. The light glowed a little ways into the woods. Caden made his way to his small dresser, the floorboards creaking as he stepped across them. He opened the bottom drawer and pulled out a handgun. Whatever was causing the light might also have answers for him. He quietly left the cabin.

Voices began to echo through the trees. One of the voices was Domblin's, and the other voice was very deep. He kept moving slowly, silently. The light was coming from behind a couple large trees.

"The whole thing has turned into a big mess. If only I had been able to spend the time mentoring Mauldrin instead of being locked away. Now the dark souls know about him, he's unknowingly released Azgiel, and there is absolutely no evidence he is tapping into who he really is. I mean he is weak." Caden could barely make out Domblin's voice as he spoke, but he could tell he sounded angry. "Our plans are falling a part and I still don't have this whole Azgiel thing under control. I just don't know. Maybe bringing Mauldrin back was a mistake, since it's only made things worse so far."

The person talking to Domblin let out a deep groan. "We have to keep hope. Is Triaad aware of Mauldrin?"

Caden finally made it to one of the trees, but stayed hidden.

"No," Domblin said. "One of the creatures mentioned that they're keeping it from Triaad, but they told Triaad about me, and supposedly he's on his way to get me as we speak, that's why I called upon you."

"That doesn't leave a lot of options for Mauldrin, does it?"

"It doesn't," Domblin said. "And Mauldrin is nowhere to the level we had hoped he would be by this point."

"What's the plan?" the deep voice growled.

Caden heard twigs snap as one of them moved.

"I'm not sure, but I do know when Triaad comes for me, he's bound to find out about Mauldrin, and we can't have that. Everything will be over then."

Caden wondered how they knew the name Mauldrin, only the strange dark creatures had called him that. He wanted to look around the tree to see who Domblin was talking to, but he was worried he might be seen. His revenge was coming, there wasn't going to be anymore nice guy, but he still had to be cautious

"Not necessarily," the voice replied, "not if you build a protective ring around this area and keep Mauldrin hidden when he comes, then allow for your own capture. That way you can keep him distracted while I get more help to get Mauldrin out of here."

"That will leave Mauldrin with no protection from the dark souls if he leaves the circle."

"Then teach him to stay inside of it." The deep voice sounded calm, but stern.

"If he's anything like what he used to be, I doubt he'll listen," Domblin muttered.

"It's our best option right now, and I can't take him with me." Caden took a deep breath and leaned over to see who was with Domblin. A huge beast was lying down in front of Domblin, who had his back to Caden. The beast had a reptile-like head, which stretched taller then Domblin stood. The creature's scale-like skin was white with gray flecks that glowed in the dark night. His eyes were a deep blue that Caden felt he could get lost in. A couple of twigs snapped as he moved his long tail across the ground and pulled it against his large body.

Caden moved back behind the tree. *Stupid fear.* He hit the back of his head against the tree trunk. Matt's words ran through his mind of his two weaknesses. Letting out a sigh, he closed his eyes, it was time to face his hallucinations and who knows what was going to happen. In case it turned into a fight, he prepared himself. A strange feeling came over Caden while his eyes were closed, like something was standing in front of him. Opening his eyes, he threw himself against the tree.

A dark creature stood in front of Caden. The same type of shadowy creature that had attacked him in the past, but once again it was a new one. Tired of hallucinations and everything else pushing him around, Caden quickly brought the gun up and shot. The bullet smashed through the creature's oily skin and a terrible smelling black liquid spattered on his face. A strange growl came from the creature as Caden let his fist fly. His knuckles made contact with the creatures face. The skin was oily as he knocked it backwards. Its red eyes blazed and Caden went to pull the trigger again. With speed that caught Caden off guard, the figure pushed him into the tree and took his breath away so he couldn't scream for help. He tried to fight back, but his arms and legs were unresponsive and the gun fell to the ground.

Darkness grew in Caden's vision as something sharp pulled at his lungs and throat. A strong light flashed, and the creature released him from his clutches. The light was so bright that Caden brought his arm over his eyes. A loud screeching rang out, hurting his ears.

Domblin stood to Caden's right; his body glowed with a bright light. Seeing him like that, Caden finally realized it was Domblin who he had seen in Dead Time. He had been the one that saved him from all the dark creatures.

The beast in front of him, screamed, and dove at Domblin. Moving with ease, Domblin held his arm out, and a glowing white staff formed out of thin air into his hand.

Before the creature reached Domblin, he swung his staff and cracked the oily monster in the head. Particles of light flew in the air. The blow slammed it to the ground. Looking frightened the creature quickly scrambled to his feet and disappeared into the dark. An oily black substance clung to the staff, but it was quickly engulfed in a white flame.

"They're getting more desperate, and unfortunately they now know where you are," Domblin said while the staff turned into particles and disappeared. He helped Caden to his feet.

"You're the one that was in the stopped time," Caden said while trying to shake off a headache from the attack. He bent down and picked up his gun.

"Yes, that was me," Domblin replied. "But there isn't much time to talk. We need to get you to a safer spot." He bent down and drew a line in the dirt. The line lit up with a blue flame—a circular boundary wrapped around the cabin.

"Let's go inside your cabin," Domblin said. Curiously, Caden bent down and ran his finger along the thin blue strip. It felt like velvet. The small strip wrapped around the cabin in a large circle.

Caden tried to pull at it but was unable to get the velvety strip out of the ground. Domblin entered the cabin and left the door open for Caden to follow. Once he stepped over the boundary, it let out an electrical sounding snap, which made Caden jump.

As Caden entered the cabin Domblin spoke up, "In a very short amount of time I'm going to leave and I need you to stay inside this cabin no matter what happens. Your life depends on it. Those dark creatures that keep attacking you will be watching this cabin and waiting for you to exit. That ring I put around the cabin will protect you from them."

"Who are you, and what in the world is going on? One minute I'm trying to take care of my wife, and then I'm at my cabin trying to figure out if this is all just a bad dream. And then I go outside to find you talking to some kind of creature that-"

"A guardian," Domblin interjected.

"Uh guard…"

"Guardian," Domblin clarified.

"Guardian, or whatever the thing is. Then some shadowy creature attacks me again, but low and behold, you pop out of nowhere and slam this creature to the ground. You were also the one in Dead Time that saved my butt, but nothing makes sense. How did you get into the same exact stopped time as me?" Caden sat on his bed, ready to draw his gun if he needed.

"I don't have time to answer all of your questions, but let me start by saying that I'm Domblin and I've been watching you since I brought you back from the eternal rest you were in. It took some time, and I had to travel the planets to figure out how, but I was finally able to."

"Travel the planets? What?"

"Yes, travel the planets. There's more planets then Myree, this planet," Domblin replied. "But I'm not going to be able to tell you much if you keep interrupting."

Caden nodded, his eyebrow twitched.

"I've never been able to make contact with you for the same reason that the dark souls, or what you call the shadowy creatures, would catch on that you're back. I've been living on another planet up until recently. The main thing that you need to know is there's a war going on that stretches across this universe, and unknowing to you, you have a very central role in it."

"So if I'm understanding you correctly, my alien friend," Caden said mockingly not in the mood for any more crap in his life at that moment, "we're involved in some alien war, unbeknownst to me, and now there are evil creatures out to kill me."

Ignoring Caden's sarcasm, Domblin continued, "Basically, but I have to explain something before I go. You can't cross the line I drew in the dirt. You'll be protected as long as you stay within the circle."

"Protected from the dead souls?"

"Dark souls," Domblin clarified. "But yes, them, and other things that will harm you if they find out you are here. Triaad is the only one that could smash through it, but he would have to identify you are even here first, which the barrier will at least block any traces of you." Domblin stopped for a second and gave a strange look that Caden interrupted to mean he was getting sidetracked. "I'm going to be taken soon and you need to stay hidden no matter what happens to me. I will be back, but by then that Guardian you saw should have you in a safer place." Domblin sounded very serious.

"What will I eat until then?"

"There will be food left for you daily," Domblin stated. "I have to go. Listen carefully, do not come out of this door until I am completely gone and out of sight, no matter what happens." Domblin moved towards the door.

"Wait," Caden said. "You have to answer one question for me. Is Bridget really dead? Did that really happen?"

"I'm sorry about your loss Caden." Domblin paused for a moment. "I have to go now. I will return soon." Domblin walked out the door, closing it behind him.

Caden jumped up to the window and watched Domblin walk to a clearing past the blue line. There were so many more questions. Anger swirled through him. The gun would be easy to draw and make Domblin stay. Then he would have to answer questions.

A loud high-pitched roar brought Caden out of his thoughts and he quickly gripped the handle of his gun. He moved closer to the window, and a loud gust of wind slammed his roof and windows making them rattle. An enormous creature flew over the cabin, but it was hard to make out what it was. A flick of light caught Caden's attention. Domblin was holding his staff again lighting the area around him. Tremors shook the ground as if something heavy crashed or landed hard.

Voices could barely be heard, but Caden could tell Domblin was talking to someone. Unable to see whom he was talking to, Caden quickly stepped over to his door and cracked it open. There was a towering dark shadow just along the tree line of the meadow, almost as tall as some of the trees.

"I'll be able to work out the mess your dark souls have created with this planet," Domblin yelled. "And if I were you, I would leave now and stay out of my way." Domblin's staff grew brighter, revealing the large shadow to be a dragon, but different then the one before. Bigger and black.

"Enough of your ridiculous words," a deep voice said. It echoed through the trees, a strange hush fell throughout the woods. Crickets, owls, and other nightly creatures silenced. The dragon-like creature moved, which caused the ground to tremble slightly. Light from Domblin's staff illuminated the creature. A dark-armored man rode on the dragons back. The dragon's golden eyes soaked in the light from the staff and his long, war-torn ears shifted backwards as he looked at Domblin.

Moving the staff forward, Domblin prepared for a fight. The dragon swiftly snapped forward, mouth open and large teeth showing. Domblin swung his staff, smashing the dragon in the side of the snout, creating a huge wall of light. Caden had to look away; it was too bright. When the light faded, Caden watched as the dragon went in for another attack, but this time with his tail. Domblin slammed his staff to the ground and used it like a shield. The large tail knocked Domblin backwards, throwing him to the ground.

Before Domblin could get up, the dragon swiped at him with his large claws, but missed as Domblin quickly rolled to the side.

Unable to tolerate any more, Caden moved to the door and swung it open, gun in hand. Domblin had finally gotten back on his feet and glanced over at Caden. A look came across his face of worry and he dropped his staff.

Before Caden could even exit the cabin, Domblin put both hands out and grabbed at the air. The door yanked out of Caden's hand and slammed shut, but before it had, Caden saw something that made his heart drop. While Domblin was using whatever magic he contained to close the door, the dragon grabbed a hold of Domblin with his giant claws and pulled him up into the sky.

Caden yanked at the door with all of his strength, but it wouldn't budge. He quickly looked out the window, almost tripping over his own feet, but it was too late. They were gone. Another high-pitched roar rang out, but it was far in the distance. He began to feel very alone and overwhelmed. The floor creaked as he moved back to the door and tried to open it again, but it still didn't budge. He sat down on his bed. He knew he could go out a window if he really wanted to, but exhaustion and utter discouragement kicked in and he allowed himself to fall asleep, feeling too overwhelmed to do anything else.

The next morning seemed as if nothing had happened the night before. Birds sang and the sun shined through the windows. Caden sat up feeling rather stiff and tired, but he couldn't sleep any longer. Bridget's blood still stained his hand brown. Tears formed at the corners of his eyes. Feeling overloaded with emotion, Caden took a hot shower. Afterwards, he felt a little better, but he was still confused and drained almost empty. His loved ones were dead. Confusion swirled through his brain from everything Domblin had told him.

Caden walked over to the front door only to find it open. Sitting on the porch was a wooden tray of food, an assortment of meats, vegetables, and fruits. Surprised by the findings, Caden placed the items in his medium-sized fridge and headed back outside. His hands shook from all the stress. The grass was matted down and a tree was knocked over where the battle had been last night. Caden stood at the edge of the blue line, not daring to pass over it. He looked over to where Domblin had stood last and noticed that his staff was lying in a thick patch of grass. He paced back and forth, wanting to grab the staff, but not wanting to cross the line. Finally his curiosity got the best of him.

A snap rang out, almost like the sound of ice on a lake cracking apart. The blue line turned black, and created a smoke ring above it. Caden watched as it dissipated into the air. *That can't be good.* A cool breeze blew through the trees and grass giving him some goose bumps.

"Caden," he spoke to himself, "there's nothing to worry about. You've been up here a million times and you've always been safe." He looked at the cabin, feeling it was far away at that moment, but he felt a little better with his gun tucked into his pants. He knelt down to pick up the staff. His hand hesitated as he could feel almost an energy coming from it. Again curiosity got the best of him and he picked it up. The staff was remarkable. It wasn't made of wood or any other material that Caden had ever seen. As best as he could guess, he thought it appeared to be made of light. The outside layer moved around and Caden could slightly see through it, like a foggy glass.

The staff immediately responded to Caden's touch glowing a little brighter. It reminded him of the flame, when it seemed to respond to him in Dead Time. Something changed and Caden could feel the light wanting to dismiss, to be free. Caden let go of the staff and particles of light dashed off into all different directions. Before he knew it, the staff was gone.

He had been so caught up in awe with the staff that he hadn't noticed a shadow looming over him. Claws tore into him. Caden threw an elbow, trying to hit the person in the head, but he was pushed forward at an incredible speed making the trees around him look like blurs.

Caden was slammed into a tree. The bark cut into his back. After he gained his balance, he searched to see if whatever had grabbed him was still there. The trees seemed darker than normal and the ground was barren of anything. The sun was gone and it appeared to be nighttime. Something scurried above. Five feet up, sat a strange beast that had a head like a dog and teeth like a wolf. The creature sat there, staring with its head cocked to the side. Slowly Caden backed away from the tree. Shadowy figures moved through the forest. Caden pulled out his gun and pointed to the fury beast in the tree, sending a bullet in its direction. Hitting it right in the chest, the creature yelped and fell out of the tree. It scrambled to its feet. Once both paws were on the ground it ran off into the dark.

After the shot, the shadows in the distance stopped moving. A dim light far away moved rather quickly in Caden's direction. *Is it the reptile-like creature he had seen talking to Domblin, or possibly Domblin himself?* As the light source passed by the shadowy figures, Caden could make out a couple of the dark shadows. One looked a lot like the large demon that had protected him, except this one was a bluish gray color and had hair around his horns and a beard on his face. The smaller creatures were harder to make out with all their leather and metal armor. A couple of the figures almost looked like humans, but their pale skin and no eyes gave Caden the shivers.

The light grew stronger and Caden put his hand up to block the brightness. His eyes quickly adjusted to the magnificent white light and he slowly lowered his hand. He was surprised to see a beautiful young woman standing in front of him. Her looks captivated him, almost seducing him. Dark blue eyes seemed to peer right through him, and her complexion glowed. She wore a white gown that illuminated everything around her and her blond hair shimmered as it flowed like water.

"Mauldrin," she smiled, "you've finally come." Even her voice was perfect.

"Why do you call me that?" Caden asked. "My name is Caden."

"That is the name I once knew you by," she said. "The name you went by before you were born as Caden."

"Before I was born?"

"Yes, before you were somehow reborn in the body you're in. You were a powerful king that watched over this world, and now you have come to grace us with your presence."

"And who might you be?" Caden asked, swallowing a lump in his throat.

"You may call me The Witch. At least that is what you would've known me before you were born."

"I don't know what you're talking about."

"So I've been told," the Witch said with a smile. "You must've been blinded to everything before you were brought back. However, we have something that might help bring back your memory. A gift in celebration of your return." She held her hand out.

Suddenly, all kinds of creatures surrounded him. He quickly pointed his gun at the closest one, a little green creature with solid red eyes. The creature looked startled and let out a chirp. Before he could shoot, his gun dissolved as the Witch made a motion with her hand.

"Please don't hurt any more of my family," the Witch calmly said. "They may look rather frightening, but they'll not hurt you. They are happy to see you." As she spoke, the large red demon that had protected Caden numerous times stepped out of the crowed and approached the Witch. The demon held a sword wrapped in a very well worn, old cloth. He held it delicately, being cautious, and handed the sword to Caden. Feeling his hands shaking, Caden tightened them a couple of times to get rid of his nervousness. After taking a deep breath, he reached out and took the sword by the sheath.

"This once belonged to you," the Witch said, while the large demon stepped behind her.

Caden looked at the demon. "Thank you for protecting me from those strange creatures, the dark souls." He remembered what Domblin had called them. The demon nodded in return. Feeling ever so slightly more comfortable Caden proceeded, "May I ask your name?"

The large demon looked at the Witch. She nodded in approval for him to answer. "My name is Kaz," he said with a deep voice.

The sword. It felt heavy in his hands. Caden began to unravel the cloth while holding it by the sheath. Once he finished unraveling, he tried to grip the handle and draw the sword, but he couldn't. It was as if it wasn't there, as if it were an illusion, a hologram. Confused, he held out the handle of the sword to the Witch wanting help. She waved her hand and an unseen force knocked him to the ground, taking his breath away.

The Witch's face seemed to go dark for a moment as Caden quickly stood. Fear gripped at him. He didn't know what to think. *How am I to know if they aren't really going to harm me?* Kaz still stood there, which gave some comfort to Caden.

"Sorry," the Witch said. "If the sword touches any of us, it will kill us instantly. I didn't mean to respond like that. You scared me." She still looked upset and didn't sound as friendly as she had before. Something was different about her, darkness behind her eyes that made Caden feel uncomfortable.

"Sorry, I didn't know." Caden still held the sword. "How do I draw the sword? I can't grab it."

"It has to respect you before you can take a hold of it," the Witch responded rather coldly. "But I think it's time for you to go, it's not safe here any more."

Caden didn't know what to say, it was rather abrupt. In a way he was grateful she wanted him to go, the whole situation had him unnerved. "How do I get back?"

"Turn around," she said, pointing behind him. As he turned he found his cabin was ten feet away. The forest was back to normal and the Witch was gone. He let out a sigh of relief. There was comfort of being back at his cabin, a sense of safety. Not wanting to waste time outside, he began walking ever so quietly back to the small dwelling.

Twigs snapped to the right of him and caught Caden's attention. A dark figure stood in the shadows of a tree. Caden squinted and held the sword close. It was Steven. Caden closed his eyes then reopened them to see if his mind was playing tricks. The way the last twenty-four hours had gone, Caden wasn't surprised to see Steven still standing there. After being encircled by beasts and monsters of all kinds, he didn't feel too startled by Steven's presence, just confused. Besides he had a sword in his hands, if he could just figure out how to draw it.

"What do you want?" Caden yelled across the meadow. Steven smiled. A flash of red caught Caden's eye; he barely made out Kaz standing in the shadows of the forest to the left of him.

Strangely, Caden once again felt comfort knowing Kaz was there. "What do you want, Steven?" he yelled out again feeling more confident.

"I see your sword has been returned to you," Steven called back. "It's nice to see it back in your hands, Your Highness." Caden looked at his sword and almost fell over in shock when he looked back up to find Steven standing directly in front of him.

"How'd you do that?" Caden said taking a step back.

"This place isn't safe for you," Steven said not acknowledging Caden's question. "We need to get far away. The dark souls will be here shortly, in large numbers. Kaz and I will protect you the best we can, but we need to move quickly because the Witch can only hide your scent for so long."

"Who are you?" Caden looked closer at him. For the first time, Caden noticed Steven didn't have the same blue eyes he used to have Instead they were black. "Or should I ask what are you?" Saying it out loud, made Caden feel idiotic, but he struggled to trust anything any longer. His whole world had turned upside down, and he felt like a lost stranger. "Are all of you with Domblin?"

Steven smiled. "Domblin shouldn't be trusted just as I shouldn't be in this body," Steven said losing his smile. "I'm an archangel, an angelic warrior, named Azgiel. I have been keeping a close eye on Domblin for some time. He played this awful trick on me, putting me into this body, which takes away most of my powers. He weakened me so I wouldn't be as much of a threat."

"So you and Domblin aren't with each other?" Caden asked trying to piece all the tidbits of information together.

"No," Azgiel responded very coldly. "If he had the chance he would kill me."

"Then why should I trust you?" Caden narrowed his eyes, analyzing Azgiel even more.

"Think about it Caden," Azgiel said. He signaled for Kaz to move closer. "Domblin put me in this body to trap me." Caden wrinkled his brow. "I was informed that he took off and only reappeared after your wife was killed, and then puts on a performance for you, acting like he was fighting the same man that he serves named Triaad. Do you know who else serves that man on the dragon?" Azgiel asked. Caden shook his head. "The dark souls. Think about it. Who sent the dark souls after you? He only pretended to save you a couple of times from them, but where was he most of the time? Especially when Kaz had to keep saving you? That blue line he put around your cabin was to attract the dark souls, but now that you have your sword back, you can bring peace to this world once again."

"They're getting closer," Kaz snorted in his low toned voice. "We need to move."

"Kaz is with you?" Caden asked with surprise.

"Yes," Kaz grunted.

"Wait, so you're saying-"

"We'll talk as we walk," Azgiel said. Kaz allowed them to reach the edge of the woods before he followed behind, keeping a little distance between them.

"So you're saying that Domblin has been ordering the attacks on me, and the times that he protected me were just an act?"

"Yes. He was completely behind the attacks on you. And those phony fights he had with the dark souls were laughable at best. You'll see what we do to the wretched things if any of them catch up to us, and believe me, they won't be walking away alive like they did after encountering Domblin."

"He seemed so sincere, like he actually cared about me and my loss of Bridget."

"Not only was he not sincere," Azgiel began, "he was responsible for your wife's death. He orchestrated that."

Bridget. Caden couldn't shake the vision of her beautiful face. *I'll never see it again. I should've killed him while I had the chance.* "How do you know all of this? Were you there, and if you were, why didn't you stop it?"

"No, I wasn't there." Azgiel said, sounding remorseful. "I wish I had been. We are sworn to serve and protect you. I would've put a stop to the whole thing. Kaz still feels horrible because he lost you in the building you were in or he would've protected both of you."

Caden clenched his fists. "How did you find out?"

"The same way Kaz knows the dark souls are getting closer. There are elements all around us in this forest that can communicate with you, if you're willing to listen. I can find out information on the last couple of days events in this very spot just by the elements talking to me. Just like they're telling me right now that we have very little time before the dark souls catch us."

Kaz now had his sword drawn and had closed the gap between them. "How do we fight them? I have no gun, and I can't draw the sword, or can we out run them?" Caden's voice cracked. All of this was too much to handle. His stomach was tightened and he felt like an ulcer was developing.

"No, we can't outrun them, but that rocky area up ahead will be a perfect spot to try and hold out," Azgiel said. He picked a leaf off a bush and held it up. "You see this leaf?" The leaf moved back and forth as if a wind was blowing it around. The green seemed to bleed out of the leaf, turning into what looked like a translucent glass. After the green left, the leaf began to expand like a balloon. "Here you go," Azgiel said while holding it out. Caden took it in his hand, bewildered on what it was and how Azgiel did it. The glassy substance was ribbed like a leaf.

"So you know magic?" Caden asked.

"Not magic," Azgiel explained as they walked around a couple of large boulders. "As you very well know, everything is made of atoms, and if you have enough knowledge and power you can command atoms to alter their state and create whatever you need or want."

"You're saying that you can altar the molecular makeup of objects," Caden asked as they came to a stop behind three large boulders.

"I'm saying that with enough power and knowledge the molecules around you will do what you ask. You were the Lord over this entire planet at one time. If you can unlock your mind, you'll be able to tap into tremendous amounts of power and knowledge, enough to draw that sword and get us out of this situation."

"How do I do that?" Caden asked, questioning the concept, not fully believing it was real.

"Drop that little glass ball," Azgiel said while taking a step back. Kaz had caught up with them and stood close by as well.

Caden looked at the ball, still holding it by the stem, amazed that the spherical object had once been a leaf. Slowly he released it, allowing it to drop to the ground. Small electric bolts came up from the ground, grabbing at the glassy bulb. Once it touched the ground, an unseen force surged through Caden making him feel lightheaded. The color around him changed and grew blurry. He blinked a couple of times. After his eyes cleared he could see the dome that had appeared. The small glass bulb had grown into something very large that surrounded them. Looking through the glass-like dome reminded Caden of wearing a pair of sunglasses—everything outside was tinted brown.

"What is this?" He touched the wall of the dome. The surface felt like the inside of a wet seashell.

"It's what's going to keep us safe for the time being."

"How'd you make it?"

"You did this, not me," Azgiel said. "It's the same way you're going to pull that sword and get us out of this mess."

A scream rang out, muffled by the dome, making Caden look past the rocks into the trees. The forest grew very dark, and the same dark soul that Caden had seen in times past appeared in front of a close-by tree.

"Tagen," Kaz growled. Caden looked at the dark soul closely, now he knew his enemy's name.

Tagen leaned up against the tree and it let out a groan that shook the ground. Pine needles slowly fell all around him. He smiled showing his black, oily teeth.

"Draw the sword, Caden," Azgiel said, but Caden was overwhelmed. Kaz tightened his grip on his heavy sword getting ready for the fight. Another scream came from behind. Caden turned just in time to see a very skinny dark soul slam into the wall of the dome and bounce off. Azgiel grabbed Caden's shoulder to get his attention. "Draw the sword."

239

Caden reached for the sword, but was still unable to take a hold of it. He needed to focus; he waved his hand back and forth trying to draw the sword, but it was as if the sword was an illusion.

"I can't grab it," Caden yelled.

Both Azgiel and Kaz were focused on Tagen and the hundreds of dark souls who were circling the dome. Another dark soul charged the dome and slammed against it with its head. Tagen let out another scream and crawled up to the dome. He gripped an edge of a small boulder that stood between them. Black-like roots spread out on the surface of the boulder, pushing off chunks of moss and pine needles. Smoke rose as the black roots climbed the wall of the dome. A loud pop startled Caden as a crack split up the side of their shelter.

"I know you can do it," Azgiel said while keeping an eye on the developing crack. "Believe in yourself and draw the sword."

One of the black roots started to come through the crack, making its way down the side of the dome toward the ground. Feeling the pressure, Caden held the sword in front of him and tried to clear his mind. His heart raced and sweat beaded his forehead. Something familiar ran through his fingers. He had felt it before when the fire had somehow responded to him when the plane crashed, and when he had picked up Domblin's staff. The handle of the sword began to turn darker, as if it were becoming less translucent. When his hand was about an inch away from the sword, something changed. The fire had responded to him in an almost a playful manner, like Mags desiring attention. Domblin's staff had almost seemed to want his attention, wanting help. But the sword gave Caden the feeling of a sadistic-minded criminal waiting for its commands to destroy. Pure evil.

Hesitating to take the finely carved black handle, the sword seemed to call to Caden, creating a feeling of dirtiness and filth like he had just done something wrong. He quickly pulled his hand away, which was more difficult than he realized it was going to be. The sword had a pull on him, as if it were controlling his muscles to do its will.

A green light caught Caden's attention, and he looked over at Kaz who held his sword up. The lettering on the sword was engulfed in green flames. Kaz pointed the blade down and slammed it into the black roots. The roots lit up in green flames, burning them all the way back to Tagen. Pulling his sword out of the ground, Kaz let out a deep growl.

Tagen let out another scream, and another dark soul ran at the dome heading for the cracks. The creature hit with such a force that it knocked a basketball-sized chunk of the wall loose. The piece of dome fell to the ground and dissipated. Letting out a scream, the dark soul quickly ran for the hole, throwing his arm through. His body contorted and slipped into the small opening. Kaz swung his sword, slicing the dark soul's arm and head off. The shadowy flesh of the dark soul seemed to drip off like an oily tar leaving behind thin, black rubbery bones. More dark souls began charging the dome.

Azgiel turned to Caden. "Draw the sword now!" His voice was harsh and demanding.

"I can't," Caden screamed.

Azgiel grabbed Caden's shirt and pushed him backwards. "You can and you will draw that sword." Azgiel started to look different. A shadow came over his face and his eyes turned a pitch black. "What kind of pathetic weakling have you turned into? Draw the sword or you're going to die. This is your world Mauldrin. Dig within and find who you truly are. There's power within you that can destroy all the dark souls around us. You just have to remember and tap into it. It's time for you to take the realm once again. Now draw the sword!"

Before Caden could respond, his head hit the wall of the dome from Azgiel pushing him backwards. He put his hands up to brace himself. The sword handle went straight through the wall. The shelter melted away at a rapid rate from where the sword handle had touched it as if acid had been pored on it.

"Kaz," Azgiel yelled, "we've got a problem." Azgiel swung Caden behind him. "Stay between us," Azgiel commanded. "If you haven't grown fearful enough to draw that sword yet, you soon will."

Before the dome was even fully dissolved, the dark souls began to charge. Azgiel grabbed a creature, holding it by its neck. It screamed and clawed at his arm. The cuts almost instantaneously healed after the creature tore at the skin. Smoke came off Azgiel's hand and then the dark soul burst into dust. As the dust fell to the ground, the rest of the dark souls stopped in their tracks. They examined Azgiel as if they were trying to figure out who or what he was.

Kaz swung his sword, slicing a couple of creatures in half. While he swung at one, another jumped on him, biting his head. He ripped the creature off, slammed him into one of the boulders, and drove his sword through its chest. Tagen took the chance to dive past him and grab Caden, slamming him to the ground and quickly dragging him into the crowd of dark souls.

"Azgiel,' Caden called out as he was being dragged away. Darkness began entering Caden and he found it hard to breath.

Azgiel pointed to the sword and yelled to Kaz. "Get the sword! If they drag it off into their cave, we'll never get it back." Kaz quickly ran, slicing through a crowd of dark souls, but they piled on top of him and Caden lost consciousness.

***

He awoke lying on some type of soft slimy ground. There was a dripping noise coming from somewhere, but he was unable to see, everything was pitch black. The air was stale and hard to breathe. A scream somewhere in the distance broke the eerie silence—not a scream from a dark soul, but a scream from someone losing their mind. Caden pushed himself up. The wall was covered in the same soft slimy texture as the floor. The substance seemed to move, and Caden felt like it was trying to soak itself into his skin. He pulled away, then placed one hand on the wall and began to walk, letting the wall lead his way.

After finding the fourth corner and no door, Caden knew he was in some type of small holding cell or prison.

Suddenly Caden felt a dip in the floor with his foot. He reached down and felt a two-inch deep hole in the slime. At the bottom of the hole along the edge of the gunk, there was something metallic and somewhat oval, but it was stuck. He played with it for a minute, feeling it out, trying to guess what it might be. After a minute of touching and pulling at it, Caden realized it was the opening to the sword's sheath. The handle of the sword was making the hole just like it had with the dome. If he could draw the sword, he might be able to escape, so Caden frantically grabbed where the handle would be, scratching at the rock floor.

With no luck of grabbing the handle, Caden felt hopeless. His fingers ached from the constant scratching at the rock surface. Rage, pain, sorrow, anger, confusion all flowed through him from everything he had just gone through and he yelled at the top of his lungs.

There was no hope. He gave up, and pushed himself against a wall. A feeling of nausea from the slimy substance as well as a feeling of being emotionally dead, drained his resolve.

CHAPTER 29

The large, luxurious bed creaked as Tagen got up. He slipped over to the window and opened it to let the sea breeze come in. The sun streaked through the gloomy clouds. It was the first time Tagen had seen the sun since he arrived at Triaad's almost a month ago. Waves slammed against the cliff-walls hundreds of feet below. Ornate furniture was purposefully placed in a couple of places along the walls. The whole room made Tagen feel a little out of place.

A young woman entered the room with two large guards. She held a tray of black oily food and set it down on the hand-carved dresser.

"Thank you," Tagen said trying to help the human feel more comfortable in hopes his kindness would get back to Triaad. She looked at him briefly with cold, empty eyes and left the room. The breakfast was made of something that Triaad must've discovered to feed to dark souls. Tagen let out a sigh. He had grown tired of sitting in the room. There was no news of the outside world, and he had no idea if he was going to be punished or honored. The days came and went with the same servant girl coming and going, never saying a word.

The treatment had surprised Tagen; it was even nicer then how he used to live before he was practically enslaved. Triaad had been so ruthless and evil ever since then, and Tagen was uncertain what to expect. He could've been thrown into a dark-matter chamber just like the one he lived in back with Snyp, but instead, they placed him in a nice room that brought back feelings of being human. Worry plagued him that it was all a trick. That all the luxury was just a manipulation.

Picking up the plate of food, Tagen shoved oily biscuits into his mouth. Outside, seagulls flew overhead, squawking. He threw a piece of the food out the window and the birds dove down to get it.

Tagen ate the last bite of breakfast; he wasn't used to being fed so well. Dark souls rarely needed to eat, so he was appreciative of all the food. It helped him to feel strong and young again.

The door opened behind him and a younger looking man with pristine silver armor entered. "Triaad will see you now." The man's voice was deeper then Tagen had expected. "If you will please accompany me."

"Did you ever give Triaad my message of what this whole matter was concerning?" Tagen asked.

"Yes, yes," the servant sounded almost annoyed. "We told him the same day you arrived."

"And he took this long-"

"No more questions please." The man motioned for Tagen to follow. "This way."

In the hallway, six guards stood along the wall, all decked out in a strange dark armor that Tagen had never seen before. One of them held chains. Tagen backed up slowly preparing for a fight.

"The chains aren't for you, so calm down," the servant said. "They're for Domblin in the next room."

"Domblin's still alive?" Tagen asked. Triaad had captured him almost a month ago, and he couldn't understand why they kept him alive. "I don't have to see him, do I?" The last time he had seen Domblin was when Mauldrin held his dead wife. After Domblin had put Mauldrin asleep, Tagen attacked Domblin and left a pretty good mark ripping his claws down his arm. Domblin chuckled evilly when Tagen attacked him, swearing that if they ever met again, he would kill him. After the threat, he was knocked on his haunches and paralyzed for the rest of the night.

"You'll get over it," one of the larger guards growled. As they headed down the hallway, Tagen quickly changed to a shadow form so Domblin would have a hard time knowing he was there, unless he was really searching.

As the door opened, Tagen could see Domblin sitting in a large chair. The room was just as nice as Tagen's, which made Tagen wonder if he had been a prisoner all this time and not an honored guest. It was starting to make sense that the food was probably prisoner food, and it would explain why every time food was brought to him there were guards accompanying the servant girl.

"You won't be a problem for us, will you, Domblin?" the guard holding the chains asked.

"I suppose I'll behave," Domblin said with a smile. He held out his hands to be cuffed.

"I'm glad to hear that. I didn't want to have to hurt an old man." Domblin's long white robe was worn and dirty. The guard lifted the shackles and placed them on Domblin's wrists. They weren't made of metal—the coloration shifted from dark gray, to black, to dark brown.

"What are these made of?" Domblin asked.

"Dark-matter and steel." The guard finished clasping them on.

Domblin pulled back but it was too late, the shackles were already on. "Don't worry, they won't hurt you," he said as he pulled at them to make Domblin follow.

"Where are we going?" Domblin asked. The guard tried to pull him but he wasn't budging.

"Triaad wants to see you."

Tagen wondered why he was asked too. As they walked down the hallway, the large number of guards clad in black body armor followed behind Domblin. Tagen walked beside the servant with the silver armor, staying at the back of the line.

The hallway curved around a bunch of corners and then into a very long stairwell. Once they reached the bottom, they headed down a shorter hallway and then into a huge courtyard. People were bustling about. Only a handful stopped to look at Domblin, but for the most part they didn't seem to care. Guards paced the lower and upper parts of the walls. Two black dragons lay resting at the far right end of the courtyard. The larger of the two was the one Triaad normally rode when he traveled.

There was a huge gateway that led outside of the castle grounds, and Tagen could see houses and cars driving on streets. Tagen hadn't been able to see the city yet. He had heard that the planet had fallen apart after the destruction of Azgiel, and had turned into a wasteland, but that was a lifetime ago. Triaad's kingdom wasn't ever talked about since Tagen was banished. *Triaad must've rebuilt the planet.* He wanted to go out there and see what the planet was like.

The guards kept Domblin marching. They headed for the oldest part of the castle. Large wood doors that towered in front of them creaked open. They walked into a huge room and dark marble pillars ran along the massive walls. Dimly lit candles lined the room, and were the only source of light. The guards stopped Domblin and attached his shackles to a chain that was bolted to the floor. Once they finished, they turned and walked out of the room, closing the large doors behind them. Fearful, Tagen stayed back.

Domblin's white robe gave off a faint glow in the dimly lit room. A deep chuckle came from a throne that perched at the top of a long flight of stairs. It was Triaad, and Tagen began to fret.

"I've been waiting to see you," Domblin said bravely.

"You have? And what would give you the notion I would ever want to bring you in here?"

Tagen didn't know what to do, if anything. He hoped Triaad would tell him when it was his turn to say or do anything.

"You made such a strong point to capture me," Domblin began, "I just assumed you wanted more then to just let me rot in that room you put me in." Domblin shifted his weight causing the chains to clank.

"I wanted nothing to do with you," the voice echoed. "I planned on letting you live your life out in that room, since your last prison didn't hold you well enough. Up there you would at least be out of my hair, and I doubt you could escape." The large figure shifted in the throne. Tagen wondered why Triaad had locked Domblin away instead of killing him. Each time he locked him up, Domblin always found a way to escape.

"Why are you pulling me out now?" Domblin asked. "Did I finally cause too much of a ruckus with my last attempt to escape, and now you're going to throw me into one of your chambers with dark-matter and turn me into one of your slaves?"

"Oh gosh no," the voice said with a chuckle. "I'm up to my eyeballs with dark souls. They manage their own creations, and goodness knows, I don't need any more strong ones." That was news to Tagen, and rather shocked him. He began to wonder if Triaad knew that he was in there, he didn't want to get in trouble or accused of spying. But he also didn't want to interrupt.

"What do you want with me?"

"I have an informant," Triaad commented casually. "He was able to sneak some information to me. He had vital news about what you were really doing on planet Myree."

"And who might that be?"

"Are you worried about what he's going to tell me?" Triaad leaned forward on the throne exposing his pale skin in the dim candlelight. He looked just the same as Tagen remembered him. Wrinkles lined the edges of his light green eyes. His strong jaw line was accented as an eerie smile stretched across his face.

Domblin repositioned and Tagen could tell he was readying himself for a possible attack. Tagen knew it was time. He slithered past Domblin. The candles flickered, fighting to stay lit as he made his way to Triaad. Some faltered and blew out, even though there was no breeze.

Triaad leaned back in his throne, his baldhead disappearing into the darkness that consumed his high-up nook. Tagen began to form at Triaad's feet, as if he were coming out from behind a curtain or wall.

Tagen wasn't sure if Triaad had really received the report, so he decided to start from the beginning. "There's more to what Domblin was doing on our planet then you may have been told. We've found Mauldrin on the planet, and Domblin had been protecting him," he whispered into Triaad's ear.

"Why am I just finding out about this now?" Triaad yelled. Tagen disappeared, scared that Triaad might take his rage out on him. After a moment of silence Tagen reappeared on Triaad's other side.

"Snyp is plotting against you and kept it from you." Tagen continued very cautiously.

"Snyp has been keeping this from me?" Triaad asked.

Tagen faded a little but kept whispering, "He has Mauldrin in a room full of dark matter trying to turn him into a dark soul. He plans to eat him to gain power and become more powerful than you. Fortunately for you, there's a huge problem. Mauldrin wasn't turning into a dark soul when I had left, and he's been in there for almost two months." Saying all the information aloud unnerved Tagen. He had done it and there was no turning back now. If Snyp found out, he would be dead.

"Domblin, would you like to know the trouble your friend Mauldrin's in?" Triaad asked.

"I left him in a place where your dark souls couldn't touch him," Domblin said confidently. Tagen couldn't help but snicker, knowing that Mauldrin had ruined the shield himself.

"He's been captured and is in a chamber filled with dark-matter being turned into a dark soul as we speak."

Domblin quickly pulled upward on his chains attempting to break them. The glow that illuminated from his robe increased to a bright light, making the walls and floor seem to bubble as if they were boiling. The chains let out a screeching noise and turned to black.

"Fool," Triaad said, "you of all people should know that you don't have any power in my chambers." His deep voice sent the chains silent and made Domblin give up his efforts. Tagen kept his distance—the whole scene made him want to bolt out of the room, not wanting to be in the middle of the fight.

There was something so different about Triaad, and yet he was still just the same. Tagen looked Triaad up and down. He was a very tall and broad man. His hands were large and well worn. There was a diamond shaped tattoo on the back of his head with a strange symbol in the center of it. His dark red robes appeared black. He slowly began to make his way down the stairs toward Domblin.

"Now tell me, was it you that brought Mauldrin back from his eternal grave?" Triaad asked, but Domblin kept silent. "It's been almost a century since I saw you last," Triaad said calmly. "It's a shame you never fought for me. I would've made you one of my generals and recognized the power and greatness that you hold."

"I would never join you," Domblin said sternly. "I've chosen good and always will. I will not follow evil."

"Good and evil," Triaad snickered with his nose wrinkled. "Where in the world did you get such a ludicrous idea? There is no good and evil. I fight for my people and their souls, to have every freedom and luxury life has to offer. And let's see, what does your *good* side do? They fight for those who follow silly rules and laws. Those rules and laws are history. They only hold us back from true power and freedom. If we're going to put the label of evil anywhere, it should go to your side, the side that tries to suppress those who aren't viewed as holy or good." Triaad circled around Domblin.

Tagen waited on edge, ready to run.

"I'm impressed with what you've done with this planet," Domblin said with a smile. "At least the little that I've seen. I heard it used to be a rather unfit place to live."

"You forget," Triaad said. "I used to be human. I still want things to be enjoyable for the flesh. I don't desire destruction and death like Azgiel did. I've gone to great lengths to rebuild the horrible things Azgiel brought upon mankind on this planet. Why do you think I helped overthrow him? I hated him for what he did here."

"You've found a topic that we can agree upon," Domblin stated. "But it doesn't mean that you're any better than him. I know there's a catch to what I've seen. It's an illusion I'm sure. Besides, you still send your dark souls out to do your bidding to help develop whatever terrible plan you have for the other worlds."

"Yes, they do serve me," Triaad said, stopping in front of Domblin. "But I'm nothing like Azgiel. I seek to give power and freedom to people, not destroy them and rule over them."

"Your ways are evil and you're not going to convince me otherwise." Domblin flared his nostrils. "I've seen more than enough of the destruction you've spread across many planets."

Tagen flinched knowing Triaad was going to do something horrible for that comment.

Triaad stopped and tilted his head. "It really doesn't matter what you think any more. You and your followers are decreasing in numbers. About eighty percent of all inhabitants on the planets follow me. Soon, you and all who believe in your old ways will be extinct." Letting out a breath he had been holding, Tagen shifted his weight while Triaad spoke. He couldn't understand why Triaad didn't attack him. His response was so calm and unusual for the Triaad he had known so long ago. It was highly manipulative, but Tagen didn't understand what Triaad was trying to get at.

"They follow manipulations fed to them without even knowing you exist." Domblin's nose flared again. "Funny though, you profess to have so much power and to be winning this war, and yet all I see is fear and evil behind your eyes." Domblin pulled his chains tight and gritted his teeth. Tagen moved a little closer to see both of them. Triaad's eyes turned a blood red and his face became dark, almost scaly looking. This was more like the Triaad Tagen knew.

Triaad lifted his hands and Domblin slammed to the ground, screaming out in pain. Taking a step back, Triaad's eyes returned back to normal. *Why wouldn't Triaad just finish him, had he grown soft?* All Tagen had ever done was give up some information after being tortured and was sentenced to a life of practically slavery. Here was a man that was out to destroy Triaad, but nothing. He wasn't doing anything to him.

"I'll let you live so you can watch me slowly turn Mauldrin into a follower of mine," Triaad said.

Tagen felt the anger surge through him. He had gone through terrible things that were worse then death to try and prove his loyalty to Triaad, to serve by him once again. And here he was giving Domblin life. A sick feeling came over Tagen, resentment towards Triaad that he hadn't ever felt before.

"Get the dragon ready," Triaad barked into the darkness past his throne. Two guards that had been unseen quickly made their way through the room and out of the building. A deep thundering roar followed after they exited through the large wooden doors.

Triaad sauntered back to his throne. "Get the gate ready for me."

A bright, blue light flashed, hurting Tagen's eyes. Guards frantically scurried around trying to get everything ready for Triaad's departure. The frame of the gate was made of black crystals that gave off a bluish light. On the inside, a dark liquid metal swirled in small waves.

Sunlight lit the room as the large front doors opened. A roar followed that shook the ground. Tagen watched as two guards brought in a massive dragon. They were holding ropes that were attached to the beast's upper neck. As they got closer to Domblin, the dragon lurched forward, pulling the guards, biting at Domblin. Its teeth caught one of the chains snapping it in half, giving Domblin more room to dodge the second attack. The dragon snapped at him two more times before the guards had the creature under control. Tagen hoped that Domblin would be eaten. At least some justice would be served if the dragon got him.

Triaad stood royally by the gate, clad in heavy armor. He mounted the dragon with ease. His armor shifted in shades of black, and Tagen realized it was made of dark-matter just like the chains around Domblin's wrists.

"Tagen," Triaad said, "you're coming with me." His dragon let out a thunderous roar after Triaad had snapped at Tagen.

Fear washed away some of the anger as Tagen realized he was going to have to face Snyp, but he quickly made his way to the feet of the dragon. Anxiety flowed through his veins. He had betrayed Snyp but there was no turning back now.

"Guards, put Domblin back in his room until I return," Triaad said. Triaad yanked on the reins and the dragon roared one last time before they jumped through the gate. Tagen reluctantly followed. He paused at the liquid bluish wall. It moved in front of him, pulling at him like a strong wind.

Going through the gate meant his life would end as soon as Snyp found out about his betrayal, but staying meant he would perish once Triaad found out about his disobedience. He had hoped his actions would get him back on Triaad's good side, but he didn't know what he wanted anymore.

Snyp was a fool—there was no way he could get enough power to overtake Triaad and Tagen knew that. It was time to follow his master. He stepped forward into the cold liquid.

CHAPTER 30

How long had it been? Caden couldn't tell any longer. There was no way of knowing days from nights. His eyes burned and his skin hurt to touch. The screams and moans that he heard now and again had become a relief because it was the only contact he had to anything living. Thoughts and memories seemed fragmented, and when he tried to remember, his head felt like it was going to explode.

The events that led him into the dark place were gone from his memory. He could vaguely recall working for the SDS, and every so often he had a dream about the downfall of the agency. Strange visions and images entered his mind, of a life that he felt he knew, where he was known as Mauldrin. They were always brief and confusing.

The only memory that seemed clear was the death of Bridget. He saw the scene vividly, over and over, causing his heart to pound. There were many times that Caden couldn't even tell if he was awake or asleep, and wondered if the whole thing was just a bad dream. *How can I still be alive when I haven't eaten or drank anything since I've been put in the room? Am I dead? Maybe this is what death is? Or worse, this is hell.*

Many times he felt like someone or something came and visited his cell. He could never prove it, but there were instances he swore he could hear breathing and something moving around in the cell with him. When he would try to find the person, he would just run into the walls. The feeling never lasted long. It was as if someone or something would pop in to check on him.

As he lay in the blackness that felt alive, a scream echoed in the distance, it was a woman's voice. It was just another thing to remind him of Bridget. An image of her flashed through Caden's mind. He stood, his heart began beating, slowly at first, and then blood began pumping through his body. Bridget seemed to be at the center of all his thoughts. Her face kept flashing before his eyes.

The images of Bridget grew clear and crisp. He could almost smell her flowery perfume. Desperately, he wanted her back in his arms. The more he thought about her, the more he felt an uncontainable fire rip through him. It started in his chest and moved out to his limbs, giving him power and energy. Strange flashbacks forced their way into Caden's memory, but strangely they weren't of Bridget. They were images of him, Azgiel, and others. They were able to control things; elements, atoms, particles. He could vaguely recall ruling over a large mass of people and the power that he held was breathtaking. Caden didn't care about those images. He worked on refocusing his mind.

Bridget.

He pushed his thoughts to the only thing that made him feel human, that grounded him. She had bled to death in his arms. The very thought of her death produced rage and shot a burning sensation through him and than his eyes seemed to open to a vision. He could see outside, but it was murky, like looking through dirty glass. Bridget was there, standing in a thick wooded area with strange creatures around her. Creatures he recognized; he had seen them before, with the Witch. He could sense the vision was real, and that he was looking at Bridget. *But how? You're dead?*

He felt as if he were in some type of wormhole or portal accessing him to Bridget wherever she was. "Bridget." Caden called out with a soft but thunderous voice that came from within, and not from his lips.

The walls screamed around Caden. He could feel himself being sucked back in. The image was gone. He became distracted with the screaming, causing his head to pound. Knowing that the image of his vision would be gone soon, he fought to keep it, but it quickly began to fade, becoming lost in the chambers of his mind. Sucked out of him by the evil that surrounded his entrapment. It was as if the oily substance on the walls clouded his mind.

There was no hope. He leaned back into the wall and began to give up. It felt as if mind-eating leaches were borrowing into his brain. His mind pounded and memories dissipated.

A strange, dim light suddenly entered the room, carving out what looked like a door. *Light, at last.* Caden moved towards the door, but before he made it, the square shape blasted open, flying past him and slamming against the back wall.

A white-cloaked figure illuminated the doorway, floating a couple inches off the ground. The light that came off the personage, burned his eyes, and he had to look away. The soft black matter that covered everything around him slowly dissolved revealing the hard rock that made up the walls.

"Follow me." The voice was a female's voice, which filled the room and had authority to it. *Bridget? It can't be.* Her voice brought strength into his body. Even his heart seemed to beat stronger.

He quickly looked up to see if it was his wife, but the figure was gone. A dim light could be seen in the hallway, lighting the cavern. He moved to follow, but tripped on the sword. He had forgotten about the sword. As he picked it up, a dark soul ran past the door toward the source of the light. Before he could yell out to warn the personage, an explosion shook the floor, and the white light in the hallway grew extremely bright.

The dark soul slammed against the ground. His flesh melted off his thin black rubbery bones.

Caden ran out of the room, his old worn shoes scuffed across the rock cave floor. His rescuer was already down the corridor and around a corner. He quickly ran after her, trying to keep up, but as fast as he ran, he couldn't catch her. She was always one corner ahead.

The tunnels were enormous, and maze like, but Caden didn't care. He had to reach the person; he had to know if it was Bridget. A noise followed him like water moving down a pipe. The noise grew louder. He turned to see the slimy dark substance returning and covering the walls and floor.

Finally, Caden saw the end of the tunnel, and for the first time in what felt like years, he could smell fresh air, which gave him a feeling of euphoria. As he exited the large opening to the cave, he saw a bright light on a hill in the thick forest. He veered in that direction, running with a speed he never knew he had.

The glow came from behind a couple of large trees. The closer he got to the bright light, the more it diminished. He ran faster, straining his muscles, trying to get there before the light completely disappeared. Like a candle being blown out in the wind, it was gone as he dove around one of the large trees.

His hands smashed into the muddy ground from a fresh rainfall. Mud splattered across his face. He quickly looked around without getting up. Nothing. *Was it Bridget or is my mind playing tricks on me?*

An emptiness crawled through his heart, and he let his head fall into the mud. He closed his burning eyes. *Is all of this just a trick, a nightmare? Am I going to wake back in the black cell?*

With disgust, he opened his eyes back up. Cool mud saturated his clothing. *I'm still free. Is this real?* He looked at his arms for the first time since he had made it outside. His veins were black under his skin. Shocked, he lifted his hand to see his black fingernails and blackness in the lines of his hands. His skin was a pale white.

Caden sat up and flinched as he grabbed his head. Memories of his past were starting to come back of SDS and growing up, but they were choppy and random. Difficult to control. His head pounded and his vision blurred for a moment.

Rubbing his head and blinking a couple of times cleared up most of the fuzziness. He shifted his attention to a small puddle, which was about a foot away. The water was clear and reflected his image as he leaned over to it. A couple of black veins ran through his neck and face. The blue color in his eyes was completely gone, replaced by blackness, which seeped into parts of the white. His clothing looked like it had just come from a dumpster, ragged and torn.

"What's wrong with me?" He spoke softly as he poked at his black veins.

A scream rang out from the cave, and Caden poked his head around the trees to see what it was. There was nothing, the outside of the cave was vacant.

"RUN!" The same voice as before, filled Caden's ears, causing him to jump. He looked around, not knowing where it had come from, but there was no one there. A familiar smell filled the area, a flowery aroma. *Bridget's perfume.* Caden hit his head. *I'm loosing it.*

A loud blast from passed the trees brought Caden out of his thoughts. A ball of fire blasted through the opening of the cave, which launched a dark soul to the ground. The second the fire stopped, a dragon's head poked out of the cave, the same dragon that had taken Domblin away, the very same that he had been told was behind Bridget's death. Anger raged in Caden, his first instinct was to attack, but he swallowed his anger and knew if he attacked now he would die. But a new revitalized energy pulsed through his body as he saw his target. Revenge.

With a quick move, the dragon tried to step on the dark soul, but the dark soul quickly vanished and reappeared further away.

"Snyp," the rider of the dragon's voice thundered. "It's no use. You might as well accept your fate for betraying me."

"Tagen's lying to you Triaad-" Snyp began but was cut off.

Caden raised an eyebrow. *Are they fighting one another? I hope they kill each other and save me the time.*

"Enough, I'm tired of your lies. Tagen is in charge here for now on," Triaad shouted. The dragon started making a strange vibrating noise and looked as if it were going to sneeze. Its long ears bent back, and it blew fire on top of Snyp, pinning him to the ground. The dirt around Snyp began to turn black, but not from the flames. Blackness spread across the ground at a rapid pace. Suddenly, a black explosion shot out from under the fire, throwing the flames back in the dragon's face knocking the beast backwards.

"If you want a fight, then it's about time you learn the true extent of my power," Snyp hissed. Black roots spread across the ground. His red eyes flared and let off a red smoke. He threw his hands forward, his claws ripping at the air. The blackness tore through the ground, throwing rocks and dirt out of its way. Before the dragon could react, the black roots shot into his legs like worms squirming into their holes. The dragon let out a screeching roar and threw Triaad off of his back.

Something tugged at Caden, telling him that he needed to leave, but he ignored the inkling and continued watching the fight. Death was inevitable for one of them and he wanted to see them die.

A black oily substance dripped out of the dragon's nostrils as he turned to Triaad and spewed fire out of his mouth, attacking his master. Triaad waved his arm at the flames and they quickly turned to steam.

The dragon lowered his head and faced Triaad, growling at him and showing his teeth. Triaad rubbed the ground, and Caden could feel tremors shaking him and the trees he leaned on. Startled he backed up a little, but still kept his attention on the fight. Triaad stood up and backed off. The dragon looked as if it was just about to attack, but the ground broke open and a huge creature emerged. A giant worm made of water. It made a high-pitched screech that was deafening.

The worm stood about six feet taller than the dragon. Blowing fire the dragon appeared to hurt the watery worm, as it shrank back into its hole. A high pitch noise rang out again, making Caden cover his ears. Like a geyser, the worm shot out of the ground and slammed against the dragon. Black liquid spilled out from under the dragon's scales, nose, and eyes as the water poured over him.

Finally the dragon fell to the ground. Snyp reappeared next to Triaad for an attack, but Triaad grabbed his neck. His movement was so fast Caden didn't even see it. The dragon got back on his feet and stepped over to his master. Triaad tossed Snyp to the ground, and with a quick movement of his right hand, a small chain flung out of a saddlebag and wrapped around Snyp. The ends of the chain dug into the ground and Snyp was unable to get up.

"What is this stuff?" Snyp hissed as he squirmed. Triaad climbed onto the dragon while he chuckled.

"It's made out of dark matter, the same stuff that created you," Triaad stated seeming rather amused about the situation. "It's one of the few substances you can't move through."

"You're making..." Snyp wasn't able to finish what he was saying as the dragon under Triaad's command placed his large claws on top of him. One claw dug sharply into Snyp's neck.

"I think your ego got the best of you," Triaad said while shifting his weight in his mount. "I've fought stronger humans than you. You've grown corrupt and I have no use for you any longer. Tagen will be able to take over here." The dragon shifted his claws ever so slightly letting up on Snyp's neck. "Now I have to decide what I'm going to do to you." Caden couldn't wait to see Snyp killed. It would leave just one to fight instead of two. He figured as soon as one was dead he would attack and avenge Bridget.

While pinned under the dragon's claws, Snyp turned his gaze away from Triaad and looked right at Caden.

"Mauldrin," Snyp yelled out. Triaad looked in the same direction, but Caden quickly hid behind the trees.

He was spotted. *Stupid, now they might stop fighting and just come after me.* Sweat broke out on his forehead as panic ran through his rapidly beating heart. Maybe he should just dive out from behind the tree and attack them, they may not expect it, giving him the advantage.

"He's out there. If you let me live I'll get him for you," Snyp pleaded.

Caden debated if he should run or fight, struggling to decide.

"I don't trust you." Triaad's voice echoed through the trees.

"Trust me or don't, but he's there and if you let me go I'll bring him back to you like I should've done in the first place. I'll rectify my wrong."

Caden listened intensely, while trying to make up his mind. It could be suicide running down there. If Snyp were going to come after him alone, he would have even a better advantage of killing one at time.

Triaad laughed. "I'll give you a chance, but I'm not sending you alone. TAGEN!"

Caden grew more and more uncomfortable, but he dared not run.

"Get a couple of younglings to follow Snyp and help him bring back Mauldrin. As soon as they get back send for me, I don't have any more time to waste here. If Snyp isn't back by morning, send a messenger to tell me so we can hunt him down and kill him." There was a slight pause before he continued, "Snyp, I may spare your life if you bring Mauldrin back to me. Don't get any stupid ideas of running for it either, I'll send a Strife out to find you and kill you, which as you know won't be difficult to do."

After hearing that, Caden knew it was time to go. Things were getting more and more complicated. Now he was going to be facing a number of dark souls instead of just one. Knowing he needed to have the fight somewhere else, in hopes of living, Caden ran for it. He breathed heavy, not from the running, but from excitement of possibly getting a chance at revenge. The sun slowly became extinct as he ran through the trees. Darkness consumed the forest as patches of moonlight pushed its way through the thick woods.

As Caden ran, something hit him from the side and knocked him to the ground. Scrambling to get the thing off him, the creature bit into his back. Caden threw his elbow and knocked the shadow to the ground. He quickly stood up and saw Snyp's two red eyes glowing in the dark.

"Nice to see you again Mauldrin," Snyp hissed while slowly moving sideways, circling Caden.

"Who are you?" Caden asked. He searched through the woods around him, looking for the other dark souls that were supposed to follow Snyp.

"I'm the one that's going to kill you," Snyp said. Without any further words, Snyp dove at Caden. Moving with incredible speed, Caden, in a moment of haste reacted out of instinct and moved a hand towards the sword to defend himself. Everything from before that had felt so wrong with the sword went out the window as Caden focused on the creature attacking him. A strange craving, an almost need came over him as his hand moved in. Power filled his body as if he had been plugged into an energy source, making it hard to breathe once he grasped the sword handle. An unseen force came from it, blasting Snyp backwards along with the vegetation and trees as if a strong wind had come off the sword.

A strange power surged through Caden and he felt invincible, almost god-like. His black veins beat strong and filled him with confidence. Not fully knowing why the evil feeling that had stopped him from drawing the sword before had vanished, replaced with this exhilarating energy and power, he felt more then ready to fight. Excited to kill the creature in front of him.

Snyp quickly picked himself up. Caden looked at him with a sinister smile. The sword's blade was glassy black with jagged edges. A purple vein ran up the middle of the blade, starting from the handle and up to a small round circle that was close to the tip. Snyp's face dropped at the sight of the sword and scrambled backwards.

The world seemed to slow down as Caden's adrenaline pounded through his body. Tightening his grip on the sword, Caden prepared to attack. Before he made his move, a sharp pain drove into his back as he was knocked down, but he kept a strong grip on the weapon making sure not to lose it.

A loud scream rang out from behind him as he quickly raised himself out of the foliage. Rustling moved around him. There was more then one. An unknown number of dark souls were circling him. Another blow hit him in the back, but this time the creature held on. Claws tore into his left shoulder.

"Enough." Caden snapped while throwing an elbow upwards. Oily skin connected with his elbow, knocking the dark soul off of him. Using quick moves, he braced himself for another attack and was just in time as a black human-like figure dove at him from the right side. Spinning with the sword out, Caden sliced the blade through the creature. Unexpectedly, the dark soul blew into a horrid smelling dust.

Two more came out him from both directions. Swinging the sword, Caden sliced through one, but while it blew into dust the other dove into his legs knocking him to the ground. Leaves crunched underneath him and a snap rang out from a branch that broke under his butt. The dark soul dove at Caden's face. With deadly skill, he swung the sword up, and plunged it into the black creature's carcass. Black dust splattered across him.

Knowing he needed to stay on his feet, Caden jumped back up, sword in hand. Nothing moved. There were no more dark souls that could be seen, including the one they called Snyp.

"Where are you, Snyp?" Caden yelled. Hate filled his chest. He was going to kill him, even if it meant his own death. They had to pay, all of them. "Come out, you coward!"

With a growl, Snyp appeared from out of nowhere in front of Caden, centimeters from his face. Startled, Caden jumped back and Snyp clawed into him pushing him backwards into a tree. The sword flung out of his hands and stabbed into the ground. Knowing he had to have the sword, Caden dove for it, but was caught by Snyp. Claws drove into his chest and flipped him backwards, slamming him into the ground.

Using excellent reflexes, Caden grabbed one of the creature's arms. The slimy skin was uncomfortable to touch. A terrible feeling entered Caden's heart as if he was touching pure evil. The feeling was almost a sense of coldness.

Snyp's arm somehow went right through Caden's hand. He was unable to contain him. Screaming again, hurting Caden's ears, Snyp pierced his claws into Caden's chest. Pain shot through his whole body followed by a paralyzed state. The greenery around him faded to black and he could feel himself losing control of his limbs.

His body was quickly shutting down. Snyp was far more powerful then Tagen had been in times past. Arms and legs were the first to go, followed by his stomach and head. Before long the only thing Caden could feel any longer was the subtle rhythmic beating of his heart. Each beat sounded as if it were echoing down a long corridor. Life was coming to an end, and Caden knew it.

Struggling to hold on, Caden tried to fight, but he didn't know how. Images began to move around him, not in front of his eyes, but in some type of conscious state. It was like he was going back to moments in his past and was able to observe without anyone seeing him. The first images were of Bridget and their life together. He could see so much so quickly. His years in the war and all the men he had lost pushed into his mind. Sorrow slowed the heartbeat down and the images grew gray, colorless.

Somehow Caden was able to shut the images off and everything went black. The beats grew even slower and quieter. Voices seemed to push there way into his mind.

"You're a filthy woman undeserving of anything." Caden was surprised to see his dad yelling at his mom. His dad followed the yelling up with a closed fisted punch, smashing her nose. Blood splattered against the wall. She fell to the floor and young Caden jumped in trying to hit his father.

"You little…" His father picked him up by the neck and slammed him against the wall.

It was strange watching the scene. Caden didn't know what to think seeing his defenseless young self, trying to fight against his pathetic dad. His younger self squirmed until his face began turning blue.

"You'll never amount to anything. You're pathetic and weak," his father said as he let him drop to the ground and then kicked him in the face while he gasped for air. Caden somehow shut the vision off feeling the pain from the horrible times of his past. It drove him further away from the slowing beat.

Matt's voice prompted him to look around once again. "I mean look at you. You think I'm wrong, and yet you don't do what it takes and kill me." With the same strange ability as before, Caden was able to see the images again. He could see himself talking to Matt in Dead Time at Matt's office. The beats grew faster.

Another voice, it was Domblin's coming from behind him, "… there is absolutely no evidence he is tapping into who he really is. I mean he is weak." Spinning somehow, he found Domblin behind him, talking to the white-grayish dragon. The pounding grew louder, echoing, and giving a feeling as if he could feel his head pounding.

"What kind of pathetic weakling have you turned into?" It was Azgiel's voice. Once again with a spin, he could see Azgiel fighting with him in the dome. "Draw the sword or you're going to die. This is your world, Mauldrin. Dig within and find who you truly are. There's power within you that can destroy all the dark souls around us you just have to remember and tap into it. It's time for you to take the realm once again. Now draw the sword!"

Images of everyone he had ever been close to or knew, began spinning around him, until it stopped on an image of Bridget dead in his arms. The beating of his heart seemed so loud that if he had eardrums it would've blown them out. He could hear the creaking of a door and a bright light shown at him. Strangely he moved towards it, but not by walking. A golden sphere appeared in the doorway. It was familiar, but he didn't know where it was from. *Mauldrin.* The sphere seemed to call out to him.

Strange numbers and signs flooded into his mind. None of it made sense, but a power began to run through him, like a river released from a dam. He could feel his heart beating once again and his lungs take in air. His arms were the first things to respond. He lifted them high and slammed them to the ground. The moment they connected with the dirt he got his vision back.

A power let loose from his hands and a shock wave blasted everything including Snyp backwards. With a loud crack, a tree slammed to the ground. *Amazing.* There was something in him, an intense power, and he didn't know where it had come from, but it worked. His whole body felt amazing, as if he had all the energy in the world.

To his right, a strange voice called out to him, but not a voice to be heard with his ears, it was felt. Looking in that direction he saw the sword. It communicated with him in a strange fashion, wanting him to call for it, to summon it. Out of a strange instinct, Caden lifted a hand and the sword flew to him, landing in the palm of his hand. A sense of security warmed Caden, feeling interconnected with the weapon.

Everything around him seemed to be whispering or communicating in some type of fashion. He struggled to make sense of it, the communications were confusing and overwhelming, accept for one part. Snyp was ready to attack, he could just sense it.

With ease, Caden shifted and brought the sword down, slicing it through Snyp's body while he was in midair trying to attack. Time sped back up and Snyp blew to pieces. Caden smiled as he held the sword out, feeling of its intense power and feeling at one with it. He looked around, peering through the darkness, seeing if there was anyone else he could fight. Confidence and an unfamiliar rage filled Caden. It was time to finish the fight. No more was he going to be pushed down or be weak.

Taking a breath, his body relaxed and his heartbeat slowed. Not knowing why, Caden found his new sense of alertness went away with the slowing of his heart. He didn't feel a connectedness with the environment around him any longer. "No, no. Come back." Caden pleaded with his body rubbing a hand up and down his chest. It was too late. He was back to normal. The power was gone.

Clenching his teeth, Caden peered into the darkness of the forest's night. He gripped the sword handle. *Power or no power, I'm still going to kill all of you.*

Not wasting any time, Caden ran back the way he had come, heading to the cave. A full moon lit the night, but the inside of the cave was pitch black. *Should I risk going in? Bad idea, I wouldn't be able to see anything.* He wanted to kill all of them, every single living creature in that cave. As he thought of what they were, he could feel his nose wrinkle up in anger and disgust.

Caden whistled loudly. "Hey, I'm right here. Come and get me." Caden smiled knowing what he said was kind of lame, but he was playing it by ear. He picked up a large rock and threw it into the darkness. It cracked off the wall and echoed down the tunnel.

Before he was ready, a dark shape dove out of the darkness, claws stretched out and black sharp teeth ready to bite. The dark soul knocked him to the ground and the sword flew out of his hands. Teeth ripped into Caden's shoulder causing him to yelp in pain. Caden gripped a rock and hit the creature in the head, knocking it off of him. Moving quickly, he rolled over and took a hold of the sword. The dark soul grabbed his leg and let out a scream. More screams could be heard in the cave in response.

Twisting his body, Caden slashed the sword through the dark soul causing the creature to explode into pieces. He chuckled, as the screams grew closer. There was no turning back now, he had their attention. They were going to pay for what they had done to Bridget. He positioned his body, readying for the fight.

Three more jumped out of the cave at him, but Caden was ready. It was like batting practice, almost too easy. More dark souls jumped out, and more dark souls exploded. There were a number of them that came out into the moonlight, but these ones didn't jump at him. They growled and began to spread out, circling Caden. He knew his position was bad, so he quickly jumped towards one of them slashing the sword through him.

All of them dove at once. Spinning, he was able to get all but one, which had been behind him. He felt the sharp claws slash his back, knocking him down to his knees. With a quick movement, Caden spun and slashed the creature's legs. In his moment of weakness, more dark souls came screaming out of the cave to get him. Their attacks were short lived as Caden swung his sword, slicing them left and right.

He could feel the warm blood run down his back from the cuts. If they encircled him again, he knew they would win. There had to be a way to cover his backside. *The cave wall.* Caden quickly ran at the next surge of dark souls, swinging his sword as he went, making for the cave wall to guard his back. One of the creatures dove off the ceiling of the cave and knocked him over.

The dark soul bit into Caden's leg. Another one grabbed his left arm, staying clear of the sword, and tried to drag him into the darkness of the cave. He went to swing his sword at the one dragging him, but another jumped on his back and pinned his right arm down. The dark soul on his leg bit him again, even harder this time, causing Caden to let out a yelp. He wasn't going to die like this, in failure to avenge Bridget. His heart pounded and a small amount of the power he had tapped into before came back, only slightly, but it felt good.

Using all of his strength, Caden ripped his arm out of the dark soul's grasp and jumped up, throwing the dark souls off him. He slashed at the air and hit two of them with the sword. The other one ducked and dove at his feet. Caden slammed down with the sword pointing towards the ground, running the blade through him.

Spinning back and forth, Caden was looking for the next fight, but no more came. *That couldn't have been all of them. He remembered there were more when they attacked him in the dome. Are they hiding in the darkness?* Caden needed to draw them out. He backed out of the opening and stood at the entrance of the cave. Finally, he noticed a dark shape that wasn't moving. It had been there the whole time and Caden hadn't thought anything of it. But sure enough, a dark soul stood just a foot into the darkness of the cave, watching.

"I see you," Caden said. For all he knew, there were hundreds more just watching him from the safety of the cave. "Don't think I won't come in there and get you."

A dark soul that Caden knew very well took a step out into the moonlight. "You," Caden said. It was the same dark soul that had attacked him so many times in the past, Tagen. The creature didn't respond. It just sat there with a look like he was trying to figure Caden out.

"Where's the others, are they all hiding in there?" Caden's tone was gruff.

"No," Tagen responded, his voice sounding deflated. "I'm the last."

"What are you talking about? There had been hundreds when you attacked me last. And where's that dragon rider, Triaad, with his dragon? Is he in there? I have a fight to pick with him." Caden felt confident and ready to finish what he had started. He was going to get revenge for his wife's death.

"Triaad took most of the dark souls with him back to his planet," Tagen said as he took another step closer to Caden. There was a look of curiosity as he stared at Caden, looking at the black veins in his face and arms.

"They just left? On a spaceship or something?"

"No. There's a gate in there, a portal, and he left taking a majority of my army that I had here, because he doesn't trust me with a large army."

"So you're all that's left huh?" He had done it. The dark souls on his planet were wiped out. There was just one left. Caden held the sword up and prepared to charge him. There was still a small amount of power that ran through him and he needed to use it soon, in case it left him like it had last time.

"Wait!"

Caden paused. "What?"

"You don't have to kill me. I can help you." Tagen looked around.

Caden figured he was stalling, trying to figure out a way to escape. "You try to bolt, I'll kill you." Caden knew that Tagen could probably out run him, but he hoped he could bluff enough that Tagen would be too scared to try.

"No, no, I'm not going to try that. I want to serve you. You, you can be my new master." Tagen stopped looking around for an escape and focused on Caden. "There is a lot I can do for you. You don't remember things. I can help you remember."

"Azgiel already offered that."

"Azgiel?" Tagen raised his brow. "Azgiel's locked away for good. How could he help you, and even if he was supposedly out, which he couldn't be, why would someone that would kill you if he had the chance, help you?"

"Enough. You're just trying to confuse me." Caden held his sword up higher for the kill.

"No. No, I promise. I'm not." Tagen dropped to the ground. "Please, please. I can be a great servant, trust me."

Caden analyzed him for a minute, debating on what to do. Just passed Tagen, Caden noticed the chain that Triaad had used on Snyp. He approached Tagen, and Tagen crawled backwards, stopping at the wall to the cave. With a couple of clanks, Caden picked the chain up. He was surprised by how light it was for such a thick chain. It was like picking up a small aluminum chain.

"Hold still while I wrap this around you," Caden said as he pointed his sword at Tagen. "Until I feel I can fully trust you, I'm going to keep you chained up."

"Very fair, Master." Tagen put his hands behind his back. Caden made quick work of tying the chain once around his torso and around his hands.

"You're going to take me to this portal and take me to the others, so I can kill all of them," Caden ordered while pushing the point of the sword into his black oily back.

"Bad idea. You go through that portal, you'll run into huge armies. Besides, Triaad alone could wipe you out," Tagen spoke quickly, turning his head to look at Caden.

Not knowing if Tagen was lying, Caden looked him over for a minute. There was no way to know, but he didn't care, he was going to finish this. He grabbed Tagen's chain and started dragging him towards the cave.

"Where're we going?" Tagen cried out while clawing at the dirt.

"To the gate. Now take me to it or I'll run this sword right through you."

"I'm not lying to you." Tagen squirmed. "If you go that way, we're both dead."

Caden held the sword up. "Make your choice, and make it quick." Tagen's shoulders slumped forward and his dark-red eyes fell to the ground. The chain clanked as he walked past Caden and into the cave. "No tricks, I have the sword right next to you. If anything happens that I don't trust, I'm not going to take any chances, you'll be dead."

"No tricks," Tagen mumbled sounding deflated. He walked as if he were on death row, which made Caden want to chuckle, but the humor was short lived as the blackness engulfed them.

With the light gone Caden was walking blind. The whole situation made him uncomfortable, his stomach tightened as he felt the hard ground change to a soft wet substance. "What is this stuff we're walking on now?"

"Dark matter," Tagen explained, "it's what creates us, and what was turning you into one of us."

Dripping could be heard in the cave, echoing down its empty corridors. It was a terrible noise to return to, a noise that would run through Caden's nightmares for years to come. The rest of the way they walked in silence, Caden being hyper-aware of Tagen's every movement. Ready for anything.

About fifteen minutes went by before Caden was able to see a dim light coming from behind a large door. Black, oily liquid covered the walls, moving around, almost responding to Caden's movements. They entered the room with the light and Caden was able to see where the light was coming from. A huge gate stood at one end of a spacious room. Inside of it was a dark liquid that swirled around. The outside had black crystals lining it that gave off a bluish light.

"I'm surprised Triaad left it open," Tagen said as he tilted his head in bewilderment. Seeing the gate gave Caden a marvelous idea and he couldn't hold back a smile.

"Let' go." Caden pulled on the chain, but Tagen didn't budge. "I'm not joking around, last chance before I slice you in half." Reluctantly Tagen followed behind. Caden could tell he was looking for a way to get loose by the way he kept looking all about.

A light breeze seemed to pull at him once they reached the twenty-foot tall gate. The black liquid swirled around inside of it creating a slight vibration in the floor. Holding the sword tight, Caden didn't waste any more time. He swung hard, running the blade through one side of the arch of the gate. A loud crack rang out through the room and Caden could feel a strong pull as the sword sliced at the liquid in the portal, trying to suck the sword in. With a quick jerk the sword came out.

"What are you doing? You're going to get us killed."

Caden didn't listen. He pulled hard on Tagen, dragging him to the other side of the gate. Tagen screamed and clawed with his feet at the ground.

Again Caden sliced through the other side of the arch with the sword. An explosion blew them backwards. Bolts of blue lightening flashed through the room as the gate fell backwards, crashing against the rock wall. Loud thunder shook the ground. The liquid in the middle of the portal began to swirl and shrink as if it were swirling into a hole that grew smaller and smaller.

Nervously, Caden noticed his sword had been flung on the ground about three feet away. He had to get it and quick. Without it, he was nothing. In hopes the dark soul hadn't seen yet, Caden lurched forward, grabbed the weapon, and quickly slid it into the sheath on his back.

"What have you done," Tagen screamed and pulled at the end of the chain. The sheer strength of the creature almost pulled Caden over. He strained his muscles, gripping the cold chain, trying to keep control of the situation.

The broken gate crackled and bolts of lightening spewed out all around them. One last large bolt flashed, striking Tagen and Caden. A plume of smoke wafted upwards from where they stood, but they were gone.

CHAPTER 31

Standing in the darkness in some woods far away, Azgiel turned to Kaz who sat on a cliff's edge just past the end of the trees. A strong gust of wind blew Azgiel's hair into a flurry.

"Did you feel that?" Azgiel asked ever so calmly.

"Sir?" Kaz snorted as he stood up, spreading his long wings out as if to stretch them.

"The sword has been released from the curse. Mauldrin's still alive. He's drawn the sword. I can feel it calling for me." Azgiel smiled. Kaz snorted and lowered his wings back down.

"Which way do we head?" Kaz cracked his neck after he spoke, his horns accidentally hitting a branch and knocking a couple of leaves off.

Azgiel moved close to the ground and placed his hand into the soft green grass that lay around them. He looked northwest and pointed. "The sword's that way. Let's get there quickly before he gets himself killed."

Breinigsville, PA USA
18 November 2010
249536BV00001B/140/P